USA TODAY bestselling author **Heidi Rice** lives in London, England. She is married with two teenage sons—which gives her rather too much of an insight into the male psyche—and also works as a film journalist. She adores her job, which involves getting swept up in a world of high emotion, sensual excitement, funny and feisty women, sexy and tortured men and glamorous locations where laundry doesn't exist. Once she turns off her computer she often does chores—usually involving laundry!

Canadian **Dani Collins** knew in high school that she wanted to write romance for a living. Twenty-five years later, after marrying her high school sweetheart, having two kids with him, working at several generic office jobs and submitting countless manuscripts, she got The Call. Her first Mills & Boon novel won the Reviewers' Choice Award for Best First in Series from *RT Book Reviews*. She now works in her own office, writing romance.

THE ROYAL PREGNANCY TEST

HEIDI RICE

INNOCENT IN THE SHEIKH'S PALACE

DANI COLLINS

MILLS & BOON

First Published in Great Britain 2020
by Mills & Boon, an imprint of HarperCollins*Publishers*
1 London Bridge Street, London, SE1 9GF

The Royal Pregnancy Test © 2020 Heidi Rice

Innocent in the Sheikh's Palace © 2020 Dani Collins

ISBN: 978-0-263-27839-2

MIX
Paper from
responsible sources
FSC® C007454

This book is produced from independently certified FSC™ paper
to ensure responsible forest management.
For more information visit www.harpercollins.co.uk/green.

Printed and bound in Spain
by CPI, Barcelona

THE ROYAL PREGNANCY TEST

HEIDI RICE

To Natalie Anderson,
who is an absolute sweetheart to work with
and a brilliant author too.

PROLOGUE

PRINCESS JUNO ALICE MONROYALE braked the hired snowmobile and wrenched up her goggles to take in the stunning view. Snow fluttered down, coating the Alpine landscape in pristine white, framing the ornate turrets and gables of a sixteenth-century castle perched on the clifftop across the gorge. The defiant structure looked magnificent against the gathering dusk of a December night. Like a cartoon fantasy made real.

Home.

Juno's heart butted her tonsils and the cold air clogged her lungs.

Had it really been eight and a half years since she had visited her homeland and seen her twin sister, Jade—the Queen of Monrova—in the flesh?

Why hadn't she come back sooner, much sooner?

But even as the question echoed in her consciousness, the disastrous events of the summer she had turned sixteen came hurtling back.

'Kiss me, Leo, you know you want to.'

'Why on earth would I want to kiss you? You're just a spoilt brat. Now leave me alone, or I shall suggest to your father he give you the spanking you clearly deserve.'

Heat rose up Juno's neck, warming her chilled skin.

She could still hear the amused contempt in King Leonardo DeLessi Severo's voice, still see the bored superiority in his blue eyes, still feel the inappropriate goosebumps as he'd grasped her wrists in firm hands and dragged her arms off his shoulders.

Good to know the memory of that summer night—when she'd thrown herself at the King of Severene at the Monrova Summer Ball and been brutally rejected—still had the power to make her cringe, big time.

Quite impressive really when she considered all the other cringeworthy moments she'd accumulated over the last eight and a half years—the most recent being the social-media snafu in her new job, which this last-minute trip into her past had been a handy way to avoid.

Some things never change.

She tugged her goggles down, and revved the snowmobile's engine.

Forget about it.

She wasn't going to think about that last disastrous summer in Monrova or the mistake she'd made a couple of days ago in New York in her new job at Byrne IT. Luckily it wasn't *that* big a screw-up and the big boss, Alvaro Byrne, knew nothing about it. It would all have blown over long before she got back to New York.

Juno headed across the gorge towards the unused entrance to the palace she and Jade had discovered during the summers they had spent together in Monrova after their parents' divorce.

But as she located the path etched into the cliff face—*result*—she couldn't seem to stop her mind from drifting to the past again.

Those summers had been so precious after she and Jade had been separated as eight-year-olds. They'd been so happy, so excited, at the chance to reconnect for two months each year, once Juno had been forced to live the rest of the year in exile in New York with their mother, Alice, and Jade—two minutes older and therefore the heir to the throne—had stayed with their father, King Andreas, to be instructed in her role as the future Queen. But as the years had passed, and Juno's life in New York had become increasingly chaotic, she'd found it harder and harder to live under her father's strict rules, and not drag Jade into mischief with her.

That cringeworthy moment with Leo had been the last straw—once her father had found out about it. Juno shivered as she manoeuvred the snowmobile along the narrow path, every single word he'd said to her that day—and the cold, flat disapproval in his eyes—still fresh...

'If you can't behave yourself in a manner befitting your status, I will have you returned to your mother in New York immediately. Do you understand me? Each summer your behaviour gets worse. You're insolent and disobedient, a bad influence on your sister, and now you've disgraced the Crown by behaving like a hoyden and throwing yourself at King Leonardo. You're becoming as much of a liability as your mother.'

Of course, she'd told her father where he could shove his ultimatum, because she'd been hurt and humiliated and struggling desperately not to show it. But the chilling way he'd nodded and then had her removed from the palace—without even giving her a chance to say goodbye to her sister—still haunted her.

No wonder she hadn't returned to Monrova while her father was still alive. Had he ever even loved her?

Shuddering, she brushed away the tear that had seeped out from under her goggles.

Jeez, Juno, dial down on the drama, before you end up freezing your eyeballs.

It didn't matter now. King Andreas had been dead for

over a year. And today she was returning on her own terms—to surprise her sister.

Jade was the ruler of Monrova now. Jade with her serene sweetness and her full open heart. Jade who loved her enough not to see Juno's many faults.

Juno huffed out a laugh as she took the final bend in the path and spotted the wrought-iron gate she had been looking for.

Bingo.

She was coming home for Christmas and nothing—not memories of Leo's brutal rejection or her father's final punishment or even her own impressive ability to screw up on a regular basis—could stop her.

All she had to do now was get to her sister's suite of rooms in the palace's West Wing—where she knew Jade would be chillaxing before tonight's Winter Ball—without being spotted by the royal staff.

And for that, she had a cunning plan.

Twenty minutes later Juno approached her sister's suite, astonished her plan—to pretend to be the Queen—had actually worked.

Decorated in garlands of fir and holly and red and gold satin ribbons and sprinkled with fairy lights, the ornate salons and sitting rooms she passed looked magical and mysterious dressed in their Christmas finery, the way she remembered them as a child.

The scents familiar from her last Christmas at the palace as an eight-year-old—fresh pine sap, wax polish and cinnamon—seared her lungs, but she refused to let the wave of nostalgia derail her.

Reaching the suite she had once shared with her sister, she opened the door.

Every one of her fondest memories slammed into her

as she spied her sister, sitting on an antique Chesterfield sofa in front of a roaring fire reading a novel. Jade's vibrant hair, so like Juno's own, haloed around her head, the cascade of chestnut curls lit by the lights from the expertly decorated tree in the corner of the room.

'Jade,' she said, her voice a rasp of emotion.

Her sister's head lifted. 'Juno?' she whispered. 'You're… You're here?'

The hope and longing in Jade's tone wrapped around Juno's heart. And joy blindsided her.

'Yes, but keep your voice down, I'm here incognito.'

A bright smile ripped across Jade's face as Juno's demure sister dumped the book on the floor and leapt out of her chair.

Juno's heart pounded so hard and fast it hurt, as her sister flung her arms around her. She absorbed the comforting scent of vanilla, for the first time in what felt like for ever. Tears stung her eyes and she hugged her twin back, as tight as she could.

Their shared laughter echoed off the luxury furnishings and seemed to make the fire in the hearth and the sprinkle of lights on the tree burn brighter.

I'm really home, at last.

'It's so, so good to have you here. Finally.' Jade laughed and tucked her feet under her butt as they settled together on the sofa.

Her sister seemed ridiculously pleased to see her, but Juno noticed Jade was thinner than she remembered her, and even more serene. Perhaps too serene, her calm reserve more ingrained—almost like a shield.

'It's good to be here,' Juno said, and meant it.

'How long can you stay? Please say you can attend the Winter Ball tonight? I'm sure we can find you a gown. It'll be so much more fun with you there. Do you need food? Tea? Wine? Champagne?' Jade asked, her excitement as infectious as her grin as she reached for the smart device used to summon the palace staff.

'No!' Juno lurched forward to stop her sister. 'Let's wait to tell them I'm here. That's why I sneaked in. I wanted to surprise you, but I thought we could spend some alone time before everything goes nuts.'

'Wait a minute... Do you mean *no one* knows you're here?' Jade put down the keypad. 'How did you manage that? Perhaps I should have a word with my Chief of Security.'

'Simple.' Juno wiggled her eyebrows. 'I snuck in via our secret entrance, then I just pretended to be you.'

'You're joking?' Jade pressed her fingers to her lips.

'Not joking, it worked like a charm too.'

'Juno you are unbelievable,' her sister said, astonishment turning to admiration. 'And you haven't changed a bit.'

'About the Winter Ball,' Juno said. 'I suppose I could come. But why don't I turn up unannounced?' she added, already enjoying the joke. 'Everyone will think they're seeing double.'

See, Father? Still not behaving in a manner befitting my status.

'That's brilliant...' Jade's grin widened. 'Except...' She hesitated, the grin disappearing and her excitement deflating. 'Except King Leonardo is going to be there as the guest of honour. He might not find it amusing.'

What the...? Was this some kind of test? Or a sick joke? Why did *he* have to be here?

'Leo the jerk's here?' Juno said, hoping Jade couldn't see the blush heating her collarbone.

She'd never told her sister about that disastrous attempt

at seduction on her last night in Monrova, and she never would. Her mortification did not need company.

'King Leonardo is not a jerk, Juno.' Jade's smile softened. 'He's a brilliant diplomat. A conscientious and extremely intelligent ruler. And a...' Her sister paused and Juno spotted the flicker of doubt cross Jade's face. 'He's a good man even if he has sowed a few wild oats.'

'A *few*?' Juno shot back. 'The guy's a player. He hasn't sowed a few wild oats, he's sowed enough to put an industrial grain conglomerate to shame since he became King...' Two months before Juno had developed that ill-advised crush on him...

'That's not true,' Jade said, protesting a bit too much. What was going on here? 'He's curbed his romantic engagements in the last few months and—'

'Hang on...' Juno interrupted, recalling the avid press speculation recently about a 'fairy-tale marriage' between King Leonardo of Severene and Queen Jade of Monrova. A rumour Juno had dismissed as hype. Jade had never mentioned Leo in all their email and text conversations over the years, not once. Because Juno would have remembered. 'Why is Leo the guest of honour? You're not...?' Why wasn't Jade meeting her gaze? 'The rumours aren't true, are they? You're not actually dating him?' Juno hissed.

The thought of her sweet, kind, gentle and totally innocent sister hooking up with Leo the man whore was the literal definition of leading a lamb to slaughter.

'No, we're not dating. I don't...' Her sister's blush subsided. 'He's good-looking, I suppose, but we just don't click.'

'Well, thank goodness for that,' Juno said, the twist of horror in her gut releasing a little. Although she had to wonder if her sister was blind.

Leo might be an arrogant jerk but, unfortunately, he'd

only become more impossibly attractive in the years since she'd fallen for his dark charms.

At twenty-two, he'd been moody and magnetic and totally gorgeous, at thirty he was even more so. Not that Juno had spent any time perusing the many, many photos of him plastered all over the celebrity press. Much.

'But...' Jade's gaze rose and Juno did not like what she saw, because she knew that expression—stubborn, loyal and scarily pragmatic.

'But...*what*?' Juno said.

Jade sighed. 'But I am considering King Leonardo's offer of a political union between us. Father was in favour of the idea before he died. And the benefits to both our countries are undeniable. A shared heir would...'

'Hold on!' Juno lifted her hand. 'Did you just say shared *heir*? As in a baby? What kind of a political union are you talking about?'

Her sister had the grace to look sheepish. 'A... A marriage.'

Juno's stomach twisted into a pretzel. 'You're not serious?' She took a breath, because she was starting to hyperventilate. 'You just told me you don't even find him attractive. And now you're saying you want to *marry* him and have his *babies*?'

Couldn't her sister see how nuts this sounded?

'*Want* would be too strong a word,' Jade said carefully. 'But I am considering it, yes. Our advisors are strongly in favour of the political union. And we wouldn't have to be intimate to have an heir. There's...' The blush returned. 'Well, there are other ways of conceiving.'

Ways Juno would bet Leo the Player King was not going to be interested in. The guy oozed hotness in every photo and news clip Juno had ever seen of him—even if Jade couldn't see it. No way would a guy like that consider getting his wife pregnant via in vitro fertilisation. Not unless it was absolutely necessary.

'Have you talked to Leo about the other ways?' she asked.

'Well, no,' Jade said, because she really was that innocent. 'We haven't negotiated anything. Yet.'

'Yet?'

'I said I would give him an indication tonight if I was willing to proceed with—'

'Good, so there's still time to stop this madness,' Juno interrupted, her mind working overtime.

She needed to figure out a way to stop Jade from making a decision she could end up regretting for the rest of her life. And fast.

Her sister had been trained for monarchy her whole life by their father, but there was such a thing as being too dutiful. And considering marriage to a guy you didn't even want to date definitely qualified.

Juno didn't have a lot of experience herself. Contrary to appearances, after Leo's humiliating rejection, too many unwanted advances as a teenager from her mom's handsy boyfriends, and one totally *meh* encounter at high school when she'd lost her virginity, she was not that fussed about sex herself... But surely there had to be more to it than making heirs in a test tube.

And, maybe it was cheesy, but what about love?

'But—' Jade began again.

'But nothing,' Juno cut her off. 'I'm not going to let you do this, Jade. Not for Monrova and certainly not because our father wanted you to. He's dead, you're the monarch now and you're entitled to a life.'

Juno glanced around the room, suddenly seeing the ornate furnishings for what they were, or what they had always been to Jade: a gilded prison. While Juno had lived a chaotic life with their mom on Central Park West, with no boundaries whatsoever, Jade had lived a life of stifling duty with nothing but boundaries.

'A life outside these walls,' she murmured as an idea took shape.

A radical idea that was fraught with possible disaster but also exhilarating and inspired and kind of cool.

Why the heck not?

Jade needed to get away from here—at least for a little while—and get a life. A real life—a normal life. Or as normal as it was possible for either of their lives to be. A life where she got to make her own choices for once—without having to factor in everyone else's priorities. A life where people weren't watching and judging her every second of every day. A life where she could be imperfect, she could make mistakes, and it wouldn't create a diplomatic incident.

A life not unlike the one Juno was busy living in New York.

Suddenly Juno knew, this idea was perfect. A Christmas gift she could give to her sister—as long as she made it crystal-clear Jade didn't have to go into her office.

But how was she going to get Jade to go for it?

'Juno, what are you thinking?' Jade said, a bit too perceptive, as always.

'Nothing,' Juno said, still thinking.

'Really?' her sister asked. 'Because you've got that look on your face you always got before getting us both into trouble.'

Instead of looking concerned at the prospect, though, Jade looked intrigued, curious, maybe even excited—just as she always had when they were children.

And suddenly Juno knew exactly how to sell her bombshell idea to her sister.

Jade had always been one hundred per cent loyal. No matter what, she had always stuck up for Juno when their father went ballistic.

Jade believed Juno would have made a wonderful Queen. Jade was dead wrong about that, of course. Juno would make a disastrous royal.

Perhaps she could be bold and tough when she had to be, but she was more likely to be reckless and impulsive and mouthy—not qualities that made you a shoo-in for the job of monarch or even princess.

But what mattered now wasn't what Juno was *actually* capable of, only what Jade *thought* she was capable of.

'I've had an idea…' Juno said. 'It's kind of nuts, but it'll give you the time and space you need to consider whether you *really* want to marry King Leo the Jerk.'

Or rather the time and space to figure out what a car crash that would be.

'Leonardo is not a jerk,' Jade repeated, but she smiled, the spark of curiosity in her eyes undimmed.

'And it'll give me a chance to see whether or not Father was right to kick me out of the kingdom with Mom,' Juno continued, riding roughshod over the 'Is Leo or Is He Not a Jerk?' debate.

Been there, done that, had my ego torn to shreds to prove it.

'Dad was wrong.' Jade's smile flatlined. 'What's your kind of nuts idea?' she asked, totally taking the bait.

Juno sucked in a breath. *Here goes nothing.*

'I think we should swap places for Christmas.'

Jade's eyebrows shot up her forehead.

'From now until New Year's Eve,' Juno added. 'I'll be the new Queen of Monrova and you can be Princess Pauper of Queens.'

CHAPTER ONE

KING LEONARDO DELESSI SEVERO of the Kingdom of Severene was so bored he was on the verge of lapsing into
a coma.

Attending official events such as the Monrova Winter
Ball were all part of the job description when you were
the ruler of a wealthy European country. That and giving pointless speeches, making dull, dignified small talk,
wearing uncomfortable uniforms decorated with too much
brocade, and hefting around polished ceremonial swords,
which you'd been taught how to wield with rapier-sharp
accuracy as a boy but had never had a chance to use.

Queen Jade's financial secretary droned on about the
remarkable yield from last year's rapeseed harvest as Leo
imagined whipping out the golden sabre banging against
his hip and slicing off the feather in the man's tricorn hat.

He stifled an impatient sigh.

Where was the Queen?

The woman was close to an hour late for her own Winter Ball.

He liked and respected Monrova's new monarch. When
he'd outlined the benefits of a marriage between them, she
had seemed intelligent and engaged, if reserved. She would
make him a very suitable wife and joint head of state. Her
status and lineage, not to mention her country's abundant

mineral reserves, and their similar dedication to civic duty would make theirs the perfect power partnership in the region—plus eventually provide both their countries with an heir. And she was quite beautiful, objectively speaking. There hadn't been much of a spark between them—and he had an unfortunate suspicion she might be a virgin. Her father had often talked proudly of his daughter's 'respectability' before he died, which Leo had assumed was a euphemism for not allowing her to date—and since she had assumed the throne there had been no whiff of any romantic entanglements… Except with him—which he knew to be fiction.

Even if he was hoping to make the rumours a reality.

He would have preferred she not be completely chaste, but he had never had a problem satisfying a beautiful woman, so he didn't see her chronic lack of experience causing too much of a problem once they were wed.

Her tardiness, though, was another matter.

He'd had to exchange more than his fair share of tedious conversation with faceless bureaucrats. And he was starving. His stomach grumbled on cue, the rumble detectable under the tinkle of champagne flutes and the strains of a chamber orchestra in the far corner of the palace antechamber where they were all waiting for the Queen's *late* arrival.

He ignored the flushed reaction of the financial secretary to his increasingly demonstrative hunger pains. What did the man expect? He hadn't had a chance to eat since breakfast due to his full schedule of talks with Monrova's trade ministers.

Talks that the Queen had chosen not to attend because her advisors had said she needed time to 'prepare' for the ball.

If she agreed to become his bride, he would have to

make it very clear that delays of this nature would not be tolerated.

A wailing bugle interrupted his internal diatribe, and a royal courtier appeared on the balcony above the ante-chamber.

About damn time.

A hush descended over the crowd as Queen Jade appeared.

But as she descended the wide sweeping staircase the strangest thing happened. His breathing became a little ragged.

Weird.

He'd considered her beautiful the last time he'd met her a month or so ago. But he had never noticed how lush her figure was before now. The sensual curves filled out the floor-length silver satin ball gown she wore to perfection, drawing his eye to the gown's bodice embroidered in gem-stones and her generous cleavage.

He dragged his gaze away as his breathing became laboured. Surprised by his reaction.

Her thick chestnut hair had been arranged in an elaborate up do crowned by a diamond tiara. The headdress's gems glittered in the chandelier light and created a halo that high-lighted high cheekbones and the sultry shape of her eyes.

His breath became trapped in his lungs as the satin shimmered, moving sinuously over her voluptuous figure.

Whatever the hell she'd been doing for the last four hours, it had been worth it.

She looked every inch the Queen, but there was some-thing earthy and elemental and much more approachable about her too, which he hadn't sensed a month ago. Which was even more surprising. He was usually an exception-ally observant man when it came to women. Especially women he intended to marry.

The spark he'd been convinced didn't exist began to sizzle.

The crowd parted and her gaze—bold and direct, and nowhere near as demure as he remembered it—locked on his. Instead of greeting the other, less senior guests first—which was the protocol—she walked past them and headed through the crowd straight towards him.

The sizzle became hot and fluid, sinking deep into his abdomen. The buzz of anticipation in his blood almost as loud as the buzz of conversation building around the room.

Was he actually getting turned on?

Her gaze roamed over him, both daring and amused, and he suddenly had the feeling she was assessing him like one of his own prize stallions. Why had he never noticed that mischievous sparkle before either? It turned the refined jade of her irises to a vibrant emerald.

'Good evening, Leo,' she said, her voice a smoky purr.

The spike of adrenaline was as unsettling as the prickle of surprise.

Every other encounter he'd had with the Queen, she had been exceptionally well versed in etiquette and protocol. She had never even called him by his given name and no one used that nickname...

No one except...

'Kiss me, Leo, you know you want to.'

The shocking memory of bright emerald eyes naked with longing, a voice full of childish demand and adult yearning, and soft fingertips trailing across his nape and detonating in his groin, sent a shaft of déjà vu through his system so uncomfortable he stiffened. The prickle of shame not far behind it.

Not the same girl, damn it.

That had been Jade's twin sister. Princess Juno. King Andreas's younger daughter, the disobedient teenager who had developed a ludicrous crush on him eight summers ago. Ludicrous, that was, until she'd tried to kiss him and—for one split second—he'd been tempted.

He'd been twenty-two and she'd been sixteen. A child and a really annoying one at that. Until that moment in the moonlight, when his libido had played tricks on him—and what he'd seen was the woman, instead of the girl.

He shook off the unsettling memory. The lack of sustenance was obviously messing with his head.

This was the Queen of Monrova. The woman he planned to marry. Not her extremely annoying—and utterly undisciplined—twin. Thank God.

A whisper rolled through the crowd. No doubt the use of the nickname was going to be all over the media tomorrow.

Leo forced a confident smile. 'Good evening, Your Majesty.'

'I hope you haven't been waiting too long,' she added, even though the mocking tone suggested she didn't care in the slightest.

What the hell?

Her breasts rose and fell, the plump flesh straining against the low-cut gown. But then a flush spread deliciously across her collarbone.

Something hot and volatile stirred, to go with the sizzle that hadn't died. And the forced smile on his lips became genuine. She felt it too, the electric chemistry that had hit him like a lightning bolt.

He gave her a mocking bow and let his gaze rake over her in return.

Whatever game she was playing, he had the urge to play it too.

'Your Majesty, believe me, you were more than worth the exceptionally long wait.' He grasped her fingers and pressed his lips to her knuckles. She shivered—and the sizzle became a spark.

'Shall we?' he said.

'Of course,' she replied, although she sounded less sure. *Touché, Your Majesty.*

He folded her arm under his, tugging her against his side to lead her into the banqueting hall.

Even in her heeled slippers, her head barely reached his collarbone, which made her shorter than the women he usually dated. At six foot four, and with a muscular physique, he generally preferred women who didn't make him feel like a giant. But while the size disparity had concerned him before, now he found it a turn-on too.

Perhaps her previously undetected boldness didn't have to be a bad thing?

They entered the large banqueting hall and he tensed.

Fresh holly wreaths elaborately finished with gold ribbons had been hung from the cornicing, while candles burned in the wall sconces to mark the upcoming festive season.

Christmas was his least favourite time of year.

She glanced at him. 'Is something wrong?'

'Not a thing,' he said, surprised she had noticed the slight hesitation. And not sure he liked it.

But when she disengaged her arm as soon as they reached their seats at the top table, he stifled a smile.

Not quite so bold now?

Waving off the waiting footman, he pulled her banqueting throne out.

As she deposited her bottom onto the velvet cushion, an unfamiliar scent teased his nostrils—citrus and musk—which was fresher and more intoxicating than the vanilla perfume he had detected before. His gaze fixed on the spot behind her ear.

Was that where she wore her scent? What would she taste like if he kissed her there? How would she react? Would she writhe? Would she moan?

Before he could think better of it, he whispered in her ear. 'Fair warning, Your Majesty. After my exceptionally long wait, I'm starving.'

She glanced round, her gaze filled with a compelling mix of surprise and awareness. The flush on her cheeks had his mind fogging with lust and his gaze snagged on her mouth. A vision of biting into that plump bottom lip and soothing it with his tongue tortured him.

He drew back, disturbed by the intensity of his reaction.

When was the last time he had wanted a woman so badly he had acted on instinct? His manners were usually impeccable.

Stop staring at her mouth.

'Just to be clear, I'm not on the menu,' she said.

'If you insist, Your Majesty,' he replied. 'Although I consider it my sworn duty to change your mind.'

Her eyes widened—and she frowned. 'Good luck with that, Leo.'

He let out a rough chuckle as the last of his restraint headed straight out of the banqueting hall's large mullioned windows and into the December night.

Game on.

CHAPTER TWO

'I BELIEVE THIS is my dance, Your Majesty. Shall we move through to the ballroom?' Leo bowed, but the formal request was as mocking as the challenge in his crystal blue eyes as they met Juno's.

It was the same challenge that had been tormenting Juno all through several courses of cordon-bleu cuisine.

What the heck had she unleashed? Because whatever this thing was between her and Leo, it was as dangerous as it was unexpected. Unfortunately, it was also exciting.

Leo offered her his arm, the dare in his eyes unmistakeable.

When had she ever been able to resist a dare?

She laid her fingers on his arm and felt the muscles of his forearm tense.

Applause followed them as he led her out of the banqueting hall and into the ballroom beyond—but she could hardly hear it over the pounding of her own pulse.

Leo is a jerk. Leo is a jerk.

Maybe if she kept repeating it, she might remember it.

Because Leo's jerk credentials had become harder and harder to remember through supper, every time he smiled at her with desire darkening his gaze; every time he offered her a taste from his plate like the Pied Piper of seduction; every time he murmured some wry observation and made her laugh; every time he made her heart thunder, or her pulse race or the hot sweet spot between her thighs throb.

Leo might be a jerk, but he was also a super-hot and super-charismatic jerk—and now he was giving her the undivided attention she had once craved, he was also super addictive.

They reached the centre of the ballroom at last, the crowd flowing in behind them to wait for their inaugural dance. Leo positioned himself in front of her, resplendent in his dress uniform, an array of medals emblazoned across his chest, his shoulders so broad and strong all she could see was him. Threading his fingers through hers, he lifted her right hand into position as the thirty-piece orchestra played the opening bars of a Viennese waltz, then wrapped his other arm around her waist to draw her into his big body.

Sensation shot up her spine, as his large palm rested on the small of her back, above the low-cut gown. The gown she'd spent an extra hour getting into to make him wait. And to irritate the heck out of him.

While Jade was en route to New York to get a life, Juno had decided her mission tonight was to make Leo reconsider the benefits of a 'political union' with the Queen.

She had thought it would be a cinch. Because eight summers ago irritating Leo had been her super power.

But not tonight.

Tonight every time she opened her smart mouth, made a suggestive comment or attempted some subtle—and some not so subtle—mockery, instead of irritating Leo, she had amused him. And he had only become more attentive.

And attentive was bad, because it only encouraged the impulsiveness that had always been Juno's downfall.

As soon as she'd descended the stairs into the anteroom and seen the ludicrously hot figure Leo cut in his formal clothes, his black hair almost blue, the tempting dimple in his chin making her want to lick it, the shot of adrenaline had become addictive.

And as the night had gone on, it had only got worse.

Because beneath his formal attire and curt mocking manners, Leo had discovered how to neutralise her super power.

No man had ever been aware of her every breath and blush and heartbeat with the same raptor-like focus. No man had ever spoken to her with such respect for her intellect while also relishing, even encouraging, her attempts to outrage and disarm him. No man had ever enjoyed her company the way he appeared to.

And as a result, the only person who had been disarmed was her.

And that had not been the plan at all.

Even as she knew her reaction to Leo was getting out of control, her body swayed in time with his as he swung her round in the steps of the dance. Her breath seized and she got a lungful of his rich exotic scent—starch, salt and subtle, sandalwood cologne.

Her pulse throbbed heavily in her sex—and everywhere his body touched hers—as the lights from the chandelier whirred above their heads.

At last the other guests began to join them on the ballroom floor. The lights dimmed, the dancers glided around in the golden glow of candlelight—their finery as dazzling as the ballroom's ornate rococo design. But all Juno could focus on was the man she clung to.

As the waltz ended, Leo brought them to an abrupt halt in the middle of the room, then leant down.

'Let's get out of here,' he murmured, his breath sending a shiver down her neck. 'So we can discuss our future plans.'

Not a good idea.

'We… We can't,' she managed, disturbed by how much she wanted to say yes. 'I'm the host. I'm supposed to stay till the end of the ball.'

I think!

His lips quirked in the super-sexy smile that had been driving her insane all evening. '*Really?* You're going to play the protocol card after teasing me to death through two solid hours of too-rich food and that never-ending speech from your minister of state?'

'Well… Yes,' she said, stupidly flattered by the thought she'd had the power to tease him at all. 'It will look bad.'

'Jade, honey.' He sighed, cradling her cheek. His calloused palm skimmed over her skin, as his thumb found the pulse hammering in her collarbone. She could feel the eyes of the assembled guests on them, hear the hushed whispers above the music at his forward behaviour. He was making a spectacle of them both, why did that only excite her more?

Was that Leo's superpower—the ability to seduce any woman into compliance at fifty paces?

'We have much to discuss,' he added. 'And everyone will think it's romantic if I drag you away after one dance.'

'But it's not romantic,' she murmured, mesmerised by the challenging light in his eyes as the hot sweet spot between her thighs burned.

'True,' he said, and her chest deflated. 'But that doesn't mean we can't create an impressive show.'

As if to prove his point, he caught her fingers, lifted her hand, opened her closed fist and bit into the swell of flesh under her thumb.

Arrows of sensation darted down, turning the sweet spot into a molten bundle of unrequited yearning. She groaned and he laughed. She tugged her hand free, brutally aware of their audience, but even more brutally aware of the insistent ache between her thighs.

'You wouldn't dare,' she murmured, the challenge issued before she could stop it.

'Watch me,' he said, then clasped her hand and began to lead her through the crowd.

The music had stopped, the eyes of everyone upon them as the guests parted to let them through.

This was madness, but it was an intoxicating madness. The reckless child inside her, who had once sneaked into another ball to kiss him, wanted to see what he would do.

As he headed towards the back of the ballroom, she spotted doors leading onto a balcony that overlooked the gorge, closed now as the snow fell in scatters of white.

It was the same balcony where she had propositioned him all those years ago, at another ball. And been discarded far too easily.

'Wait.' She tugged him to a stop, a laugh trapped in her throat when he shot an impatient look over his shoulder.

'We've waited long enough,' he said. And she had the terrifying thought he knew who she was. That he recognised the rejected girl she'd been. But then he added, 'I thought that waltz would never end.'

'Could we go that way?' she managed, pointing towards the secluded balcony. If he was going to kiss her, she wanted it to be there. Where he'd refused to kiss her all those years ago.

It was nuts, but somehow she felt she owed it to that reckless child. Apparently she still had something to prove to that love-struck girl.

He frowned, his gaze drifting over her ball gown. 'Are you mad?' he said. 'You'll freeze.'

'Perhaps you can find a way to keep me warm,' she

said, a little stunned by her own boldness. Her pulse leapt as arousal flared in his eyes.

'Excellent point,' he said, but as his grip tightened and he changed direction towards the balcony doors her sister's chief of staff—Major Something or Other—stepped into their path.

'Your Majesties…' The man introduced himself and bowed low, effectively blocking their escape route.

Juno scrambled to recall his name. Jade had told her who he was in the list of details they'd exchanged that afternoon, about their respective lives, but…

'Garland? What is it?' Leo said, his impatience obvious. *Garland. Hallelujah.*

'Perhaps you would both like to repair to King Andreas's former study, so we can discuss…' Garland leaned forward, lowering his voice so their crowd of inquisitive onlookers couldn't overhear '… the latest trade agreement.'

Say, what now? Panic ricocheted through Juno. A trade agreement? Jade hadn't mentioned anything about having to negotiate a trade agreement tonight?

'Queen Jade and I wish to speak alone about our trade agreement,' Leo said.

Relief rushed through Juno as she figured out what trade agreement they were discussing. Otherwise known as the political union with heirs attached. Leo's large hand landed on Juno's hip, his palm skimming over the satin, possessive and provocative. Sensation rioted over her skin.

'But, Your Majesties…' Garland began. 'The advisors are ready to discuss—'

'We can have this discussion without our advisors, Garland,' Leo's commanding voice interrupted.

Dismissed, Garland bowed and turned to leave.

'Wait, Garland, take this with you and give it to my valet,' Leo said.

He let go of Juno's hip, and lifted the ceremonial sword and scabbard he had been wearing all evening over his head. Then handed it to the astonished advisor.

As Garland held the sword, Leo flipped open the buttons of his uniform jacket.

'Leo? What are you doing?' Juno murmured.

To her total astonishment, he winked at her as he took off the jacket, then draped the heavy brocade garment over her shoulders. The fabric was warm from his skin, the jacket large enough to reach her knees, enveloping her in the scent of soap and sandalwood and clean male. An older female guest nearby sighed, the hum of approval from the crowd matched by the strange glow suffusing Juno's chest at the chivalrous gesture.

'Let's go.' Leo grasped her hand and headed towards the balcony doors.

The colour rose in her cheeks as he led her through the adoring crowd. She felt like the head of the cheerleading squad, wearing the captain of the football team's letter jacket after a winning game, times about a hundred. Except she'd never been a cheerleader in high school and never been on the captain of the football team's radar.

It was a heady feeling, but also kind of shocking, not just to be singled out by Leo, but to know it could make her feel important, when she had always laughed at those girls in the past.

Leo grasped the crystal handle and pulled open the heavy glass door to the balcony, then executed a sweeping, mocking bow.

'After you, Your Majesty,' he said as the blast of cold air chilled Juno's flushed cheeks. 'Our private sanctuary awaits.'

Memories of that night eight years ago clogged Juno's throat. She'd surprised him out here then, having snuck down from her room to catch a glimpse of her crush. She'd grown up since then, a lot, because she'd had to, hiding her mother's addictions while dealing with all the responsibilities her mother had abandoned over the years. And lost any belief in fairy tales.

But as she stepped outside, the frozen air misting her vision, a part of that wild, troubled but still innocent child stepped into the night with her. And a lump got lodged in her chest making it hard for her to breathe.

Let it go. You're not that besotted kid any more.

This wasn't romantic, she told herself staunchly. Leo had an agenda—he wanted a political union, and probably to get into her pants.

But even as her natural cynic tried to control her breathing, the lump grew, threatening to block off her air supply, as Leo stepped onto the balcony behind her. His big body shielded hers as he rested his hands on her shoulders.

The door slammed shut behind them. And suddenly she was alone with him in the still night. Her pulse accelerated to warp speed.

He pressed his face into her hair, and inhaled.

'Your new scent is killing me,' he murmured. 'It reminds me of summer. What made you change it? Because I definitely approve.'

'I wanted to torture you…' she said, pushing the words out past the ever-expanding lump—she'd started wearing this scent eight years ago to impress him with how grown up she was. It hadn't had the desired effect then.

'It worked.' The rough chuckle against her nape was a salute to that desperate teenager. 'Vanilla doesn't suit you.'

She tensed, the moment of panic not helping with her breathing difficulties. Jade had told her during their long exchange of details to be careful of Leo, that he was an exceptionally observant man.

Juno had dismissed the warning. If Leo was so observant why hadn't he been aware of her long campaign to get him to notice her that summer?

But Jade had been right. And whatever happened tonight, she couldn't afford to have their ruse exposed.

But the danger of discovery only increased her excitement as Leo gripped her hand—his fingers warm, hers already chilling—and led her away from the prying eyes of the crowd inside the ballroom, to the far end of the snowy balcony.

Towering over her, his body heat warming her, he cupped her cheek, then ran his thumb over the line of her lips. 'How did I not notice how exquisite you are until tonight?' he murmured.

Her cheeks heated, panic and exhilaration combining in the pit of her belly, as his gaze lifted to her tiara and then glided down.

Was it her sister he saw now? Or her?

She shivered.

'How are you not freezing?' she managed, trying for mocking but getting breathless instead.

He barked out a laugh. 'Great circulation,' he said, but then he framed her face in both hands and tilted her head up to the torchlight. 'And hours of anticipation.'

He lowered his mouth, his wide sensual lips hovering over hers—the tantalising promise hurtling her back in time.

'Kiss me, Princess,' he demanded.

Her mouth opened on a sob of longing and welcomed him in.

Leo threaded his fingers into the silky locks at the Queen's nape and claimed her mouth. At last.

Her lips softened, her throaty moan a siren call to his

already overwrought senses. He captured the sultry taste of wine and desire, as the kick of need throbbed in his groin.

The woman had bewitched him, all evening, and the only way to break the enchantment was to give them both what they needed.

Her fingertips settled on his waist, making the muscles of his abdomen tense and the burgeoning erection throb as the kiss became carnal in a heartbeat.

He grasped her hips to draw her closer. The satin glided under his hands like a whisper, but the feel of the firm, toned body beneath, the lush curves shivering under his touch, sent the twist of need into his gut.

His tongue tangled with hers, exploiting, demanding, so hungry for the taste of her he doubted he would ever be sated. He found her nipple with his thumb, rigid beneath the thin satin of her dress; she gasped but arched towards him in an instinctive cry for more.

He drew the bodice down, ducked his head to warm the taut pebble with his lips, her scent surrounding him now. He drew her breast into his mouth, felt her buck in his arms, as her nipple engorged. The frantic need echoed in his groin. Holding her in place, he found the apex of her thighs through the gown, pressed the heel of his hand where he knew she would need it the most. He heard the tortured sob. The sudden desire to pull up her gown and find the slick nub with his fingers was so sharp and shocking, he tore his mouth away from her breast. Lifted his hand to her hips.

This was more than temptation.

Too much more.

They were on a balcony, in the snow, damn it.

He dragged a staggered breath into his lungs. Her eyes were fixed on his, glazed with arousal, but also shadowed with shock as he drew the bodice of her gown back up to hide the reddened nipple.

What the hell had just happened?

He'd planned to seduce her, to charm her into agreeing to the marriage—or at least to debating it—but this sudden, visceral connection, this stark hunger didn't seem charming or expedient.

This wasn't a seduction. It was something more. Something he did not recognise. Something he wasn't even sure he could control.

She shuddered and stepped back, out of his arms, the dazed look replaced by wariness.

'That was a mistake…' she said.

Gripping the coat, *his* coat, she wrapped it tighter around her body, the body he was suddenly far too eager to explore.

'Why?' he demanded, even though a part of him agreed with her.

The taste of her had been too real, too addictive.

The benefits of a political and financial union had been the last thing on his mind as he'd fed on her surrender.

The truth was, he was finding it hard even now not to drag her back into his arms and finish what they had started. Her flushed face, and the reddened skin on her chin from his kiss, the memory of her hard nipple engorging in a rush made the throbbing in his pants painful. But why be coy?

He wanted her and she wanted him. That didn't have to be a bad thing. In truth it could be a very good thing.

Her gaze darted away as she sank her teeth into her bottom lip.

The pounding in his pants intensified.

Not good.

He grasped her chin. 'Answer me, Jade,' he said. 'Surely

discovering there is some chemistry between us—' And wasn't that the understatement of the century? '—will make a marriage between us even more beneficial.'

And hot and wild and…

Focus, Leo.

He curbed the insistent ache. And dropped his hand, to stop himself from devouring her all over again.

Her eyes flickered with something that looked like panic.

'I'm tired. I should…' She hesitated, and it occurred to him the kiss had shocked her too, as she jerked a thumb over her shoulder. 'I need to go to bed. I'm exhausted.'

Really?

But the ball wasn't over yet. It had barely begun. And they had not even discussed the marriage.

He forced himself not to voice his impatience though. Her flushed face and wide eyes made her seem younger than she had a moment ago. The sense of déjà vu niggled at the back of his mind—why did he feel as if he had been here before with her?—but he dismissed it.

'As you wish, Jade,' he said, shoving his hands into his pockets, to control the desire to drag her back into his arms.

She was an innocent, he needed to remember that. What had just happened had shocked him as well.

'Let's continue this discussion tomorrow.' *Once we've both calmed down enough to have a conversation.*

'Yes, let's… Thank you.' Her visible relief made him smile.

She would be his, all he had to do was wait.

'I'll… I'll see you tomorrow. When do you leave?' she asked.

He frowned; didn't she know the schedule? 'Noon.'

'Okay, good,' she said, then rushed past him.

He watched her disappear around the side of the building—the sight of her in his jacket as appealing as everything else he had discovered about the woman he was now determined to make his bride.

Before tonight, all he'd seen were the political and economic benefits of their union. But tonight he had discovered that there would be considerable fringe benefits too.

The Queen was skittish, that much was obvious. But perhaps that was to be expected. Until tonight there had been no hint of any chemistry between them. Especially not a chemistry of this magnitude. The truth was the intense passion between them had blindsided him; he wanted to be able to control it, before they took this further.

But if it had blindsided him, what must it have done to her? After all, she had no experience of men.

He strolled to the balcony door, the chilly air prickling over his skin. But instead of returning to the ballroom he took the path she'd chosen around the side of the building.

The chivalrous thing to do would be to return to the ball.

But despite outward appearances he was not a chivalrous man, he was a realist. And if he did not return to the ball either, rumours would be rife tomorrow about their joint disappearance.

Rumours he could exploit.

CHAPTER THREE

JUNO AWOKE THE next morning, groggy and disorientated.

Am I dreaming?

Her brain and body struggled to adjust to the alien feel of luxury cotton sheets, and the unfamiliar sight of thick velvet drapes, antique furniture and the view through a tall mullioned window—not of the fire escape of the apartment block opposite hers, but of an enchanting Alpine vista blanketed in snow.

Then her gaze alighted on the uniform jacket draped over one of the armchairs, the memory of hot lips had her nipples drawing into tight peaks and reality came rushing back.

Monrova. Jade. The swap. The ball. *Leo.*

She pressed her fingers to her chin, where Leo's kiss had left a mark.

The man was a born kisser. That kiss had been more than worth an eight-year wait.

But the memory of what had happened next had the heat flushing through her system again. She cupped her swollen breast, felt the molten spot between her thighs where his hand had pressed for a few terrifying seconds of bliss.

A light tap sounded on the bedroom door, jerking her out of the erotic trance.

'Your Majesty, it's Serena, I'm here with Jennifer. Are you awake?'

Serena? Jennifer? Oh, yes, her sister's personal assistant and her personal maid.

'Yes. Give me a minute,' she said, dragging her still-aching body out of her sister's bed.

She checked her sister's phone.

It was past noon. Leo and his entourage had been due to leave by noon.

A strange combination of relief and disappointment echoed through her confused body. It was for the best, she told herself staunchly—as soon as he had told her the time of his departure she had intended to avoid seeing him again at all costs.

Leo was a dangerous man. Not just observant, but demanding and so hot he had incinerated her control and her common sense last night. One kiss and she had been his, revelling in his touch, his taste, her body not her own. She couldn't afford to get that close to him again.

She tugged on a silk robe. Tied her hair back, so that neither woman noticed it was shorter than her sister's, and tried to calm her racing heartbeat. Not easy, considering she was hopelessly jet-lagged, she was still struggling with last night's kiss bombshell and, unlike Jade, she had never been a morning person.

'Come in, Serena,' she called out.

The middle-aged woman hurried into the bedroom with a harassed look on her face, followed by the younger woman who was carrying a tray loaded with...

Breakfast... *Yum.*

And coffee.

Praise the Lord.

'Your Majesty, are you well?' Serena said, clutching a bunch of the morning papers, while Jennifer proceeded to put the tray on a small table by the window and set out her breakfast. 'I have taken the precaution of making an appointment with the palace physician.'

'I'm great, Serena, no doctor needed,' Juno said, grabbing a slice of toast off the tray and slathering on some butter.

Note to self: set an alarm tomorrow.

Her sister probably got up at dawn no matter what time she'd been up the night before.

'You can cancel the appointment. Sorry I overslept. Last night was...' *What?* Intriguing? Astonishing? Terrifying? Dangerously exciting? 'Quite tiring,' she said, as she sat down in one of the room's armchairs. After finishing the toast in a few quick bites, she grabbed the coffee cup Jennifer had just finished pouring.

'Thank you, Jennifer, you're a lifesaver.' She inhaled the delicious scent before swallowing a life-saving gulp. 'Perfect.'

'Thank you, Your Majesty.' The maid curtsied. 'Would you like me to add the cream and sugar now?'

Juno plopped the cup back down on the tray. *Oops.* 'Oh, yes, of course.'

She'd totally forgotten her sister's sweet tooth.

Juno watched, dismayed, as the maid loaded the coffee with enough cream and sugar to give any normal person tooth rot. She took another sip and tried not to gag.

'Mmm, lovely, Jennifer. Thank you, that's just how I like it.'

Really, Jade?

Serena finished talking on the phone. 'I've cancelled the appointment, Your Majesty, if you're absolutely sure you're well?'

'Yes, really.' She could not risk getting examined by the palace doctor. She and Jade were identical, but she had a small scar on her knee she'd got skidding into home base aged twelve—and a unicorn on her hip.

She'd got the tattoo on her eighteenth birthday—a month after her mom's death, and the day after their Central Park apartment had been repossessed.

At the time it had been a statement of purpose. Proof that she was a survivor. Right now it would be an even bigger statement she was an imposter.

'Okay, wonderful,' Serena said, but she still looked harassed. 'His Majesty will be so pleased. Could I tell him you'll be down in twenty minutes?'

'Sorry? What?' Juno said, dumping the cup back on the tray.

Leo was still here?

Suddenly swallowing the sugary coffee without vomiting was the least of her worries. The twist of anxiety in her gut was nothing compared to the incendiary buzz of sensation firing over every inch of her body.

'I'm sorry to rush you,' Serena said. 'But he's been quite insistent. Apparently he has been speaking to Major Garland about your schedule and he wants to discuss a significant change after last night's events at the ball.'

Last night's events at the ball?

Juno's skin began to heat. The memory of Leo's lips on her breast—so firm, so forceful, so demanding—far too vivid.

The woman laid the papers she had under her arm on the breakfast table. 'The reaction to the news of your romance has been overwhelmingly positive, by the way.'

Their romance! What romance?

Juno blinked, the heat exploding in her cheeks, and several other places besides, as she scanned the newspapers— her breathing becoming increasingly difficult.

Check Mate: Has the King Finally Taken His Queen?
Is Royal Romance Confirmed at Last in Monrova?
Having a Ball, All Night Long!
Look of Love for King Leo and his Future Queen?

Each headline was illustrated with tons of candid shots…
Of her and Leo looking loved up as they flirted during the
banquet and danced far too close together. But the worst
were the shots taken from a variety of angles as he followed
her out onto the balcony, her body swamped by his coat.
The anticipation on her face would have put a child who
had just been given their very own candy store to shame.

No. No. No.

How had she managed to trash the reputation of Monrova's monarchy in one night?

Not that she usually gave a damn about the reputation
of the monarchy, not since her father had made it clear
it was more important to him than she was. But she was
giving a damn about it now—because trashing the monarchy's reputation meant trashing her sister's reputation too.

She'd messed up. Again. And Jade would be the one
to pay the price.

'While he has been rather impatient this morning, I
suppose it is to be expected.'

Serena's words interrupted Juno's mental walk of
shame. 'Excuse me?'

The woman's blush had faded, and her expression had
softened. 'I should have congratulated you, Your Majesty.
I really had no idea the negotiations had gone this far. But
you do make such a romantic couple. I don't know why I
didn't see it before. Everyone will be overjoyed when you
set a date.'

Negotiations? Date? What. The. Actual…?

Juno slapped her hand on the papers. 'Right, I see,' she

said, trying to think round the wodge of panic threatening to choke her.

She hadn't agreed to anything last night. Had she?

The end of the evening, after that clinch on the balcony, had been a blur, her senses still reeling from the shock of discovering Leo was a kiss ninja.

She pursed her lips, the tingle returning full force.

Stop thinking about him and start thinking about how on earth you're going to get out of this—without everyone finding out that you are not your sister.

'Your Majesty, we really must get you ready.' Serena's beatific smile had faltered as she whipped out her phone. 'I promised His Majesty faithfully he would not have to wait too much longer to see you. He's a rather forceful man, is he not?'

Forceful? Yeah, that was one way of putting it.

She pushed the tray to one side. She'd lost her appetite anyway. She really did not want to see Leo again. He was her kryptonite, the unpredictable effect he had on her something she wasn't sure she had any control over. But from the look on Serena's face, she knew she didn't have a choice. How could she get out of this meeting without making Jade's assistant and everyone else suspicious?

'Okay, Serena,' she said. 'Could you let Leo know I'll be there as soon as I can, I promise?'

Juno headed for the shower, hoping against hope she could come up with some kind of a plan—to handle her catastrophic fall from grace last night and the rumours about their 'romance' but, most importantly of all, Leo's devastating ability to make her forget everything except the promise of pleasure.

'Her Majesty, the Queen of Monrova.'

Leo turned from his contemplation of the snowy landscape—a view he had been admiring for over an hour now—to see Queen Jade enter the room with her personal assistant.

Wearing designer jeans and a sweater, her hair tied up in a knot, she should have looked neat and pretty and demure—the same impression she'd made on him during their meeting a month ago. But as she walked towards him, his gaze snagged on the way the skinny jeans and sweater clung to her curves, and his fingers burned to free her hair from the prim topknot. It didn't suit her now, the way it had before, some tantalising tendrils already escaping from confinement to cling to the line of her neck.

How would she taste if he placed his mouth on the pulse point?

'King Leonardo, I'm so sorry to have kept you waiting so long,' she said.

King Leonardo? Not Leo?

He frowned at her strained smile as she held out her fingers in greeting. So she was going to pretend last night had never happened.

He captured her fingers in his, lifted them to his lips and watched the smile falter.

'You seem to be making a habit of it, Jade,' he said as he released her.

She brushed the back of her hand against her jeans, probably trying to ease the sensation still lingering on his lips. He smiled, glad to see she was as incapable of controlling that buzz as he was.

'I'm afraid I overslept, Your Majesty,' she said, the snap in her voice amusing him.

There she was, the spitfire from last night. Demure be damned. This woman was about as far from demure as it was possible to get. Who would have guessed he would find that so hot?

'But there was no need to delay your departure,' she added, the stubborn tilt of her chin telling him to back off. 'Your Majesty.'

Unfortunately for her, he had the upper hand here and he intended to use it. The media had happily spread the story this morning, insinuating in that adorable way they had that he and Jade had already consummated their marriage plans last night after their joint early departure from the ball. Little did they know how close they had almost come to doing just that.

No way was he backing off now.

While she had been lying in bed—he stifled the image of her lush body, naked, beneath the sheets—he had been busy devising a plan with the obsequious cooperation of Jade's chief of staff, Major Garland, who it transpired was very keen to facilitate the marriage, because it had been her father's wishes.

Leo did not like the man. Officious and opinionated and old school and happy to ride roughshod over the Queen's wishes if he thought it suited her dead father's agenda, Garland reminded Leo of his own father's advisors, men he had been quick to fire as soon as he had acceded to the throne.

Humiliation closed his throat, as the phantom pain of his father's riding crop stung his backside.

Perhaps Garland wasn't as bad as those bastards, who had turned a blind eye to his father's excessive attachment to corporal punishment, but the major was in the same mould. Right now, though, Garland's support was useful.

'Of course I delayed my departure, Jade,' he said.

She scowled at the deliberate use of her given name and he had to bite down on his lip to stop a chuckle bursting out.

I swallowed your sobs of pleasure last night, and felt

your body soften as mine hardened. Do you really believe
we can pretend that never happened?

'We have much to discuss about our impending nup-
tials,' he finished.

Her eyebrows shot up her forehead.

'But... We haven't agreed anything,' she said, looking
flustered and unsure.

She really was very different from the woman he remembered, who had been so placid, so pragmatic about
discussing this topic. But they hadn't known then what
they knew now. That this did not have to be simply a ster-
ile political union.

'The press would disagree, after last night,' he said.

'But nothing happened last night,' she said as a guilty
flush illuminated the freckles sprinkled across her nose.

He stifled the urge to tug her towards him and kiss
each one in turn.

Focus, Leo.

'Really?' he said, raising a brow. 'Nothing at all?' he
murmured, letting his gaze drift to her breasts and enjoying her answering blush.

'Well, nothing much.' She pursed her lips into a tight
line.

Yup, she was still being tortured too.

'Regardless, I believe the judicious course of action now
would be to capitalise on the positive publicity from last
night and take this opportunity to explore our connection.'

'Our... Our connection?' she said, her eyes widening—
with horror but also awareness. And awareness he could
use.

'Yes, our connection.' He took her hand, which hung
limply by her side, and ran his thumb across the back of
it—to soothe her nerves, while also staking his claim.

She was young. And inexperienced. Her understanding

of men a lot less than her understanding of monarchy…
Although even that seemed to have deserted her last night.
But to be fair, it had deserted him, too.

He wanted to reassure her that he would not push her
the way he had last night, but make her aware that, at the
same time, theirs was a physical connection they could
both enjoy.

'I've spoken to Major Garland and suggested a state
visit to Severene for the next week. All the usual protocols
will be observed but it would be an excellent opportunity
for you to be introduced to the Severene people and for
them to meet you.'

And an even better opportunity for him to persuade her
this marriage would have some excellent fringe benefits.

'But I can't.' She tugged her hand free and stuck it into
the back pocket of her jeans, doing interesting things to
her bust.

'Why not?' He forced his gaze back to her face.

Still focussing, Leo.

'Because I'm busy here,' she said. 'It's Christmas and I
have stuff to do. Official stuff. And lots of it.'

'On the contrary, Your Majesty.' Garland stepped forward on cue. 'There is nothing in your schedule that can't
be postponed or rearranged.'

The stubborn chin was comprehensively contradicted
by the flash of panic in her emerald eyes. 'Are you sure?'

'Absolutely, in fact I have taken the liberty of already
making the necessary arrangements. Given our recent discussion of the huge benefits of your political union with Severene and its King—and how much King Andreas wished
this marriage to take place—I felt sure you would be very
much in favour of taking advantage of this opportunity.'

'But it's Christmas,' she said, sounding exasperated as

well as panicked now. 'Surely I should be here with *my* people, not Leo's.'

'You'll be back in time for Christmas,' Leo cut back in, stupidly pleased by her use of his given name again. 'Garland and I have arranged a seven-day visit culminating in the Severene Christmas Ball on December the eighteenth, at which you will be my guest of honour. You would return to Monrova the next day.'

He stemmed the twinge of regret that she wouldn't be in Severene over Christmas itself, when she would have provided an excellent distraction from the dark thoughts that always assailed him at that time of year.

'But…' she began again, clearly searching for something…*anything* to get out of this situation.

It was a good thing he had such a robust ego—her reluctance to spend a week with him something she was not making any effort to hide.

But he found her skittishness as captivating as he had last night.

Jade's reluctance could not be about the official visit. She was an expert at participating in these kinds of events, so her reluctance had to be about him, and the chemistry they shared.

He was glad their physical connection had unsettled her so much, because it had unsettled him, too.

'But I didn't agree to this.'

He stifled the sting of sympathy.

'Your Majesty,' the overbearing Garland butted in again. 'As you know, your father was keen for this match to—'

'Enough.' Leo lifted his hand, seeing the flash of something in her eyes that surprised him. Stubborn refusal, yes, but more than that… Distress. Garland's intervention was hindering his cause now, rather than helping it.

'I wish to speak to the Queen in private,' he said, giving

his own advisors a nod. They left the room immediately, knowing not to contradict their King's orders. 'Leave us, Garland,' he added.

'As you wish, Your Majesty,' the major said, and finally left too, because Leo suspected he was a chauvinist as well as a self-important stickler.

'Miss…' Leo turned to Jade's personal assistant, to dismiss her too, if he could remember her surname.

'Jenkins, Serena Jenkins,' she said, then, instead of obeying his order, she turned to her Queen. 'Your Majesty, are you happy to participate in a private audience with His Majesty?'

'I… I suppose so.' Jade blinked, as if she'd been pulled from a deep well. A well that intrigued him now as much as the rest of her. Perhaps her relationship with her father had not been as comfortable as appearances suggested? 'I suppose it can't do any more damage.'

He smiled despite the tension in the room. Damn but she was refreshingly outspoken.

Jenkins curtsied and left them alone together.

The hunger that had kept him up half the night surged. No longer able to resist, he pressed his palm to the flushed skin of her cheek.

She stiffened, but didn't draw away.

'Relax, Jade,' he said. 'I'm not going to devour you,' he murmured, even though he had to admit he wanted to.

Which was not like him at all.

He enjoyed women, and he enjoyed sex. But he had never felt this visceral need before.

He let his hand drop. Disturbed by the thought.

'I don't want to go on this state tour or visit or whatever,' she said, the flash of anger in her eyes a potent partner to the arousal.

'You have made that very apparent, Your Majesty,' he

said, determined not to be charmed by her candour again. They had a shared purpose, which had only been enhanced by what had happened on that balcony, and he was struggling to understand why she could not see it. 'To which I would have to ask, why? Garland is a pompous ass, but he is your advisor, and until last night you too understood the political value of our union.'

She blinked, clearly dismayed by the reprimand. He hadn't intended to be quite so blunt with her, but he'd be damned if he would allow her to ignore the huge benefits of the plan he had outlined with Garland.

'Right…okay,' she said, clearly flustered. Turning, she walked to the window, and wrapped her arms around her waist. He could see the tension in her body, and thought he understood it. 'I just…' she murmured, her voice so low he could barely hear it. 'I just didn't want to spend a week in Severene. I was looking forward to having no official duties now until after Christmas.'

He followed her to the window, his gaze roaming over her hair as he stood behind her. He shoved his hands into his pockets, resisting the desire to place his lips on the sensitive skin of her nape and breathe in the enchanting scent that had intoxicated him the night before. Now was not the time to claim the spoils of victory—or ignite a spark he still wasn't entirely sure he could control.

He understood what her real reservations were about joining him on this tour, even if she did not. This wasn't about the burden of the official duties. Jade had always been prepared to do whatever it took to benefit her kingdom. Her reluctance to spend the week with him was to do with the strength of the physical connection they had discovered last night. It scared her, he got that. As much as he planned to use it to his advantage, at the same time he needed to reassure her that he would not ravish her, the way he almost had yesterday.

All of which meant, he would have to be patient now, if it killed him.

'I want you to come to Severene with me, Jade. To see the kingdom properly, to get a chance to meet my people and for them to meet you.'

She swung round, her gaze both wary and tense. 'Really, is that all?'

'Not quite,' he said and, before he could stop himself, he touched his thumb to the tendril of hair that had slipped from her topknot and dangled enticingly over her cheekbone. Testing the texture between his thumb and forefinger, he hooked it behind her ear. 'I enjoyed last night immensely,' he said, the husky tone as raw as the desire searing his throat.

Arousal had darkened her irises to black, something she could not hide.

He tucked his hand back into his trouser pocket.

Don't push, Leo. Not yet.

She reminded him of an unbroken colt. What she needed now was persuasion, not pressure.

'And I want a chance to take it further,' he added, gratified when her cheeks coloured. 'Much further. But I will allow you to set the pace.'

'Really?' she said.

'Yes, really,' he concurred, prepared to give her the time she needed.

'But what if I don't measure up?' she said. 'As Queen, I mean. To your people?'

He frowned. What an odd thing to say. Of course she would make a good queen. She'd been trained for the role her whole life, just as he had. And she was already doing an exemplary job with her own subjects. 'I doubt that will be a problem.'

'You don't think so? After the scandal I've already caused?' He detected the note of vulnerability he'd found so fascinating the night before.

'*We* caused,' he corrected her. 'And the results of which we both enjoyed, so I'm not going to lose sleep over it,' he said, because he had lost enough sleep already over the memory of her lips opening for him, her nipple engorging under his tongue, that soft sob of…

For goodness' sake, focus, Leo.

'Okay, I'll do it. I'm come to Severene,' she said, as if they hadn't already agreed on it. 'But if the visit is a disaster, there'll be no more talk of marriage. Okay?'

It sounded as if she thought she was striking some kind of bargain.

He nodded, deciding to humour her. 'Absolutely. Not another word on the subject,' he said.

Because he intended to ensure, at the end of those seven days, their decision to marry would be nothing more than a formality.

CHAPTER FOUR

How DID I get here? And how do I get away again without messing everything up?

Juno stepped out of the private jet and stopped dead.

The barrage of flashes from the herd of press photographers held behind a cordon blinded her. The shouts and clicks became deafening.

How does Jade stand it?

'Jade, is there a problem?' Leo's steady voice interrupted her thoughts—until his palm landed on the base of her spine to direct her out of the plane and a whole new level of panic exploded along her nerve-endings.

'No, not at all,' she said, forcing herself to move.

He took her arm to lead her down the steps to a series of dignitaries lined up on the tarmac. She shook their hands, her mind dazed and her body far too aware of Leo's nearness.

Since he'd pressed her into going on this trip approximately five hours ago, he'd ignored her, while she'd been bombarded with instructions and information from her staff. But she'd taken barely any of it in, because she'd been completely unable to ignore him in return.

He'd greeted her at the airport and then spent the forty-minute flight over the mountains being briefed by his advisors while she was going over the schedule of events that had been arranged for her in Severene with Serena.

What the heck did she know about how to conduct herself during a walkabout of Severene's old town or a carol concert in the cathedral or the state opening of the capital's famous Christmas market? She wasn't a queen. She was a fraud.

But as Leo did the introductions, keeping her close by his side, her concern over all the things she did not know about her new role was nothing compared to the major pheromone freak-out going on because his big body and that tantalising scent were totally invading her personal space.

Having introduced her to the last of the dignitaries—all of whose names she instantly forgot—Leo directed her to the waiting limousine.

A uniformed chauffeur bowed and opened the door.

She stopped, Leo's hand still causing havoc on her back.

The dark leather interior looked warm and intimate. Way too intimate.

'Shouldn't I travel with Serena?' she managed to ask, glancing back to see her PA standing several yards away with the other advisors. 'I've still got a ton of work to do on the schedule briefing,' she added. It wasn't even a lie; she had no clue what she was doing over the next week.

Leo's dark brow lifted. 'You'll have time for that this evening. The first item on the agenda was our sleigh procession through the old town to the palace—the crowds are already assembled.'

They were?

She hadn't noticed that item on the agenda, but then she'd been too busy trying to ignore Leo and the effect he had on her to notice much of anything.

'Then why are we getting in a limo?' she asked, still delaying.

His hand shifted on her back, sending the shivers into overdrive. 'To drive to the barracks where the procession is ready for us. Are you scared to be alone with me, Jade?'

Absolutely.

'Of course not,' she lied, trying to sound outraged despite the heat in her cheeks.

His lips quirked at her indignant reply. She wasn't fooling him any more than she was fooling herself.

'Then get in the car, Your Majesty,' he demanded, calling her bluff.

Left with no choice, she scooted into the limo.

The leather interior only became more intimate as he joined her. They were several feet apart on either side of the large car, but even so she was too aware of him as the chauffeur sealed them in together.

Her pulse beat harder as the car drove off, winding down the Alpine gorge through the forest. She stared out of the window. She had to find a strategy for dealing with her reaction to Leo.

'While I find it remarkably flattering,' he began as she tried to concentrate on the incredible scenery outside the car, instead of inside it, 'there is no need to be quite so jumpy when you are alone with me. I promise not to touch you again... Unless you ask me.'

'It's not that...' *It so is that.* 'I'm just not sure we should present ourselves as a couple. I don't want everyone to be disappointed when the marriage doesn't happen.'

Leo's rough chuckle sent the shivers straight back up her spine. 'They won't be,' he murmured... And she heard the words he hadn't said.

Because the marriage will happen.

'But you can also rest assured you won't be required

to do more than you would normally do on these occasions,' he added.

She turned, to find him watching her.

The panic sprinted up her spine to join the inappropriate shivers.

Leo is an exceptionally observant man.

'Right, great,' she said as her sister's warning echoed in her ears.

Relax, Ju, or you'll blow your cover.

Stressing about what she didn't know about being a queen—which was pretty much everything—was the least of her worries. The truth was making a bad impression on this trip might not be a bad thing. It might be the only way to put Leo off the prospect of their 'political union with benefits'.

Being herself—without giving away her real identity—shouldn't even be that hard, because she'd effectively been doing it for four years, while building her social-media profile as the Rebel Princess.

She'd created the illusion of being a princess in exile—pampered and privileged and yet streetwise enough to connect with the general public—without ever letting on how tough her life had been. Aspirational was good on social media, micro celebrity even better; a homeless eighteen-year-old with debts she couldn't pay and a mother who had died of chronic alcohol abuse, not so much.

Her social-media activity had been a lifesaver after her mom's death. She'd bartered her Rebel Princess brand, such as it was, into enough of a money-spinner to keep herself afloat with the help of several dead-end jobs, without ever having to ask her father for a handout. But she'd been only too happy to jettison it a month ago when she'd been recruited to head up Byrne IT's Social Media Engagement Team. She'd come to hate the fakeness of everything she posted as the Rebel Princess. But her ability to project an image, play a role, would come in handy now. All she had to do was be convincing as the Queen of Monrova while also turning Leo off the idea of marriage.

The limousine pulled into the gates of an army barracks and stopped in front of a parade of uniformed horsemen—resplendent in the red and gold colours of Severene's national flag—and an ornate sledge complete with a team of six white stallions.

She swallowed. The chauffeur opened her door and she stepped out.

The dusky light shone off the snowy landscape and she could see the palace of Severene, tall and majestic, perched above the old town in the distance.

Leo got out of the other side of the car and walked round to offer her his arm.

'Your Majesty, your carriage awaits,' he said, the mocking tone almost as captivating as the sizzles of sensation that leapt up her arm and sank deep into her belly.

She had to play the role of Queen—enough to be convincing, but no more than that.

But as Leo escorted her to the carriage, the uniformed cavalry all saluting him as they passed, she knew not having her cover blown wasn't her biggest challenge.

Resisting Leo and avoiding a repeat of what had happened on the balcony was going to be the much bigger ask.

'Ready?' he asked, after they had settled in their seats in the sleigh, a fur rug covering their knees.

As I'll ever be.

'Smile, Jade, and relax, they love you already,' Leo murmured to his travelling companion as the royal sledge passed the crowds of spectators lining the route through Severene's old town towards the palace. The crowd were cheering, excited to see the woman they were keen to believe might become their new Queen.

He knew how they felt.

He turned to the crowd, threw a salute or two as they passed through the old town's central plaza and the sledge glided over cobbled streets buried under a layer of snow.

He noticed that Jade directed her attention to specific people in the crowd. The crowd clearly enjoyed the personal connection, but he wondered why her father's courtiers hadn't taught her the best way to conserve her energy? Exerting too much effort when waving could give you arm-ache.

She waved enthusiastically at a small boy being held on his father's shoulders. She swung round as they left the child and his father behind, her eyes sparkling with exhilaration.

'Did you see that little boy?' she said. 'I think he was waving at you.'

'Doubtful,' he said, surprised by her enthusiasm. 'You're enjoying yourself?'

'Actually, I am. It's exhilarating, isn't it?'

Is it?

Seriously? What was so exciting about a royal procession? Hadn't she done a million of these before?

He'd never found this part of the job appealing. 'I told you, they love you already,' he said, willing to use the evidence to his advantage.

'They don't love me, they don't know me,' she said, looking momentarily surprised by the idea. 'But they obviously love you.'

He frowned, taken aback by the observation. Was she mocking him?

'They don't love me,' he said. 'That's not my role.'

The one thing he could congratulate his father on was

that he had always ensured the Kings of the Royal House of Severo were respected, not loved. Maintaining distance and dignity with people you had been born to rule was important. Maintaining your privacy even more so. Or this circus could consume your life.

She watched him, her scrutiny making him uncomfortable. 'Then whose role is it?'

'The Queen's,' he murmured, but even as he said it, the brutal spike of memory—from another Christmas, a long time ago—made a strange band tighten around his chest.

'Why don't you join the other children, Leo? I'm sure Santa has a present for you too.'

'Papa said I must not. That my job is by your side, Mama.'

'Papa isn't always right, my sweet boy.'

'Why is it only the Queen's role? Isn't that a bit sexist?' Jade said, pulling him out of the uncomfortable memory.

He preferred not to remember his mother, especially at this time of year.

He smiled, amused by how direct she was. 'You disapprove?'

She stared at him. 'Of course, if they can love your Queen, why can't they love you too?'

'Perhaps that's the way I prefer it,' he said, noting her reference to 'your Queen'—as if that Queen was not going to be her.

He had work to do. Then again, he had always enjoyed a challenge.

'Why would you prefer them not to love you?' she asked.

'Because I'm not a sentimental man,' he answered honestly. 'And love isn't something I require.'

It was her turn to frown. 'Doesn't everyone need love?' she asked.

The statement was so guileless, it wrong-footed him for a moment.

Should he lie? And give her some appropriate platitude? After all, he was trying to woo her into marriage. But if she agreed to this marriage, he reasoned, she needed to be aware of the limitations. He certainly did not want her to believe their union could go beyond the physical and the political.

'Not everyone needs love, no,' he said. 'Some of us are self-sufficient and don't require that kind of connection. And emotional self-sufficiency is an invaluable commodity in a monarch, wouldn't you agree?'

Surely her own parents' marriage and the scandalous way it had collapsed was proof of that.

Her father, King Andreas, had made as much clear to Leo all those years ago, the summer he had been in Monrova on a trade mission, just after he had acceded to the throne of Severene. That was the summer the King's unruly younger daughter had developed a crush on him, and Andreas had first suggested a marriage to Jade.

At the time, his older daughter and heir had only been sixteen though, and Leo had baulked at the suggestion. He was not a cradle snatcher.

And in truth, the younger twin was the only one of Andreas's daughters he'd noticed that summer, probably because she had been so persistent in trying to get his attention.

But Leo still remembered the conversation he'd had with King Andreas the evening after the younger girl had tried to kiss him. He hadn't mentioned the incident to her father, but he had wondered if the man had discovered the truth somehow, because he had made a point of warning Leo off any entanglement with Princess Juno. At the time, Leo had found the suggestion amusing.

But he could still remember Andreas's candid words of warning because it had spoken volumes about the failure of the man's marriage.

'Juno is undisciplined and reckless and she always has been. She lacks the temperament for monarchy and since she has been living in New York I'm afraid she has become as much of a problem as her mother. Take it from me, Leonardo, pick your Queen with care and with a level head. Infatuation is never a good basis under which to make those crucial decisions. I speak from bitter experience.'

It was all Andreas had said on the subject that night, but Leo knew the story of his ill-fated marriage to Alice Monroe—the beautiful young actress Andreas had met at a UN reception in New York and then married less than a month later. Alice was a media darling and their whirlwind romance and fairy-tale wedding had captivated the press the world over. But not long after their twin daughters had arrived almost exactly nine months later, the cracks had begun to show.

By the time Andreas had finally divorced his Queen eight years later and sent her packing back to New York with their younger daughter, Alice's increasingly scandalous behaviour had come close to bringing down the Monrovan monarchy, and Leo was not surprised the man had regretted that initial infatuation.

Jade, his heir, had been the only good thing to come from it.

'Do you really believe that being royal means you don't need to be loved?' Jade asked, incredulous.

'That's not what I said,' he murmured, even though it was what he believed. 'But I do believe it can be an inconvenience that is better avoided.'

Her frown was replaced by something that looked disturbingly like pity. 'I see,' she said and looked away.

He stiffened, annoyed. Was it *him* she pitied? Why? Surely she of all people must know that love—or rather infatuation, for that was the emotion people often mistook for love—had no place in a royal marriage?

The sledge glided into the palace courtyard where a line of dignitaries and the palace's two-hundred-strong household staff waited to greet their arrival.

A young footman in the palace livery approached and opened the sled door, then unfolded the step. Bowing his head as was customary, he raised his hand to help Jade alight.

Taking his offered assistance, she bounced down from the carriage. But then to Leo's utter astonishment, she turned her attention on the young man.

'Hi, and thank you,' she said.

The footman blushed, glancing up from his bowed position, not used to being addressed directly.

'Your Highness,' the young man murmured, bowing so low Leo was surprised he didn't topple over. 'We are so honoured to have you in Severene.'

'And I'm honoured to be here,' she said. 'What's your name?'

'It's…' The young man's gaze connected with Leo's, the flush on his cheeks turning scarlet.

Leo nodded as he climbed down from the carriage behind Jade, giving the boy permission to speak to the Queen.

'It's Klaus, Your Majesty,' the footman said, looking completely nonplussed, but as he bowed again he shivered visibly.

'It's lovely to meet you, Klaus,' Jade murmured. 'Can I ask you how long you've been standing out in the cold?'

'About an hour, Your Majesty.'

'You're not serious, in that outfit?'

The boy nodded. And the Queen of Monrova turned, her gaze fierce as it connected with Leo's.

'Leo, this is ridiculous. Look what he's wearing. He hasn't even got proper gloves on,' she said.

'Yes, I see your point,' he said. She was right. The staff uniforms, although ornate, were hardly substantial enough for sub-zero temperatures. But it was the passion flashing in her eyes that fascinated him. Even though it was a cliché he had never subscribed to, he had to admit the Queen was quite breathtaking when she was mad.

'Who's in charge here?' she demanded.

'I suppose that would be me,' Leo said, even though strictly speaking it was the palace's Head of Household, Pierre La Clerk, who would have made the decision to have the staff stand outside. But he preferred to have all her passion directed at him.

An urge so perverse he would have to examine it later.

'Then don't just stand there, Leo,' she snapped. 'We have to get these people indoors immediately.'

He should have been outraged, of course. No one spoke to him like that and no one gave him orders. But instead he was captivated. Her unconventional approach—and her passionate determination to protect the young man shivering in his uniform—making him realise what a formidable queen she would make him.

Nodding, he clicked his fingers. And called over his head of household as another thought occurred to him.

Would he even have noticed the boy's discomfort? Highly unlikely, he realised. Ever since he could remember, state visitors were greeted in this way. Why had he never considered changing this arrangement before now?

Le Clerk approached with a stiff smile on his face—telegraphing his disapproval at the delay. Leo didn't care. The man had made a mistake.

'Your Majesty, if there is a problem with the—' Pierre began.

'Pierre, move the introductions indoors,' Leo interrupted him. 'Klaus here is freezing and no doubt so are the rest of the staff.'

'But, Your Majesty, it is tradition for—'

'Tradition be damned if it is going to give the staff frostbite.'

Pierre's lips pursed, but he bowed low. 'Absolutely, as Your Majesty wishes.'

Pierre, the palace butlers and the other senior staff members set about moving the welcoming committee indoors.

'Come on, Klaus, I think you probably need a hot toddy,' Jade murmured as she smiled at the young footman. 'I know I do.'

Leo watched the boy smile back at her—the worship in his eyes unmistakeable.

To think he'd once thought her reserve and her dignity were her main assets as a wife and a queen. Her unconventional style of leadership—which he hadn't even realised existed until last night at the ball—was surprisingly appealing.

The footman nodded, clearly shocked by the Queen's familiarity—weren't they all?

Leo placed his palm on the small of Jade's back—the desire to touch her undeniable.

She shuddered beneath his touch as he guided her into the palace. The electric energy that had been so provocative the night before arched between them again.

Once they had repaired to the palace's cathedral-like reception room, Leo whispered in her ear. 'Can I have a private word, Your Majesty?'

She glanced at him—and he could see the wariness in

her expression, but also the heat. The recollection of her mouth hot and eager on his fired through his system.

His palm remained on the small of her back as he directed her towards his private study. Getting her alone again might not be the wisest plan, but he'd be damned if he wasn't going to press his suit every chance he got.

Here it comes.

'Why did you want to see me alone?' Juno stepped away from Leo as soon as they entered his study, hating the defensiveness in her tone. And the strange sense of loss when he lifted his guiding hand from her back.

She'd been expecting the reprimand as soon as she had acted on instinct and demanded the introductions be moved indoors. But he'd lulled her into a false sense of security. To her astonishment Leo had agreed with her in public. Even gone so far as to make arrangements immediately with his staff. But she had seen his surprise at her actions. And that should have been a massive clue—that he was simply waiting for a more private moment to let her have it.

She waited for the axe to fall. But he simply stared at her, then said: 'Why are you so defensive, Jade?'

Juno's anxiety increased. A part of her knew she had to be more subservient—or he might figure out the truth about her identity. But another part of her knew she had not been wrong to protect his footman.

Surely Jade would have done the same, although probably more diplomatically. But the result would have been the same.

'I know what you're thinking,' she said, seeing the inscrutable twist of his lips.

Was he trying to torture her, to make her more acquiescent? Was this some kind of regal power play? Or was he

trying to soften the blow because he still wanted to persuade her to agree to the marriage.

The knot in her belly tightened.

Not knowing what the heck he was thinking only made
this worse.

She should never have agreed to come. Because her
clever plan—to persuade him she would make him a terrible queen by being herself—was already working... But
she'd just discovered it had one massive flaw.

She knew who she was. Even if Leo didn't.

So when she screwed up—either by accident or design—and Leo reprimanded her, it would be like dealing
with her father all over again.

It would be a replay of all those shattering blows to her
ego, and her heart, she had endured as a child, when he
had looked at her with cold, disapproving eyes and told
her—in actions as well as words—that she could never
be royal, could never be as important as her sister, could
never be worthy of his love. Dating right back to that day
when she was sixteen and he had kicked her out of his life
for good. She'd spent her life since that day convincing
herself her father's disapproval didn't matter, that it could
only hurt her if she let it matter. And now she was going
to be forced to relive it. For seven days straight. When
she was found wanting by a man whose opinion shouldn't
matter either... But somehow it did. And she didn't even
know why it did.

The anxiety began to strangle her. This whole situation
was so super messed up.

Propping his butt against the desk, Leo folded his arms
over his broad chest, his eyebrow lifting in challenge. 'You
know what I'm thinking? Why don't you tell me what that
is, then?'

Leo's disapproval did not matter. She wasn't trying to

impress him. In fact the opposite was true, she was trying to persuade him she'd make him a terrible wife. And a disastrous queen.

But somehow that goal had got lost in the surge of longing that had swamped her when he had supported her decision in the courtyard. And she'd wanted to believe he really did think she'd done a good thing.

'You're going to tell me I shouldn't have been so outspoken about Klaus,' she said, because she just wanted the axe to fall now so she could deal with it. 'I know you think I should have found another, more discreet way to suggest the introductions be done indoors. That there's a right way and a wrong way to do these things and I chose the wrong way.' How many times had her father told her the same? And okay, she got it, she was not a natural at this stuff. But she was right to have done what she did. If it meant no one froze to death just to observe protocol, so be it.

'Klaus was freezing, Leo. And I refuse to apologise for making that call.'

'I see,' he said.

She braced herself for the tirade of indignation, the anger at her recklessness. The tedious lecture about her overstepping her authority and letting her emotions rule her judgement.

She should have seen this coming much sooner. Why hadn't she? As soon as he had told her during their sledge ride he didn't think emotional connections were necessary in a royal marriage, that... How had he put it? That...

'Emotional self-sufficiency is an invaluable commodity in a monarch, wouldn't you agree?'

She'd actually felt sorry for him at the time. Why would anyone believe something so sad? Sure, love could be messy and difficult and it didn't always solve everything, in fact sometimes it solved nothing at all. She'd loved her mom and she knew, in her own screwed-up way, her mother had loved her. But that love had never been enough to stop Alice Monroe loving the bottle more...

But even with all its imperfections, love was still important. It could help and it could heal. Seeing Jade again and wanting to do this swap for her sister's sake as well as her own had proved that much. And she refused to believe that anyone could survive without needing love.

Unless they were a man as cold and unfeeling as her father.

That had been her mistake. To feel sorry for Leo because she'd somehow convinced herself he wasn't that guy. When actually he was.

After all, he wanted to marry her sister to give his country a political advantage and to have a shared heir. Any man who could even contemplate something so bloodless had to be seriously messed up—no matter how much her body might desire him.

'You know, Jade,' Leo said, tilting his head to one side now as if he were studying something particularly fascinating, 'I really do not know what to make of you. And, much to my absolute astonishment, because I usually prefer predictability, I'm finding that aspect of you even more irresistible than the memory of what happened yesterday night.'

What?

Juno barely had a chance to register her shock before he had pushed off the desk, unfolded his arms and crossed the room.

She took another step back, but couldn't control the swell of relief. Or was it longing? At the dark passion in his eyes.

He cupped her cheek, the soft brush of his palm making the tangle of raw nerves in her belly unwind in a rush.

'You're not angry with me?' she heard herself say.

'Angry? Not at all,' he said, and the inscrutable smile became a genuine smile. Her heart expanded. 'You did the right thing, Jade.'

The words seemed to reach inside and touch the heart of the child she'd been, all those years ago, when her father had chastised and rejected her.

'You really think so?' she said, immediately realising how needy she sounded when he gave a rough chuckle.

'Yes, I'm not quite the bastard you seem to think I am,' he said. 'The boy was freezing and if we'd waited much longer he might well have become hypothermic. I hate to think what the press would have made of that. And how much it would have cost the palace if he had sued.'

He was making light of the incident. But even so she could hear the respect and admiration in his tone.

He caressed her cheek. His thumb drifting across her lips.

'You should trust your instincts more,' he said, as if it were the easiest thing to do in the world. 'I don't know why you're insecure about your abilities, but, just in case no one else has ever told you this, you are an exceptionally good queen.'

She wasn't an exceptionally good queen, she wasn't any kind of a queen. But she found herself leaning into the caress anyway. And letting the joy at his heartfelt comment wrap around her heart.

His praise shouldn't mean this much to her, objectively she knew that. She didn't want it to mean this much. But subjectively, she couldn't stop herself from indulging that rejected child.

But then the needs of the woman came from nowhere. She pressed her palms to his broad chest, felt his pecs tense beneath his uniform.

His heart was beating in strong, steady punches. Her desire rose like a phoenix from the flames, making her want him so much it was almost painful.

He swore softly, then threaded his fingers into her hair and drew her face close to his. His mouth hovered over hers, tantalising, tempting, torturous.

'Ask me,' he demanded.

And so she did. 'Kiss me.'

His mouth slanted across hers, capturing her tortured gasp. Their lips locked in a battle of dominance and submission. She opened for him, losing the war. The need became painful as it throbbed between her thighs. He clasped her head in his hands, holding her in place as he devoured each sob, each sigh, each groan.

The kiss was firm, seeking, commanding, but beneath the hunger was something more. Something both brutal and tender.

She needed this; she needed him. His praise, his validation, his acceptance.

She grasped his waist, wanting more, and he groaned.

Passion shivered through her, hardening her nipples and making her body soften, the pounding in her sex so hard now it hurt.

That she could make him ache, the way she ached, that she could make him want her, so much, strengthened the surge of vindication. The surge of triumph.

But then his calloused palms slipped under the hem of the cashmere sweater she wore, and his thumbs traced the line of her waistband igniting the skin across her back. And he bit softly into her bottom lip.

The light nip was like a bomb, detonating in her sex.

She wrenched herself free and stumbled back, coming up short when she hit a leather armchair.

Her ragged breaths matched his as they stared at each other.

She touched her fingers to her lip, aware of the sting from his teeth.

He looked devastatingly gorgeous, with his chest heaving, his dark hair mussed, the dimple in his chin even more lickable than usual and the thick ridge in his pants prominent enough to make her mouth water.

'We shouldn't have done that,' she managed on a raw gasp.

I'm not the woman you think I am.

'But we did.' He ran his tongue over his lips. Could he still taste her? Because she could taste him.

She brushed her hand through her hair and became aware that the elaborate chignon the stylist had insisted on that morning had escaped its moorings.

'We should…' She attempted to repair the damage herself, frantically repinning the unruly locks as she spoke. 'We should return to the reception, before anyone notices we're gone, and gets suspicious.'

'Everyone will have noticed by now,' he said, the wry twist of his lips impossibly hot. 'And I hate to tell you this, but I think the speculation about our relationship is a horse that bolted out of the paddock yesterday evening.' He glanced down pointedly at the evidence of his arousal. 'And is now doing a victory lap in my pants.'

The rush of heat and adrenaline racing through her body made it hard for her to concentrate. And a smile at the outrageous comment lifted her lips before she could stop it.

He huffed out a strained laugh. 'I'm glad you find my discomfort so amusing.'

'I don't, I just…' She tried to regulate her breathing, the flirtatious comment making her aware of the danger again. This was not funny, at all. He wanted to get her into compromising positions. Why had she let him? 'It's just, it's complicated…'

So *so* complicated and getting more complicated by the second.

Having Leo want her wasn't exciting. Or wonderful. Or cool. That was her sixteen-year-old self talking. It was a disaster.

Giving in to this…this explosive chemistry…would be wrong. Both ethically and emotionally and every which way in between. She wasn't the woman he thought she was, but even if she were, the kind of marriage he was suggesting was a cold, clinical abomination of the term.

Nobody should be prepared to marry for the sake of securing a political union between two countries, or to provide an heir. It was nuts. And she was here to make him realise that, while her sister discovered the same while getting a life in New York. She was not here to obsess about his lips, or his chin dimple, or his delicious smile, or that magnificent…

Look away from his pants!

He was watching her again in that inscrutable and unbearably hot way he had, the twist of his lips more than amusement now. There was heat there too, and calculation. As if he knew exactly what her body craved and was figuring out the best way to use it against her.

Her pulse spiked.

She finished pinning up her hair as best she could and rubbed her finger across her lips hoping that her lipstick wasn't too smeared.

'Why don't I go back in first, then you can follow when…?' She glanced at the prominent ridge again that hadn't softened at all.

'You can follow when you're ready.' She made a beeline for the study door.

But as she passed him, he caught her wrist and drew her to a halt.

'Not so fast.' His thumb pressed into her pulse point, which went haywire as he tugged her round to face him. 'I want this marriage to happen. I think it will be hugely…' he paused, his eyes darkening with arousal '…beneficial for us both. And I'm not averse to persuading you how beneficial by whatever means necessary.'

It was a warning, plain and simple. She needed to be careful. To keep her hormones and everything else in check, or she might well end up doing something reckless and unforgivable… And Jade would be the one to pay the price.

Leo was a dangerous man. Arrogant, entitled, super goal-orientated and unbelievably hot. He'd already proved what a devastating effect he could have on her libido, and her best intentions, not to mention her self-control. He was a man who got what he set his sights on… And she was now in the firing line.

She dragged her hand free of his grip, rubbed her wrist where his touch had burned. 'Point taken,' she said, as haughtily as she could while her insides were giddy with a disturbing combo of nerves and guilt and…anticipation. 'But don't worry, I won't ask you to kiss me again.'

She headed for the door, ignoring the ripple of sensation that travelled up her spine from his mocking laugh. She had been warned, and she had to do everything in her power now to resist Leo, not just physically, but emotionally too.

CHAPTER FIVE

'Wait, Leo, there's a little girl over there we missed.'

Leo glanced round as Jade touched his arm, to see a small child in the thousand-strong crowd who had turned out to greet them at the opening of the Christmas market in Severene's old town. The little girl was huddled behind her mother's skirts, clutching a bunch of wilting hothouse flowers.

'You go ahead,' he murmured, surprised again by the Queen's innate ability to spot spectators who didn't push themselves forward—even if they were only two feet tall. It was a particularly impressive feat given how much the crowds had swelled in the last four days—ever since Jade's fierce defence of his freezing footman had been broadcast over the local media.

'She's your subject, Leo,' she said as she grasped his hand. 'Why don't we go and talk to her together?'

It wasn't the first time she'd suggested such a thing. She seemed to be on a mission to break down the barriers he had always had around his interactions with Severene's population. He suspected it originated in the conversation they'd had in the sledge on her arrival, right before Freezing Footman Gate. She was testing him to see if he would buckle.

He should have found her behaviour infuriating. The request to familiarise himself with his subjects went against every tenet of his monarchy. He simply was not a people pleaser—unlike Jade—and he was not required to be. The monarchy in Severene did not rely on a sovereign grant, so there had never been any need to schmooze the public. All that was required of the royal family was that they be visible.

He also suspected this was a distraction technique. An attempt to ignore the heat that had only grown between them since she had arrived in Severene.

The more he attempted to command her attention, the more she managed to deflect or frustrate him. And it was starting to drive him more than a little insane.

Had any woman ever been so damn evasive when he was attempting to pursue her? Especially when he knew the passion between them was entirely mutual. She might be managing to resist his attempts to seduce her, but she couldn't hide the shivers of response every time he settled his hand on her back, or kissed her knuckles in public. The only problem was he had a sneaking suspicion those PDAs were tying his libido in knots, more than hers.

'To hell with it,' he murmured under his breath. 'Let's get this over with, then.'

He could see his capitulation had surprised her—the truth was he'd surprised himself. He would never normally single out individuals the way she was so adept at doing. And he found conversing with children particularly problematic, especially shy children. He didn't mean to be intimidating, but somehow he was. During these past four days, though, he'd watched Jade build an easy rapport with the people of Severene—*his* people. So really, how hard could it be?

'Are you sure?' she said, and he had to stifle a smile. However awkward this was going to be, it would be worth it to have finally wrong-footed her for the first time in four days.

'Absolutely,' he replied, with a fervour he didn't really feel, but was more than prepared to fake.

She nodded. But then to his surprise, she smiled. An artless smile, devoid of her usual wariness. What he saw in her expression stole his breath in a way that made no sense. Because her green eyes were shadowed with something that looked very much like approval... And he didn't require anyone's approval.

They reached the line of people pressing against the ropes, and his breathing became uneven, something tugging at his memory that he knew he needed to resist.

The little girl pressed closer to her mother's side as they approached. But Jade squatted down on her haunches—not easy in the pencil skirt and heeled boots she had worn for the walkabout—so that she could converse with the child eye to eye.

'Hello, are those for me?' she asked, indicating the wilting flowers.

The small child nodded, her thumb now stuck resolutely in her mouth—was she trying to suck off her thumbnail?

'They're beautiful,' Jade said, the genuine warmth in her voice doing even stranger things to Leo's breathing, especially as he watched the child's eyes brighten.

The little girl thrust the bunch out.

'Thank you, so much,' Jade said, accepting the offering as if she'd been given a crate full of priceless jewels. How did she do that? How did she sound as if she cared when this had to be the fifth bunch of flowers she had been offered already today—and these were easily the most bedraggled?

'I'd love to know your name, so I can thank you properly,' she said, lowering her voice, ensuring that the child knew she had all her attention.

He found his own anticipation mounting, the pressure in his chest increasing, as the child considered the request and then popped her thumb out of her mouth.

'Ella,' she whispered, before stuffing her thumb back.

Jade laughed, the joyous delight in the sound making the pulse of anticipation in his chest turn to something sharp and unbidden. He tensed, shocked by his undisciplined, instinctive response.

What was wrong with him? Why was his reaction to Jade still so volatile?

'Ella? What a beautiful name,' Jade said. 'Thank you so much for these, I will treasure them.'

As she rose back to her feet, the child's mother curtsied. 'Thank you so much, Your Majesty. Ella picked them herself this morning—she was desperate to meet you after seeing you on the television. I know this means a lot to her,' the woman said, the moisture in her eyes making Leo feel uncomfortable.

How many of these walkabouts had he done in the past, without connecting with anyone? He'd always been taught to maintain a formal distance. But Jade's approach seemed so effortless, so enchanting, so...

He frowned.

He was supposed to be the one in control of this seduction. Not her. He had planned to exploit their physical desire for one another, nothing more.

But from that first day, when Jade had rescued Klaus the palace footman from frostbite—hell, that first night, when he had placed his jacket over her shoulders and seen her eyes go a little misty—he was becoming captivated by every unpredictable move. And all the qualities in her he was discovering.

'It means a lot to me too,' Jade said graciously to the mother. 'You have a lovely child.'

The uncomfortable sensation spread under Leo's ribs. Warmth yes, admiration yes, but more than that, a disturbing feeling of connection.

And a question that he had begun to ask himself rose to the surface again.

Why did he want to marry this woman? Because the reasons that had been so simple before he had seen her again at the Winter Ball didn't seem so simple any more.

All the reasons why their union would be a good one—politically and economically for both their monarchies—still applied. In fact they had been exponentially enhanced by her visit. But beneath the expediencies was the yearning—for something that went beyond those reasons. And that disturbed him.

No woman had ever fascinated and excited him the way she did. And he knew his desire to see her each morning at their breakfast table for their schedule briefings, and his reluctance to bid her goodnight at the entrance to her suite of rooms after their evening meal, weren't just to do with his campaign to get her to agree to the marriage.

'Leo, say hello,' Jade prompted, sliding her hand into his.

The mother beamed—it had been duly noted in the press on several occasions already how romantic the people found Jade's use of the nickname. But as he heard a barrage of camera clicks, he recoiled at the thought that their observers might have seen more in his expression than he wanted them to see. More than he wanted to feel.

He bowed to the child's mother.

Do the job and then you can leave.

'A pleasure, *madame*,' he said to the mother, who curtsied and then blushed. But as he prepared to leave, the niceties handled, Jade tightened her grip on his hand.

'Didn't you forget someone?' she said. She slanted her gaze to the little girl. 'I'm sure Ella would like to say hello to you too, Leo.'

There were more clicks, and flashes and the whir of cameras—and for a hideous moment he hesitated, trapped in the glare of the spotlight. A spotlight he had become accustomed to over the years, but had always been careful to keep at a distance.

He stood frozen, the memory that had prickled at his consciousness exploding in his mind's eye.

The brutal winter wind, the sombre wail of a trumpet dirge, his father's hand gripping his hard enough to hurt, the pain in his throat as he struggled to swallow the tears.

'Your mother is dead, Leonardo. Now stop simpering. It is your job as a prince to maintain your dignity at all times.'

'Leo, is everything okay?' Jade's gentle voice dragged him free of the prison of memory.

Everyone was staring at him. The child, her mother, Jade and the press, many of whom were still firing off their shots.

'Yes, yes, of course,' he said, wanting it to be so, humiliated beyond belief.

Where the hell had that come from? And why? His mother's death had been a lifetime ago. So long ago he hardly even remembered her.

'Are you sad?' He heard a small voice and looked down to see the child staring up at him with patient, perceptive eyes. And for one weird moment, it was almost as if she could see into his soul. Or rather the soul of that little boy, who had been cast adrift in a sea of other people's tears, looking for the one face who could rescue him—only to discover she was lost for ever.

'Not any more,' he said, his voice rough with emotions he didn't want to feel—fear, panic, loneliness—but didn't seem able to stop.

The child nodded, with a gravity beyond her years, then she smiled, a sweet, innocent, inquisitive smile devoid of judgement.

'Do you love Queen Jade like me?' she asked, adoration shining in her eyes.

I hope not.

The answer sprang from nowhere, rattling him almost as much as the cruel slap of memory.

'Ella, you mustn't ask questions like that,' her mother interrupted. 'It isn't polite.'

'Have a good Christmas,' he murmured to the child, and her mother, then, grasping Jade's hand, he led her to the waiting carriage, cutting the walkabout short.

He had to escape… The crowd. The press. The scrutiny. The messy emotions he didn't want to feel. The need he did not want to acknowledge. And the miserable memory of that day, which he thought he'd buried a lifetime ago—along with his mother.

'Leo, what's wrong? What happened back there?' Juno asked, staring at the King of Severene's rigid features as the limousine drove off towards the palace.

'Nothing.' He glanced her way, then stared back out of the window, the muscle in his jaw clenched so tight it was twitching.

This was not nothing. Even though he had the outward appearance of control, this was Leo freaking out.

'The walkabout wasn't finished,' she said. Since when did Leo not stick rigidly to the schedule?

'It was getting cold,' he said, by way of explanation for the sudden change of plans.

But he didn't meet her gaze, and she knew he was lying. Something had seriously spooked him.

And that was her MO, not his.

Or it had been four days ago, until she'd begun to find her niche as the fake Queen of Monrova.

Maybe she would never be as good as Jade at this stuff. But she'd found—much to her astonishment—that she wasn't completely horrendous at it either. As they'd been ferried around a series of events and engagements in the last four days, she had discovered she enjoyed meeting the citizens of Severene. Of course, it didn't hurt that they were all so eager to meet her. That had thrown her at first, because she knew she wasn't the person they thought they were meeting. But she'd dealt with the guilt by deciding she was Jade's stand-in, doing a job that Jade couldn't do because she was busy discovering herself in New York.

Perhaps it was dishonest, but it wasn't hurting anyone. Especially if she did a decent enough job. And the numerous formal engagements had also been a brilliant way to keep her desire for Leo at bay.

So she'd thrown herself into the events, and made a real effort to win over the people she met, so as not to disgrace her sister—while at the same time keeping Severene's King and his delusions about a marriage of convenience between them at arm's length.

The only problem was that as she threw herself into her charm offensive her biggest ally, and supporter, had been the very man she was trying not to fall for, in any way, shape or form.

In fact, she never would have been able to pull off being the Pretend Jade effectively if not for Leo. His encouragement over the last few days had been invaluable.

Trying not to let his approval mean too much had been something of an emotional minefield. Every time he looked at her with that fierce purpose in his dark gaze. Every time he touched and kissed her in public and her panties melted. Every time his lips lifted in that inscrutable smile, or something she'd done turned his deep blue eyes to a rich turquoise, she risked falling a little bit harder.

The only way to ensure Leo's attention—and her reaction to it—didn't derail her completely had been to remember three important truths. First Leo had an agenda, second, Leo thought she was a real queen, and finally, Leo's loyalty wasn't to her—or Jade—it was to the kingdom of Severene and his role as its monarch.

Remaining aware of his emotional detachment—to his subjects as well as her—had been the best way to keep that reality front and centre. Until he'd torpedoed it approximately five minutes ago. First by finally agreeing to meet one of his subjects, then stopping dead in the barrage of camera flashes, and giving her a glimpse of a man she hadn't known existed.

He'd recovered quickly, so quickly she was fairly sure no one else had noticed. But she had… In that split second, he hadn't been Leonardo DeLessi Severo, the smart, erudite, intimidatingly cool and collected King of Severene. Or Leo the scarily gorgeous man who could turn her inside out with lust. He wasn't even Leo, the arrogant charmer who wore his confidence and his cynicism like a badge of honour…

No, for that moment suspended in time, Leo had been lost and alone and in pain.

And Juno had realised for the first time the man she thought he was wasn't the whole Leo. That was only one side of Leo. And the other side was someone who could be vulnerable too, just like her.

Her heart rammed her chest wall as the sympathy and compassion and affection for Leo she'd tried so hard not to feel overwhelmed her.

'It wasn't that cold, Leo,' she replied. 'Something upset you. Was it…? Was it something I did?' she asked, feeling guilty for the way she'd badgered him to go say hello to the little girl.

His head swung round. His lips quirked.

'Actually, yes, it was,' he said, but the devastating charm she had become so used to was gone. In its place was something studied and deliberate, almost as if he were trying to deflect the conversation. 'I'm becoming rather tired of going through the motions of this visit, without ever talking about the particulars. And I'm even more bored of sharing you with all these people.'

His gaze dipped to her mouth.

Her heart bobbled in her throat. And the hot spot between her thighs pulsed, as it always did when he looked at her mouth like that… As if he wanted to devour it in a few quick bites.

She stared right back at him. 'What happened back there? You looked…' she swallowed, the compassion making her throat hurt '…so sad.'

He blinked and then frowned. But she knew she'd hit the mark when he turned back to the view of the streets as the limousine headed back towards the palace grounds.

'Just an inconvenient moment of déjà vu,' he said, his voice rough, as if he'd had to wrench the words from his throat.

The deep frown as he continued to stare out of the car window made it obvious he wasn't seeing the huddle of traditional shops—their mullioned windows alight with Christmas lights—he was back in that moment of déjà vu.

She reached across the car and placed her hand over the fingers he had fisted on the seat between them.

He jerked round—the contact like a lightning bolt.

'If you want to talk about it, I can listen,' she said.

The furrow on his brow deepened, and for a moment she was sure she'd overstepped. But as she lifted her hand, he released the fist and captured her fingers.

'Don't…' he murmured.

His thumb stroked her knuckles, absently, as he contemplated their joined hands.

'What was it about? The moment of déjà vu?' she coaxed gently.

'Stupid really, it was so long ago. And I barely remember her.'

She squeezed his fingers, desperate to reassure, because she could hear the pain he was trying so hard to hide in the flat conversational tone of voice.

'Who?' she asked.

His gaze lifted to hers. The puzzled frown like a bear coming out of hibernation, unsure of where he was. Whatever dark place he had gone to during their walkabout, he had been back for a return trip.

'Who do you barely remember?' she asked again.

He sighed, then looked away, but he didn't let go of her hand.

'My mother,' he said on a huff of breath, so soft, she could hardly hear him.

His mother?

Juno racked her brains, trying to remember what she knew about Leo's mother. She'd met his father, as a very young child, during a state visit, and remembered she hadn't liked him. Where her father had been detached, Leo's father had been downright scary. A tall, muscular, darkly handsome man who wore his superiority like a shield and had been dismissive of her and her sister because they were girls.

But she had never met Leo's mother, because she was pretty sure the Severene Queen had died before she and her sister had even been born—which would have made Leo a very young child when his mother passed.

'She died, when you were little, didn't she?' she asked.

'Yes, a long time ago,' he said. 'Her funeral procession was held in the old town a few days after Christmas.' The frown on his forehead softened. 'Perhaps that's why today's event reminded me of it?'

'How old were you?' she asked softly, not wanting to interrupt too much. The way he was talking, she wasn't even sure he was aware of her presence.

He shrugged. 'Five, I think. The stupid thing is… I didn't know at the time, as we walked behind the casket, with the press taking photos, and the crowds staring at me, and weeping, that she was dead.'

'They made you walk behind her casket?' she said, shocked.

What kind of monster would make a child of five walk behind his own mother's coffin? No wonder Leo had an issue with connecting with his own subjects. No wonder he treated the walkabouts and other chances to meet the crowds as a chore. No wonder he had no desire to let down the mask.

'I asked my father where she was, and when he told me I started to cry. He was furious,' he said, his voice so controlled, Juno felt her heart implode.

'Why was he furious?'

He turned, his distant expression becoming quizzical. 'Hmmm?'

'Your father, what was he angry about?'

'Public displays of emotion were not permitted behaviour for a prince,' he said, his voice so distant, so controlled and unemotional, her heart broke. 'When we returned to the palace, he punished me accordingly.'

'He punished you?' The horror turned her question into a hoarse whisper. 'How?'

She'd thought he was cynical, pragmatic, even a bit of a snob, a man completely unable to connect with ordinary people, when in reality it was so much more complicated than that. Leo didn't have a superiority complex, he was wary of public displays of emotion. And now she knew why.

'By taking a riding crop to my backside.'

'He *hit* you? On the day of your mother's funeral?'

Leo's face heated at the shocked sympathy shadowing Jade's eyes. He'd said too much. Far too much. He'd never admitted his father's dedication to corporal punishment to anyone. Because it would dishonour the monarchy and embarrass him. And it was ancient history now. But it had been so hard to resist her coaxing, and the squeeze of her fingers on his.

'My father was a hard taskmaster,' he murmured. 'I think he believed it was for the best, that I needed to learn early the importance of dignity at all times.'

'But you were a five-year-old child. Who had just lost his mother, Leo. That's absolutely hideous—how could he punish you for grieving?'

He shrugged, but the movement felt stiff. Why should her compassion for that unhappy boy mean something now?

'No one ever accused him of being a kind man, or a loving father,' he said, the rawness in his throat spreading up his neck. 'But he was a well-respected king.'

As the words left his lips, they sounded hollow and inadequate.

One thing Jade had shown him in the last few days, as he'd watched her engage with the crowds, treating them as equals instead of inferiors, smiling and laughing and connecting with his subjects in a way he never had, was that his father might have been well respected, but he had never been loved. And somehow he had taken that mantel on too, not by accident, but by design. In defending himself, defending that traumatised child, he had closed himself off from all but the most tenuous contact with anyone outside his inner circle.

'Who cares if he was well respected?' she said, the certainty in her voice making his ribs ache. Her trembling fingers squeezed his hand, and his heartbeat accelerated. 'He was still a monster.'

The fierce statement had a lump forming in his throat.

A lump of raw emotion…

He swallowed heavily, trying to force it down.

Don't let her see you bleed.

He'd become infatuated with the Queen of Monrova in the last week. Not just by her body and her scent and the way she responded to him so instinctively without even realising it. But also by her spirit, her intelligence, her smart mouth, her decidedly wicked sense of humour—and the unconventional way she seemed capable of sharing so much of herself with everyone she met.

But as she stared at him, with that fierce compassion in her eyes, and her fingers gripped his, the lump continued to grow.

'You deserved so much better,' she added. 'You were his son first and foremost, not a prince.'

He let go of her hand, and thrust his fingers through his

hair, the tight feeling in his chest becoming unbearable as the car entered the palace courtyard.

'There's no need to feel pity for that boy,' he said, struggling to talk now around the ever-expanding lump. 'He died a long time ago.'

'But, Leo, what he did is still sickening and you're still suffering because…'

'Stop…' He pressed a finger to her lips.

Her instinctive shudder of response ignited his senses in ways he understood.

'I don't wish to talk about it any more.' He couldn't talk about it. Couldn't think about that lost child. Couldn't let her see how much her defence of that child meant to him, or she would have even more power over him—and she had enough already. 'I want you, and you want me,' he said. 'Perhaps it is time to stop talking altogether?'

He clasped her face and tugged her towards him. Her hands covered his, but she didn't resist. Instead she softened against him.

He slanted his lips across hers.

This was what he needed from her, not pity or compassion, only this. And he'd waited far too long to take it.

His tongue delved deep, to capture her sob of need. The pent-up hunger of the last four days released in a rush as he gorged himself on her soft moan, her sweet mouth.

He angled her head to take the kiss deeper, to demand more. She clung to him, her fingers fisting in the cotton of his shirt, her tongue meeting his in a dance of temptation and desire.

The loud tap on the window had her jerking against his hold.

'Your Majesty, we have arrived at the palace,' the driver said through the tinted window.

'Leave the door closed,' he shouted, but he was forced to let her go.

Her hair fell around her face in disarray, her lips reddened by his kiss, her breathing as rapid as his.

'Let's stop overcomplicating this,' he said. 'I'm not a child anymore and neither are you. There's no earthly reason why we shouldn't make the most of the chemistry between us...'

Panic clouded her gaze. 'But I can't... I can't marry you, Leo, that hasn't changed.'

'To hell with the marriage,' he said.

Right now all he cared about was getting her into his bed. And stopping this need getting out of control. He'd revealed things about his past, his father, that made him feel more exposed than he had as a child, walking behind his mother's casket and feeling so alone in a crowd of strangers. That had to stop, but the only way to do that was to put this *thing* on a level he could control.

Sex was simple, uncomplicated. Emotion not so much. He had become obsessed with her; to break that obsession he needed to feed the hunger, stop trying to deny it.

'Do you...? Do you mean that?' she asked. 'You won't expect more from me if we...' he watched her throat contract as she swallowed '...if...if we become lovers?'

The wariness in her gaze made him reach out, to cup her jaw, and run his thumb across her lips.

'*If*, Jade?' he said, the surge of possessiveness undeniable when she leaned into the caress instinctively. 'Don't you mean, when?'

She pulled away from his touch, but the staggered passion in her gaze was all he needed to know.

She would be his. Before the week was out. But this was a big step for her. He needed to remember that. However instinctive her responses to him, however much she might desire him, she was innocent. He would be her first lover.

The surge of possessiveness—protectiveness even—at the thought shocked him to his core. He had never slept with a virgin before, had never wanted to, and had certainly never prized a woman's virginity. Why would he? It would be the height of hypocrisy, given that he was not a virgin himself. But somehow he couldn't deny that with Jade it was different.

He wanted to be the first man to hear her sigh, to hear her moan, to watch her come apart in his arms. But to do that, he needed to calm the hunger inside him.

'I just don't want you to think I've agreed to marry you by default,' she said. 'If we sleep together it doesn't mean more than that.'

He huffed out a strained laugh. Captivated all over again, despite his best efforts not to be. When were her honesty, her integrity, her directness going to stop surprising him?

'You have my word,' he said. '*When* we sleep together,' he corrected her again, 'it will be for our private pleasure and nothing else. The marriage is something completely separate.'

The truth was, he still planned to press the case for marriage. And he was more than willing to use their shared passion to his advantage in that regard. But he could do that at a later date. If the only way to get her into his bed now was to agree to her terms, he would do so gladly.

'*Can* we keep it private?' she asked. 'From the media? The public?'

He smiled, he couldn't help it. How could she be this naïve? After a year as a queen and even longer as a royal princess? How could she not know it would be all but impossible to keep such a liaison a secret for long? But even so he humoured her. He wasn't about to lose the chance to satisfy this maddening hunger on a technicality. 'We can certainly try.'

'When?' she asked, her directness surprising him yet again—and sending a new wave of desire south. 'When do you want to…to do it?'

Now.

He clamped down on the visceral urge to take her in the back seat of the limo.

She was putting him in charge. That she trusted him enough to do that would have to be enough for now.

'Is that a yes, Jade?' he asked.

Her cheeks flushed a deep scarlet, but she nodded, her gaze wary but forthright. 'I… Yes, I want you too.'

He curled his fingers into fists, to stop from grabbing her as the heat pumped into his shaft.

Her forthright attitude to sex was going to kill him.

'How about after the Christmas Ball, in three days' time?' he said, thinking fast, a plan already forming that should satisfy the need for privacy. 'That's our last official engagement. It will be easier to keep our liaison private once your state visit is over.'

No one need know that she had not returned to Monrova.

Three more days of having to control his desires and limit himself to PDAs was going to be nothing short of torture—especially now she had agreed to sleep with him. But keeping this next step private was important. Once they had become lovers, he could use their physical intimacy to his advantage in any marriage negotiations, but why expose themselves before it was necessary? Surely, they both deserved a little time to enjoy this aspect of their relationship first?

'I'll make all the necessary arrangements,' he said. 'Do you trust me, Jade?'

Guilt flashed in her eyes, surprising him. What could she possibly have to feel guilty about?

'Yes,' she said. 'Yes, I do.'

He smiled, dismissing the ripple of unease. No doubt the guilt was subconscious, and a result of her father's Neanderthal attitude to marriage and virginity. After all, Andreas had boasted about his daughter's untouched state to Leo on several occasions while trying to promote a marriage between their two dynasties over the years. At the time, Leo had thought the whole concept archaic and frankly sexist, proof of a double standard that he had never adhered to.

But the irony wasn't lost on him now as his libido responded enthusiastically to Jade's guilty flush.

Not only was he turned on by the thought of being Jade's first lover, he intended to be her only lover too.

'Excellent,' he said, lifting her fingers to his lips, and buzzing a kiss across her knuckles. 'I'll see you tomorrow.'

'Won't I see you tonight?' she said, the disappointment in her voice a sop to his ego. 'For the briefing dinner?'

'Not tonight.' He tucked a knuckle under her chin, stroked the pulse point under her jaw. It fluttered deliciously. 'I think for the next three days it might be wise if we limit our meetings to public engagements. So we're not tempted to jump each other ahead of schedule.'

'Oh, yes, of course,' she said, the freckles on her nose igniting all over again. He could not wait until he got to kiss every one of those freckles. 'Then I'll see you tomorrow,' she said.

He allowed himself one last quick kiss on the tip of her nose, before turning and opening the limousine door himself.

He didn't look back as he slammed the door then headed across the courtyard towards the palace.

The next three days were going to be agony, but Jade was a precious gift who was worth the wait to unwrap.

Anticipation fired through his system—making him feel like a child on Christmas Eve waiting for Santa to arrive, even though he'd never been allowed to believe in Santa as a child.

He would whisk Jade away to his father's old lodge. It was beautiful and secluded. And would allow them the privacy they needed—heat blasted through his system—to finally feed the hunger that had been building for the last five days. And in the days afterwards, he would have Jade all to himself to get her to accept his proposal of marriage.

CHAPTER SIX

'Juno, it's so good to hear your voice.'

Juno pressed the phone to her ear, the sound of her sister's breathless voice turning the butterflies in her stomach into a battalion.

'Sorry I couldn't get to the phone straight away,' Jade added. 'It's... It's pretty early here. And I thought we agreed we wouldn't contact each other, just in case?'

Juno had started to panic when her sister hadn't picked up immediately and the call had gone to voicemail. Why hadn't Jade answered straight away? Her sister was usually so on it, especially first thing in the morning?

Chill out, Juno. You're projecting.

'Jade... I... It's wonderful to hear you too,' she said, the sting of tears roughening her voice. She took a calming breath to beat down the butterfly battalion. 'I'm sorry I woke you up,' she added. 'And I know I'm not supposed to call, but...'

But what, exactly? Juno stalled.

She'd rehearsed this conversation a thousand times since she and Leo had agreed to a no-strings affair three days ago and she still did not know what she wanted to say to her sister...

She was so confused, so conflicted—racked with guilt

and yet at the same time full of excitement, anticipation… yearning.

Agreeing to jump Leo and let him jump her tonight after the ball was wrong on so many levels it wasn't even funny but at the same time felt so right.

She had so many questions she didn't have answers to, the most glaring of which was like a ten-ton elephant that wasn't just in the room any more, it was now sitting on her chest and twirling.

Should she tell Leo who she really was before they did it? After they did it? Not at all? Wouldn't the truth risk ruining everything, not just for her, and Leo, but for Jade, too? But if she didn't tell him, would she be able to live with herself? Live with the guilt?

If this connection was just about sex, would it be so wrong to continue to pretend to be her sister? If they'd already agreed that the discussion about marriage wasn't a part of this development? And really what she'd discovered about Leo, and what Leo had discovered about her, was all true. He'd loved the way she handled herself during their engagements, and they'd found it harder and harder to keep their hands off each other in the last three days. Why couldn't tonight's ball and what happened afterwards be about who they were, instead of who they were not…?

The hypothetical arguments had spun around in her head over the last three days like out-of-control dodgems at a fairground, getting faster and faster, banging into one another, but never finding a place to stop.

'Juno, what's wrong?' her sister said, picking up on her unease from over four thousand miles away, and the hypothetical dodgems slowed, momentarily.

'Something, something's happened,' Juno blurted out. 'Something… I really did not expect…' Her voice trailed off. How to explain that combustible chemistry and the connection she'd established with Leo in the last seven days? How did she make sense of it to Jade? When she didn't really understand it herself?

'Is this about Leo, and your state visit to Severene?' her sister said. 'You make a great couple.'

'We're not a couple,' Juno said, instantly. Not only were they not a couple *yet*, but even if they became one, tonight, after the ball, as planned, it could never be more than a fleeting, physical connection. That she knew for sure.

'Are you certain?' Jade's voice was gentle, coaxing— and so devoid of judgement, the dodgems started revving their engines again. 'You look happy together in all the press coverage. And by the way you're doing a stunning job impersonating me. Better than I could do myself.'

'I'm just good at faking it,' Juno said.

'You're not faking anything, Ju, you're a natural,' her sister replied, the wistful tone confusing Juno more. 'I always told you Papa was wrong not to consider you as his successor, and now I get to say I told you so.'

'Aren't you angry with me?' Juno asked.

'Why would I be angry?' Her sister sounded genuinely puzzled.

'Because I'm not supposed to be in Severene? Because this swap was never supposed to get this complicated? Because I could end up completely screwing up Monrova's diplomatic relationship with Severene.'

If Leo found out who she really was—and went ballistic— which was a distinct possibility.

The truth was, she had no real clue how Leo would react.

He might think it was funny, sexy, cool. But what if he didn't? What if he got super mad and ended up hating her? What if it caused a diplomatic incident? And he punished

Jade, too? If this was just about sex would it be better never to tell him the truth? Just in case? To protect herself and her sister? She'd been rejected before, she knew just how much that hurt. And did she really have the right to risk Jade's reputation, when she had been the one to push for this swap in the first place?

Every day she'd kept the secret, every day she'd got closer to Leo, discovered more about him, and herself, the stakes had got higher. It had never been her intention to hurt anyone. But in the last week, all the possible ramifications of what could happen if she told Leo the truth— good and bad—had begun to torture her.

Three days ago, Leo's offer of a private no-strings fling had seemed like the perfect solution. If the marriage was off the table, how could sleeping with him do any harm?

And Leo was the one who had suggested it.

Now every time he looked at her as if he wanted to devour her, and she melted in response; every time he winked at her or smiled at her, and she became breathless; every time she looked at him and saw the traumatised child as well as the man he had become, she knew this thing between them was about her and Leo, not Jade and Leo, and certainly not some arranged marriage…

'No, I'm not angry about any of that,' her sister said at last, interrupting Juno's frantic qualifications. 'I've come to realise, seeing the press reports of you two, that Leo and I were never meant to be together,' Jade added. 'I'm really glad you persuaded me to come to New York.' She paused. 'It's been an eye-opening experience for me. I also think it's super cute that there seems to be something developing between you two.'

'There's nothing developing between us. Nothing permanent anyway,' Juno murmured.

Whether she told Leo who she really was or not, nothing could come of their liaison. 'It's just… There's a lot of chemistry between us,' she said. 'And I like him more than I ever expected to.'

Leo wasn't the man she had thought he was. He had depth and layers, he was complicated, with a past not nearly as easy and entitled as she had assumed. He had struggled with his place in the world, just as she had. In fact, he'd struggled more.

She had been dismissed by her father because she was never going to be Queen, and King Andreas had considered his responsibilities to the Crown more important than his responsibilities to his daughters. But Leo had been abused by his own father; if King Constantin had believed that maintaining a dignified front at a funeral mattered more than comforting a grieving child she very much doubted it was the only time he had hit his son.

Their shared pain had given them a connection—but they had dealt with that pain in very different ways. While she had rejected her royal heritage and reacted to her father's neglect by being more rebellious, more reckless, more irresponsible, Leo had done the opposite. He didn't even seem to acknowledge the extent of his father's abuse, nor did he resent his duty to the Crown. And while a week ago she would have thought less of him for that, now she felt more. She'd watched Leo in the last week taking on his responsibilities, refusing to shirk them, even though she now knew how hard some of that was for him. And that had made her think of Jade too, and how Jade had done the same.

While Juno had always taken the easy route, the selfish route, the path of least resistance and done precisely what she chose.

If this week with Leo had done one thing, it had given her a maturity she hadn't realised she lacked. Made her realise there was more to life than personal freedom, that some things were bigger than yourself. Leo had taught her that. And she hoped in return she'd helped Leo to lighten up a little, to not take every element of his job so seriously, and to forgive that little boy for crying at his mother's funeral.

'Are you sure there's nothing more between you?' Jade said, sounding wistful. 'From the press reports I've seen, he looks at you in a way he's never looked at any of the other women he's dated.'

Juno's heart galloped into her throat at the softly spoken question. She swallowed heavily, trying to push down the foolish bubble of hope.

That's because he thinks I'm a real queen.

'No, there's nothing more,' she said.

Don't go getting even more delusional than you are already, Ju.

As much as she had come to care for Leo, anything more than satisfying the chemistry that had been driving them both nuts for seven days was not going to happen. Because she would always be a fake... And he was the real deal.

'Jade, I just...' Juno began again. *Just get to the point.* 'What I need to know, the reason I called, is...' Juno swallowed—could this actually get any more awkward? 'If Leo and I jump each other tonight. I mean, he's asked me and I... I really want to go for it. Because, you know, chemistry,' she said, trying to sound pragmatic when she was struggling to breathe. 'We've agreed it won't mean anything beyond the physical. That it won't have any political implications. That the marriage is a whole separate issue. But if you'd rather we didn't... I mean, I don't want to mess things up for you... With Leo.'

'Juno, you're not serious—what possible claim would I have on Leonardo?'

'Well, you know, you were considering marrying him a week ago,' Juno said.

Jade laughed, interrupting Juno's guilt trip.

'The marriage was always just about securing a trade relationship and uniting our two kingdoms,' Jade said easily enough. 'I can't believe I ever thought that would be okay.'

'Jade, you don't sound like yourself,' Juno said, noticing the strange tone in her sister's voice for the first time, a tone she'd never heard before. Jade had always been so certain about her role in life, her duties and responsibilities. Juno had wanted to shake things up with this swap, but now she wondered if she'd shaken them up too much. 'Are you sure everything is going okay in New York?'

As usual she'd made this call about her. Why hadn't she asked Jade for details about what was happening Stateside?

'It's… Yes, it's been really transformative in a lot of ways,' Jade said, but Juno couldn't tell from her sister's tone whether that was a good thing, or not.

Juno's concern increased.

'I'm discovering things about myself I didn't realise,' Jade added. 'Not all of which I like.'

'What things?' Juno asked, getting more concerned by the second. 'There's nothing about you not to like.'

'I used to think the same thing.' Jade laughed again, but the brittle note jarred.

'If something's happened, Jade, you can tell me, or we could swap back. Now.'

'No. I don't want to swap back, not yet. I'd really like to stay until New Year's Eve, like we agreed,' Jade added. 'Unless you want to…'

'No, I don't want to swap back yet either,' Juno admitted, glad that Jade at least seemed very sure about staying in New York as long as they'd originally agreed.

'Listen, Ju, I've got to go,' her sister said. 'I've got a busy day ahead of me. But whatever you and Leo do, or don't do, you have my blessing. Okay?'

'Okay,' she said, knowing she should be pleased her sister had given her carte blanche to do whatever she wanted with Leo tonight.

'But do me a favour, don't underestimate your feelings for him,' Jade added. 'They might be stronger than you think.'

Before Juno could reply, the line was dead, and her sister was gone.

Juno's heart rate increased as she put down the phone. The giddy rush of anticipation at what tonight might bring ramping up.

But as she spent the next hours getting primped and prepped to within an inch of her life, she couldn't shake the growing feeling of vertigo, as if she were standing on the edge of a precipice and Jade's blessing had just brought her one step closer to the fall.

CHAPTER SEVEN

THE CHRISTMAS BALL was Severene's premiere event of the year and one of Europe's most sought-after social occasions. Dignitaries and VIPs, politicians and A-list celebrities were flown in from all over the globe to attend. The palace ballroom—considerably larger than the one in Monrova—glowed with the twinkle of a thousand tiny lights, the walls festooned with ribbon and garlands, silver baubles and gold leaves, to ring in the festive season. A thirty-foot fir tree from Severene's pine forest stood like a beacon in the far corner aglow with green fairy lights and scarlet bows.

Beautiful people danced to a thirty-piece orchestra in the main ballroom, and mingled in the adjacent antechambers while being served cordon-bleu cuisine created by a battalion of Michelin-starred chefs and vintage champagne and wine curated by a world-renowned sommelier.

Juno floated through the evening on a wave of desperate hope and frantic excitement—while burying the unanswered questions deep.

As soon as Leo's hand had folded over hers at the top of the wide sweeping staircase, where they were the last guests to be announced, and he led her down onto the marble floor of the ballroom, she'd made a conscious decision to live for the moment and deal with the decisions she had to make on an as and when basis.

She would play it by ear. Figure out what was the right thing to do when she needed to, and not before. Tonight was about living the dream and forgetting about the reality. Whatever happened it would be her last night with Leo; tomorrow she had to return to Monrova and, whether she told him who she really was or not, she could never see him again.

Whatever she did or didn't tell Leo though, it gave her a giddy thrill to know that no one here even suspected a girl from Queens was masquerading as a queen among them tonight.

See, Father, for all my wild ways, I could have made a good queen. Just not your sort of queen.

Leo monopolised every one of her dances, and she could see the assembled throng going glassy-eyed at the romantic couple they made. Him in his red dress uniform, and her in a ball gown of rich emerald velvet that matched her eyes.

Their romance might be fake, but tonight the fairy tale felt real. And even if none of these people would ever know who she really was, she would know. And that was enough.

He'd helped her to prove her father wrong. And that mattered, even if tonight was their last night together.

She would miss him. In many ways he was the ultimate Prince Charming, handsome, dashing, demanding, unknowable, larger than life in every respect. But she couldn't fall into the same trap as her mother—believing she could have more—when this was all there was.

She'd seen the press photos from the Christmas Ball over the years, a ball her sister had rarely attended, and locked the yearning to be here inside her—determined to believe she didn't want the life that had been denied her.

But tonight she could indulge every single one of those secret desires.

As the guest of honour at the ball, she had to mix and mingle, but Leo made no secret of the fact he wanted her in his arms as often as possible, so their royal duties were cut to a minimum.

Giddy with her new confidence, Juno fed on the adrenaline rush as he whisked her round under the twinkle of lights, and they played out the last of her Cinderella fantasy.

Anticipation skittered over her skin, every time his strong arms held her a little too close, or his subtle cologne filled her lungs, or his large hand rested on the small of her back.

As the clock struck midnight, and the revellers let up a cheer, a golden sleigh was hauled into the centre of the ballroom by six footmen, loaded down with elaborately wrapped gifts. As the guests began to help themselves, sighing and gasping at the kingdom's largesse, Leo grasped Juno's hand and tugged her towards the staircase they had descended together four hours before.

The adrenaline rush became turbocharged. Finally, they could be alone. The ball would wind down now, her state visit over. And the night they had committed to three days ago could begin.

There was nothing to stop them doing whatever they wanted into the early hours of the morning—and no one to see it.

He leaned down, his hand settling on her back, and whispered against her ear: 'I have to say goodnight to a load of boring diplomats. But I'll see you upstairs in fifteen minutes.'

The intense gaze that had been focussed on her all evening made her pulse jump and jitter. 'But I'll need to get Jennie to help me get out of this gown,' she said.

His gaze dropped to her cleavage, and the emerald velvet compressed her ribs. 'Give her the night off. Getting you out of that gown is a job I've been looking forward to all evening.'

Bowing, he made a point of kissing her knuckles and bidding her a formal goodnight. The camera clicks from a nearby photographer faded into the background, as Juno's heart pummelled her chest in hard, heavy thuds.

She watched him disappear into the crowd. She would have to tell him who she really was. But did she have to tell him right away?

She waited the required five minutes to cover the fact they were leaving together, then summoned Serena. Ten frustrating minutes later, she had said all the necessary goodbyes and headed up the stairs towards her suite of rooms, so hyped she could hardly breathe.

There had been no sign of Leo. She hoped he had managed to escape faster than she had. And that he was waiting for her as planned. She didn't want to have too much time to think alone in her rooms.

As she took the last turning towards her suite, a warm hand clasped her wrist and tugged her to a stop.

'About damn time, what took you so long?'

Leo! Her heart bounced into her throat.

She struggled to keep pace with his long strides as he led her down the hallway, past the double doors leading to her private suite.

'Where are we going?' she managed as she stumbled.

He paused just long enough to scoop her off her feet.

'To my rooms,' he said, his voice so husky, the wry, mocking tone had become raw.

She knew how he felt as she clung to his shoulders.

'Where I intend to ravish you,' he added, marching towards his suite with purpose in every stride.

The hot sweet spot between her thighs burned as her breath released.

Ravish! Did he just say ravish?

The last coherent thought flew out of her head and she leapt over the edge of the precipice.

Did it really matter who she was?

Surely all that mattered right now was feeding this hunger?

'The Severene monarchy…i.e. me…has some standards,' Leo growled as he carried Jade down the corridor to his suite of rooms. 'And *not* popping the Queen of Monrova's cherry in a corridor happens to be one of them.'

Did you actually just refer to popping the Queen's cherry?

But as Jade smothered a shocked laugh against his chest—and he finally reached the sanctuary of his rooms—Leo decided he'd be damned if he would apologise for the crude language.

The woman had bewitched him, and the only way to break the enchantment was to give them both what they'd waited far too long for already.

The velvet gown glided under his hands as he placed her on her feet, but the feel of her firm, toned body beneath, the lush curves shivering under his touch, sent the twist of need into his gut.

How had she managed to stay a virgin for twenty-four years?

Doesn't matter.

She was his now, and only his. And he was glad she'd waited. Because he wanted to be the first man to uncover her secrets.

He started with the diamond tiara, which he had dreamed of divesting her of a week ago on the balcony in Monrova. Locating the pins in the room's half-light, he plucked them out of her elaborate hairdo to toss them across the room.

She sighed as he lifted the jewelled headpiece and dumped it on a nearby chair. He took off his jacket, unbuttoned his shirt as her hair tumbled down in a glorious wave of chestnut curls. Her breathing became fast and jagged as he lost his shirt.

Clasping her neck, he caught the silky locks at her nape, and dragged her mouth to his. Her lips softened, her moan making his erection throb as the kiss became deep and elemental. His tongue tangled with hers, exploiting, demanding, so hungry for the taste of her he doubted he would ever be sated.

He ripped his lips away first and drew a staggered breath. Her eyes fixed on his, glazed with lust and longing, but also shadowed with what he could only assume was shock.

Slow down, be gentle.

He'd joked about ravishing her, but it didn't seem funny any more. The fact of her virginity roared in his head, as he gathered every last ounce of his control to force the words out of his mouth.

'Are you sure this is what you want?' he murmured. 'I don't want to hurt you.'

For a moment he saw guilt flash across her face—which made no sense—but then she said, 'You won't.'

His hands were clumsy in his urgency to locate the zip on her gown. The sibilant hum as he drew it down seemed deafening above the crackle of the fire and her staggered breathing.

The velvet slid down to collect in an emerald pool at her feet, revealing a banquet of treasures even more breathtaking than he had imagined.

Damn, but she was exquisite. The swatches of purple lace did nothing to disguise the shadow of her areolae and the neat triangle of hair at the apex of her thighs.

How could he have been so unmoved by her beauty a month ago? When he had become obsessed in the last week with gorging himself on every gorgeous inch?

The last molecules of blood still in his brain pounded beneath his belt, the desire to claim her so powerful and all-consuming his body burned. He unhooked the front fastening of her bra and stifled a moan as her breasts spilled into his palms.

He cradled the swollen flesh, circling the rigid peaks with his thumbs. His erection stiffened to iron as her sobs became pants of need. He bent to capture one plump nipple in his mouth, drowning in her delicious scent, determined to prolong the torture for them both as long as was humanly possible.

Her fingers fisted in his hair, tugging and pulling as she begged. 'Please… I need more.'

The last threads on his control snapped at her breathless plea. Leaving the banquet of fragrant flesh, he lifted her into his arms and carried her through the suite's living room and into his bedroom.

He placed her on the large four-poster bed in the centre of the room. He watched her watching him, her chestnut curls rioting around her head, her beautiful body pale against the golden quilt, the ripe flesh gilded by the firelight as he stripped off the last of his clothing.

Her dark emerald gaze drifted down, and the flush on her cheeks darkened.

He was a large man in every respect and her wary look gave him a moment of concern.

'Don't worry,' he said. 'I promise to be gentle.'

Her gaze met his. 'You don't need to be gentle,' she said, the fearless comment as bold and brave as the rest of her.

His heart swelled, making his ribs feel uncomfortably tight. He shook off the unfamiliar emotion and climbed on the bed. After dragging off her panties, he cupped her to capture the wet heat.

This was sex, and phenomenal chemistry. He liked her, had grown accustomed to having her by his side, and she had made the usual roster of Christmas engagements less of a chore than usual in the last week. But he didn't require more, and certainly didn't want more.

She bucked as he delved, circling, testing, his thumb finding the slick nub of her clitoris. She writhed as he exploited it, drawing forth her sobs. Watching her enjoy her own pleasure was so erotic he had to grit his teeth to stop from embarrassing himself.

'Come for me,' he demanded, and she responded instinctively, her body bowing back as she shattered.

His heart thundered in his chest, his ribs like a vice now as he positioned her hips. Her eyes fluttered open, dazed with afterglow as he notched the head of his erection at her entrance and pushed.

She was unbearably hot, unbearably tight, her sex clamped around him, but her body stretched to receive him, her nails scoring his shoulders, her pants becoming sobs as he pressed deep.

'Are you okay?' he managed.

She hadn't flinched. And he hadn't felt any impediment.

Puzzling questions clouded his mind, but then she nodded, and the need for answers dimmed. He had to move, to claim her fully, before he exploded.

Clasping her hips, he rocked out, then thrust back, filling her to the hilt this time. He continued to move, slow and careful at first, still mindful of his size, digging deep to work her G-spot. He established a brutal rhythm, clenched his teeth to ignore the orgasm licking at the base of his spine. Desperate to hold on, determined to make her shatter first. And brand her as his.

His Queen, *his* woman, *his* lover.

She cried out, the vicious pulse of her climax triggering his own unstoppable release.

His seed exploded into her womb as he soared over the high wide ledge and let himself fall.

Sweaty, exhausted, sated, he collapsed into her welcoming embrace, drenched in a pleasure so intense, so fierce, he was afraid he might never be able to get enough of it.

Juno's eyes drifted open. Dazed, disorientated and floating in a shiny sea of afterglow, she lay cocooned in a delicious cloud of sandalwood cologne and man.

Her tender sex twitched and she became brutally aware of the thick intrusion, still firm, still *there* inside the tight clasp of her body.

The heavy weight pressing into her collarbone grunted.

'Stop that, or I'll have to ravish you again, and it will probably kill us both.'

Her instinctive chuckle at the wry observation choked off as the delirious fog dissolved. And a strange new reality came flooding in.

The man lying on top of her, his black hair illuminated by the firelight, his masculine scent intoxicating, had just given her so much more than she had thought possible.

A vicious shudder racked her body and she had to bite down on her lip, hard enough to taste blood, to stop the shocked sob buried in her chest rising up her throat.

Emotion slammed into her like a freight train.

What had she done? She had known sex with Leo would

be good, the best she'd ever had. Because that wasn't much of a competition.

But she hadn't expected it to mean anything more than that. And yet it had. Because as well as the stupendous, breathtaking orgasms, there had been the staggering wave of intimacy.

'Hey, what's wrong, Jade?' he murmured, the gruff use of her sister's name only making her feel more exposed. More compromised.

She hadn't told him the truth. Had convinced herself it didn't matter. And now suddenly it did.

Her flesh released him with difficulty as he withdrew.

He frowned and cradled her cheek. 'Did I hurt you?'

She shook her head, unable to speak past the huge boulder forming in her throat.

She'd ruined everything. She had never thought sex could be so overwhelming.

And now she had to deal with the consequences.

She'd always been impulsive. And she'd paid a high price for that in the past. But this time, *this* time, she'd gone too far, way too far to ever be forgiven.

'Speak to me, Jade,' he said, brushing his thumb down the side of her face, shaming her even more as brutal yearning echoed in her sex. 'You need to tell me what's wrong.'

'I… I…' The tenderness and concern in his expression only shamed her more. She'd lied to him, convinced herself it was just a little lie, a convenient omission, but now she knew it wasn't. 'Really, I'm fine,' she managed. She pulled his hand away from her face, so she could move away from him.

The flight instinct was a familiar one. So she went with it.

She needed to think, figure out how to break the news to him—that she wasn't the woman he thought she was.

She scooted off the bed, brutally aware of the sticky residue of their lovemaking. He hadn't used a condom.

Doesn't matter. You can deal with that later, once you've told him the truth.

Her heart lodged in her throat. But how did she do that? He had treated her with such respect, such warmth, such care, and it was all based on a lie. She'd seen the puzzled look cross his face when he'd entered her, had known in that instant exactly what he was thinking.

Why isn't she a virgin?

She made it to the edge of the bed, swung her legs to the floor, but just as she prepared to make a dash for the bathroom he grasped her wrist.

'Everything's not okay, Jade,' he stated, his voice strained but firm, his frown deepening. 'That much is obvious.'

Please stop calling me that. I'm not Jade, I'm Juno.

'If I hurt you, if I was too rough with you, you need to tell me,' he said.

Please, just stop.

'You didn't… You didn't hurt me, Leo. The sex was phenomenal… It's just, I've never had an orgasm during sex before and…' A blush blazed into her cheeks as she babbled to a halt. Had she just admitted that? Out loud?

'Before?' he said. He didn't sound angry or upset, simply surprised. Even so, she wanted to curl up into a ball and die. 'So I wasn't your first?'

'Yes, I mean, no. There was only one other guy. When I was sixteen in high school,' she said. At least this was the truth.

'But no orgasms?' he asked and she noticed the slight quirk of his lips. Was that good? Even if she felt brutally humiliated?

'He'd bet his pals he could deflower a princess,' she

said, forcing herself to give him the miserable details of that furtive, uncomfortable night eight years ago, which had left her feeling sore and dissatisfied. Brad had boasted to his friends that the Princess wasn't all that. And she'd been forced to take the walk of shame the next day in gym class. She'd held her head up and ignored the sniggers, and the scathing looks. She'd done nothing wrong—why should she be ashamed? Brad had been the villain in that scenario. The liar.

But she was the liar now.

'It made me think sex was totally overrated. And I thought it always had to be like that...'

The sensual smile on Leo's lips became more than a little smug.

Shut up. This isn't helping.

He squeezed her wrist and rubbed his thumb across her rampaging pulse.

'The guy sounds like a bastard, Jade,' he murmured. 'I'm glad I got to be your first in the only way that matters.'

The comment was kind, when she knew she didn't deserve kind.

'It was a long time ago, now,' she said, staring down at her hands, aware of her nakedness. 'I can barely remember him.'

Tucking a knuckle under her chin, Leo lifted her face. 'I'm glad I didn't hurt you,' he said gently. 'Although if you'd told me sooner we could have jumped each other three days ago.'

Her heart scrambled. Really? That was why he'd suggested waiting? Because he'd been concerned about her virginity? The wave of tenderness built again.

Followed by the nauseous wave of guilt. She had to tell him the truth. She'd lied and lied, to him and to herself, because she'd wanted this to happen. But now it had, every single one of those qualifications and justifications and excuses had been exposed for what they were—bare-faced, self-serving lies, so she could trick a king into se-ducing her.

'I… You thought I was a virgin,' she said, trying not to wince. 'I'm sorry.'

'Your father boasted about your untouched state quite a lot.' The mild amusement in his tone only damned her more. 'I guess he didn't know about the bastard.' His brow furrowed, his gaze direct and probing. 'When did you go to high school? I always thought you were homeschooled, like me?' The quizzical tone, and the easy affection behind it, made panic tighten around her ribs.

Tell him. Tell him now.

But somehow the words wouldn't come out of her mouth. Instead her heart rammed her throat and started to choke her. Her mind whirred in frantic circles, acceler-ating like a merry-go-round spinning out of control.

His grip tightened and he moved to sit next to her. His naked hip bumped hers as he placed his hand on her back. And rubbed.

'Breathe, Jade,' he murmured.

She sucked in a juddering breath past constricted lungs, his voice an anchor as the merry-go-round juddered and jumped and finally started to slow.

'I'm sorry,' she mumbled, dropping her head into her hands. 'This is super awkward.'

'Awkward?' He gave a husky chuckle. 'I disagree.' He tucked a lock of hair behind her ear. She turned her head at the gentle touch, to find him watching her. 'More like fascinating and charming,' he murmured, the rough ap-preciation in his tone making her heart swell painfully in her chest again. 'You just keep surprising me, Jade.'

You have no idea.

Her sister's name knifed into her gut and she straightened. 'I'm so, so sorry, Leo,' she said, because what else could she say?

Her mind began to race through all the possible ways to tell him what she should have told him ten minutes ago. Ten hours ago. A week ago. As soon as she'd kissed him on the snow-covered balcony, let him bare her breast in the frozen night and set them on this path.

I'm not Jade, I'm Juno. I went to high school in New York. Because I'm a nobody, not a queen. Jade's the virgin, not me.

'Don't be sorry.' The sensual smile made her heart leap in her chest. 'I'm not,' he continued, his thumb resting on the rioting pulse in her collarbone. 'In fact, I'm probably the one who should apologise.' His blue eyes focussed on her face, the sincerity making her stomach tangle into a knot. 'I didn't use a condom. And I didn't ask if you're using birth control?'

'Umm… No, but we should be okay, my period is due very soon,' she whispered.

Could this actually get any more awkward?

'Maybe we don't have to worry either way.' He smiled. 'After how good that just was, my offer of a union between us is still very much on the table.' Bracketing her hips, he drew her towards him.

What?

Just as her panic started to spiral out of control again, he pressed his lips to the rioting pulse in her collarbone. She jolted, let out a broken sigh, the tantalising butterfly kisses making the heavy weight in her stomach sink into her sex.

He lifted his head, cradled her cheeks.

'How about you stay here and we can negotiate the details over the holiday?' he said, his mouth hovering over hers. 'I thought we could take a trip to my father's old hunting lodge. It's secluded, and private, and it will give us a chance to get to know each other even better.' He lifted his brows, the heat in his gaze making her want to cry.

That sounded so good, but it could never happen.

She flattened her palms against his chest as he lowered his head. The misery helping to smother the knot of shame as heat bloomed in her core.

'Stop, Leo. We can't.' She pushed him away.

'No?' he said, the confident, mocking tone making the knot in her gut grow to impossible proportions.

'I told you, we can't get married,' she blurted out. 'Ever. I told you that before I agreed to tonight.'

'Why not?' His lips twisted and the devastating smile did crazy things to her equilibrium. 'We're terrific together, in every way that counts. We just proved that beyond a doubt.'

You have to tell him. Now.

But how?

She'd screwed up so badly, she didn't know if there was a way to make this right.

'I need to take a shower.' *A cold shower. A very long, very cold shower.*

'Do you want me to join you?' he said, in that too sexy voice that made her want to say yes, when she knew she couldn't.

'Maybe next time,' she said, as she shot off the bed and made a dash for the bathroom.

She slammed the door and pressed her back against it. His confused look at her erratic behaviour imprinted on her brain.

She was a coward, as well as a liar, but she had to figure out the right way to tell him the whole truth and nothing but the truth—to minimise the enormity of her betrayal. And she couldn't do that while he was looking at her as if he wanted to devour her, and her sex was still humming from the feel of him deep inside her.

She jumped as the door bumped against her back. 'Jade, what's going on? Can I come in?'

'Nothing, *really*, I just need a minute…' *Or fifty.* 'I'll be out soon.'

As soon as I've figured out how to defend the indefensible.

CHAPTER EIGHT

LEO RESTED HIS forehead against the bathroom door. He heard the shower and realised he had been dismissed. He frowned.

The woman was more capricious than a wild stallion, but while Jade's unpredictable moods had been a major turn-on for days now—hell, ever since he'd seen her marching towards him at the Winter Ball a week ago with that bold, reckless light shining in her eyes—the trickle of unease had started to become a flood.

Something about this whole thing didn't add up. Had never added up. He'd dismissed that gut instinct a week ago, and every day since, because he'd wanted her, more than he'd ever wanted any woman. She had captivated him, bewitched him even, and the sex they'd just shared had been... Frankly, mind-blowing.

But that realisation only made his uneasiness increase.

He'd never had a sexual experience like it... One so intense he hadn't even remembered to use protection. He'd had a couple of condoms burning a hole in the pocket of his jacket all evening, but when he'd watched her body brace with pleasure, the need to bury himself deep inside her had been so overwhelming he hadn't stopped to think.

She'd been artless and eager, responsive to every touch, every taste, every look, the chemistry between them as explosive as ever. And she hadn't been experienced, but at the same time he wasn't her first.

He had wanted to throttle the bastard who she had lost her virginity to—and wished that it could have been him— which didn't make a lot of sense either.

The questions just kept coming—the inconsistencies, the surprises, the strange feeling of déjà vu that first time he'd kissed her.

Why had she seemed so naïve and insecure about her role as Queen? Why had she been so unconventional in her approach to their royal duties, when she had seemed to be so serene and controlled when he had met her on previous occasions? Why had she turned him inside out with lust, and longing, this week, when she never had before? Why had he trusted her so easily with the truth about his father, blurted out all that revealing stuff about his mother's funeral? And why had the mention of marriage caused her to freak out, when she'd discussed the offer with such pragmatism less than a month ago?

So many questions. Questions he'd put to one side but which were bombarding him now. Questions he needed answers to.

He walked back to the bed, scooped up his boxers and trousers and put them on. The sound of pounding water from the power shower covered the click as he tried the bathroom door.

It wasn't locked. He stepped into the room.

She stood in the shower cubicle, with her back to him.

Soap suds slid over skin flushed pink under the pummelling jets and the familiar heat pounded back to life. He sank his fists into his pockets and leant back against the door to enjoy the show. He needed to calm down before he quizzed her.

He'd always been a cynical man, but whatever was going on here, it probably had a reasonable explanation.

She went about the ritual of washing all those beautiful curves. And he had the strange thought he could happily spend the rest of his life watching a show like this every morning.

Strange, because, even though tonight had only confirmed for him how much potential a marriage between them had, he doubted even the stupendous chemistry they shared would lead to a lifelong commitment to his royal wife.

He just wasn't built for that kind of emotional investment...

He had wanted this marriage, not just because of the diplomatic and financial benefits for both their monarchies, but also because a marriage based on expediencies would not require him to give more than he was capable of. This week's events, though, had created something of a problem in that regard, because Jade intrigued and fascinated him enough to complicate his feelings towards her.

Not only did he want her more than expected, he was now even more invested in getting her to agree to the marriage.

She lifted her arms to finish rinsing the shampoo from her hair, giving him a tantalising view of her breast in profile, the puckered nipple still reddened by his attentions.

The heat spiked and he forced himself to banish the unhelpful thoughts. Just because he wanted her, in bed as well as out, theirs would still have to be a marriage of convenience.

'We can't get married. Ever.'

He recalled the panicked expression on her face when she'd refused him. Again.

Why couldn't she marry him? She hadn't given him an answer.

The flood of unease helped to dampen the heat as she switched off the jets and reached for the pile of towels on the vanity. The steam that had obscured his vision was sucked away, giving him a view of every luscious inch as she dried herself.

She bent forward to dry her legs, and he spotted something on her hip that he hadn't noticed in the shadows of the bedroom.

What was that? A birthmark? No, a tattoo... A faded tattoo of a unicorn...

His heartbeat kicked up another notch, and the erection stiffened.

Jade had a tattoo... Of a unicorn? How had she managed to get that past her father?

'I love unicorns, they're a symbol of magic and freedom. I think I'm going to get a tattoo of one as soon as it's legal.'

The passionate voice of another princess stabbed at his consciousness from eight long years ago.

What the...?

The shocking truth barrelled into him—and the knot in his gut became a nuclear bomb.

He shuddered so violently, the door behind him rattled against the frame.

She swung round, letting out a shocked gasp as she clasped the towel to her chest.

'Leo? How long have you been standing there?'

Rage rose up his torso as he strode across the bathroom, positively shaking now. He'd been taken for a fool. Tricked, exploited and humiliated.

'Long enough,' he ground out, the rage all but choking him as he grasped her wrist and tugged her towards him, so he could re-examine the evidence up close.

He swore, furious that the sight of her bottom—and the

saucy mythical creature etched into her skin in faded colours—caused the inevitable rush of desire.

'Leo, stop.' She wrestled her arm free and scrambled to cover her backside from his inspection. But she couldn't disguise the guilty flush burning across her collarbone and spreading up her neck. Or the panic darkening those emerald eyes. Panic he'd been so desperate to soothe five minutes ago, after they'd made love. Panic that suddenly made sense now too.

He fisted his fingers, stuffed them into his pockets, to resist the urge to throw her over his knee and give her the spanking she deserved.

Breathe, damn it.

'Why?' The one word came out on a broken breath, only humiliating him more. He fought off the twist of pain in his gut, forced the fury to the fore, to cover it. He'd told her things he should never have told anyone. She'd tricked him, manipulated him, lied to him, but he'd let her. '*Why* did you do it? Why did you lie to me for seven days straight? Is this some kind of sick joke?'

Kiss me, Leo. You know you want to.

The memory came flooding back, and with it the hurt that had shadowed her eyes when he'd told her he didn't want her. And suddenly he knew. His fury became huge and all-consuming, but it still couldn't cover the ache in his belly.

'It was payback, wasn't it? Because I refused to kiss you all those years ago. Well, congratulations, Princess Juno, you got me.'

The horrified guilt in her eyes gave him a grim sense of satisfaction, but did nothing to ease the pain in his gut.

It had all been a lie. Every damn thing. He'd been captivated, enchanted, overwhelmed… And she'd been laughing at him all along.

* * *

'I… I'm sorry,' Juno sputtered, but the apology felt weak at best. And no defence against his fury.

Her mind raced to catch up with her accelerating pulse and the anxiety threatening to close off her air supply.

His eyes narrowed. 'You're *sorry*?' The scathing look burned into her skin. 'You were always a spoilt, wilful brat, but this… This is something else.'

The insult cut through all her tough-girl bravado to the child she'd been, branded the Problem Princess and kicked out of the palace by her father.

'I know I should have said something sooner.' She wrapped the towel around herself, but how could she shield herself from his judgement, and how could she protect her heart from the great big black hole forming in her chest and threatening to suck away the last of her confidence and self-respect?

She deserved this. She knew that. She'd been a liar and a coward, he was right. But hadn't any of it been real? Not one thing? Where was the man who had looked at her with such approval, such hunger, such tenderness?

'I wanted to tell you, but I was scared you wouldn't… That you wouldn't…'

'That I wouldn't what?' He sank his fists deeper into his pants pockets, making his pecs bulge and tense.

She could feel his fury pumping off him in waves. Unfortunately it wasn't the only heat she could feel.

Fire flared through her oversensitised body, tightening her nipples into hard peaks and sinking like a heavy weight deep into her abdomen.

She edged back a step, her butt bumping into the vanity, disgusted and humiliated by her body's response.

'What?' he barked, making her jump.

'That you wouldn't want me…' she said, the broken sob of need impossible to disguise. 'The way I wanted you.'

They were both breathing too fast, the vicious arousal darkening his gaze as real and vivid as the melting sensation going molten at her core. But she knew, even though she'd only just acknowledged it, this had never been just a physical need.

Why hadn't she had the courage to admit that to herself until now?

'It was never you I wanted though, was it?' he ground out, stepping away as if she were contaminated. 'It was your sister.'

The rejection lanced into her heart, cutting through every last one of her defences. Defences she had built up over years, to seal herself away from the pain.

She looked down. So ashamed now she felt as if her heart were being ripped out of her chest. 'I know,' she said.

Who the heck had she been kidding? How could what she felt for him, what she had hoped he felt for her, ever have been authentic when it had always been based on a lie?

'Do you have any idea what you've done?' he snarled.

'I'm so sorry,' she said again, her voice a whisper of pain.

He grasped her chin, dragged her gaze up to his. 'Sorry isn't good enough,' he growled, the controlled fury in his tone making her flinch.

Her breath got trapped in her throat as the panic and pain roiled in her gut.

'I know,' she said. 'But I'm still sorry that you hate me now.'

I don't hate you. I wish I did.

The truth bounced into Leo's brain, but he managed to stop himself from voicing it. Juno Monroyale had caused this crisis, with her asinine little charade, and he'd be damned if he'd let her get away with her thoughtless, reckless behaviour.

Maybe he didn't hate her. How could he, when she had been so vibrant, so alive and intoxicating in his bed? When he still wanted her so much? And when a part of him couldn't seem to get it through his head that the woman who had captivated him had never been real...in any of her guises?

Not the fierce goddess who had protected a freezing footman. Not the natural nurturer who had crouched down to charm a little girl. Not the compassionate friend who had comforted the lonely boy who still lurked inside him.

But even if there was some truth in there somewhere, how could those women make up for the one who lurked beneath all of those guises? The spoilt brat who had never had to give a damn about anyone but herself.

While the real Jade had stayed in Monrova and been groomed to become Queen, her twin sister—from what he could remember of what he'd read about her over the years—had swanned off to New York with her feckless mother and become the darling of Manhattan high society, carving out a niche for herself as the Rebel Princess on social media that was as vacuous and self-absorbed as she was.

Perhaps it was about time the Rebel Princess learned actions had consequences. That honour and duty meant something. And that being of royal blood gave you responsibilities, not a licence to do precisely what you chose.

Nobody knew that more than he did; he'd had that mantra literally beaten into him by his own father. And he'd be damned if he'd allow Juno's latest prank to have any lasting impact on him or his monarchy—which meant keeping this disaster out of the public domain, by whatever means necessary.

'Where is your sister?' he demanded, disgusted all over again that he'd been forced into this position. How was he supposed to clean up the mess she'd made?

'In New York, pretending to be me.'

'So she was in on this too?' he said, not sure whether Jade's involvement made him even madder or not. 'Whose idea was it?'

'Mine,' she said.

'Figures.' He stared. Why was he not surprised?

'We swapped places on the afternoon of the Winter Ball. It wasn't really planned, it just sort of happened. The idea was to give Jade a chance to spend some time thinking about whether she really wanted to go through with the marriage... To you.'

'Uh-huh. And whose idea was it for you to sleep with me?' he snarled, the fury starting to choke him again. How could he have been such a fool? To fall for their little scheme. Why hadn't he questioned much more vigorously all the things about the new Queen of Monrova that didn't fit?

Because you wanted her so damn much. That's why.

'No one's.' She gasped, looking genuinely shocked at the suggestion; why that should calm his racing heartbeat, he had no idea. He'd still been taken for a fool, by them both.

'I didn't... I didn't think we would hit it off the way we did.'

So that much at least had been real. His temper and outrage downgraded another notch. But her admission wasn't going to solve their main problem. He'd trusted her before he knew who she really was; he didn't trust her any more. And the only thing he cared about now—the only thing he could allow himself to care about—was preventing this mess from becoming a media scandal.

She sighed, drawing his attention to the soft swell of her cleavage over the towel.

The shaft of longing was echoed in the bright blush that seared her face.

He forced his gaze back to her eyes. He needed to figure out how best to handle this situation now. And he couldn't do that when the basic elemental need was still echoing in his groin.

'Does anyone but Jade know about this?' he said.

She shook her head.

'Are you sure? How the hell did you keep it a secret from Garland, and the rest of your staff?' he asked, astonished all over again at her recklessness.

'I suppose people only see what they want to see,' she said, the blush flaring over her cheeks.

Wasn't that the truth.

'You need to leave, so I can think,' he snarled.

She swallowed, her face a picture of embarrassment— which would have been oddly charming, given what they'd already done to each other, if the situation weren't so dire. 'Okay, would you mind staying here? So I can get dressed, and go back to my own rooms.'

He stepped back so she could pass him. 'I'll tell you how we're going to proceed tomorrow,' he said, just in case she had some idea he was going to let her run off without facing the consequences of her actions.

She nodded, but as she walked past him—her head lowered—he had to shove his hands back into his pockets, to resist the powerful urge to touch her.

But he couldn't resist the opportunity to admire the sweep of her spine and the soft swell of her backside, barely covered by the towel.

She opened the door, and glanced over her shoulder, catching him watching her.

Her blush ignited, while his own skin heated.

'I really am sorry,' she said. 'This wasn't ever supposed to get so complicated. I just wanted to give my sister a chance to live like a normal person, for a little while.'

It was a ludicrous thing to say. What did she even mean by live as a 'normal' person? How could Jade ever be normal, or Juno for that matter, when they were of royal blood?

But he stifled the urge to berate her further; there would be more than enough time to do that tomorrow. Right now his feelings were too damn volatile. He needed her gone.

'Get out,' he said.

He listened for a moment to her moving about in the adjoining bedroom.

Images of her dropping the towel tortured him and the heat in his pants became painful. He stripped off his clothing and stepped into the shower.

Taking himself in hand, he worked the strident erection in fast, efficient strokes under the punishing spray. After finding his release, he rested his forehead against the wet tiles.

When he turned the water off, the sound of her movements had gone. But as he began drying himself, while considering how best to deal with the fallout from tonight's events, he had the disturbing, but persistent thought that he was already anticipating seeing Juno Monroyale again in the morning.

CHAPTER NINE

'YOU'RE NOT SERIOUS?' Juno stared at Leo, her heart beating so fast it was threatening to leap right out of her chest.

'Do I look as if I'm joking?' Leo replied, the words bitten out in short staccato punches as if he were talking to a disobedient child who needed to be disciplined.

Nope, he definitely did not look any more amused than he had last night. If anything his uber frown had got a whole lot worse since she'd been summoned to his study this morning. She'd been up most of the night panicking about what he was going to do this morning, how he might choose to punish her... And Jade...

And on the rare occasions she had managed to fall asleep she'd woken again hot and sweaty, tortured by dreams in which Leo was the star player...

But of all the worst-case scenarios she'd envisioned during the night, what he'd just suggested hadn't even been in the top hundred.

'But... Why...?' she murmured. 'Why would you want to spend seven days alone in a secluded cabin with me? I thought you never wanted to see me again?'

'Because it's the only way to solve both our problems,' he said, not denying that he didn't want to see her again.

The foolish little bubble that had formed under her breastbone when he'd made the suggestion popped.

'I want you to stay out of the public eye until your sister returns, at which point you can swap back.'

Leo raked his fingers through his hair and she noticed the smudges under his eyes—and the shadow of stubble on his chin. So he'd had a sleepless night too.

Unfortunately, in a pair of dark jeans and a black sweater that clung to his impressive chest, he looked as hot as ever—which made the wave of sympathy tangle with the wave of sensation that had tormented her most of the night.

'I can hide in Monrova until Jade returns,' she offered. She couldn't spend seven nights alone with him in a cabin—because the yearning, the need and, worse, the feeling of connection were all still there. 'Jade didn't have any public engagements planned in Monrova over Christmas—which was why it seemed like a good time to do the swap.'

His eyes narrowed dangerously. 'If you're trying to imply I put you at risk of discovery because I persuaded you to come to Severene for a state visit, you can think again.'

'Persuaded?' she said. 'You ganged up on me with one of my father's advisors and practically kidnapped me.'

His brow lowered ominously. 'At the time I thought I was kidnapping a queen. Not her identical twin. If you had deigned to tell me the truth, I would not have had the slightest interest in kidnapping you in the first place.'

The cutting put-down sliced neatly through her indignation.

'Well, anyway…' she said, scrambling to shore up what was left of her self-esteem. 'The point is if I return to Monrova now, I should be able to keep well out of the public eye, until Jade returns.'

Winning the blame game with Leo wasn't going to happen, so it was probably better to stop playing it, because all it was doing was grinding what was left of her ego to dust.

'So you don't need to worry about my identity being discovered or causing a scandal.'

'Except that's not our only problem,' he said, the sarcasm in his tone as cutting as the earlier put-down. 'I didn't use a condom last night.'

His gaze skimmed down to her midriff, and the sensation that would not die chose that moment to swell between her thighs.

She wrapped her arms round her waist, assailed by the memory of his hard, heavy weight inside her.

Terrific. As if she needed any more reasons to feel lower than dirt.

'According to the internet research I did last night,' he continued, his hot gaze doing diabolical things to her already shaky equilibrium, 'we must wait seven days to take a pregnancy test to ensure we don't risk a false negative.'

'Okay,' she said. She wasn't going to be pregnant, she was sure of it. Even *she* couldn't be that unlucky. But even so… 'I could take a test in Monrova in a week's time and let you know the result.'

'That's not going to work for me,' he said, the flat tone tearing at what was left of her self-respect. 'Assuming you can even source a test there without the Queen's doctors finding out you're not the Queen, do you really expect me to trust you to get it done without screwing it up?'

'Yes?' she asked, hating the plea in her voice. And the slicing pain in her heart at his contempt.

Why had she let his approval mean so much to her, when it had always been conditional on her being the Queen?

'That wasn't a question, Princess.' The muscle in his jaw jumped, his lips pursing into a tight line of dissatisfaction. 'Just to be clear, I'm not letting you out of my sight until the test is done to my satisfaction.'

The rigid, uncompromising tone made her stomach hurt. The hollow ache was one she recognised.

'But what would we do? For seven days alone in a mountain cabin? When you can barely stand to talk to me?' she asked, her desperation getting the better of her.

She couldn't spend a week with him treating her the way her father always had, like a reckless, unruly child who needed to be brought to heel. Not only would her ego never survive it, but she was very much afraid her heart wouldn't be able to survive it either.

He studied her, but then to her astonishment the tight line of his lips lifted into a sensual smile. And the disapproval in his gaze turned into something a great deal more disturbing.

'I can think of several ways to amuse ourselves that would not involve unnecessary conversation.'

'What?' Heat flooded up Juno's torso and hit her cheeks. 'You're not… You're not serious? You still want to sleep with me? Even though you detest me.'

And why was the hot spot between her thighs erupting like Vesuvius at the thought?

'I don't detest you. Unfortunately.'

'Gee, thanks,' she said, trying to channel her indignation and getting breathless instead.

Why was that foolish bubble of hope rising back up her torso? Because that was even more delusional than the volcano in her panties.

His gaze raked over her, the heat as caustic as the disdain. Then he shrugged. 'Obviously it would be your choice, but I see no reason not to explore the chemistry between us while we're there. There'll be little else to do, and that much at least was real.'

She stared back at him. She should tell him where he could stick his insulting offer. She should demand to know where he got off treating her like a disobedient child on the one hand, then suggesting a seven-day booty call on the other.

But the outrage and the anger got stuck in her throat, trapped behind that foolish bubble of hope. And something else entirely came out of her mouth. Something that had tormented her ever since last night.

'Why didn't you use a condom?'

The muscle in his jaw flexed, but his eyes widened.

'Was it deliberate?' she asked. 'Were you trying to get me pregnant so you could force me to marry you, when you thought I was Jade?' The accusation was so atrocious, she wasn't sure she even believed it herself, but something about his failure to use contraception didn't make any sense.

He was a cautious man. How could he have made that mistake?

Guilt flashed across his features, but it was accompanied by a wary tension that only confused her more.

'No,' he said. 'By the time I got my hands on you I wasn't thinking about anything at all. I would never do something so…' He stopped abruptly, his eyes narrowing. And then swore softly under his breath. 'Point taken,' he said.

'What point?' she asked. She hadn't intended to make a point.

'I guess you weren't the only one who got carried away last night,' he said grudgingly.

The bubble of hope under her breastbone pressed against her chest.

Perhaps he didn't totally hate her after all. Relief flooded through her. It felt like progress of a sort.

She tried to swallow down the bubble of hope but it wasn't going anywhere.

Hope was not her friend.

Things had got hot and heavy with Leo over the last week because he had believed she was a queen, and with majesty came great responsibility in Leo's world. But now he knew she wasn't, the pressure was off. Did that mean…?

'Okay, I'll go with you,' she said, the heat spreading into her cheeks as his intense gaze darkened.

'Excuse me?' he said, with the supreme arrogance that had always been a major turn-on.

'I can hack seven days alone in a cabin if you can.'

She could see she'd surprised him again when his brows launched up his forehead. But then he laughed. The sound husky enough to scrape over her nerve endings.

His lips twisted in a sensual smile that had the heat pulsating into her panties.

It was probably nuts to agree to go with him—she wasn't entirely convinced he didn't still detest her—but she didn't want things to end like this. She wanted a chance to show him the real her. And that the real her wasn't really that different from the fake her. That was all. Perhaps it was super self-serving, wanting to make up for the mistakes she'd made, wanting him to like her, at least a little, but so be it.

'You make it sound as if I was giving you a choice, Princess,' he said.

She'd begun to realise Leo always liked to have the last word.

He *had* given her a choice, though. The choice to jump him or not to jump him. And more importantly the choice to have this mean something, or not mean something.

This time she intended to make the right choice, on both counts, by sticking to one simple rule.

Hot was allowed, heavy never.

CHAPTER TEN

LEO CIRCLED THE Puma over the hunting lodge's heliport. The lights blazed from the luxury cabin's porch, illuminating the hot tub built on a platform under the trees, which had been fired up, as per his instructions.

Anticipation powered through his system as he brought the big bird down and switched off the ignition. Juno sat beside him. Her beautiful body, the one he'd had in his arms only last night, was cocooned in a ton of clothing topped by a heavy quilted jacket.

They hadn't spoken much since they had agreed to the trip this morning. But as he waited for the blades to power down, and his libido continued to rev up, he questioned his decision to bring her here, again.

All the arguments he'd given her this morning were real. Or real enough. But if this trip had really been about limiting the risk of scandal and making sure she took a pregnancy test, why the hell had he suggested they jump each other while they were here?

That hadn't been smart or sensible. It had been an impulse. And he was not an impulsive man. Well, not until he'd met Juno Monroyale.

Maintaining his anger with her would have been a whole lot safer... But as soon as he'd seen the dazed awareness in her eyes at his suggestion... The dangerous decision to indulge their baser instincts had come out of his mouth regardless.

The dusk lingered on the horizon, the stars already winking above the forest canopy. He should be exhausted, after all he'd had a virtually sleepless night, but even so, as she sat quietly beside him—for once silent—and he contemplated seven long days and nights alone with her, he'd never felt more alive, more alert.

She dragged off the headset.

'This place looks incredible.' The smile that tipped up her lips was both tentative and tantalising—a sign that she was as unsure about this as he was. But then one thing he had learned about Juno in the last seven days, she was a great deal more reckless than he was.

Which meant it was up to him to take charge.

'The landscape around here is so beautiful,' she murmured, the flushed pleasure on her face unguarded. 'I don't think I ever realised how much I missed my homeland until I came back.'

'How long ago is it since you were in Monrova?' he asked.

Her surprise at his question made him realise he'd never asked her anything about herself—even before discovering her true identity.

'Not since my father kicked me out of the palace at sixteen for molesting a king,' she said, the wry amusement in her tone sad somehow. So he'd been the cause, inadvertently.

'How did your father find out about that?' he asked.

'You didn't tell him?' she said.

'Absolutely not,' he said. 'Do I look like a tattletale?'

She sent him the quick grin. 'Actually, no, you don't, Your Majesty.'

He laughed, the chuckle strained as it rumbled up his

chest. And it occurred to him he'd probably laughed more since he'd met her than he had in his whole life up to now.

Not helpful, Leo.

'We should get inside before we freeze,' he said, pulling off his own headset, more keen than he should be to see her out of that shapeless clothing.

Climbing down from the cockpit, he grabbed their bags then helped her down.

He followed her along the path that had been cleared in the deep snow. With the helicopter blades finally silent, he could hear the crunch of their footsteps, and Juno's shallow breathing, the silence of the forest as night fell annoyingly romantic as the lights strung across the porch reflected in the fresh snowfall.

As they entered the lodge, he stopped on the threshold. His breath froze in his lungs as he took in the cabin's décor. It looked as if Santa had vomited over the luxurious furnishings.

Who had done this? He would have them fired.

'Oh, wow.' Juno's gasp of excitement broke through the chill seeping into his bones.

She spun round to take in the fire burning in the open hearth, the pine bows arranged on the mantel, and the six-foot tree in the corner festooned in fairy lights and red and gold ribbons and bows.

The musical lilt of her laughter echoed around the room, warming the chill in his chest.

'Leo, it's fabulous,' she said, before she spun to a stop. 'I didn't know you were a Christmas junkie.'

'I'm not,' he said, dumping the bags on the floor, the strange glow starting to disturb him. 'This wasn't my idea.'

'Oh,' she said, the smile dying—and he felt mean for ruining her moment of joy. Then annoyed with himself for caring.

'Are you hungry?' she asked, her eager expression only increasing the pressure in his chest. 'I could cook us some supper? I had a job as a short-order cook in a diner not so long ago. I'm pretty good.'

He frowned. Why would she have needed a job?

'You go ahead, the fridge should be fully stocked. I've already eaten,' he said, stifling his curiosity. He needed to get a handle on the feeling crushing his ribs.

'Is something wrong, Leo?' she asked.

'No,' he said, and watched the light in her eyes die. He refused to feel guilty about it. They were here to get through the next seven days, do the damn pregnancy test, hope to hell it was negative, then leave and never see each other again. Satisfying the chemistry between them was one thing, encouraging an emotional connection something else entirely.

Keeping things cool tonight made sense. They needed to establish firm boundaries before they enjoyed any fringe benefits. Juno Monroyale was a force of nature—wild and undisciplined. She'd captivated him without even trying when he'd thought she was a queen. He wasn't about to let her do the same now he knew she wasn't.

'I've got work to do,' he said, picking up his own bag. 'I'll take the bedroom at the back. You can have the master. Do you want me to take your luggage in there for you?'

'No, that's fine,' she said, extending the handle on her case.

He could see the confusion clouding her eyes.

'I'll see you tomorrow, then,' he said.

He was going to get through tonight without touching her, just to prove he could. Whatever happened in the next seven days, he was going to be calling the shots from now on. Not her.

But as he lay on his bed twenty minutes later, staring

at the wooden rafters on the lodge's ceiling, and heard her moving around in the cabin's state-of-the-art kitchen, the delicious scent of herbs and grilled lamb making his stomach growl, the memory of her bright smile and her little gasp of joy when she'd seen the Christmas decorations was still doing strange things to his chest.

Juno awoke the next morning to a white-out. The snow was falling outside the cabin in fat, fluffy chunks, covering the trees in a blanket of pristine white.

You never got pristine snow like this in Queens, and she'd missed it.

She showered and changed into her outdoor clothes and made herself some coffee, then headed out into the living room. She'd heard Leo the evening before in the kitchen making himself a midnight snack, had debated whether to surprise him. Then decided to let him sulk. Something had spooked him, something about the Christmas decorations. And it had made her sad to see it. Was it something to do with his mother's death?

She'd wanted to ask him more about it. But ultimately she'd decided against it. She didn't want to break her 'no heavy emotions' rule on the very first night.

She switched on the Christmas tree lights—which she realised Leo must have switched off.

After rinsing out her coffee mug, she found a carrot in the fridge and headed outside.

Juno breathed in the clean, clear pine-scented air, the peaceful morning. The beauty of the snow-laden forest was a gift she wasn't sure she deserved but was determined to make the most of.

She formed a snowball, then began to roll it across the ground in front of the cabin. She hadn't made a snowman since she was eight years old, and she'd still lived in Mon-

rova with her sister. They'd escaped from the palace every
chance they got that Christmas, to escape from their overbearing governess and the sound of their parents arguing
in the adjoining suite. They hadn't realised at the time
it would be their last Christmas together. The snowman
they'd made just before the thaw had been the last they
would ever build. But Juno hadn't forgotten how.

'This one's for you, Jade,' she whispered as she set to
work.

Thirty minutes later, she had lost the feeling in her fingers and toes, her jeans were soaked through at the knees,
she'd discarded her hat and scarf and her anorak and was
only wearing a thin camisole, because the sun was warm
and building a snowman was a lot sweatier than she remembered it.

After perching another snowball on top of the larger,
misshapen lump she'd made earlier, she retrieved the carrot
and screwed it into the middle. She tilted her head to one
side, to admire her handiwork, then grabbed her discarded
scarf and wrapped it round where the head and torso joined
together—calling it a neck would be a bit ambitious.

She stood back to check him over again.

He looks kind of grumpy.

'What is that?'

She swung round to see Leo standing on the porch,
wearing nothing but a pair of sweat pants, some boots, a
T-shirt, and a frown.

Heat infused her already sweaty body—and all the
pheromones she'd put on hold the night before went into
party mode.

How does he do that?

With his dark hair rumpled, the soft cotton outlining
his impressive chest and his expression as sulky and im-

perious as it had been the night before, he looked good enough to eat. Or certainly nibble.

Relax, pheromones, and get a clue. He doesn't want you.

'Actually, I think it might be you,' she shouted back. 'He looks almost as sulky.'

'He?' came the distinctly unimpressed reply. 'That thing has a sex?'

'Yeah, I'm gonna call him King of the Grumps—sound familiar, Your Moan-esty?'

His brows rose, but then the frown was back. 'I'm hungry. How about you come in here and make me some breakfast?'

'Not until you ask me nicely.'

'Stop being contrary,' he demanded, as if she were one of his subjects. 'You must be hungry after all your...' he paused just long enough to be deliberately insulting '... hard work.'

How could he even sound suggestive when he was disparaging her perfectly good snowman? And why had her pheromones gone into party overdrive at the words 'hungry' and 'hard work'?

That was so wrong. On so many levels.

'Cook your own breakfast,' she said. She'd wanted to cook for him last night, but she was through sucking up to him. Sulking Leo might be sexy as all get out, but that didn't mean she was going to put up with his 'I'm the King of Everything' behaviour.

'Now who's sulking?' he said and turned to go back into the cabin.

Her temper spiked and, grabbing a fist full of snow, she flung it as hard as she could.

Much to her astonishment, because she'd always been a terrible pitcher in high school, the missile hit its mark, smacking into the back of his head and showering him in snow.

Oops.

He turned slowly, flicking the already melting snow off his damp T-shirt, the sulky frown now catastrophic. 'Are you mad?'

The giggle burst out of her mouth, part amusement, part shock, mostly hard-partying pheromones. 'You have a problem, King of the Grumps, come get me?' she said, then bent to grab some more ammunition.

Big mistake.

A freezing ball thudded into her chest, soaking the front of her camisole as soon as she straightened. And suddenly six feet four of enraged King was heading her way, stocking his own arsenal en route.

She shrieked and started pitching from behind the snowman.

It was a declaration of war.

Ten minutes of screaming, yelling, running, slipping, sliding, and some actual snowball-throwing later, and Leo scooped her up and threw her over his shoulder.

'That's it, I'm putting you out of action,' he declared as he headed back to the lodge, but she could hear the laughter in his voice.

She stuffed her last snowball down the back of his T-shirt.

'You little witch!' he roared, and shuddered violently, nearly shaking her off his shoulder.

She shrieked some more as he hefted her up the porch steps.

They were both breathless, laughing, covered in snow— well, she was covered, he was mostly dry, because her surprise pitching skills had totally deserted her as soon as war had been declared. He carried her into the lodge, scattering snow and ice onto the polished wooden floors. Then dumped her onto the large couch.

'It's payback time, Princess,' he growled. And the partying pheromones joined forces with the giddy beat of her heart as his gaze dropped lower.

Even wet and sweaty and flushed she is irresistible.

Leo's heart thundered as he took in the pebbled nipples under Juno's wet shirt. Was she braless? Heat shot into his groin.

Her riotous hair tumbled down around her shoulders. And her green gaze blazed with emerald fire.

He needed her naked, like yesterday. He'd woken up grumpy as hell, she wasn't wrong about that. After two nights of unfulfilled erotic dreams, was it any surprise? But he was through controlling his hunger—he'd established who was boss and that was enough.

He lifted her foot, tugged off one boot, and the other. Then kicked off his own boots as she watched him, the eager anticipation already firing through his system.

She hadn't objected to sleeping with him on this trip, so what was he waiting for?

The mood changed, from playful to intense. But it didn't matter. This was all about sex, always had been. Sex and chemistry and getting it out of their systems before they both went back to their real lives.

He lifted her and she wrapped her arms around his neck, hooked her legs around his waist and buried her face against his collarbone, her lips finding the pulse point beneath the stubble on his chin. Her scent—citrus and spice and warm, playful woman—surrounded him, her kisses so artless and enthusiastic his heart stumbled in his chest.

He staggered towards the lodge's master bedroom as he found her mouth. She shivered deliciously in his arms as they finally crashed into the bedroom together and he dropped her on the bed.

The frantic battle to divest themselves of their clothing took less than a minute but felt like an eternity as he watched her wrestling off her wet jeans, socks and panties and then tug the sleeveless T over her head. Her bare breasts bounced, the flushed nipples sending the heat pounding straight into his groin.

He stripped off his sweat pants and T-shirt and kicked off his boxers in seconds flat.

At last, they were naked, her eyes locked on his rampant erection as he grabbed the sweat pants and pulled out a condom with trembling fingers.

He ripped open the packet and rolled on the protection, aware of her eyes on him.

But as he climbed on the bed, and she scrambled back to give him room before lifting her arms to wrap them around his shoulders, he could feel his control slipping again. Grasping her hips, he pulled her under him, but as her hands fell to his shoulders, her eyes dark with a longing that matched his own, the shaft of longing—and desperation—was so intense, the squeeze in his chest so sharp, it began to scare him.

What was happening here? Because what should have been simple and straightforward sex, and nothing but sex, felt like more again.

He could see the glow of affection in her eyes, could feel their hearts beating in unison. She opened her mouth and the fear sharpened.

'Leo...'

He pressed a finger to her lips.

'Don't,' he said, his voice so thick with emotion it was starting to terrify him.

Her eyes became shuttered, and he had the strangest

feeling he'd broken something that might never be repaired. But the hunger, the longing, the physical yearning leapt in to take its place.

He gripped her hips and flipped her over, then lifted her, until she was positioned on all fours, ready to be plundered. Need surged through him, the desire so strong he could hardly breathe. He didn't want to see her face, didn't want to see the emotion that he was terrified might match his own as he took her.

'Leo?' she whispered, her voice thick with arousal, but also trembling with need.

He nestled the rigid erection in the swollen lips of her sex, not penetrating, but stroking the slick seam, playing with her, to refocus her mind on what he could give her. Instead of what he could not.

She jerked, and he tightened his grip on her hips. He found the font of her pleasure and exploited it with the smooth strokes.

She sobbed, the guttural sound thickening his shaft even more.

At last, he could feel her shattering, bucking against his hold. He reared back, unable to wait a moment longer, and plunged to the hilt. The tight clasp of her sex milked him as she cried out. He moved, his thrusts deep, branding every last inch of her, revelling in her surrender. As her orgasm pulsed around him, his own climax built from the very reaches of his soul, shocking in its intensity.

The orgasm rushed towards him then slammed into him with the force and fury of a runaway train. He shouted out, the pleasure wrenched from him, and clung onto her slender frame as he let himself fall.

Juno lay like a limp noodle on the bed, Leo's big body covering hers, the scent of sweat and sex surrounding them, the imprint of him still humming in her tender sex. She closed her eyes tight, not wanting the blissful wave of afterglow to end. Not wanting to revisit the words she'd nearly blurted out.

Thank God he'd stopped her.

You can't go there. He doesn't want that.

She heard him shift, the words that had formed in her head, a declaration of need, longing, desire, replaying in her head despite her best efforts. But then a light kiss on her shoulder had her swinging round.

'Come on,' he said as he climbed off the bed. After discarding the condom, he reached down to lift her over his shoulder.

'Leo? What are you…?' She choked out a shocked laugh, pathetically grateful for his playful mood. 'Put me down! I'm exhausted.'

Not entirely true—getting a bird's-eye view of his naked butt from her position on his shoulder was having a restorative effect. And helping her forget about everything other than the sex.

'Tough,' he said. 'Now stop wiggling or I'm going to drop you.'

Pressing her hands against his back, she lifted up and twisted. 'Where are you taking me?'

'Outside.'

'You're… *What?*' She shrieked and began to wriggle in earnest as he pulled open the porch door and stepped out onto the snow-covered porch.

'Leo… Are you nuts? We're naked.' She carried on shrieking and wiggling, with him laughing until she was dumped unceremoniously into a pool of steaming bubbling water. She slid under the delicious jets, letting the water envelop her body, her senses as alert as the rest of her. When she popped up, he was sitting beside her on the ledge of the wooden hot tub, the steam bubbling up to guild his handsome features in a luminous film of moisture… And smugness.

She slapped the water, covering him in the steamy froth. 'You jerk,' she said, but couldn't resist the smile at his outrageous behaviour.

'Hey,' he said as he caught her wrist and tugged her towards him. 'It's Your Moan-esty to you, Princess.'

She laughed as he dragged her up and over his lap, until she was straddling him. Her shoulders above the water felt the bristle of cold air, but it only heightened the sensations rioting through her body as his erection pressed against her belly, and his heavily muscled thighs tensed beneath her butt.

'I can hear you thinking,' he murmured as he cradled her cheek with his palm, threaded the wild spray of hair behind her ear. 'Stop it.'

She glided her thumb down the side of his face, felt the delicious rub of stubble already beginning to darken his cheeks.

'Could I ask you a question?' she said as the curiosity overwhelmed her—she'd never seen him so relaxed or so open and it enchanted her.

He had forgiven her and there were so many things she wanted to know about him. Just small things, nothing major, maybe if—

'No questions, Juno,' he said, cutting off the eager thoughts. 'Unless they're about what I want for breakfast or how to construct a snowman properly.' He captured her hand, bit into the swell of flesh beneath her thumb. 'Or when you want me to ravish you next.'

She could see the fierce determination in his gaze and hear what he wasn't saying.

They had six days together. Six days to explore this intense physical connection. But deepening the emotional connection that had begun in the past week was out. Because all that would achieve was to hurt her more when they parted.

She swallowed past the lump of regret in her throat, forced herself to concentrate on the exhilaration of being in this beautiful place with this super-hot guy. And not the feelings threatening to hijack her breath and destroy her equilibrium.

It was Christmas, they had a week to enjoy this gift and she was not going to ruin it.

Or forget that by the time Christmas was over, what they had together would be over too.

CHAPTER ELEVEN

JUNO STUCK RELIGIOUSLY to the no questions rule as if her life depended on it in the days that followed, and developed a rhythm of sorts. She did all the cooking, because she loved to cook, especially for Leo, who it turned out had a voracious appetite, not just for her, but also for food.

The sex too was a revelation for her. She had never believed her body was even capable of this level of pleasure... And each day Leo ramped up the demands he made on her and she found herself meeting those demands with demands of her own.

For a woman who had always been outspoken, she'd never realised she'd had so little awareness of her physical needs, but with Leo there to tempt and tease and tantalise her, to wring every last drop of pleasure out of each encounter—whether it be fast and furious on the kitchen counter, or slow and languid in the shower—she began to realise what she'd been missing.

The more she fed the craving for him, though, the more she seemed to need—but what scared her the most was that the questions just kept multiplying.

And the more she contained them, the more desperate she became to know the answers.

To stop herself from breaking the rules, she badgered him into snowmobile rides into the forest, evenings in front of the fire, or card games to fill up the time when they weren't making love.

But even so, each night when he left her bed to return to his, after their last sex-capade of the day, it became harder and harder not to ask him to stay. And tougher still to wake up alone.

She knew why it had to be this way. Increasing the intimacy between them would be a lie, and she had to keep those questions at bay, to deal with the longing that clutched at her chest each morning when she woke to her empty bed.

Activity helped. So she established a routine for those empty mornings. Get up, get dressed, then head out to make another snowman.

Who knew she would discover she could be a morning person after all?

She loved the cold crisp mornings and building a snow-man meant she didn't have to dwell on all the unproductive thoughts, all those questions she wasn't allowed to ask or all the emotions Leo stirred, which she couldn't acknowledge.

There were no more snowball fights. And she suspected she knew why, as each day the intensity of the sex, and the agonising tension of tiptoeing around all the things they weren't allowed to talk about, increased.

Leo didn't want to give her another opportunity to blurt out her feelings.

As those feelings had begun to terrify her, she was on board with that. Avoidance was definitely the answer.

Christmas morning arrived, and she built her last snow-man—but there was no sign of Leo. She tried not to get upset or anxious that he was sleeping away this special day, when it was their last full day together.

Not a big deal, Ju. This is just an epic booty call. You've got no claim on him and the good news is he has no claim on you.

Luckily, she'd spotted a project that should keep her busy for most of the day.

Taking the turkey she had pulled out of the freezer the night before, she hefted it into the state-of-the-art kitchen. She was busy stuffing the bird an hour later when Leo's deep voice rumbled down her spine and his large hands settled on her stomach.

'What's that?' he murmured, as his face appeared over her right shoulder and he tugged her into his embrace.

'A snowman,' she said, aware of her pulse hammering too hard. 'What does it look like?'

He laughed. 'I thought as much.'

She twisted her head and smiled at him, her heart stuttering in her chest at the sight of his jaw darkened by beard scruff, his face so handsome her breath caught every time she looked at him.

Maybe they weren't a couple, but was it wrong to grab these moments of closeness so she could remember them when they parted?

Sympathy pulsed in her chest as she noticed the sadness in his eyes.

Christmas was hard for him; it was when his mother had died. But she could fix that today. No questions asked.

She shifted out of his arms and reached into the fridge to snag the box of fresh eggs, the sliced ham and a quart of milk. 'Here, why don't you make us breakfast this morning while I concentrate on this?'

'Breakfast, huh?' he said, standing back and holding the produce as if he had his hands full of a couple of armed grenades.

'Yes, ham and eggs...' She frowned at his perplexed

expression…as a strange thought occurred to her. 'Leo, you do know how to cook ham and eggs, don't you?'

'Why would I know how to cook ham and eggs?' he asked, as if she'd just asked him if he knew how to soufflé a pheasant or make sushi from scratch.

'Because everyone knows how to cook breakfast,' she replied. Unable to prevent the little jolt in her heart rate at what an endearing figure he made.

She'd never once seen Leo out of his depth. But that air of authority had slipped—as he stood barefoot in a kitchen, wearing boxers and nothing else, with his once perfectly styled hair sticking up on one side and his jaw darkened by a week's beard scruff, staring at the eggs and ham as if they might bite him.

'I've never cooked anything in my life,' he declared, as if that were perfectly normal.

'Not even an egg?' Juno asked, actually kind of shocked. She'd done all the cooking, but that was because she enjoyed it. She'd assumed he didn't—she hadn't realised he couldn't.

'Not even an egg,' he said without hesitation. He put the supplies on the kitchen counter. 'Why don't you cook as usual and I'll watch?' He gripped her wrist and pulled her into his arms, his hand landing on her butt under the silk robe she'd thrown on after her shower.

She snorted out a laugh, despite the leap of desire coursing through her sex-obsessed body. She'd become addicted to Leo, that much was obvious, but she knew a distraction technique when she saw one. 'Nice try, Your Majesty,' she said.

Drawing out of his embrace, she picked up the groceries. 'I've got a much better idea,' she added. 'Why don't *you* cook while I tell you how? It'll be my Christmas present to you, teaching you some basic cooking skills.'

She could see he wanted to object. And it occurred to her how tough it was for Leo to admit a weakness.

Up till now, Leo had been the expert. On everything. How to behave as a monarch, encouraging and supporting her while they were on her fake state visit. He'd even been the expert in bed, teasing out her pleasure and sending her senses soaring to heights she'd never believed possible. But now the tables were turned.

'You're not going to let this go, are you?' he said.

Juno's grin widened; this was one more precious memory she would be able to keep from their time out of time here. 'Nope.'

He swore softly under his breath. 'Fine, but don't blame me if you get food poisoning,' he added.

She laughed as she drew out a large metal mixing bowl from the impressive array of kitchen equipment. 'I won't.' She smiled at his frown and passed him an egg. 'Now let's break some eggs.'

'I think this has been my best Christmas ever,' Juno murmured, stifling a yawn, as she placed her bare feet in Leo's lap and relaxed into the sofa cushions, so tired and full of food she could barely keep her eyes open.

'It has been mine, too,' he said. The glow of firelight and the twinkle of lights from the tree in the corner of the room played over the planes and angles of his face.

Her heart expanded, the sincerity in his gaze making her chest ache with all the things she hadn't been allowed to say, but knew now to be true.

This was Leo with his guard down, the man without the crown who she'd only been allowed a few rare glimpses of before—while talking to a small child, at the height of passion, over a snowball war—and he was adorable.

Her heart pulsed painfully but she pushed the emotion to one side.

Sensation returned as he played with her toes and she thanked God for the timely distraction.

Don't ask for more, Juno. When this is all you can have, and all you're entitled to.

'Seriously, we cannot do it again. I'm exhausted,' she said as the familiar tug of desire centred in her sex.

His rough chuckle made her insides hurt. 'I never knew I had a foot fetish.' His smile warmed the ache in her heart. He dropped her foot back into his lap, caressed the instep. 'You have delicious feet, Princess.'

She grinned back at him, refusing to let the melancholy in.

The remnants of their Christmas feast—roast turkey, roast potatoes, a medley of vegetables and a red wine jus—lay on the coffee table where they'd devoured it after spending the afternoon and evening devouring each other in between bouts of industriousness in the kitchen.

Who knew Leo would look so cute learning how to make ham and eggs?

She resisted the tug of longing. They only had a few hours left—twelve at the most—before they would have to return to the palace. And Leo would be forced to don his crown again.

The unfairness of that pinched her heart, but she refused to let it in.

Not forced. Leo wore that responsibility willingly, because that was the kind of man Leo was. Overwhelming, tender, hot as hell, and loyal, but also damaged in ways she recognised, because she had been damaged in the same way. Never loved unconditionally, always knowing that, other than her sister, there was always a price to pay for affection. For approval.

Leo would never give up the throne—because his father had made him believe that was what gave his life value. And she knew that made a union between them impossible, because she knew she would always be second best. The way her mother had been, to her father.

She'd spent so much of her life resenting the monarchy. Resenting the choices her father had made, the decision to choose duty instead of family. In a strange way, being with Leo these past two weeks, discovering that she wasn't as rubbish at pomp and circumstance as she'd thought, had been a revelation, a confidence boost, a way of finally putting those demons to rest. That she could tame her recklessness, control her rebelliousness, if she was given the right support, the right help and guidance.

Look at me now, Father. I didn't disgrace you after all.

Jade had told her at the start of all this that she needed to come to terms with her past. Their past. All that she'd lost all those years ago. And she hadn't believed her. But her sister had been right.

She'd needed Leo, needed to prove she wasn't a nobody, that she was her father's daughter after all. And that should be enough.

Unfortunately, it wasn't, because she'd fallen hopelessly in love with Leo in the process.

A part of her wanted to blurt out the truth. But she couldn't, because however strong her feelings were, she knew he didn't return them.

She couldn't bear to expose herself again, to beg for someone's love and be rejected. To be told by another man she loved that she was not enough.

He stroked her feet with his thumbs, sending sensation shimmering into her sex, as he turned to her. 'Why did you get a job as a short-order cook?'

The pulse around her heart intensified at the off-hand

question. She'd abided by his rules, and now… Did he know he was breaking them?

'Why do you ask?' she said.

'I just wondered if you did it because you enjoyed cooking so much.'

The question was loaded.

She could answer with the platitudes she had always used before, when disguising the reality of her life in New York with her mother. And the financial fallout after her death. She shouldn't want Leo to know the truth, when no one else ever had. But the memory of what he'd called her on two different occasions came rushing back…

A spoilt brat.

And suddenly she wanted him to know that wasn't who she was. It was dangerous. Perhaps he wouldn't believe her, he might not even care, but he'd asked. And that was enough.

'I needed the money,' she said. 'By the time my mother died we were in a lot of debt. The penthouse had to be re-possessed. I'd had a waitressing job at the diner since I was sixteen,' she added, seeing the stunned surprise in his gaze. 'But the cook's position paid more.'

'Why did you need money?' he said. 'Did Andreas not give your mother a fair divorce settlement?' He sounded outraged. Why should that mean so much?

'He did. In fact, he was more than generous. He wanted to be rid of her, and he was willing to pay,' Juno said, the familiar bitterness tightening her voice. 'But by the time we'd been in New York for a few years, her drinking had become a problem. She couldn't hold onto any acting jobs, she'd lost her looks and the constant partying became an excuse to spend everything he sent her and borrow more. By the time I was sixteen we were in tons of debt.'

'Why didn't your father help you?' he said, straightening in his chair.

'Because she never acknowledged she had a problem and I'm not even sure he would have helped us if she had. He'd made it very clear that last summer in Monrova that I was a problem he didn't want to be bothered with either.'

She'd been too scared to ask, because she'd been sure the answer would be no.

Leo stroked her feet absently, his gaze locked on her face. 'Juno, that's appalling. I had no idea.'

Her throat thickened and she felt stupidly close to tears. To know that he believed her, that he cared, felt so huge. When it really shouldn't.

'Do you know what the toughest thing was though?' she said.

'What?' he asked.

'She still loved him. I always thought it was just drunken ramblings, when I'd be pouring her into bed, she'd say over and over again how much she missed him. How she wished she hadn't messed up. But I think now she really meant it. I guess it didn't matter to her that he had never loved her in the same way.' More than duty, more than scandal, more than his responsibility to the monarchy. 'Maybe if he had he wouldn't have discarded her so easily.' *Or me.*

'I am sorry I called you a spoilt brat,' he said, with a forcefulness that made her heart swell even as she acknowledged the dangerous parallels in her own life. She'd always known falling for Leo would be a mistake. Why hadn't she been able to stop herself? 'It seems that your childhood was a great deal harder than mine.'

'I doubt that,' she said. 'My father never hit me.'

'I should never have told you about that,' he said, his voice brittle with purpose. 'He wasn't a loving man, but I survived. And it taught me self-sufficiency.'

Did he really believe that?

She cradled his cheek, felt the muscle tighten in his jaw and her heart broke a little more. They'd both said too much. But even if he regretted it, she never would.

'I wish I could have met that little boy,' she said, seeing his eyes becoming shuttered. 'I would have loved to give him a hug.'

'Don't…' He clasped her wrist and drew her hand down from his face. And she felt the deep sense of loss.

She shifted off the sofa, knowing she'd broken the rules, and paced over to the fireplace. She shouldn't have let that slip. Especially when she felt him step behind her, his voice husky.

'Don't be sad, Juno. That child is long gone.'

Is he…? Really? When you still tense at the sight of a few Christmas decorations?

She should leave it at that. She'd made a promise to herself she wouldn't beg. Wouldn't ask, so he could reject her. The way her father had.

But suddenly it all became too much. The need, the want, the heady emotion scraping against the raw spot he had revealed that still existed in her heart. And not telling him felt like the height of cowardice. What if all she had to do was ask? What if he didn't reject her, what if he loved her too?

She turned, to find him watching her. She gathered every last ounce of her courage and made herself tell him the truth.

'I've fallen in love with you, Leo.' The words released on a tortured huff of breath.

The flicker of shock in his eyes appeared before he could mask it and stabbed right into her heart.

CHAPTER TWELVE

'LOVE IS JUST a word. It doesn't mean anything.'

Leo hadn't wanted to say it, but what else could he do? The last few days—hell, the last entire week—had been torture. And the torture had only got worse. He'd known this might be coming, and he had dreaded it, ever since they had made love the first morning in the cabin and he'd seen the words she wanted to say in her eyes.

It had become so hard to stick to his own rules. But it was even harder to do so now he knew she was nothing like the woman he had assumed even a week ago.

She had continued to captivate and inspire him. But what the hell did he do with that, when he had nothing to offer her?

She blinked and swallowed. 'Is that all you have to say?' she whispered, the shock in her voice only making his desperation worse.

He cupped her cheek, drew his thumb across the line of her lips, unable to stop himself from touching her, even though he knew now it wouldn't stop the yearning, it would only make it worse.

'We can't have any more than this week. I thought you understood.'

She pulled away from his touch. Her eyes darkening, the longing still there, but beneath it was the sadness.

'Why can't we?' she asked, so simply his insides turned over. 'I know you don't love me back, not yet,' she added, and the understanding in her voice pierced his heart. 'All I'm asking is that you let me in, Leo. Is that really so hard?'

She waited a beat, and the words were on the tip of his tongue. But the rush of emotion, of need, of yearning was so deep and visceral it terrified him.

He could not expose himself to that need, or it would leave him defenceless. The way he had been after his mother's death.

Something he had strived his whole life never to be again.

'Yes, I suppose it is,' he said, absorbing the desperate yearning he could not give in to.

'I see,' she said, a heartbreakingly poignant smile on her face. 'Thank you for being honest with me.'

She stepped back, the shutters coming down over her expression.

No. Damn it.

He grasped her arms, pulled her back into his embrace. 'Why do you need any of that, when all that matters is this?' he said. But he could hear the desperation in his own voice as he framed her face and pressed a kiss to her lips.

She opened for him instinctively. Their tongues tangled in a dance of desperation and desire. He felt her shudder of need. He tugged off her sweater and bra to reveal the full breasts, swollen with need. He'd devoured her body so many times already, why was it never enough?

He placed her on the sofa, stripped off the rest of her clothes and tore off his own, then knelt in front of her, to find the heart of her pleasure with his lips. She cried out, sobbed as he worked the slick, swollen nub, feeding on her pleasure, knowing exactly how to touch and tempt her to make her shatter.

This, he could give her this, why wasn't it enough? It had to be enough.

She rose up, bucking and shuddering beneath the sensual torment, her scent surrounding him, her surrender complete as the orgasm gripped her.

He rose over her, plunged the iron-hard erection deep into her welcoming heat, her sheath still pulsing with the brutal orgasm.

The firelight flickered over her body, the Christmas lights turning the chestnut curls to a mass of colours—her emerald eyes absorbing every ounce of his fear until all that was left was the need.

He plunged deep, took more.

He could not be the lover she wanted, could not let himself be that vulnerable ever again.

As her second orgasm gripped him, he felt his seed—hot, hard, unstoppable—gathering at the base of his spine. He pulled out just in time to spill it on her belly.

She lay exhausted on the sofa, her emerald eyes glossy with afterglow, but the sadness remained. He gathered his strength, to stand and lift her into his arms. She curled into his embrace, the shuddering sigh making his heart ache. He'd hurt her, and he wanted to make it right.

He carried her into the bathroom, switched on the power shower. And washed her with gentle, supplicant hands.

They stood together under the steamy water and he saw the water run down her cheeks, her expression so lost he couldn't tell if tears were mingled there.

She shivered with the emotional impact of their joining, and he felt like a bastard.

He placed her in the bed, and prepared to leave, but she reached out and caught his arm. 'Can you stay with me tonight? Just this once? I won't ask any more. I promise. But I don't think I can be alone.'

It was such a small thing, and so easy for him to acquiesce. So he broke his own rule and moved into the bed beside her, held her gently in his arms and felt her fall into a deep dreamless sleep.

But he stayed awake for hours, thinking of the young girl, left destitute by an alcoholic mother. And the boy, who might once have been able to open his heart to her—but had been lost long ago.

CHAPTER THIRTEEN

JUNO WOKE THE next morning, her body aching, but her heart hurting more. The bed was empty beside her.

She closed her eyes as the pulse of pain wrenched a hole in her chest.

She'd risked everything, and it hadn't been enough. When would she ever learn?

She was going to miss Leo. So much. And this beautiful Christmas. But it had always been a fantasy, a time out from reality, a moment she couldn't trust.

We can't have any more. I thought you understood.

Leo was a forceful man, and every inch a king, was it really any surprise it wasn't her he wanted?

He had so much love to give, she was sure of it, trapped inside him with that little boy, but she wasn't the one who could find it. And she had to accept that now, or she would end up like her mother, pining after a man who could never love her back.

She stretched, her body protesting slightly.

As if conjured by her thoughts, Leo appeared in the doorway carrying a tray laden with something that smelled delicious and her aching heart leapt painfully into her throat.

'Good morning, Princess,' he said.

Wearing nothing but boxer shorts, his hair ruffled, the

scruff on his cheeks having turned into the beginnings of a very sexy beard, he looked like a man instead of a king.

She forced a bright smile to her lips. Maybe she couldn't have him always but now, today, this morning, he was hers and no one else's.

'Good morning, Your Majesty,' she said, dragging herself into a sitting position, and holding the sheet to her breasts, strangely shy as his gaze dipped to her cleavage.

He set the tray down on the bed beside her.

'Mmm…' She took a deep breath in of the aromas, trying not to let on that the last thing she wanted right now was food, her stomach too jumpy and unsettled. 'It smells really good. You're obviously a natural.'

But as she lifted the napkin he'd placed by the plate, she spotted the plastic stick in clear wrapping resting beside it.

Her jumpy stomach somersaulted up to her throat.

'I thought we could do the test after breakfast,' he said, matter-of-factly, as her stomach went into freefall.

How could she have forgotten this had always been the plan? And why did the thought of the pregnancy test feel fraught with so many more problems now than it had yesterday, before she'd blurted out how she felt?

'The instructions suggest it is best to do it first thing in the morning, when the hormone levels are strongest.'

She put the fork back down on the tray, her fingers trembling.

Maybe, if she were pregnant, he would want her? But as soon as the thought struck, she hated herself for it. A baby couldn't make him love her. And even thinking that would just make her more pathetic.

'If you don't wish to eat, I will understand,' he said with his typical pragmatism.

Why did the easiness with which he read her only make the yearning worse?

She nodded. He lifted the tray off and placed it on the side, then handed her a robe as she climbed off the bed.

She wrapped the robe around herself as he passed her the pregnancy test.

But as she reached for it, instead of releasing it, he pulled her close and cupped her cheek. His gaze roamed over her face, the affection, the desire, so bold and unabashed it only made her feel sadder and more inadequate.

'Whatever the result, we will deal with it together,' he said, his voice steady, his eyes kind. 'Okay?'

She nodded, and he placed a kiss on her forehead, then let her go.

It was the honourable thing to say. And she knew that he meant it, because he was an honourable man. But as she walked into the bathroom alone, the pregnancy test burning a hole in her palm, she knew that, whatever the result, it couldn't alter the fact he hadn't known who she was when they had made love without protection.

And he could never love her, even if he had.

Leo had never believed that one's heart could actually get lodged in one's throat, but something was definitely beating heavily there and threatening to strangle him as he waited for Juno to come back out of the bathroom.

He had tried not to think about the possibility of a pregnancy, had certainly not gone so far as to imagine himself and Juno parenting a baby. But as he showered in one of the lodge's other bathrooms and got dressed, he found himself imagining Juno's slender frame ripe with his child, and the tidal wave of possessiveness, protectiveness, was unmistakeable.

He tried to even his breathing as he waited on the bed they had shared twenty minutes later, the door to the bathroom still closed.

He heard the tap running, then cutting off. At last the door opened.

She stepped into the bedroom, still wearing the silk robe he had given her what felt like a lifetime ago, tightly knotted around her waist, the stick swaddled in toilet tissue in her hand.

Her head lifted and he could see the shattered shock in her eyes.

'It's positive?' he asked, but it wasn't really a question.

Her head bobbed. 'I… I think so. I reread the instructions several times.'

He strode across the room and lifted the stick from her trembling fingers. She looked so fragile, so he slung a steadying arm around her shoulder as he read the result for himself.

The wave of possessiveness peaked as he stared at the two clear blue lines.

'Yes,' he said. 'I read the instructions several times myself,' he admitted as he handed the stick back to her. 'Have you decided if you wish to have the child?' he asked.

Say yes.

He wanted to watch her grow heavy with his child, wanted to hold her and support her as she gave birth. But most of all, he wanted the chance to keep her by his side— warm, compassionate, honest, funny, forthright. Why had it never occurred to him that this could be a solution, not a problem?

He had wanted a queen. Why could that queen not be Juno?

She moved away from him and stood staring out into the snowy landscape beyond the bedroom. With her arms clasped tightly around her midriff, and her shoulders slightly hunched, he sensed her battle to hold in the swell of emotion too.

She seemed smaller somehow, and so young. This was a huge step for both of them, and something that had been forced on them by accident.

'You don't have to decide yet,' he murmured, his heart threatening to choke him as he waited for her answer.

She looked over her shoulder. 'I… I want to have it,' she said.

Even as relief washed through him, he could see the fear in her eyes.

He wrapped his arms around her waist and lifted her into his arms, ignoring it.

'Juno, I'm overjoyed,' he said.

Her eyes widened. The flush of stunned pleasure on her cheeks when he put her back on her feet made his heart stutter.

'Really, you're not angry?'

'Why would I be angry? We are to be parents. And Severene will have an heir. We must be married as soon as possible,' he said. He held her waist, the smile he knew was plastered all over his face echoing in his heart as her gaze met his, still uncertain, still wary. He touched her chin. 'Don't look so worried, this is excellent news,' he said, the possibilities suddenly endless.

He hadn't considered such an outcome, but now it all seemed so obvious.

'I will release a press statement first thing tomorrow. I expect there will be something of a diplomatic incident when we reveal the truth of your identity—and my chief of staff will have a cow when he realises he is going to have to arrange a state wedding in a matter of weeks instead of months. But when they hear about the child…' He pressed his palm to her flat stomach, marvelling at the thought of the child that already grew inside her. *His* child.

He wondered feverishly when she would start to show, when he would be able to feel his child kick.

'They will be overjoyed,' he said, stroking her stomach. 'There is no better press for the monarchy than a royal baby. Really, I could not have hoped for a better outcome. Once we have—'

'Stop, Leo.' Her hands covered his on her stomach. And he was forced to raise his head. What he saw shocked him. The flush of pleasure was gone from her face to be replaced by sadness, and pain, the same grinding pain he had seen the previous evening—when he had been forced to tell her the truth, about what he could give her, and what he could not.

'We can't… We can't be married. You must understand that?'

'What?' The word came out on a broken huff of breath.

Surely he could not have heard that right? She was refusing him? Now? Why?

'Because nothing has changed,' she said.

'*Everything* has changed,' he said. 'You are having the royal heir, Juno. The future King or Queen of Severene. Surely you can see there is no other option now but for us to be married, so I can offer you and our child the full protection of the Crown.'

She stepped back, and his hand dropped from her stomach. 'It's not a king or a queen. Or an heir. It's just a baby. *Our* baby.'

'And as such it has a birthright,' he snapped, the anger surging to protect him from the pain. She didn't want him? When she had professed to love him? 'A birthright I will not allow you to deny.'

'What are you saying…?' She pressed a hand to her forehead, her distress so clear at the prospect it only hurt him more. 'That you'll take this baby away from me if I refuse to marry you?'

'Of course not,' he said. She was twisting his words, twisting everything around, making him into a villain, when he was simply trying to do what was right, for her and his child. 'But that doesn't alter the fact this child is the heir to the Severene throne. You might wish to shirk your duty and pretend you can be free from responsibility, but that isn't an option any more.' Frustration and fury rose up inside him, but beneath it lurked the empty space in his stomach, which told him without duty, he was nothing.

The pregnancy had forced his hand, and hers—and if she couldn't see that he would have to show her.

'Is that all this means to you? Duty? I don't want that for me or my child,' she said frantically. 'You told me yesterday you could never love me, can't you see that—'

'Stop it.' He gripped her arm, dragged her back to him. 'Stop being so damn selfish,' he said, his fear now almost as huge as his fury. 'You're talking nonsense. Naïve romantic nonsense. This isn't about that any more.'

'Please, Leo, let me go,' she said, her voice breaking on the word.

He dropped her arm, the sheen of moisture in her eyes like a bolt to his heart. He thrust his fingers through his hair.

'Please, could you leave me alone, while I get dressed and pack?' she said, her voice so small and exhausted the bolt twisted.

He hesitated. He wanted to push the point, wanted more than anything to make her see how foolish she was being, but she still looked so fragile, so wary, he knew now was not the time. She was still in shock from the result of the pregnancy test. She needed time to come to terms with the reality of what this all meant. She was being rash and unpredictable and impulsive. Perhaps the pregnancy hormones were already affecting her reasoning? Who knew? This did not have to be decided right here and right now.

So he nodded. And tried to force himself to relax. Now was not the time to demand and insist. He could do that later, if he had to.

What he wanted to do was pick her up and cradle her against his chest. Make love to her again the way he had last night. But that would have to wait too.

'Okay, Juno. Once you're ready we can head back to Severene. We can discuss things on the way,' he said, determined to make her see reason. 'There are many things about this situation I don't think you understand.' Things he would make her understand calmly and sensibly, once she'd digested the news.

She wrapped her arms around her midriff, as if she were shielding herself from him, and nodded. 'Thank you.'

It was hardly an agreement, but it would have to be enough, for now. Calling her names and losing his temper weren't going to make this situation any less volatile or easy to control.

Even though it was one of the hardest things he had ever had to do, he turned and left the room.

He headed straight to the lodge's study, to contact Severene's flight control centre so he could plot a flight path back to the palace. The sooner they got back, the sooner he could get Juno to accept—by whatever means necessary—that the only solution now was for her to become his Queen.

CHAPTER FOURTEEN

TEN MINUTES LATER, Juno crunched through the snow towards the back of the lodge. She shoved open the door to the garage. Her hands shook and her breath misted the air as she lifted the hood on the snowmobile Leo had used earlier in the week and ripped out the belt drive.

She pressed a hand to her abdomen, cocooned in the snowsuit.

A child grew inside her. A child who she could love. A child who would love her even if Leo could not.

What she had to do now was go home. Back to Monrova—which was less than fifteen miles across the border. And then back to New York. Back to her real life.

Her Cinderella story was over. He didn't love her, had told her he could never love her, and being pregnant with his child couldn't change that.

She hid the belt drive under a tarp at the back of the garage. Then she mounted the snowmobile parked nearer the entrance.

Frozen air filled her lungs as she drove the cumbersome machine out of the garage and hit the freshly fallen snow.

She headed past her family of snowmen and into the drifts that had fallen the day before—as she and Leo had made a Christmas feast together. And thought of that moment when she'd thought she could have it all, just by asking. What a fool she'd been.

She heard a shout from behind her. But refused to look back.

'Juno? Come back here. What the…?'

The curse words were muffled as the snowmobile headed into the trees and she revved the throttle to increase her speed.

What else could she do but run? She couldn't give him the power to destroy her. The way her father had destroyed her mother. Especially not when her child was at stake.

But as she sped into the forest, took the path towards the border, the tears fell freely down her face, chapping the exposed skin.

And she mourned, for a future that might have been real.

If only he'd been able to love her the way she loved him.

Leo swore loudly as he slammed down the snowmobile's hood. The words Juno had left for him on a notepad in the bedroom still echoing in his head.

> *Please don't follow me, Leo. I will be in touch. But*
> *I can't be your Queen. I'm so sorry.*
> *J*

'Damn it, Juno. What have you done?'

He ran into the house, the fury he had tried to keep at bay earlier, when they'd argued, starting to consume him. But beneath it was the black, agonising, all-consuming wave of fear.

How the hell was she going to navigate her way to Monrova, which was surely where she was headed? She didn't know the terrain, and she was pregnant, damn it.

Was the thought of being his Queen, of having his heir, really so terrible?

Grabbing the satellite phone kept in the lodge's office in case of emergency, he stabbed in the number for his chief of staff at the palace.

'André, we need to send out search-and-rescue helicopters to the area on the Monrova-Severene border along the Aberglast pass. And deploy a ground team, too. Also, get in touch with the authorities in Monrova. We need to co-ordinate our efforts.'

'Your Majesty?' André sounded confused.

'You heard me. Princess Juno has run away and we need to find her.'

'Princess Juno, sire? Surely you mean Queen Jade?'

'No, I mean Princess Juno.'

'But, Your Majesty—'

'Juno has been posing as her twin sister for two weeks,' he interrupted the man's conversation. He didn't have time to explain this mess. None of that mattered now, if it ever had. 'Inform all the relevant parties of her true identity,' he said, his head starting to explode with the logistics of finding her.

'What about the media, Your Majesty?' the man said.

How ironic, Leo thought, that averting a scandal had once been his main concern. When it was the last damn thing he cared about now.

'I don't want them informed, yet,' he said. 'They'll only get in the way. The important thing right now is that we find her. She's pregnant with my child.'

But even as he said the words he knew the child was an abstract concept at this point. He had been overjoyed at the news of Juno's pregnancy less than an hour ago.

But suddenly, the child, its future, the monarchy's future didn't seem all that significant. None of that mattered any more. What mattered was Juno. And getting her back. Safe.

Didn't I pass this clearing an hour ago?

Juno brought the snowmobile to a juddering halt and assessed the terrain. The trees had all begun to look the same hours ago, but as she stared at the long shadows falling over the snow, she knew she'd been through this section of forest before.

Her hands ached and her arms were so heavy they felt like lead weights attached to her shoulders. She fisted her fingers, the cramps making the numbness painful. The cold had seeped into her bones hours ago.

The goggles began to mist from her body heat, so she thrust them up. The freezing air hit her chapped cheeks, increasing the pain.

She shouldn't have run. She should have stayed—Leo had been right to call her selfish.

Thoughts of Leo battered her tired brain—his face, so harsh, so handsome; his body, sculpted muscles, firm skin so beautiful she could feel its softness under her frozen fingertips; his scent, man and musk and sandalwood, invading her nostrils; his voice, low and husky and so confident about everything…

Why did I run? Why did I leave him?

He was safe, secure, strong. So much stronger than she had ever been. And warm; he could give her the warmth she yearned for. Except…

'We can't have any more than this week. I thought you understood.'

'If you can't behave yourself in a manner befitting your status, I will have you returned to your mother in New York immediately.'

The emotionless words—from so long ago, and only hours before—echoed in her head, becoming one voice, one man, one brutal reality that chilled her heart.

Leo didn't want her for herself. He wanted an heir, a queen.

Her father hadn't wanted her either. He'd wanted to protect the monarchy and to free himself of any scandal she might cause too.

The buzzing in her head became louder and she looked to the skies, to see a large black bird hovering overhead. She squinted into the setting sun, the frozen skin on her face prickling in the wind as the bird became wider, louder, its outline changing into something mechanical. Not a bird, a helicopter.

Snow flew up from the earth as she watched the mechanical beast set down at the far end of the clearing. The trees shuddered and shook, the bladed wings lifting the drift into a maelstrom.

Her mind blurred. Her heart pounded so hard the pain became one in her body, as the wings stopped spinning and a figure jumped out of the cockpit.

It ran towards her, a voice carrying across the frozen air. But the words made no sense, her mind too numb, too confused, too dazed to decipher what they meant.

'Juno, stay where you are. Don't move. I've come to take you home.'

Home?

But she had no home.

She watched, her body frozen in place, her mind spinning as the figure became a man running through the snow towards her.

His face became visible, blue eyes piercing, determined, full of accusation... Or was that fear?

Her heart slowed from a gallop to a crawl as he reached

her. Flinging off his gloves, he cupped her cheeks; the warmth burned her skin and seared her soul.

'Juno, you little fool, you're freezing,' he said, the hot breath making her eyes water. 'Are you okay?'

But she couldn't make sense of the words, the pain so real and vivid now, the numbness starting to consume her.

Why had she never been enough? Why couldn't she be loved?

'Talk to me, tell me you're okay.' The voice begged, bullied, but it was so far away now she could hardly hear it.

She just wanted to sleep. To be warm again. To be safe. To be loved.

So she closed her eyes and let herself fall.

CHAPTER FIFTEEN

'IF THE PREGNANCY is weakening her, you must terminate it.' Leo grabbed the doctor's lapels, his fear starting to consume him. 'Do you understand me? I don't want you to take any risks with her life.'

'Yes, Your Majesty. I understand.' The doctor disengaged Leo's fingers, her eyes kind. 'But as I told you, the pregnancy is not an issue. Princess Juno had mild hypothermia. But we have warmed her body gradually, and are monitoring her vital signs and she should—'

'Why hasn't she woken up then? It's been nearly twelve hours since I brought her back to the palace.'

Twelve hours that had felt like twelve years as he'd sat by her bedside and willed her to open her eyes, to talk to him. To forgive him.

The fear had become so huge he hadn't been able to eat, or sleep. The truth was he was barely functioning.

He could still recall every minute detail, which had played over and over again in his mind since the moment he'd reached her in the clearing.

The way her eyes had lost focus, the chill on her cheeks, how she had gone limp and then collapsed into his arms. The flight home had been a blur as the terror that he might have lost her, that he had driven her to this, became too huge to control.

The hours that had followed had stretched into eternity as he'd struggled to keep the fear at bay, not leaving her side, as the doctors worked to keep her comfortable, to assess her condition. And she slept.

Why had he been too scared to tell her the truth?

'Your Majesty.'

He turned to see the nurse from Juno's bedside standing at the entrance to her room.

The terror engulfed him all over again.

'Is she dead?' he murmured, ploughing his fingers through his hair, the despair destroying him.

'No, Your Majesty, I believe she is waking up.'

'Juno, please wake up.'

Juno could hear a voice, a deep husky voice, beckoning her out of the darkness. Her eyelids felt so heavy, she didn't want to lift them yet, the lethargy that permeated her body so warm and comforting. But the voice was so insistent... And so familiar.

She forced her eyelids open, to see his face.

'Leo?' she whispered, her throat like sandpaper.

'Princess,' he murmured.

Where was she? And why did she feel so disconnected from reality? What had happened and how long had she been sleeping?

'You're going to be okay,' he said, his voice rough with purpose. 'And the baby too.'

The baby?

The only reason he wanted her.

The sharp blast of reality ripped through the fog and she blinked furiously, trying to stop the cruel memories flooding back, but it was already too late.

She looked away from him, the tears welling up now misting her view of the beautifully appointed bedroom.

She'd run, like the coward she'd always been. And he'd rescued her. She pressed her hand to her belly.

Her baby was safe. The baby she'd almost accidentally killed.

I can't marry you.

It was what she wanted to say. But the words refused to be released from her throat. The guilt and sadness were suddenly too much to bear. The tears flowed freely down her cheeks.

She had ruined everything. Perhaps this was a fitting punishment—that she would have to marry him now and live for the rest of her life loving him and knowing he could never love her in return.

Juno forced herself to look into his eyes, absorb his dishevelled appearance and the heavy beard.

She loved him, and she would marry him. And maybe one day he could learn to love her in return.

The silence seemed heavy as Leo took her hand and squeezed it in his.

'I'm so sorry,' she said.

At exactly the same time as Leo murmured, 'You must forgive me.'

He frowned then smiled, but it was a smile with no humour in it, only regret. The same regret that had wrapped around her heart.

'I can't imagine what you would have to be sorry for, Princess,' he said, the use of the endearment piercing her heart.

So many things.

'I'm sorry for swapping places with my sister,' she said, knowing the list was endless. 'I'm sorry for running. I'm sorry for putting our baby's life in danger,' she said, her heart so heavy it was hard to talk. 'I'm sorry for trapping you into a marriage you can't possibly want.'

The crease on his forehead deepened, the smile flatlining. 'Why would you think that?' he said, as if it weren't perfectly obvious.

'You don't love me, Leo. But you're being forced to marry me because of the baby and—'

'Don't.' He pressed a thumb to her lips to silence the rush of confession. 'Don't apologise for something that is lacking in me, not you.'

'I don't… I don't understand,' she said.

But instead of explaining, he lifted her hand, threaded his fingers through hers, and slowly brought her hand to his lips, pressing his mouth against the skin.

The prickle of sensation, the ripple of hope was almost more than she could bear. She could see the shadows under his eyes as he moved into the light. Why was it so much harder to face the truth of their situation knowing that he cared for her, just not enough? He stroked her knuckles with his thumb, finally lowering her hand and raising his gaze to meet hers.

What she saw there shocked her to her core.

This wasn't regret, or sadness, it was pain.

'Leo?' she whispered, her heart so full now she was scared it might burst.

What had she done to this strong, steady, beautiful man? What had they done to each other?

'It's not that I don't love you, Juno. It's that I was too terrified to admit it.'

The bubble of hope inflated against her breastbone, making the pain increase. 'But—'

'Please, let me finish,' he interrupted, but the roughness in his tone wasn't impatience, she realised, it was regret. 'I hadn't thought of a pregnancy, hadn't really considered how I would feel about it. What we would do. But when you came out of that bathroom with the positive result, everything inside me... It all felt so right. So wonderful.'

She nodded. 'I know, because you need an heir.'

He shook his head, the emotion in his eyes so real and vivid now the bubble of hope expanded even more. 'That is what I told myself. That is what I told you. And that is what I wanted to believe, but when you collapsed into my arms in the forest, I knew it was not the truth.'

'It wasn't?' she heard herself say.

'No.'

'What is the truth?' she asked, scared to hope now, but so much more scared not to know the answer.

'It's really very simple. I wanted to have a reason to demand you stay with me, that you marry me, without ever having to reveal my feelings for you. Feelings which I think began to develop the moment I first laid eyes on you at the Winter Ball.'

His head bowed, as if the weight of the world were on his shoulders. 'I told myself I didn't want you to love me, that I could never love you in return.' He traced his thumb over the back of her hand, then lifted it to his lips again in an act of supplication that stole her breath. And made her heart expand with the bubble of hope now bursting under her breastbone. 'The pregnancy was just another excuse. Not to confront those feelings.'

His gaze met hers, the shattered blue so full of longing her breath caught in her throat.

'And this is why you must forgive me, not the other way around. You told me you loved me, and I refused to say the same—refused to even admit it might be a possibility. Because I'm a coward. If you wish to have this child in New York, away from me, you can. I would never take the child away from you. Never force you to marry me for the sake of a duty you don't feel.'

'Oh, Leo!' She forced herself up on her elbows, to cup his cheek.

He was wrong. He wasn't a coward, he was just scared. She'd been a fool not to see that the love they shared—so rich, so sudden, so vibrant—had terrified him when it had scared her so much too.

They had both been terrified. And the only reason she'd told him first was because she'd never been able to guard her feelings. The way he had been forced to guard his.

'You idiot. Can't you see none of that matters now?' she whispered, her voice raw.

'It doesn't?'

'Of course not. Not if you love me too.'

He gripped her cheeks, pulled her towards him, until his lips hovered over hers. 'If being terrified of losing you is love? If wanting to listen to you breathe every day for the rest of my life is love? If wanting to go to sleep with you in my arms every night and wake up beside you each morning is love? If wanting to hear your voice, even when you are calling me an idiot, is love?' He placed his hand on her abdomen. 'If wanting to watch you grow round with our baby, and plant many more inside you, is love?'

She nodded, the tears cascading down her cheeks turning to happy tears at last.

'Then I guess I am in love too,' he said.

'Good,' she said. 'Now please shut up and kiss me, Your Majesty.'

EPILOGUE

Two days later

'YOUR MAJESTY, IS it true that the Queen is not the Queen?'

'Queen Jade, how are you in two places at once?'

'Which Queen is the imposter?'

Juno blinked furiously, overwhelmed by the barrage of camera flashes and shouted questions that greeted her and Leo as they stepped onto the podium at the hastily arranged palace press conference. Her stomach jumped into her throat, the guilt threatening to make her vomit as she gazed out into the sea of faces—their expressions ranging from curious to astonished to stunned to excited.

She had caused this media storm. This was all her fault. She might even have destroyed the monarchy of the man she loved beyond reason, beyond…

But just as her panic threatened to outpace the breakfast she'd barely eaten an hour ago, as the advisors had briefed them on how to handle the news that Jade had appeared in Monrova that morning two days ahead of schedule, Leo's grip on her hand tightened and his arm wrapped around her shoulders.

Leaning close, he whispered in her ear, 'Breathe, Juno. It's okay.'

She glanced up at him and whispered back, 'Are you sure? Isn't this the disaster you wanted to avoid?'

But he didn't look angry or concerned, instead a grin split his features that made the warm glow in her heart intensify. 'Please don't remind me what a boring idiot I used to be.'

She smiled back at him.

While this love was still so new and scary, the thought of the baby growing inside her newer and scarier still, somehow she knew, with that look of bone-deep approval on his face, she could conquer anything. Not just her fears, but also her flaws.

They were all still there, of course, but somehow they'd lost their power to define her in the last two days. While she and Leo had talked and laughed, and made love, and he had reassured her constantly that, whatever happened next, he had her back.

She'd been alone for so long, it felt strange knowing that she wasn't any more. She knew it would take her a while to fully accept it. But all he demanded of her, because he was as astute as he was wonderful, was that she concentrate on believing him.

'Are you sure you don't want me to handle this alone?' he murmured as the palace press officer announced them and attempted to silence the crowd of over-eager journalists. 'I don't want you overtaxed,' he added.

She shook her head. 'I got us into this fix, I think it's up to me to help get us out of it, don't you?'

He pressed his forehead to hers, in a gesture so full of love and affection her heart expanded in her chest. The room went quiet, the world's press holding their breath. 'We got into this fix together, Juno. Don't ever forget that. And it's a fix I will be grateful for, for the rest of my life.'

He kissed her softly, and she kissed him back, not caring as the barrage of camera flashes and shouted questions went off again.

Her skin had heated to what she thought was probably an impressive shade of scarlet as Leo turned to the assembled crowd and—having waited for everyone to finally quieten down again—addressed them.

'I have a statement to make on behalf of myself...' he sent Juno a smile so full of love she was surprised she didn't start floating '...and the woman I very much hope will become my Queen. Eventually. But first of all I should introduce her to you properly. Her name is Princess Juno Alice Monroyale, and I love her unconditionally.'

The room erupted again, the inevitable questions being fired at them both. Juno felt her heart swell to impossible proportions as the press officer attempted to outline the arranged explanation that had been agreed with Jade and her advisors that morning—that Juno and her sister had swapped before the Winter Ball to give Jade a break from her royal duties, Leo had been in on the ruse, but then he and Juno had fallen hopelessly in love.

As the questions followed, Leo answered most of them, but when he deferred to her, his hand in hers and his presence beside her made her aware that, no matter what she said, or how she said it, he wouldn't stop loving her, or supporting her.

It was a heady feeling. And one she intended to spend the rest of her life getting used to.

After ten minutes, the time limit Leo had insisted on, the press officer brought the conference to a close. And then a screen behind the stage lit up with Jade's press conference in Monrova, which had been timed to coincide with theirs.

That was their cue to leave.

Leo ushered her backstage, then led her through the

crowd of advisors—ignoring every one of their attempts to waylay them—and into his private study.

He slammed the door, leaving them alone together, then gathered her into his arms.

'Thank God that's over with,' he said, his mouth lowering to hers. 'Now I plan to spend the rest of the day ravishing you.'

A delighted giggle escaped before she could stop it, but as his mouth lowered to hers she stifled the yearning and pressed her palms to his chest. Something that had been bugging her since her phone call with Jade that morning niggled at her again.

'Leo, wait. I'm worried. I think something's going on with Jade.'

He lifted his head, his lips twisting into the tantalising grin she had become totally addicted to.

'Uh-huh.' He nuzzled the spot under her ear that he knew would drive her wild. 'You mean apart from the fact...' his lips travelled down, trailing fire in their wake to land on her collarbone '...that she's been playing hooky for three weeks in New York...' Juno gasped as his hand drifted under her blouse to tantalise the place on her back he now owned unconditionally while his lips kept wreaking havoc on her pulse point '...while the man she was supposed to be marrying has fallen in love with her incorrigible twin.' His roving hand slid down the back of her jeans.

The laugh at his behaviour choked off in her throat, but the niggling guilt refused to go away.

'No... There's something else...' Juno's breathing became staggered as she tried to keep her mind and her hormones on track under Leo's relentless onslaught. 'When we talked this morning, she seemed...sad. And she didn't tell me why she came back from New York two days early.'

It was the reason why they had been forced to arrange a press conference so suddenly. The cat—or rather the Queen—had suddenly been out of the bag. 'I'm worried about her,' Juno admitted. 'I hope I didn't screw things up for her with this swap—when everything turned out so brilliantly for us.'

Leo leaned back and sighed. He dropped his forehead to hers. His hands stilled. 'You know what I think, Juno?'

'No, what?' she said.

'Your sister is a grown woman and an extremely competent queen. *If* there's anything she needs to tell you, she will, because she loves you and she knows you love her. I adore your compassion but sometimes you just have to give people space.'

'Are you telling me to back off and stop being so nosey?' she asked, the guilt releasing its grip on her throat. Leo was right. Jade was smart and sensible and she knew Juno had her back. If Jade needed her, she'd let her know.

He smiled. 'That too.' He lifted her into his arms as the giddy laugh popped out after all. 'Now let's start celebrating the new year early.'

She held on to his shoulders and found his lips with hers.

Ready to celebrate this new year, and the next, and all the years to come as soon as humanly possible.

* * * * *

INNOCENT IN THE
SHEIKH'S PALACE

DANI COLLINS

For my editor, Megan Haslam, who brought up some key points when I pitched this book (e.g. Make sure there aren't any other stray samples!). And for you, Dear Reader. Social isolation is my normal, but it's so much easier to bear knowing you're here with me in these fantastic fictional worlds.

CHAPTER ONE

DRIVING IN NEW YORK WAS, hands down, worse than taking the subway, even on a Sunday. Hannah Meeks hadn't had much choice, though. She had come straight from a weekend research trip upstate and the clinic had been adamant she arrive by ten, offering to send a car for her if she couldn't get there on her own steam. They'd even given her a special code to open the gate to their private lot, promising her a spot.

None of that was a win when she had to be outside at all. Today was the sort of weather her grandmother would have said was "great if you're a duck." Ducks weren't dumb enough to be gadding about in this, though. Only her.

Hannah couldn't imagine what the emergency was. She'd paid all of her instalments on time and her pregnancy was progressing without hiccups. Well, a few actual hiccups on the baby's part, which she'd been assured were normal.

She punched in her code and nearly froze her hand off. The rain was turning to sleet, bogging down her wipers as she entered the mostly deserted parking lot. The drive to her small walk-up would be even worse, and she would need every type of good luck charm to find a parking spot within a six-block radius.

Maybe they would let her leave her car here for the night, not that walking to the subway station would be a picnic, either.

She sighed as she carefully turned her car's nose into a spot to the right of the entrance steps. Her sedan fishtailed as she touched the brakes, leaving her car at an angle that probably took up two stalls. She didn't bother trying to fix it. Frankly, she needed the extra space to open her door all the way. Her belly had her sitting so far back from the wheel that she could barely touch the pedals.

Checking her reflection, she heaved another sigh. She rarely wore makeup and had a few more months before her adult braces could be switched for a retainer. Why had she thought this pixie cut was a good idea, though? Her hair had just enough curl that the little wisps turned up on the ends, especially where they landed against the frames of her glasses. No matter how she smoothed the front, her bangs sat crooked. She looked like a six-year-old who had cut her own hair with garden shears, then put on her grandfather's horn-rims.

She jammed her hat on, pulled on her gloves, buttoned her coat and gathered her phone and keys into her bag. Her windows were starting to fog, and when she tried to open her door, she found it had—seriously?—frozen shut! Well, now what?

She dug into her bag for her phone, thinking to call into the clinic for assistance, but just then, an SUV pulled in a few spaces over. A man leaped out of the passenger seat and popped open an umbrella before he opened the back door for another man.

The door was slammed, and the men would have hurried into the clinic, but she snapped to her senses and gave her horn an urgent series of toots, then squeakily rubbed a hole into the foggy window beside her.

"Help! Excuse me! Can you help, please?"

She heard one ask a question in a language that might have been Arabic. They wore woolen overcoats and their heads weren't covered, but they both had dark skin, black hair and closely trimmed beards.

"I need help!" she shouted louder as they stood there. "My door is frozen."

And I'm going to need a powder room ten minutes ago. Panic stations, gents.

The one with the umbrella grumbled something, but the other impatiently took it. It was useless anyway. A gust of wind drove the sleet sideways, turning the umbrella inside out. He shoved it back at the other man and came to glower at her through the little circle she'd made in the fogged glass.

Her heart leaped in surprise, alarm, fear. Maybe a hint of desire?

He was a blurred impression of height and intimidation, thirtyish, and good-looking despite his frown. His overcoat gaped and showed a dark blue suit that appeared to be tailored and probably was. The clinic catered to the supremely wealthy. She was very much a charity case who'd got in on a *who-you-know*, after doing a huge favor for the head administrator's wife.

"What are you shouting about?" he demanded.

"My doors are frozen. I'm stuck!" She demonstrated by trying the latch and giving the door a shove with her shoulder.

He frowned and tried it himself. Then he circled her

car, trying all the doors with enough force to make the car rock. None opened.

He said something to the man trying to fix the umbrella. A third man emerged from the SUV while the first came back to her window and asked, "You're sure it's unlocked?"

Oh, dear God. She wanted to die then. She pressed the button and heard it release.

Her would-be knight yanked opened the door to let in an icy blast—and that was just off his thunderstruck expression.

"I am *so* sorry." Had he ever heard of pregnancy brain? "I forgot that I hit the locks when I came into the city. You never know when a carjacker will try to jump into your car at a stop light, you know?"

He did not know. He *dared* carjackers to even think about looking in his direction. He continued to glare at her with exasperated disgust while the wind tried to tousle his short, thick hair. Silly wind. Nothing tousled him. He thrust out a hand, glance hitting her belly as she twisted to get her feet onto the ground.

"I can manage," she lied, feeling even more ridiculous as she tried to shoulder her bag and search out a safe place for a firm grip while the parking lot looked to be an ice rink.

"Can you?" he asked with scathing sarcasm. "Give me your hand. I'm not going to be responsible for a woman in your condition slipping and falling."

"Thank you." She begrudgingly took his hand and her heart leaped again, this time with a sharper, higher skip and a resounding thump as it landed back in her chest.

She had expected his palm to be smooth, but his grip

was calloused and incredibly strong, making her feel ultrafeminine even as she heaved herself out of the low car with the grace of a baby hippo. She tried a nervous smile, but he was the furthest thing from interested in anything beyond getting her into the clinic and out of his un-tousled hair.

All three of the men were swarthy and handsome, wearing expensive overcoats and deadpan expressions. But the one who had helped her seemed to be in charge. While he held her hand, the other two made themselves busy. The guy with the umbrella rushed to close her door and steady her other elbow, and the third man raced ahead to trigger the automatic doors as Hannah kept a waddling pace across the slippery sidewalk and up the snow-caked steps.

"This is very heroic of you, thank you," she said, gripping her rescuer's firm arm.

The umbrella-holder followed behind them, trying really hard to keep the umbrella over his partner, but it was moot. They were all soaked and her dark knight in woolen armor spoke impatiently again in Arabic, brushing him off.

They stepped through the first set of doors and she sighed with relief as they all wiped their feet on the mat. She hurried through the second set of doors, past the reception desk, blurting, "Hannah Meeks" as she headed straight into the powder room she had used on previous visits.

A few minutes later, considerably more comfortable, she tried again to do something with her reflection. It was a lost cause. Her hair now had a dose of static thanks to her hat. Fine brown strands stood straight up, making a halo around her red-nosed face.

Hopefully, she wouldn't have to face her rescuer in the waiting room. If she did, perhaps she could smooth things over by offering to take on any urgent research projects he might have. It was basically her only marketable skill beyond her paid position as a university librarian, but it had come in handy with the making of junior here. But who was her savior? And who were the other two men he was with? It seemed like they could be his bodyguards. With those signs of wealth, it definitely fit that he might need protection, but why was he coming to a fertility clinic without his partner?

Making a donation? She snickered into her hand at her own pun and decided to quit speculating about him since he'd likely already forgotten about her. She was extremely forgettable, as she had been reminded as recently as a year ago, when she'd bumped into the young man who'd taken her virginity her freshman year of college. He'd stared at her blankly, flummoxed that she'd greeted him by name. Humiliated, she had wound up lying and saying they'd met at a faculty event.

Ignoring the scorch that arrived against the back of her heart, she tugged her thick brown pullover down her belly, as if that would change anything. The knit bounced right back up, revealing the plain black camisole she wore tucked into the stretchy panel of her maternity jeans. So classy.

Hannah was not one of those women who glowed through pregnancy while transporting a cantaloupe behind their belly button. Nope. Her front was as big as one of those giant yoga balls some of her colleagues sat on at their desks. Her butt was wide as a delivery truck while her breasts had barely grown a cup size. She was the opposite of a figure eight—an egg. She still wore her hiking boots—having visited Grammy's resting place before driving back to the city—and the shoes that were good for tramping through the cemetery reading gravestones didn't exactly lend grace or comportment.

It's a girl, her grandmother would have said. *Girls steal their mother's beauty.*

Hannah gave a wistful sigh at Grammy not being here to meet her great-grandchild, but she doubted Grammy would have approved of Hannah's method of conception.

At twenty-five, Hannah had quit waiting for Prince Charming. She had never had any beauty to be stolen. Boys had been cruel, and men forgot her. Even women failed to notice her enough to ask, *Can I help you find a size?*

Hannah was that dreary cliché: a spinster librarian. But she had recently taken her future into her own hands. She had always known she wanted a family. She was confident her child wouldn't care if she had crooked teeth and freckled skin, a few extra pounds and a tendency to sniffle her way through allergy season. Being a single mother wouldn't be easy, but it would be easier than being alone.

For the first time in her life, she was optimistic for her future. Excited and confident. She refused to let anyone make her feel insecure about how she looked, even herself.

She quit fussing with her reflection and left the powder room. A nurse stood at the counter, waiting expectantly for her.

The Crown Prince of Baaqi, Sheikh Akin bin Raju bin Dagar Al-Sarraf, was trying not to allow the unthinkable into his head, but he didn't lead his country's military so successfully by failing to add up the evidence before him. In fact, his keen intelligence and ability to recognize and defuse small conflicts before they grew into wars was one of his greatest assets.

The facts he'd been gathering the last few days were foretelling only one disastrous, explosive outcome. It was a circumstance so infuriating that he cast about for any other explanation, but he instinctively knew he was wasting precious brain power and time.

A sperm sample was unaccounted for. An urgent meeting with the head administrator of the clinic had brought him from his father's sickroom. The nurse had insisted on waiting for the very pregnant woman toddling toward them to reappear before showing *both of them* into a meeting.

What a bizarre woman. She seemed utterly, cheerfully ignorant of the gravity they faced as she flashed a mouthful of metal and said, "Thank you again for your assistance."

His bodyguards had been alarmed by her honking and demand for assistance earlier. Akin, however, had instinctively known what he faced the instant he glanced at the lone woman arriving for an appointment on a day when the clinic was otherwise deserted. It wasn't a round of gunfire, but the next few minutes would tear gaping holes through his life. He knew it.

His second impression of her wasn't any more reassuring than his first. She had her overcoat over her arm but was still very bulky with heavy pregnancy. She had removed her hat to reveal an asymmetrical punk rock haircut that was the furthest thing from flattering. Her face was round and bare of makeup behind dark-rimmed glasses that turned her eyes into mousy brown beads. Her lips thinned into a self-conscious line as she succumbed to what he imagined was a habit of hiding her teeth.

"Hi, Hannah." The nurse's smile faltered as she swung her attention toward him. "Dr. Peters will see you now."

Hannah flashed Akin another oblivious smile as she swept past him.

Akin might be in deep denial, but that didn't stop him from taking every sensible precaution. He issued a few brief orders in Omid's direction.

Omid nodded and took out his phone.

When he fell into step behind her down the narrow hall, Hannah glanced over her shoulder with confusion and tried to see past Akin to the waiting room.

"Do you work here?"

"No," he said flatly.

"Then why—?"

"Here we are." The nurse knocked once and pushed into an office.

Dr. Peters rose and greeted them with a tense, apprehensive nod. His balding head was shiny with perspiration. His hands nervously smoothed the lapels of his white coat. He started to come around to shake Akin's hand, but Akin stopped him with a flick of his wrist, silently telling him to skip the niceties.

"Your Royal Highness." The doctor bowed slightly. "Have you met Ms. Meeks?"

Ms., not Mrs. A small mercy? Akin's mind raced to the next steps in what he needed to do to recover from this ambush.

"Not officially. Hannah. And you're a Royal Highness?" Hannah's surprise was filled with confusion as she looked between them. When the door clicked closed behind the nurse, Hannah finally began to look concerned.

"Sheikh Akin Sarraf," he introduced himself, using his simplified English address to save the doctor bumbling through his full name. He and Hannah were about to become closely acquainted. No use standing on ceremony.

"The Crown Prince of Baaqi," the doctor impressed on Hannah.

"Am I, though?" Akin asked in a light tone that made generals shake in their boots.

The doctor went white.

"I don't understand why we're both here," Hannah said in bafflement, glancing warily at the closed door.

"You will. Have a seat," Akin said.

The doctor sank back into his own, hands trembling as he shifted a couple of file folders on his desk.

Hannah took the arms of a chair and lowered herself into it, but Akin remained on his feet, arms crossed, bracing himself for the bombs that would land in the next few seconds.

"I presume you found the misplaced sample?" he prompted.

"What sample?" Hannah blurted, snapping her head around and proving herself not completely lacking in the ability to make a deduction. Her hands took hold of the arms of her chair so tightly her knuckles went white. She leaned forward as though ready to leap back onto her feet.

Dr. Peters drew a shaken breath and sent a *deeply* remorseful look toward Akin that did not move him one iota. The doctor swallowed.

"To bring you up to speed, Ms. Meeks, I should tell you that Sheikh Akin's brother—"

"The late Crown Prince," Akin interjected.

"Yes. Um… Crown Prince Eijaz was a client. Sadly, he succumbed to a lengthy battle with cancer in March. Before he began his treatments, he had us store six sperm samples, in hopes he would survive and marry. He wanted to ensure he could produce an heir."

Why Eijaz had chosen a New York clinic would remain a mystery. He had been diagnosed while visiting here, so it might have been an impulse or convenience. The clinic had an excellent reputation, but it was clearly not infallible.

"I'm very sorry for your loss," Hannah said, sounding sincere. "But I'm sure that news has nothing to do with me." She spoke firmly, rejecting the obvious conclusion the way Akin had fruitlessly tried to do. She was pushing her whole body deep into that chair now, shoulders rounding defensively, hunkering down for the inevitable that she could sense was about to befall her.

"The royal family recently made the difficult decision to destroy the Prince's samples. Prince Akin is—" the doctor cleared his throat "—*currently* the acknowledged heir."

At no time had Akin coveted that role, despite all his father's failings and his brother's glaring lack of capacity for ruling a country. Akin had long moved past any opinions whatsoever on being "the spare." He had no feelings beyond grief at being called upon to take up the duties of king.

He had begun to prepare for the responsibility, though.

And now he was being relegated to the shadows again. It wasn't that it stung; it was just so damned cold there. Bleak.

Hannah was looking at him with a small frown, as though she could see past his hardened expression into the turmoil he worked so hard to ignore.

"In the course of our task, it was discovered we only had five of the Prince's samples in our bank," Dr. Peters continued.

Hannah brought her attention back to him. Her color had been leaching from her skin through the last minutes. She licked her lips and spoke in a voice that was very careful, as though she was fighting to hold on to her composure.

"Are you asking me to bring my dogged librarian skills to bear and help you find it?"

"Please, Ms. Meeks. Let's not have jokes. This is an extremely serious matter." The doctor shot Akin a look that was downright terrified. "We had the blood sample you donated last month for our research database. We used it to run a DNA test and can confirm that Prince Eijaz's sample was used to inseminate you. I'm very sorry."

Akin had been expecting exactly this, but it still punched a curse from his lips. The profanity rang loud and clear in the small room. He didn't apologize. His brain was folding in on itself with the ramifications. He began formulating his best plans of action, seeking a win while protecting his flanks.

Hannah only gave a disbelieving huff.

"You're sorry? Why? I didn't know the donor's name

and now I do. That will be nice if any health concerns arise in future, but nothing changes. I have the baby I wanted and I'm the furthest thing from sorry for it."

Akin had to admire her bravado. It wasn't true confidence. Her voice quivered. Behind that poise, she understood that reality as she knew it had been altered irrevocably, but she was pretending she still had choices. Autonomy. If he was a man with a heart in the metaphoric sense, he might have found it endearing and called her "cute" for it.

"When are you due?" Akin asked her.

She jolted. He realized he was using the tone that snapped young soldiers into following orders.

Not a single enlisted man would dare refuse to answer him, but she stubbornly set her jaw and sealed her lips, as though refusing to speak would somehow help her keep that baby all to herself.

"Six weeks," Dr. Peters provided after a glance into one of the files before him. "December 29. The sex is…a boy. Congratulations." He threw a smile toward Hannah. "Everything is progressing normally."

"What the *hell* are you doing? *I'm* your patient," Hannah interjected with a tap against her breastbone. "I don't know him." She pointed at Akin. "I did not give you permission to share my confidential information. *I* didn't even want to know the sex. Are you completely abandoning professionalism and embracing full clown car?"

Apt description, and Akin empathized with her flare of temper. He really did. But he controlled his own as Dr. Peters continued to speak.

"We understand this is distressful and will be taking responsibility. Our lawyers have been notified and will be in touch to work out fair settlements with both of you."

"How charmingly American," Akin said tersely. "Throw lawyers and money at a problem to make it go away." The clinic would suffer a higher premium on their future malpractice insurance, but otherwise remain unscathed. If anything, their reputation would benefit. Women would line up for a chance at accidentally carrying royal blood. Whatever was awarded to Akin's family would be a drop in the bucket of billions they already possessed and would provide no real compensation for all that was about to happen.

Because he and Hannah faced a lifetime of reckoning with this error.

"It doesn't matter how this happened, since it *has*, but how did it?" Akin asked.

"We had a flu sweep through the clinic. Hannah's doctor was sick along with other key staff. Once a woman has prepared for the procedure, we don't like to ask her to wait. We're very tightly booked and had an intern—"

"I get the picture," Akin cut in, already bored with the perfect storm of incompetence.

"Whether I'm awarded a settlement or not, I intend to continue paying my instalments." Hannah set trembling fingers atop her bump. "So there's no question this baby is completely mine."

So cute. Truly.

"Is she safe to travel?" Akin asked.

"If the appropriate precautions are taken." The doctor used a handkerchief to dab the beads of sweat from his brow as he glanced at Hannah. "I have a nurse standing by to accompany you."

"To go where?" Hannah pinched her arm. "Am I even awake? Did I slip on the ice and I'm in a coma?"

"Hannah, the Sarraf family is very wealthy and powerful. I recommend you cooperate—" the doctor began, but she cut him off.

"No," she said resolutely. She flattened her feet to the floor and thrust her belly into the air as she pushed herself to stand. "I don't care what your inept intern did or how formidable your deceased client's family is. This is *my* baby. Not *yours* to give away to someone else. Definitely not *his*. I'm going home. I will drink my cup of chamomile tea and have a nap. When I wake up, I will discover this didn't even happen."

"Prince Eijaz didn't approve this use of his sperm," Dr. Peters said in an urgent effort to reason with her. "If you weren't so far along, we would insist on termination—"

"Don't you *even*." Hannah had one hand splayed on her belly. She slapped the other onto the doctor's desk, looking as though she would vault over it and tear out the man's throat. Her face turned red. Her expression was the most threatening thing Akin had ever seen on a woman. It was a sight to behold and he had to respect her for it.

"The doctor is wrong," Akin interjected. "Termination would *not* be an option. Your son is the next ruler of Baaqi. That wouldn't change no matter what stage of pregnancy you were in. I would die protecting his life, today or any other day, as is my honor and duty."

Hannah straightened and looked at him with confused mistrust. "That won't be necessary."

"You don't know that, Ms. Meeks," he said with dry irony. "The future is extremely unpredictable, as our present circumstance demonstrates. Neither of us expected this would be our destiny an hour ago, did we?"

"My destiny hasn't changed."

"It very much has," he informed, experiencing an uncharacteristic shred of pity. He might have spared some for himself if he didn't know what a useless emotion it really was. "Our rulers are born in Baaqi, Ms. Meeks. Therefore, you are coming with me. You may stay as our guest and provide the loving care and guidance you clearly intended to bestow on him as he grows up there, but that is where he will grow up."

"*Counteroffer.* You ask Dr. Peters for a referral to a psychiatrist, because you're clearly delusional. Goodbye."

CHAPTER TWO

HANNAH WAS SHAKING so hard she could barely walk.
She had to set a hand on the wall as she made her way
down the hall, feet heavy as lead while her heart raced,
and her vision going in and out.

It didn't matter who the father was. That was the conclusion she had reached when she had decided to seek
artificial insemination. All she'd wanted was a healthy
specimen and she had been assured she had one.

She had been *happy* not knowing who the father was.
It meant the baby was all hers. There wouldn't be any
troublesome interference from a deadbeat father or an
interfering mother-in-law. She had had a very special
relationship with her grandmother, and she had looked
forward to that same unconditional embrace of familial
love. The kind that made a home a home. That made
life worth living.

Dear God. The umbrella guy from the SUV had rep-
licated into six more. They were all dressed in flawless
dark gray suits with black-and-silver striped ties. One
melted through the exit when she appeared. The pair
stationed at the door each set out a hand to indicate she
couldn't pass. Two more stood next to the only other

doors that led from the reception area. They all looked past her as she appeared.

Because the prince, or sheikh, or whatever Akin was, had practically stepped on her heels the whole way down the hall. She refused to look at him as she shrugged into her coat, but it didn't change the fact her heart was hammering so loudly it threatened to knock her over. Or that she felt his presence looming like a cloud that would envelop and smother her.

"Ms. Meeks will be traveling to Baaqi with us. She will be shown every consideration." He didn't touch her but halted close enough behind her shoulder that she felt the warmth off his body, even through her coat.

"I'm not getting on a plane with you!" Hannah looked to the reception desk, but the waiting area was deserted. What the *hell*? She thought about shoving her elbow into Akin's gut and making a run for it—as if his rugby team of bodyguards wouldn't tackle her.

"Give your keys and address to Omid. He'll ensure your things are forwarded."

His voice had the most authoritative ring of *Do it* she'd ever heard, but she had a lifetime's experience of standing up to chauvinists, misogynists and bullies. She straightened her spine—which only stuck her belly out further—and bluffed a complete lack of intimidation.

"No." What was he going to do? Beat her up and risk this precious baby he was sworn to protect?

"Hannah." Along with the musical lilt intrinsic to his own language, his English held a crisp British pronunciation, as though he'd learned it at a fancy boarding school. It added an annoying note of condescension to his air of superiority. "You're a vulnerable woman who is heavily pregnant. You've just received very shocking news, so I'm overlooking your insolence, but don't mistake my patience for weakness. You have arrived at the limit I possess. If you want a power struggle, we can engage in one. I will win. That won't be good for any of us, most especially the baby."

"What am I supposed to do? Defer to whatever you decree?" She waved a wild hand.

"Most people do. It makes everything run more smoothly."

The arrogant ass wasn't even joking.

"Let's speak somewhere with more privacy," he suggested.

She didn't move, aware in the back of her head that, much as she wanted to, she couldn't pretend this wasn't happening. Tears of panic were hot behind her eyes, but she fought them just as she fought to remain rational. Surely they had options that didn't include overturning her life?

"You can follow me to my apartment." She turned and swept past his door guards but was pulled up short by the snow falling like clumps of mashed potatoes beyond the second set of doors.

One of the bodyguard clones stood in that soppy mess next to Akin's SUV, ready to open the door when his boss appeared.

"You can't drive in this." Akin arrived beside her. "Come with me. One of my men will take your car."

"I can drive myself. I drove here, didn't I?" She closed her lips over that. If he said one word about how she had locked herself in her own car…

"My vehicle is safer. My driver is trained for inclement conditions. You already know I'm chivalrous. I helped you out of your car and walked you in, didn't I?"

Worst mistake of her life, relying on him for five seconds.

"I'm not going to let you talk me into anything," she warned.

"But you do understand we've been put in a remarkable position. It needs further discussion." He offered his arm.

After a final moment of hesitation, she went outside with him, down the steps, and clumsily climbed into the back of his SUV.

He came in beside her and offered, "Seat warmer?" He pressed a button, then held out his hand. "Keys."

It was a relief not to have to drive. She excavated her keys from her bag, letting him relay them out the door before she realized—"I need those to get into my apartment."

"They'll be there before we will."

The doors shut and the SUV pulled away. She pondered that comment, looking back to see two of the men climbing into her messy car, moving her laptop case into the back seat. But just as she began to fear she was being a complete ninny and had participated in her own kidnapping, one of the men in the front asked for her address and relayed it to the other men.

She relaxed a little and glanced at Akin. He was bringing his telephone to his ear, speaking in Arabic.

She could point to Baaqi on a map, but she didn't recall much about it beyond it being incredibly rich in oil reserves. It was one of those small lynchpin countries that had suffered unrest over the last decade, from both inside and along its borders. Everyone knew who Crown Prince Eijaz was, of course, and not just because he was a photogenic playboy with millions of online followers, forever vacationing with beautiful women while caught up in one sexy scandal after another. No, he was notorious for his petulant social media post a few years ago, when he'd been stranded in the Maldives. It had sparked a meme that was regularly reposted in response to tone-deaf First World problems.

My avocado toast is scorched.
Oh, muffin. It's like the time your private jet broke down in the Maldives.

She was having a hard time comprehending that *that* man had fathered her baby. It didn't fit in her head that her baby's father was an infamous philanderer and his brother was…? She hadn't even realized there was another Prince of Baaqi.

She pulled out her own phone to learn more, but Akin reached out to cover her screen.

"We'll keep this between us for now."

"I was only going to look something up." *Him.* She dropped her phone into her bag.

It was nice, though, that he thought she had the kind of friends whom she would text *Guess what just happened to me?* She did have people in her contacts list. She wasn't the isolated child she had once been. These days she had colleagues who were polite enough to invite her to retirement parties and baby showers. Students brought her a latte when she saved their bacon by sourcing a book or other reference document they needed. She was friendly with some of the authors she worked with, but only with the sort of online chatting that was mostly superficial. *Do you have kids? No, but I want one.*

Friendships had never been her strong suit any more

than suitors had. Growing up, Hannah had had her grandmother to ease the sting of friends turning on her or dropping away, but after Grammy passed and she'd rented out their bungalow in Syracuse to take her current job at Columbia University, loneliness had become her most steadfast companion.

That first year had been a backslide into her worst self-denigration. When she had found herself alone in bed at the end of it, greeting the New Year by watching a classic rom-com for the millionth time, she had resolved to quit waiting for someone to want to spend the rest of his life with her and fall in love with herself instead.

She had made a list of all the things she wanted out of life, including nicer teeth. "Family" had topped it and she'd been ticking things off, one by one, slowly making her best life come true until—

Her best life *was* coming true, she assured herself, setting a hand on the side of her belly where a little foot was giving a restless nudge.

Akin said a final few words and ended his call, then spoke to her without inflection. "My parents are looking forward to meeting you."

That wasn't how it had sounded. She might not know how to swear in his language, but that had definitely been the gist in the other man's weak, gruff tone.

This was the moment to say something pithy about them visiting New York in the winter, but he continued speaking.

"I presume you're unmarried, since no one came with you to the meeting. Do you have a partner who was expecting to help you raise this baby?"

She frowned, not liking his phrasing, as though he

was saying that whoever might have expected such a thing could kiss that scenario goodbye. She had a brief impulse to claim she did, but his cool way of looking down his hawkish nose sent reverberations through her, warning her against making silly mistakes.

Besides, they were going to her apartment, where it was plain she lived alone.

"No," she replied.

"Family?"

"My mother died when I was young. My father wasn't in the picture and my grandmother raised me. She's also gone."

"What was your plan? What sort of work have you been doing?"

Again with the past tense. She deliberately answered as though her plans were unchanged. Her plans *were* unchanged, she insisted to herself.

"I'm a librarian at Columbia. I'm taking a year's leave of absence beginning at the end of this month. I'm going to Syracuse, to live in the house where I grew up. For the last few years, I've been building an online business doing research for authors. If that continues to go well, I may quit the university altogether and stay home until the baby starts school, but I haven't ruled out coming back to work here or taking a position at another library elsewhere. I like to have options."

"Don't we all," he said with an ironic curl of his lip that struck foreboding in her soul.

Which was when she realized they weren't anywhere near her apartment and were, in fact, crossing the bridge into New Jersey.

"You said we would meet your men at my apartment!"

"I said they would get there before we did. We are not going there."

"That's still a lie! Is that how we're doing this? Because I can lie, too. I haven't, but I'll start," she warned.

His cheeks went hollow. Otherwise he sat very still, hands resting on his thighs. After a moment, he nodded once. "Lying is counterproductive. You're right. I won't mislead you again."

"And I'm supposed to believe that as you kidnap me to… Where do you think you're taking me?"

"My private jet is waiting to fly us directly to Baaqi. I've arranged our own nurse. I can't trust anyone from that clinic. Our flight plan ensures we'll have suitable places to land should any emergencies arise."

"I was being facetious. This *is* a kidnapping!"

"It is."

She could only choke, too flabbergasted to find words.

"You asked me not to lie," he said without a hint of sarcasm or remorse.

"I asked you to take me home."

"I know." His hands made one restless stroke to his knees and returned to the middle of his long thighs. "I understand you want your life to carry on as normal, Hannah. It can't. You are carrying the next ruler of my country. My nephew. If you think that doesn't matter to me, you are deeply mistaken."

Everything about him was very stoic, but he had lost his brother recently, she recalled, then stamped down on any compassion that incited in her.

"I liked it better when you lied," she muttered.

"That ship has sailed."

She studied him, wondering if he really did feel some connection to this baby.

"You miss him? Your brother?" Maybe it was a test of his willingness to be honest. Would he crack and admit to such a human emotion?

"I do," he said after a very brief hesitation, sounding pensive. "But I don't wish to talk about him right now." He glanced at her. His expression was unreadable, but it was probably the most believable thing he could have said.

Impulsively, because she had been dying to share this with someone who might actually feel it as the stunning miracle it was, she picked up his hand and brought it toward her belly. "Was your brother a boxer? Feel what his son is doing to my kidneys."

Akin's hand tensed and he started to pull away.

It was probably overstepping royal protocol for her to touch him without permission. It was definitely unwise. There was something in the feel of his hand that made her bones melt and her head swim, but his gaze dropped to her bump. His brow flexed in a glimpse of agony and he let her set his hand in place.

"Wait for it." She kept one hand over his and used her other to press into the other side of her belly, coaxing the baby, "Don't be shy. Say hello to— *Oof.*"

His breath rushed out and his hand jerked away before he pressed it back into place. "Did that hurt?"

"Like an elbow on the subway," she joked, realizing he wouldn't have any experience with such things.

His brow remained creased and his gaze grew more absorbed as he looked at the roundness of her belly. He circled his thumb, soothing the spot where the baby had kicked.

No man had ever moved her, not in a sexual way. It was another reason she'd asked a clinic to help her make this baby. Akin's absent caress wasn't even meant to be erotic, but it awakened a sensual response in her, one that sent swirling tenderness through her while embarrassing her at the same time for having such a reaction.

"Do you…um…have a wife and children?" she asked.

"No." Maybe he heard some of her confused reaction in her voice, because he withdrew his touch. His cloak of distance returned. "Why did you want to have a baby alone?"

"I still do," she said pointedly.

He didn't move, but his stillness suggested thinning patience and made the air between them crackle with animosity.

Look at me, she wanted to say. *That's why I'm having a baby alone. No man wants me.*

She was horrendously aware of his staff in the front seat, who seemed to speak English, though. And it made her so *sad* that people cared more about how a person looked than who they were inside. She hated to admit she'd always been one of the people society rejected for no good reason at all.

When she answered, she kept her voice low, hoping only Akin could hear her.

"I dated when I first went to university, but relationships aren't all they're cracked up to be." Especially when so many young men had only been looking to score—sexually or on an exam—and cheating had been the goal in both exercises. "My grandmother was elderly and needed help, so I didn't have much time outside of school for socializing anyway. After she passed, I moved to the city and haven't connected with anyone, but I miss having family. The fact is, this pregnancy kind of fell into my lap. Ha-ha."

"How so?" He turned his head to regard her.

"One of my author clients is married to Dr. Peters. I made a joke one day that I wanted children but needed to find a husband first. She said maybe not and told me about the clinic. One thing led to another, and even though the clinic has a wait list and charge through the roof, I was given a consult and taken on as part of their research program. I'm required to give occasional blood samples and answer health surveys for the rest of my life, but I'm happy to contribute to science, so…" She shrugged.

"The samples and questions will discontinue. My brother did not consent to being a research project and nor has my future king."

"Akin—may I call you that?"

"Of course."

She could have laughed at how accommodating he sounded when he was such a giant brick wall in every other way.

"I've decided to pick my battles with you. I'll let you have that one, so you'll be more inclined to compromise on really important issues. Like the fact I am not going to Baaqi."

"Do you know that I have spent more than a decade commanding armies, Hannah? Winning battles is my day job. Perhaps don't pick any with me."

She could have sobbed. She swallowed back her panic and sat straighter and tried to keep her head while fighting for her life with as much civility as she could muster.

"I have to fight you, Akin. Take a walk in this pregnant body of mine for a moment. Whatever you feel for this baby because he's a remnant of your brother, I feel a thousandfold because he's a part of *me*."

"I understand that," he said politely and waited, but she didn't know what else to say, because she could already tell that whatever she came up with, he would counter and override. On the one hand, it was refreshing that he was willing to let her have her say before he told her she was only a lowly woman and should mind her place, but it still made her want to scream.

She huffed in despair and threw up a hand.

He gave a pained nod. "You begin to understand."

"No! I don't. No one has to *know* this was his sperm."

"*I* know. My parents know. *You* know. I would hope you understand that this baby has a birthright you don't have the right to withhold. What are you going to do? Wait until he's eighteen, then point to a spot on the map and say, *That's yours. Go rule it*?"

"Don't lecture me on my rights." The frustrated burn behind the backs of her eyes grew to near unbearable. She turned her attention to the view out the window, where a lack of tall buildings suggested they were nearing a private airfield.

She pressed her lips flat so they wouldn't tremble, but her voice still held a creak of emotion. "Once I decided to have a baby alone, I realized how much better that is. Simpler. I wouldn't be undermined by the other parent, wouldn't have to argue over which in-laws to spend Christmas with. I don't expect big things from my life. All I want is a little family. Me and my child, maybe a goldfish or a cat someday. It's unfair of you to say I'm asking too much by asking for that. I have a right to give my baby the life I planned. It's a good one."

"I don't disagree. For many it is. I envy you for having experienced such a simple life. But this is bigger than either of us, Hannah. This is where we both step up for the greater good of the baby."

"Oh?" she scoffed. "And what great sacrifice will you be making?"

"I'll be marrying a stranger, same as you. I'm becoming a parent when it was the last thing I expected or prepared for."

"What? *No*." Adrenaline sent her hand shooting for the door latch.

He struck like a rattlesnake. His big body loomed over hers, pressing her into the seat while his hand encircled hers. He had caged her so quickly, it took her a moment to realize he was being incredibly gentle about it, even as she sensed his grip couldn't be broken and she had no hope of shifting the wall of his body so much as a fraction of an inch unless he wanted her to.

She panted in alarm, torso brushing his. He was very warm, his eyes like black coffee, the tip of his nose grazing hers as he held her stare. He smelled like spicy aftershave and snow and damp wool.

"I did say I will protect this baby, Hannah. Even from you, if it comes to that. Will you give me your word you won't do anything foolish?"

"No." She blinked hard to see him through a blur of angry tears. "We are *not* getting married. I am not marrying a stranger."

"It doesn't have to be forever, but our marriage will benefit the baby and—you'll have to forgive how cold-blooded this sounds—will help smooth things over in the press."

"That *is* horrible. All of this is!" She wriggled against

him, trying to free her hand and only succeeded in feeling all the more ineffectual for it.

"This is reality, Hannah."

He held her for an extra second to prove the point that he was in charge, she was sure of it, because he waited until she settled before he gently brought her hand away from the door and set it into her lap. He settled back in his seat but continued to watch her closely.

"Our modern world can accept a woman having a baby out of wedlock. My people can even accept a monarch conceived with an unknown foreign woman. Both? That is a tough sell. More important…" His cheeks hollowed. "I trust I have your complete confidence?"

She snorted. "Who am I going to tell any of this to and be believed?"

"Fair point."

The SUV came to a stop near the stairs to a sleek private jet. She dug her back deeper into her seat and clenched her hand around her seat belt, ready to fight being pried out of here and thrust onto that plane.

"Give us privacy," he said.

His men promptly left the vehicle to stand in the gathering dusk and falling snow.

"For health reasons, my father was about to abdicate to Eijaz before my brother's diagnosis made that impossible. My father's health has declined steadily since Eijaz's death. My mother is equally devastated by grief. We were waiting until after the anniversary of his passing before I officially took over from my father. Now…"

Akin's palm swept through the air in a far too subtle gesture toward the earthquake that had occurred a mere hour ago, altering both of their lives.

"Now what?" Her hands instinctively tightened further on the belt.

"Now I will rule as Regent," he continued without emotion. "Until my nephew is old enough to be crowned. Given that enormous responsibility and the influence I will have over your child, it would behoove you to be recognized as my partner. Otherwise you'll be dismissed as a paid surrogate and treated accordingly."

She gasped. "Don't you ever, *ever* suggest that I am some sort of brood mare that carried this baby for any reason except a very deep desire to have a child *of my own*. You don't have any rights to him. Do you understand that?" She was near shouting.

He was completely unaffected, and merely shook his head at her as though she was a recalcitrant toddler.

"What are you going to do, Hannah? You can't abdicate on your son's behalf. That's for him to decide eighteen years from now. How are you going to raise him 'normally' now? How are you going to raise him *securely*? Are you refusing to prepare him for the challenge of taking the crown? Tell me what you think the options are for any of us."

The bastard sat there with that patient, patronizing look on his face because he knew he had her. She didn't have any choice. Not really. She might receive a settlement from the clinic for this mistake, but it wouldn't match the resources he had at his disposal. She would be lucky if all he did was drag her into court. She'd never had the pleasure of being sued, but she knew time was measured glacially in that forum and lawyers were obscenely expensive.

She had nowhere to go, so she escaped the only way she could. She buried her face in her hands. She was a smart woman, but no matter how hard she racked her brain, she came up with nothing. She couldn't even find anger. It was definitely there, simmering at the injustice of life and Akin's casual assumption of authority over her, but she had the rest of her life to wallow in bitterness over that familiar foe.

Right now, she had to fight for what self-government she could retain.

"I don't want to marry you."

"It's just a formality. We won't consummate it."

Oh, there was a surprise! She couldn't help her choke of hysterical laughter and was startled when something soft touched her hand. She lifted her head to see he was pressing a silk handkerchief on her.

"I'm not crying," she muttered, blowing her nose into it. "I'm trying to keep my head from exploding. You don't want to marry me. Do you? Me," she stressed. "I am not a bride you would choose for yourself, am I?" It was a type of self-harm to spit it out like that, but she wouldn't delude herself into believing anything less.

His long silence was damning, but there was something in his hardened expression that made her think he was wrestling with his own demons behind that mask, not intentionally reinforcing hers.

"I have never enjoyed the luxury of choice when it comes to such things. The expectation has always been that my brother would made a selection from my mother's vetted short list of potential brides and produce an heir before I would do the same."

"That's pretty cold-blooded, isn't it? What about love or basic attraction?"

"This from the woman who chose the most dispassionate way possible to conceive her child? A successful marriage merges interests, not hearts." He somehow grew even more shuttered as he said that. "You and I share a common interest in someone who is of the utmost importance to both of us. Marriage is the best action for all of us."

"This isn't your baby."

"He's still my family."

"But…" She hesitated, then forced herself to say it because she had to know exactly how he envisioned things would be. "Don't you want children of your own?"

"We can discuss that at a later time, if you decide you'd like more children."

"And then what? Our marriage ceases to be platonic?"

"As we're both aware, the father is no longer required to be present when his children are conceived." He sent a sardonic glance to her belly.

"So you don't ever want to have sex with me," she said, speaking as plainly as she thought the situation warranted. "Are you going to have sex with other people? Are you gay?" she asked.

"Why would you think that? No, I am a straight man who has gone without sex for various lengths of time in the past. I'm capable of doing it again. Are you?"

"Yes." Duh. She was having a baby without having had sex, wasn't she?

"You planned to stay home and work at your online job. You can do that from Baaqi."

Not all of it. Sometimes she needed feet on the ground, but she could do a lot of it online and through correspondence to various library collections and other archives.

He was doing it; he was talking her into it! And she

was already too exhausted to continue their war of wills to keep resisting his cutthroat logic.

"I can't just *leave*, Akin. I still have a few weeks of work—"

"It will be handled. My staff will close your apartment and ship your things within the week. Your employer will be notified." He was probably making all of that happen as they spoke, cutting all her ties to her old life, leaving her no path to go backward.

"What exactly will happen when I get there?" She hated herself for asking. It sounded too much like she was surrendering.

"We'll marry in a private ceremony, immediately. Then a single announcement will go out encompassing all of this. You needn't appear in public until after the baby is born."

"Every girl's dream." To be forced into a marriage that would be a paper-only footnote to bigger news, her existence hidden from view like a shameful secret. A brand sat against her heart, scoring deeper with each slighting word and potential action. "I don't want…" Her throat was so tight she could barely force any words out. "That. I don't want any of that."

"I know." Why did he have to sound so pitying? If he'd been outright mean, she might be able to hate him. That tone was far more cruel. It carried the same pained pitch Grammy had used when sharing hard truths. *Life isn't fair. We don't always get what we want.*

Hannah drew a breath, wanting to protest, but after a moment the air left her body in a rush. She deflated like a balloon, drooping forward, desolate but still refusing to cry. She had never missed Grammy more in her life.

"You will be well cared for, Hannah. Your child will have an incredible life."

"But it won't be *mine*." She sat up straight. Not her child. Not her life. "I won't ever forgive you for this, Akin."

He was only the messenger. She knew that. And he didn't look too bothered either way, but she was in agony because she knew what she faced would be hell. She had had to work really hard to find her confidence and turn the other "chipmunk cheek" to the incessant litany of insults that had come her way all her life. Bucky and Four-Eyes and Fats were the least offensive.

Now she would be in a new place, already a stranger who didn't know the language or customs. She might be educated and have basic manners, but she wasn't a polished diamond the way Akin and his family were. People like him didn't know what it was like to be someone like her. They didn't want to, not when they could point and laugh instead. Her suffering would have to be swallowed and endured, the way she'd done through each level of hell called "school."

And how would her son be treated if he didn't come out looking look like some Botticelli cherub—

She snapped an accusing look at Akin.

"What?" he asked with caution, sensing the change in her.

No one would ever bully her child. *No one.* Not ever. Not without earning her unmitigated wrath.

Not that she knew how she would protect her son no matter which world they occupied, but being the mother of a future monarch would bestow a lot more power on her to quash attacks against her child. Her *son* would be less of a target, growing up in that role.

"If I go with you, I expect to sign a prenup that outlines clear and fair terms for our marriage and eventual divorce. It must include stringent language that declares my absolute right to oversee every single stage of his upbringing. If you agree to that—"

"I do."

"I'll hold you to that. No lies," she reminded, pointing her finger at him.

"You have my word."

"Fine." She reached for the latch again, pausing to take in the red carpet that was collecting snowflakes as it trailed up the steps into the jet.

What on earth was she thinking?

But here he was, coming around and offering his arm to guide her into his world.

CHAPTER THREE

AKIN HAD THOUGHT Hannah was staging a sulk, setting her head against the window the minute she sat down, but she fell asleep before the plane left the tarmac.

A pang of something that might have been guilt or concern struck against the dented shell of honor he wore to shield against less tolerable states of mind.

She'd spoken briefly with the nurse when they'd boarded, but aside from a bit of breathlessness after climbing the stairs, he hadn't heard any concerns raised by either of them. If he had realized how tired she was, he would have sent her to the stateroom. He started to nudge her awake to do so, but she must be exhausted if she was crashing so hard and fast.

He waited until they'd leveled off, then signaled for a pillow and pressed the button to recline her seat. She barely stirred as he eased her from the window into a more comfortable position. He accepted the blanket from the attendant and draped it over her.

He tilted his own chair back alongside her, wishing sleep came as easily to him, but it never did. He felt as though he'd been on an adrenaline high for twenty years straight. It had grown worse, not better, as time passed.

He had chided Hannah that she couldn't expect to

raise her son in America and have him ready to take over Baaqi at eighteen, which was true. Ironically, Akin wasn't much better prepared at thirty-two.

In his country—in his *family*—the first son was groomed for that role. Pampered and encouraged and revered. When not at school, Eijaz had sat with their father, learning the fine arts of diplomacy and protocol.

Akin had merely been an insurance policy, acknowledged as a member of the royal family but sidelined as expendable. When *he* was home from school, Akin had trained with the army, beginning with the foot soldiers at twelve. Nepotism had played little part in his rise through the ranks. He'd had to prove himself capable before he'd been given command of their forces.

Part of that stark contrast in treatment was due to the fact their father had once been challenged by his own younger brother for control of Baaqi. His father had not only become a hardened autocrat as a result, but he would brook no similar mutinies. He had made clear that Akin's value lay in his unquestioning loyalty toward his brother.

Akin had been devoted to Eijaz. For all of Eijaz's faults and sense of entitlement, he'd been the only one to truly care about Akin. Their mother had been broken by grief when Akin had been very young, and she'd developed a resentment toward him that was lately exacerbated by her eldest son's death and her declining mental health.

So Akin had suffered a constant message of inferiority as a child, but he had never begrudged his brother for his higher station. When their father's heart trouble was diagnosed, however, and the King had begun giving more responsibility to Eijaz, Akin had wondered if Eijaz's temperament was up to the task. The more money he was given to control, the less he controlled himself. Had drugs or mental health issues played a part? Akin couldn't say, but it had all come to a head two years ago when Eijaz had attempted to turn Baaqi into a beacon of modern ideals—something even their own father had opposed. The seismic political shifts had *not* made their country a darling in a part of the world that clung to its traditional values.

Akin had found himself in an impossible situation. The few times he attempted to discuss the matter, his father had accused him of dancing close to treason. His only choice had been to put out fires—often literal ones started by dissidents throwing Molotov cocktails.

He had dreaded what would happen when his father stepped down completely and Eijaz took the throne. That did not mean he had wished his brother dead, but a weight of guilt now cloaked him heavily for his doubts.

Eijaz's cancer had been aggressive and cruel. While his parents supported Eijaz, Akin had taken on even more responsibility. When the unthinkable had happened far more abruptly than they could absorb, they were all devastated, but there had been no time for Akin to grieve or ruminate or show any emotions. He had to prepare himself to take the throne. His father was weaker than anyone outside their need-to-know circle could imagine, and the stress of ruling was shortening the little time he had left.

Even so, the old man had spent what energy he had left on clinging to power, using that power to argue that Eijaz's sperm samples could be used to produce an heir. The logistics had been a blurry prospect. Could they ask a wellborn lady to conceive a future monarch without taking the baby's father as her husband? Did Baaqi want a ruler born to a stranger hired for the express purpose of carrying a child? What if conception was tried and failed? Then what?

After much discussion, his parents had resigned themselves to accepting Akin in the role for which he had been conceived—the fallback heir. He would produce their next monarch the old-fashioned way, via an arranged marriage with a woman of appropriate rank.

It had fallen to Akin to enact that difficult decision. He had made the call to the clinic like a ruthless Shakespearean king, one who ensured his bloodline would not be threatened by his brother's issue. It had made him sick. Nothing about taking Eijaz's place felt good or right.

Within hours, the clinic had relayed the message that five samples were confirmed as destroyed. One was unaccounted for.

That had been three days ago, and he had known immediately that his loyalty to his brother was once again being tested. Nevertheless, Akin had rushed to New York to await the results of their prompt investigation.

Was Eijaz laughing, wherever he was? Because Akin had done the math. If Hannah was due at the end of December, she'd been inseminated shortly after Eijaz had passed. Akin didn't believe that those in the afterlife could reach into this world to shake things up, but this was definitely the sort of practical joke his brother would have laughed himself weak over.

Why Hannah, though?

Akin turned his head, studying her round, pink cheeks. The way she was slumping, her chin had doubled and her glasses were sitting crooked. He gently removed them and set them aside, noting the frown she wore even when fast asleep.

Such a strange bird, so dull and brown and unassuming, but when provoked, her feathers ruffled up like she was ready to win a cockfight. She reminded him of the geese in the park next to his English boarding school. When they felt territorial, they wouldn't think twice about nipping someone's butt.

I don't want to marry you.

Like being goosed by a goose, her words had stung his ego more than doing real harm, but did she not know who he was? Even as second son to a king, women wanted him.

I am not a bride you would choose for yourself, am I?

A long-buried bitter agony had arisen in him when she said that. Although his mother had begun tracking potential brides for Eijaz and him even while they were still young boys, making note of social triumphs and bloodlines and dodged scandals, Akin had always been expected to wait until his brother had secured his own heir before Akin produced one of his own. The one time he'd thought to defy that expectation, he'd been quickly reeducated.

So he had dismissed marriage as a far-off thing, even when his mother's faculties began to fail. When he had affairs, he confined them to those times when he was outside Baaqi. He always ensured the woman in question understood their relationship was temporary. If she wasn't fine with that, they didn't progress beyond dinner, but most took him to their bed anyway. A prince was a catch, even if he only gave her bragging rights on a brief affair.

But future kings, apparently, were even more of a

catch. Legions of eligible women had been reaching out since his brother's death, wanting to "check in" and offer "a quiet night in." He'd been exhausted with the courtship chase before it even started, but that didn't mean he wanted to marry tomorrow. Or to marry Hannah, a librarian who wore cheap pullovers and locked herself in her own car.

Why recalling that made laughter build in his throat, he didn't know. He'd been annoyed as hell when it happened. Delirium, he supposed. This had been a hell of a day, but for a moment his heart felt lighter than it had in a long, long time.

As was his habit, he cut short his straying thoughts and forced his mind back on task. He tried to anticipate all the possible versions of the future he faced, all the moves on the chessboard and all the ways he could react. What result would each produce?

The exercise was enough to induce a migraine, and his gaze unconsciously drifted to the roundness of her belly. He re-conjured that simple moment when she had set his hand against her taut warmth and let him feel the small piece of his brother, alive and kicking. The most perfect, unsullied parts of his brother, free of vanity and venality.

As he tried to recall exactly how that strange moment had felt, the fingers of slumber reached out to draw him under. His grasp on clear thought slid away and, for the first time in years, he drifted into a heavy sleep without any trouble at all.

The Queen's disappointment was palpable. Her pained expression as she skimmed her gaze over Hannah went into Hannah like a knife. She forced a polite smile to remain on her face while the older woman said something in a plaintive tone to Akin.

"Please speak English, Ummi. Hannah is American."

To be fair, his mother looked about as wretchedly unhappy as Hannah felt. And after sleeping in her clothes and coming off the plane in them, Hannah looked like a crumpled ball of sandwich wrap.

Queen Gaitha's face was lined with deep grief, but there was no mistaking the wrinkle on her nose as anything but an expression of dismay. She waved at a servant to show Hannah out.

Hannah refused to let anyone see how much the old woman's disdain affected her. She looked to Akin for guidance.

He nodded distantly to send her away, which stung, but he was about to be her husband in name only. She couldn't expect him to be some kind of savior who would make this easier. She would have to navigate it on her own.

A pretty young woman close to her own age introduced herself as Nura. She seemed kind and efficient and spoke several languages including English and Arabic. She explained that the wedding would take place as soon as Hannah and Akin had bathed and changed, then she would be able to rest until the baby came.

"Change into what?" Hannah asked with a semi-hysterical laugh. She didn't even have the overnight bag she'd left in her car when she had walked into the clinic.

"Oh, there are many choices." Nura drew her through a beautiful entry foyer that had an intricate mosaic floor and gold-framed mirrors on the walls. They reflected the round table in the center that held an enormous arrangement of fragrant flowers.

Hannah glimpsed a spacious waiting lounge with a view to a beautiful courtyard that had a free-form pool and abundant greenery casting shadows across the water. It looked like the Garden of Eden.

Nura brought her down a short hallway to a salon of some kind. This must be the palace spa, Hannah deduced. It had a professional hairstyling chair with a huge mirror surrounded by lights. Scissors and brushes and styling tools were all at the ready. There was a manicure station and a pedicure massage chair like at a beauty parlor. On the other side of the room, there was a carpeted dais surrounded by full-length mirrors.

Nura slid aside a pair of doors and walked Hannah into a boutique. There was a selection of gowns in every color, shelves of shoes and handbags, scarves and belts and other accessories.

"I thought this one, but there are many beautiful choices." Nura produced a stunning caftan in silvery gray matte satin. It was demure, with long sleeves and a high neck, but beautifully embroidered with silver and gold beads. There was a matching veil that was so gracefully pretty that Hannah couldn't help exclaiming over it.

Since when was she such a *girl* who couldn't wait to try on a pretty dress for her forced marriage? Especially when she knew her figure left everything to be desired?

"Thank you," she said warmly to Nura, who was clearly pleased that Hannah approved of her taste. "If you could show me where I'll be staying, I'll bathe before I try it on."

"We're in your home, Princess."

"I don't think I made myself clear," Hannah said with a laugh of genuine amusement. "I know I'll live here in the palace, but I meant my bedroom. Is it close to this shop?"

"This isn't a shop, Princess. This is your dressing room. I am your personal attendant."

"I don't need an assistant," she said with confusion.

Nura looked at her with concern, as though she feared Hannah was spiking a fever. "Your assistant comes tomorrow, Princess. She will discuss with you your desires for the nursery and help you hire the nannies and the rest of your staff. I am your maid within these rooms, to help you dress and ensure your comfort—although your nurse will also stay in a room next to mine until you deliver, to ensure you and the baby remain in perfect health."

"But I don't need any of that!" Hannah blurted with real panic.

"You don't like me?" Nura's face fell in shocked hurt, as though Hannah had physically slapped her. "My mother attends the Queen. She has trained me my whole life to serve our future queen." She blinked wet eyes.

"Oh, Nura. I didn't mean to hurt your feelings." Hannah grasped her arm, realizing this might be her one chance to make a friend and she was blowing it. "This is all very new to me. I will very much need someone who understands how the palace works and what is expected of me. Of course, I like you and need you here to help me."

Nura gave her a trembling smile. "My mother likes to say a woman wears the spirit of the child she carries. If so, our future king will be very strong-minded and independent."

Hannah had thought she'd heard every old wives' tale possible, but that was a new one. She couldn't even laugh, though.

She dumbly followed Nura as she showed her into a palatial—ha-ha—bedroom. The *bed* was bigger than Hannah's old apartment. Massive windows looked onto the beautiful courtyard full of ornamental trees and vines and lushly blooming flowers. There was a fountain directly outside her bedroom window, creating a soothing sound and a screen of privacy should anyone be in the pool looking in.

Like who? she wondered with a half-crazed snort.

When she moved through the huge glass doors to take in the enormous space, she heard birdsong and saw several birds flitting about in a huge gilded cage.

Nura pointed out a door off the far end of the courtyard, barely visible behind its own bower of greenery. "Prince Akin's rooms. And this one leads there also."

She brought Hannah back inside and opened a slatted door from the bedroom into a private passageway.

Hannah felt as though the baby did a somersault. She grew warm at the proximity to Akin while also experiencing an urge to release a fully hysterical cackle. Might as well nail that shut, she wanted to say. He wasn't coming through it. Ever.

"The nursery is on the floor above. The elevator is near the kitchen."

Speechless, Hannah followed Nura into a ridiculous bathroom where the bath was a six-person jetted tub surrounded by marble columns. The shower was big enough to host a carwash. The extravagance of space was one thing, but the details! Gold faucets, hand-painted tiles, etched mirrors and silk rugs to drip her bubble bath froth upon. There was a velvet-covered bench in case she needed a rest between washing one hand and the other.

I can't do this was the uppermost thought in Hannah's mind as a muted bell sounded.

"The doorbell." Nura excused herself and hurried away.

"I have a *doorbell*?" Hannah muttered. She plopped down on the bench, head pounding. She couldn't even begin to process this, especially when her skin felt coated by travel, her mind still cottoned with jet lag.

She stripped down and turned on the shower, hoping it would clear the cobwebs. The soap felt like silk and smelled of vanilla. The shampoo was a caress of tingling pineapple and rich coconut as it slid down her body. This would have been the most incredible shower of her life if Nura hadn't walked in and patiently waited with a bath sheet outside the cubicle.

"I'm not…used to having people see me naked," Hannah stridently told her, turning her back on the woman.

"Pregnant women are the most beautiful of all. Be proud that you carry a future king."

Clearly Nura's main duty was to bolster her mistress's fragile ego, and Hannah was feeling brittle enough to accept it. She let Nura dry and fuss and pamper her. When Nura rubbed moisturizer into her feet, she decided it was as good a reason as any to marry Akin.

Was she really marrying him?

Nura got her into a satin robe and slippers and they returned to the fancy dressing room. Nura pointed out the envelope that had been delivered. As Hannah sat in the chair to read it, feeling like a movie star refreshing her lines from a script, Nura began combing and drying her hair.

The document was their prenuptial agreement. When

had Akin had time to prepare it? And how could he justify giving her half a mi— Wait. That was half a *billion*
dollars for every year of marriage!

Hannah nearly fell out of the chair but kept reading.
Along with granting her complete control over inci-
dentals like decor in the nursery and whether her baby
would be fed by bottle or breast, she was charged with
the hiring and supervision of nannies and other infant
caregivers. Provided she gave appropriate consideration
to the teaching of Baaqi's language and customs, she
had veto power on nearly every aspect of her son's early
schooling. His later education would require a consul-
tative process with the palace's best advisers, but her
opinion would hold "profound weight" in those matters.
There were stipulations for the baby's visitation with
the Queen and time with Akin to learn how to rule,
along with an expectation that her son make the palace his home. In all other ways, her son was regarded
to be in Hannah's custody from birth until he was ma-
ture enough to make his own decisions.

The cordless phone rang and Nura stepped away to
answer it, bringing it to Hannah.

"Will it suffice?" Akin asked.

Her heart gave a hard thump at hearing his voice.
She looked at herself in the mirror, her reflection blurry
because she wasn't wearing her glasses. She was prepared to agree. How could she refuse? But did he really want to attach himself to her? What did she bring
to this marriage? Certainly not billions of dollars or in-
ternational influence or even a sexy body that he could
make use of via their shared secret passage.

"I don't understand," she said truthfully. "Are you

really willing to give me this much power?" His mother had hated her on sight. Hadn't he noticed?

"Hannah." He had a way of saying her name as though he found her the most curious creature he'd ever come across and didn't know what to make of her. "You are the mother of our future king. All of those powers are yours regardless. I spelled them out because you asked me to."

"I'm…" She looked at the contract, but her thoughts were scattered. "I'm overwhelmed, Akin."

"Focus on the immediate. Sign it. Marry me. Then worry about the next task."

"I love how you act like our marriage is as simple an undertaking as registering to vote."

"It is. Polls close in one hour. I'll see you then."

One hour later, she was shown to a large hall where at least two hundred people were assembled. This was his idea of a small, private wedding?

She had felt self-conscious when she had realized he would see her like this. Nura had done her best, but lipstick didn't hide her braces. Heavy eyeliner only marginally helped her eyes look bigger behind her glasses. There was no way to look anything but near-popping pregnant, because that was what she was.

Akin looked incredible, of course. He wore a dark green robe with gold edging over a traditional white robe and headdress. His gaze skipped restlessly over her, showing no reaction, but her heart did a few twists and turns all the same, hoping he saw a little of something he might like.

At least the veil hid her butchered hair, but she still felt as though she was trying too hard. Like it was obvious she was trying to be pretty yet had nothing to work with.

Don't, she reminded herself. She'd spent too many years maligning herself, but she wished he was marrying her for some reason more than her baby. She wished he liked something about her. His dispassionate acceptance was almost worse than a stronger emotion like contempt or hatred.

The ceremony was conducted in Arabic. A young woman stood off to the side, quietly translating for Hannah. Parts of it seemed to follow his traditions, while others were more familiar to her as western customs. He didn't seem like a man who did things on a whim or out of sentiment, so she assumed there was a message for the gathered guests in the merging of their cultures.

She was so busy trying to track all those things she didn't feel the weight of her marriage sink in until Akin slid a ring on her finger. The split band setting lined with diamonds held a massive, glittering stone in the middle.

Her hand trembled in his and her breath grew uneven. He squeezed lightly as though offering reassurance, then gave her a similar ring to thread onto his finger.

It surprised her he would wear a wedding ring, especially one that was a masculine match to hers. His was a more robust setting with fewer diamonds on the band but an equally giant stone that was more deeply set.

It was heavy, and pressing the ring into place on his finger made her eyes sting. She blinked and the false eyelashes she wore fluttered against the lenses of her glasses.

Moments later, they were pronounced husband and wife. He lifted her veil.

That was the most difficult moment of all, when she felt as though all her shields were removed. She was as vulnerable as she could possibly be. He looked on her before all these people and she knew herself completely inadequate in every single way. He had let her put a ring on his finger as though this meant something, but it meant nothing.

Yet, his grave expression told her this marriage meant everything. He had made vows, same as her. For one tiny second, she almost believed they had truly promised themselves to one another.

His gaze slipped over her expression, likely reading all her silly dreams and hopeless insecurities. Her attempts and failures. Her hard-won pride and every humiliation she had ever suffered.

He gently cupped her cheek and his thumb caressed once, twice. He loomed closer. He was so tall! Her belly nudged into him and he paused with surprise right before his mouth touched hers.

Then his lips were against hers and her mouth trembled. How did such a sweet gesture make her feel as though she clutched lightning with her bare hands? Scorching heat suffused her, and her eyelids fluttered closed over her damp eyes. He started to draw back and she drew in the barest breath of protest, not ready for their kiss to end.

He returned with another sweet graze of his mouth over hers, lovely and tender and brief. He drew back, expression still solemn, but with a curious light in the back of his eyes.

Perhaps it was simply the flash of the cameras as they began to burst around them.

He turned her to face the crowd and it was done.

Hannah rose in the night, as she did about a thousand times every night. This time she knew she wouldn't get back to sleep. Maybe it was jet lag, maybe it was the baby, maybe it was a mind that had decided it was time to sift through the last thirty-six hours or so.

She and her "husband"—how surreal to think she had one—hadn't stayed long at their wedding celebration. She'd been introduced to a sea of faces and had eaten a few bites of unfamiliar foods that would have intrigued her if she hadn't been so overwhelmed. She had felt like an oddity in a zoo and was relieved when they made their escape.

She was hungry now, though. She searched up a banana from the bowl in the lounge and wandered outside to the courtyard to eat it, not bothering to pull a robe over her filmy blue nightgown. It was gorgeous out here. The birds were quiet, the stars twinkling, the fountain glowing and the air soft and warm. She lowered herself onto a well-cushioned lounger in the shadows beneath a tree and wondered if she had done the right thing or made a horrific mistake.

Just as homesickness and doubts began to prickle at her, there was a quiet movement from across the pool, the sound of a door sliding open.

Akin appeared in a loosely tied bathrobe, a drink in his hand.

The way he eased into a lounger and exhaled made her think he hadn't slept yet. He sipped, set the drink aside and let his head fall back.

She should say something, let him know she was here, but there was something companionable in silently sharing the night. Marital bliss? She smiled to herself in the dark, relaxing as she gazed on him.

He slid his hand into the opening of his robe to give a lazy scratch and she bit her lips against an embarrassed giggle. Maybe she should yawn loudly and pretend to wake up, then act surprised to discover he had joined her out here. She would just wait until he'd stopped...

He seemed to be scratching a long time. Was he—

Oh, good grief. He was. He was caressing himself!

She *really* needed to let him know she was here, but she was too mortified to move. Her mouth went dry and her throat locked up. She closed her eyes, but that was worse, because it only made her aware of the most luridly sensual feelings that were awakening inside her. Her nipples tightened and a pulsing, reflective ache accosted her loins.

She hadn't done what he was doing in ages, not feeling the least bit sexy lately, but suddenly she desperately wanted to touch herself and she wanted to watch him touch himself as she did.

What kind of pervert was she? At the very least, she definitely ought to keep her eyes closed!

But she didn't. She opened them to see if he had noticed her. He hadn't. She couldn't *really* see what he was doing, but his legs had shifted open. His hand moved beneath the drape of his robe. Tension increased its grip on him, and his hand moved faster...

She heard him inhale. She was right there with him, taut with anticipation.

He stilled and time stopped. Then his breath left him in a shaken exhale. His bunched shoulders relaxed.

For a moment, all she could hear was her heartbeat in her own ears. It was so loud he ought to be able to hear it clear across the pool.

He sighed again. It sounded more like relief than pleasure. Then, in a perfunctory move, he swiped the edge of the robe across his stomach, rising to remove it in essentially the same motion, as though he was well practiced at staining his robe and leaving it on the lounger. Then he walked naked to the steps of the pool.

Hannah sat there in astonishment, hot with voyeuristic lust, especially as she caught an eyeful of him stark naked, like he was part of some kind of man-candy calendar. The pale blue glow off the fountain threw shadows onto his brown skin, delineating his muscled chest and sectioned abs and *wow*. Sculptors were never that generous when they recreated a body like his.

Of course, he was still thick with his recent arousal, but her inner muscles clenched in longing as she drank her fill of the sight of him. She was still reeling from watching him, still ashamed that she'd done so, but not nearly as regretful as she ought to be.

She felt a bizarre kinship toward him, too. The matter-of-fact way he'd done it, as though it was one more chore like brushing his teeth, struck her as very forlorn. Was he as lonely as she was?

The water climbed to his knees, the middle of his thickly muscled thighs, and cut across his narrow hips to his waist.

She hadn't moved, but he suddenly stiffened. His arms flexed and his fists closed as he snapped his head to look directly at her.

Oh, dear. She braced herself for the worst dressing down of her life, one she absolutely deserved.

"I forgot you had access to this courtyard." His aggressive tension dissipated. "Go to bed. You need your rest." He stretched his arms before him and dove under, beginning to swim laps with tuck turns as if he did this as often as he did the other.

She husked out a laugh of relief, but... What had just happened? Why wasn't he angry?

Baffled, she shifted on the lounger, curling her legs up so she was more on one hip, the side of her face tilted into a small pillow so she could watch him. She wasn't sure why she did. She was still aroused, still terminally embarrassed, but there was something soothing in watching his body slide through the water in that rhythmic way. A splash of a turn and the long pull of his arms again.

Maybe she just wanted to know she wasn't alone here after all?

After about fifteen minutes, he stopped near her and folded his arms on the ledge. Here it came. She braced herself.

"Can't sleep? Why not?"

She blinked. "Why can't you?"

"Too much to do."

Dare she ask if manhandling himself was on his to-do list? To think she'd only put braces and making a baby on hers.

"Exercise is a waste of time," she said in a weak attempt at humor.

"It helps me clear my mind and fall asleep."

She bet it did. Oh, she was dying over here, glad the dark hid her fiery cheeks, trying to think how to smooth things over and coming up dry.

"Do you need something?" he demanded in a clipped

tone that she imagined had entire regiments standing up straight.

Clarity. Reassurance. "I'd settle for a cup of tea, but I don't want to wake Nura."

"Your maid? Wake her. That's what she's there for."

"It's not important," she protested, touching where the baby was elbowing for more room. "This is all very strange. You have to know that, Akin."

"You'll get used to it." Zero compassion there.

Oh, she was going to have to grab the bull by the horns, wasn't she? "You must be angry with me. You have a right to be."

A single beat of surprise, then, "Anger, like all emotions, is a waste of time."

She frowned. "Do you really believe that?"

"I've been in combat, Hannah." Here was the quiet tone that refused to pull punches. "Anger provokes foolish acts of bravery. Rational thought keeps you alive. As you wisely put it to me, pick your battles. I don't pick unnecessary ones."

She let her head settle back onto the pillow as she absorbed that.

"But in future, if you want to watch me touch myself, *ask*. You owe me one." He slipped under the water and began swimming laps again.

Was that a joke? She covered her mouth, able to feel how hot her face became at the thought of owing him a reciprocal performance, but she couldn't help laughing into her hand. He had made a *joke*.

CHAPTER FOUR

AKIN WAS TAKEN aback each time someone congratulated him on his recent marriage. It was pro forma, and he had far more pressing matters to deal with. Immediately after his brother's death, various factions had decided Baaqi was at a weak point. Skirmishes had broken out on several fronts. Akin was still quashing them, but as the world absorbed the news that the much-harder-assed brother would be taking control while a recognized heir was weeks away from coming into this world, a tentative stability was beginning to settle over his country.

The fact that Eijaz's blood would eventually rule stirred up old feuds, though. Those who had admired Eijaz as dynamic and modern were elated. Those who had seen him as profligate and careless wanted nothing to do with his surprise heir.

And even though Akin's interest in such things as gossip, social media and fashion was less than zero, he was forced to sit through a report on how the world was taking the announcement of his marriage to the woman who was bringing that baby into the world.

"'I can't believe Hannah the Hag bagged a prince,'" one of his mother's minions read aloud while the palace public relations team wore appalled expressions. A handful of his closest advisers frowned with concern. "'She must have paid someone or switched the samples herself,'" the reading continued. "'There's no other way she could get a man to knock her up.'"

"She is my *wife*," Akin said through clenched teeth. "Never repeat those things. Sue them for libel."

"We've been taking steps, Your Highness, but these sorts of posts have persisted for weeks. We can't continue to ignore them in hopes they'll go away."

"What do you suggest I do?"

"Speak to her about making a statement? She's been refusing—"

"You *told* her these things are being said about her?"

"She was aware. They're online."

"These attacks are aimed at *me*. They're an effort to undermine my global standing and authority over Baaqi. But you had the audacity to take that to *her* doorstep and told her to solve it? She didn't ask for this! What the hell is wrong with you?"

"The Queen—"

He stopped short of dismissing his mother in front of the staff. There were certain lines he refused to cross no matter how ill formed his mother's views were these days. He walked out on the meeting, though.

He hadn't actually seen his wife much. They had dined with his mother twice since their wedding. Both occasions had been painfully stilted affairs where his mother refused to speak English. He couldn't discount that she was outright forgetting how, so he hadn't made an issue of it. He'd also traveled more than once, but he had daily reports from Hannah's nurse. He understood her to be uncomfortable and tired, which was regarded as normal when she was three weeks from delivery.

She hadn't emerged in the night again to watch him swim. He had confined his self-help activities to his shower. He was still perplexed—and yes, titillated—by the fact she had watched him. He didn't want to be tantalized by her. He rarely indulged himself with sexual imaginings. The desire for orgasm was an annoying appetite, like hunger for food. Yes, his body needed it eventually, but he wouldn't actually die if he went without sex, so he shouldn't be experiencing a twitch between his thighs right now, picturing an unpregnant Hannah gripping him while he stroked her slippery folds. What would she do if—

He yanked a halt on those lascivious thoughts as he arrived at her door. He hit the bell in warning and walked in.

Her maid appeared, widened her eyes in startled recognition, then dropped her gaze deferentially as she hurried to lead him into a small parlor where Hannah was sitting, reading her tablet. She set it aside when he appeared.

"Hello." She looked pale. Her eyes were bruised with lack of sleep. She wasn't smiling, which he suddenly realized she had done every other time she had seen him.

He found himself at a loss, not certain how to approach what needed to be said when there was no way to avoid hurting her with it. He should have been working through it on his way here, not pandering to explicit fantasies.

"How are you feeling?" That seemed a safe start.

"Let's just say the air conditioning is saving lives right now." She wasn't meeting his gaze and he didn't think it had anything to do with their intimate encounter the night of their wedding. They'd spoken several times since then and she'd confined her reaction to a self-conscious blush. This was shame, but from a different source.

He sighed and paced, waving the maid from the room.

"I'm not particularly intuitive, Hannah. Not when it comes to emotions. Dwelling on what someone might be feeling in a given circumstance has never served me in any profound way. I tend to let them deal with things however they wish and focus on taking action." He turned back to her. "But there are times when I must recognize that a sacrifice has been made. I realize you are giving something to our country at great cost to yourself." He nodded toward the tablet she'd set aside.

"I knew it would be awful, I just didn't expect it to be *this* awful." The break in her voice hit his chest hard enough to crack his breastbone. He didn't know how it hit so dead center, but it did. He quickly shored up inner walls against what felt like a sneak attack.

"You shouldn't have been told what people are saying. People in my position are targets. It's nothing to do with you."

She snorted. "It's *everything* to do with me. It's *about* me."

"It's not. You're the catapult they're using to throw stones at me. Dismiss it. Never think of it again."

"Oh, okay. I didn't realize it was that easy." She looked to the window onto the courtyard. Her throat flexed as she swallowed.

He might not be intuitive, but he knew intense pain when he saw it.

"They are strangers, Hannah. Their opinion of you means less than nothing."

"They're not strangers! They're people I knew from

high school and college. People I worked with. The ambassador of my own country, who shook my hand at our wedding, called my pregnancy an 'unfortunate twist of fate.' *Your* people hate me. One of your PR people asked if I could go on a *diet*. What kind of *idiot* doesn't know how pregnancy works? Your mother can't even stand to look at me. She knows I'm not good enough to carry your brother's baby. Don't even try to tell me that's not true," she warned hotly.

"My mother is not in the market for new friends," he said flatly. "Do not take her cold shoulder to heart. That way lies madness, trust me."

Her gaze flashed up from beneath her crinkled brow. Another shift occurred. He had the sense of having revealed too much and reminded himself he had stopped caring about his mother's indifference long ago.

However, it was one thing for his mother to hurt him, and quite another that she was hurting his wife.

"Fire anyone on the staff who speaks to you in a way you don't like," he said tersely.

"I'm not going to fire anyone! That's not my place. And I'm not like that. I don't *retaliate*. It spurs them to act even uglier next time."

"There won't *be* a next time."

"There is *always* a next time," she hurled back at him. "And it's not like I didn't expect it. I'm just having trouble shaking it off this time."

He let that sink in. "You've experienced something like this before?"

"For God's sake, Akin, open your eyes! Of course, I've experienced this before. My entire life has been one bully after another. Except this time, I can't run home to Grammy or change schools or reinvent myself in a new job. I'll have to live with this sort of thing the rest of my life and my baby will—"

She closed her eyes, mouth pinched. A single tear tracked down her cheek and she struck it away before he had absorbed that he'd seen it.

"I'm the kind of person people want to pick on. I've never understood why. I'm nice. I shower," she defended on a choke. "But I've always been Lice Girl and Horseface Hannah and That Frigid Librarian. Why?" she demanded, eyes glowing with a sheen of angry, agonizing tears. "Explain to me why. Then maybe I'll be able to stop whatever it is that I'm doing wrong. Is it because I'm not pretty?" she asked with a pang in her voice. "Is that all it is? Because I can't change that."

The fractured crack in his chest was turning into a chasm. He knew this pain. He knew rejection so intimately; he couldn't see small red cars and snap-together train tracks without reexperiencing it.

Why was Eijaz exalted for his misbehavior and Akin's efforts to excel ignored? Why was his brother, who made jokes and pitched tantrums, so much better than he was, when he minded his manners and did as he was told? Akin had been given reasons for it at different times, but none that he had understood. Ever.

"Ignore me," Hannah said through a mouth that trembled, swiping impatiently at her wet cheeks. "I haven't been sleeping and I'm hormonal as hell. I'm not usually so weak."

She wasn't weak. He was having trouble figuring out exactly what she was. She baffled him continuously and put such an ache in his chest he couldn't speak, but she was the furthest thing from weak.

"Normally when I get maudlin, I go write a grant or

work through the stacks to be sure all the books have been shelved correctly," she said with a weary sniff. "Got a library that needs cataloging?"

Don't do that, he wanted to say of her deflection, even though it was very much his own coping strategy. He would far rather take action than suffer the emotions that were trying to take him over as they stood here.

"We do have a library," he said, clearing a thickness from his throat. "It is scrupulously organized, but it contains books in several languages. You might find something that interests you. I can show you if you like."

"You're a busy man. As I've been told every time I've asked about you," she said with a faint smile that died on contact.

Remorse pinched him. She was lonely and struggling and he had had no idea.

"I've seen the library," she dismissed with another faint smile. "It's beautiful." She inched herself to the edge of the cushion. "But right now, I need the potty. *Again*."

He moved to catch beneath her elbows and helped her to her feet.

"This is why I'm exhausted." Her mouth trembled between wry amusement and fraying courage. "Making a baby is hard work. Remember this some future day when I'm under your skin and you want to walk me into the desert and leave me there."

He did something he couldn't recall doing outside of a sexual encounter. He slid his arms around her and embraced her. Her belly made it awkward. He felt the small jolt of surprise that went through her as she realized he was hugging her and not letting her escape it, but after

a moment, she obeyed his light touch on the back of her
head and let her brow come to rest on his chest.

"It will be okay, Hannah." He didn't know if he was
telling the truth, and his conscience twisted, because
what if it wasn't?

"Every time I convince myself you're a grouch who
is avoiding me because you hate that you had to marry
me, you do something I couldn't possibly expect."

"I don't hate that we're married." He tucked his chin
to look down at the top of her head. Her hair wasn't a
plain mousy brown as he'd thought. There were glints
of cinnamon and copper and sable.

When had he become a poet, picking out strands of
color in a woman's hair?

"You barely talk to me," she mumbled in accusation.
"I'm pregnant with the baby who will usurp what you
thought would be yours. You have to resent us."

"Oh, Hannah." He found himself playing with one
little tail of downy soft hair that curled up near the base
of her skull. "I barely talk to anyone unless I'm issuing
orders. As for coveting that crown... I am filled with
pity for your son. My only hope is that together we'll be
able to mold him into a person who is strong enough to
bear up under the pressure without being warped by it."

His deepest worry was that this baby would turn
out like Eijaz, and all his efforts to maintain Baaqi's
independence would be thrown away on a playboy's
impulse.

"I'm counting on you being a good mother," he told
her, running a hand down her spine, massaging her
lower back. "Because I have no idea how to be a good
father."

She stiffened and jerked back in what he read as

rejection, even though he'd only meant his touch as comfort.

Her face wore shock and panic and the most belea-guered look as she said, "My water broke."

Akin called the nurse, who had Hannah transferred to the medical wing. He went back to work. He wouldn't be any use to her. The closest he'd been to a birth had been a feral cat in the back of a tent when he'd set up a presence near a vulnerable village some years ago. He had called his medic to keep an eye on things and remove the animals to a better home when it was all over. It had taken several hours, so he knew to expect that much.

But when he woke to a lack of announcements and arrived to an office going about their day, he blurted, "Is there any news?"

A sea of blank faces stared at him and someone tried to turn on the television.

"On my *wife*." It rolled off the tongue, but he didn't understand why. He suspected it was a possessive thing. His country belonged to his ruler. Virtually nothing in his world was his alone. Even Hannah would have to be shared with his future king, but he still liked being able to call her *his*.

One of his assistants picked up a phone and soon re-layed that things were progressing normally. "A transfer to hospital should not be necessary, but they are pre-pared to do so if need arises. Every precaution will be taken so our next king arrives safely."

All the gazes dropped to the screens in front of them, signaling Hannah was forgotten.

She was actually quite small. Had no one noticed

that? She only stood as high as his armpit and she was all belly. His brother had been built like him, an ox of a man.

She is not disposable, he wanted to shout.

That rush of inexplicable rage was enough to have him trying reflexively to compress his emotions back into their tightly packed bottle, but it only took an inane question about a political matter to snap his temper again.

"Who told her to lose weight? Find out who it was and fire them," he bit out to his assistant and shoved to his feet. "Tell the American ambassador he should go home and get control of his news outlets. He's not welcome here until he has personally apologized to my wife for the insults they've printed." He jabbed his finger on the table in front of the man in charge of his calendar. "Tell my wife's secretary that, under no circumstance, is the American ambassador to speak to her, in person or over the phone. If he writes to her, return his letters."

"I'm sorry," his assistant stammered. "I don't understand. How will he apologize if—"

"He'll have to speak to me, won't he?" Akin said in his deadliest voice.

Every single person who heard him slunk his head into his shoulders. His assistant, a stalwart servant of more than a decade, swallowed loudly.

"As you command, Your Highness. I'll attend to it immediately."

Akin was already stalking away, barking at the nearest person that he would be in the palace surgery, where the royal medical staff treated the family for all but the most serious ailments.

When he arrived, he was halted from proceeding down the hall to the delivery room by the nurse who'd been with Hannah since her arrival from New York.

"She's pushing. It's going well. Fast, which can be distressing. There's not much chance for her to catch her breath between contractions, but she's coping."

"She's in pain?" Why did that slice into him like a broadsword?

"Yes," the young woman said gently, her smile calling him a dimwit. Of course, Hannah was in pain. It was *childbirth*.

He looked past her. "It sounds like a party." Was that *punk rock*?

"It's her birthing playlist. The staff are enjoying it. But it will take some time," the nurse said. "I'll notify you myself the moment there's news."

The nurse hurried back down the hall and he stood there like a chunk of furniture. A thousand priorities danced through his head, but he found himself cocking an ear, trying to hear the lyrics on the next song and the next. There was a string of angry-sounding "Hey, hey, hey!" and something about a bad movie and another complaining of times like this.

He pinched the bridge of his nose. What the hell kind of woman had he tied himself to? He had been worried enough to lose his temper and she was in there laboring like the world's biggest badass.

An angry scream, the kind he'd only heard in the throes of battle, ripped through the air, stopping his heart. The music abruptly silenced.

He shot down the hall and burst into the room, hand reaching for the gun he wasn't wearing.

She was naked on the bed, a sheet draped over her

waist, and an inchworm of a newborn, bright red and mewling, was being settled on her bare chest.

The music had been switched to a gentle piano over waterfalls and dolphins. It was so surreal he could only stand there in shock.

"Your Highness," the doctor said in a scandalized scold, even though he was the one looking up Akin's wife's skirt! A nurse draped a towel across Hannah so only the top of her chest and the baby's head were visible.

Hannah gently cradled her shaking hand around the damp wet hair of the infant. Her cheeks were tracked with tears. Her hair stood every which way and stuck to her sweaty face. She was florid with exertion, but when she smiled her metal teeth at him, he felt it like a punch in the heart. He had never seen anything so beautiful in his life.

"Come see him," she invited in a voice that rasped.

He was drawn forward as though pulled by a spell.

"I was convinced the scans were wrong and he would actually be a girl. I always wanted a daughter, but look at him. He's everything I could ever want or need."

The bond between a mother and her daughter was special. Perhaps one day, Akin found himself thinking, he might give her that girl she secretly yearned for. It was a foolish, wayward thought when he was quite sure the last thing she wanted to think about was childbirth again. He brushed his whimsy aside, but he couldn't resist touching her, gently squeezing her shoulder and letting his hand linger to caress her soft, damp skin.

"Well done, Hannah. Well done."

CHAPTER FIVE

HANNAH HAD DELIVERED early and even though it had been the most intense experience of her life, she and her baby were pronounced well two days later and sent back to her wing.

She then had a brief appearance where she presented the baby to the King so her son could be officially recognized. She'd been photographed looking wan and squishy, but she was too caught up in being a new mother to care what people were saying about her.

Officially her son was named for his father with a string of references to his family, the King, and the fact he was considered a miracle. Privately, Hannah called him Qaswar, which meant "lion," because he roared so loudly when he was hungry.

He always settled the minute she took him, which made her feel like the most powerful person in the world, but he slept as hard as he cried, and with his army of devoted nannies to change and bathe him, Hannah was able to get her rest. He also had a standing appointment to visit the Queen for thirty minutes every day, which Hannah began filling with gentle yoga.

She hadn't realized what a wet rag she'd become in those final weeks of pregnancy until, two weeks postpartum, she began to feel like her old self. Her energy returned along with her determination to steer her own destiny.

Everything had gone off-script with the discovery of her baby's father. This wasn't Syracuse. Her son was a future king and she was married. Although, who could tell? She hadn't seen her husband since the day she'd presented her baby to his parents. That stung, but she refused to let it get her down. This was her life now.

This was her *only* life. Two years ago, she had decided not to wait around for a man to "make" her happy. Akin might have barged into her delivery room like some kind of frantic new father ready to lay down his life for hers, but that had been out of concern for his nephew. She refused to read into it.

In fact, this scorned yearning that kept dancing in her periphery was exactly why she had chosen to have a baby by herself! She didn't want to spend her life looking at herself through a man's eyes, thinking, *If only I could lose ten pounds...* Well, it was *forty* now, if she wanted to be catwalk class. She already knew the futility of molding herself to a man's tastes. She would wind up shoring up his ego at the expense of her own sense of self-worth. She had done that her graduate year, when she had learned not to mention her grades because they outshone those of the man she was dating.

Her job was to love her son and herself. This might not be the life she had imagined, but she would not only own it, she would rock it.

To that end, she went through the things that had arrived from her apartment. She kept a few special items that added a personal touch to her living quarters and gave the rest to Nura to use herself or disperse among the rest of the staff. Nura acted as though it was Christmas, but that was still a few days away.

In fact, when Hannah unearthed the tiny tree she'd used in her apartment, she set it on her coffee table. It was only a foot tall, but it was sparkly and delighted her.

For the first time in years, she had a loved one to shower with gifts. Not that Qaswar needed a single thing—including Christmas. Baaqi was a Muslim country and her son would be raised with that faith, but thanks to his father's modern attitudes, Baaqi was broadminded toward other religions. Hannah only observed Christmas as a tradition anyway, not for holy reasons, but this was her baby's first one. She wanted to celebrate it.

One detailed list to her assistant later, everything she needed arrived forthwith, but wrapping it all had to wait. She had an appointment.

Hannah was finally out of maternity clothes and tied on a pale blue wrap dress with a nursing bra beneath. *Wow*, she noted as she stood in front of the mirror. Between the padding in the bra and the swell of milk, she had a chest that could get her hired in a booty bar.

Meanwhile, not only had she delivered a small monster of nine pounds, her body had stopped retaining the Persian Gulf. Her breasts were the part of her that stuck out most, not her waistline. She *had* a waistline.

Welcome back, she greeted it with a twirl, tempted to put on a pair of heels and see what that did for her figure, but who wanted to walk in those torture devices?

She did indulge herself by opening her private safe and having a rummage through it.

To mark Qaswar's birth, the Queen had presented Hannah with an opulent necklace. Its platinum setting was lined with round and baguette diamonds. The front was a remarkable fall of three strings with nearly two dozen massive sparklers interspersed with smaller diamonds. It was meant to be passed along to Qaswar's wife on the birth of his first child, she understood that, but she was still in awe that she possessed such a thing.

She didn't know when she would wear something that ostentatious, but she tried on her wedding ring. It fit! Pleased, she took out the other necklace she'd received to mark her son's birth. It had arrived with less fanfare and, compared to the behemoth from the Queen, this pear-shaped aquamarine pendant surrounded in diamonds was positively modest, but she had fallen in love with it the moment she saw it. Maybe it was the note that had endeared it to her.

With my deepest respect, Akin.

Respect, not regard, she had noted.

Oh, hush, she chastised herself as she asked Nura to fasten the necklace.

She returned to the lounge, where Qaswar was in the buggy that the nannies used to bring him from the nursery. Two hovered nervously, one armed with a diaper bag. Nura was giving Hannah an "Are you sure?" look as she helped her into an abaya and arranged a scarf to lightly cover her head. Nura would stay behind, but Hannah's assistant was pressing a brave smile across her face as she shrugged into her own abaya.

Hannah ignored their misgivings and said, "Hold the door, please." She thrust her chin into the air and sailed through it. Four men waited beyond the foyer doors of

her apartment. Two accompanied her son to his grandmother's each day; two were her own bodyguards.

Everyone fell into step behind her.

Hannah was reasonably sure she knew where she
was going. She'd come back this way in a wheelchair
after her stint in the private room where she'd delivered.
The halls had been lined with smiling staff the whole
way, all of them quietly and tearfully waving as they
caught a glimpse of their future ruler.

Today, Hannah earned startled looks as she strolled
along, taking a moment here or there to study a sculpture or painting. This place was a museum, loaded with
stunning pieces. The floor tiles were art in themselves.

Each time she paused, her gaggle of ducklings would
shuffle to a stop and wait patiently, then fall into step
behind her for another few feet until she stopped again.

When she reached the main gallery, she couldn't help
standing amid the rays of sunlight shot with rainbows
as it poured through the colored dome.

"Isn't this beautiful?" she said with delight.

An elevator pinged nearby and she glanced over to
see Akin stride out with his own entourage. Despite
her stern pep talks, her heart leaped at the sight of him.

It was deeply unfair that he was so effortlessly gorgeous. His beard was scrupulously trimmed, his white
kaffiyeh falling casually to flutter against his broad
shoulders and frame his sculpted face. He wore a black
robe with gold trim and an air of impatience as the sight
of her stopped him in his tracks.

Those eyes! Nearly everyone she met here had dark
brown eyes, but Akin's were like polished ebony framed
in long, thick lashes. On anyone else, they would be
pretty, but he wielded his gaze like a weapon, cutting

his glance down to her toes and back up, sweeping across the people around her, then clashing back into her blinking stare.

"What are you doing here?"

"Good morning." She refused to let her good mood falter in the face of what she sensed was intense disapproval. "I'm going to the dentist."

"The dentist will come to you." His stern gaze flicked to her assistant, who cleared her throat, then to her guards. She heard what he was asking. Had no one thought to tell her that? "And the baby has no teeth."

"Yes, I know that," she said breezily. "But we felt like a walk."

"Did we." Akin's gaze stubbornly pulled hers, seeming to steal her breath as he did.

"Yes." She refused to ask him if that was okay. *Stop apologizing for existing* was definitely part of her happy-life plan, but it took all her mettle to stand there and clench her molars against the old habit. "Would you like to see him? I'm sure you'll notice he's grown since you last saw him." Akin had said he didn't covet the crown, but his lack of interest in her and Qaswar suggested otherwise.

"Since yesterday?" he asked dryly. He moved to peer down at the boy.

"You saw him yesterday? When?" she demanded.

"When he was with my mother. I see him every day when he's with her."

"I didn't know that." She could hear the accusation in her tone and his brows lifted in a subtle warning.

"Did you need to?"

"Are you hiding it?"

"No."

"Do you hold him?"

"Why?"

"Why should you hold him?"

"Why do you want to know?"

Because she wanted to see that, didn't she?

His cheek ticked. "I'm needed elsewhere. We'll talk about this another time."

The word "this" was barely inflected, but it left a deeply ominous dread inside her.

He turned away and she told herself, *Don't say it*, but it came out anyway.

"Have a nice day at work, dear!"

His shoulder blades flexed as though her words had struck like a stone between them. He walked away.

Akin had spent too many years cleaning up after his brother's impulses to be charmed by capriciousness on anyone's part.

After the day of Qaswar's birth, when he'd suffered a roller coaster of uncertainty as he awaited the birth, and then had his heart briefly ripped from his chest when he feared the unthinkable had happened, he had been forcing his world back onto an even keel.

It had only taken the act of stepping out of an elevator and finding Hannah strolling the palace like it was Central Park to feel as though the rug had been pulled out from under him. He couldn't countenance it.

He wouldn't dress her down in public, but he intended to impress on her that he expected her to make his job of raising a competent king easier, not harder. He couldn't concentrate on human rights legislation when half his mind was taken up by wondering where she would take the baby next.

He stalked the shortest distance between their living quarters, the passageway between their bedrooms. Something about using it made it a clandestine act. He didn't know why. Her rooms had been set aside for his wife when he had arrived at adulthood and was given this wing. Hannah was his wife. There was nothing sexual about walking over to speak to her.

Except, despite his best efforts, he continued to have sexual thoughts about her. He blamed her doctor. In those moments after he had seen his nephew for the first time, Akin's mind had been stacked with thoughts of what needed to be done, like informing his parents and ordering public announcements. He'd still been reeling from the heart-punch of seeing Hannah holding that tiny baby. He'd been vaguely annoyed with himself that he hadn't been with her the whole time.

The doctor had drawn him aside and said something about realizing Akin was newly married and under many pressures, but Hannah couldn't meet the expectations of her new role until she had recovered.

It had taken a moment for the doctor's meaning to penetrate. When it hit, Akin had brushed the whole thing aside. He had told Hannah their marriage would be platonic, and he had meant it.

At the time.

Then she had watched him on the night of their marriage, and he'd been fighting to concentrate ever since. He regularly imagined coming outside to find her naked in the pool. The fantasy always ended with him seducing her among the ferns and orchids.

It was annoying to be so distracted, and then, bam! There she was, right in front of him, dressed modestly like one of his countrywomen, but where the *hell* had her breasts come from? Mail order? They were spectacular. It had taken everything in him not to stare like an adolescent encountering his first underwear ad.

His loins twitched in remembrance. He should have showered before he came here, but no sense turning away now. He was at her door.

There was no bell. This passage was for their use only. The doors on either end were only decorative privacy screens of vented slats that allowed airflow and light into the windowless space.

He started to rap his knuckle, but that felt foolish. She was his *wife*. He might be second in line for the throne, but he was the height of authority in this wing.

He walked in and startled the maid who was plumping a pillow on the bed.

She squeaked with surprise and bobbed a quick bow, nervously directing him to the dining room, where he could hear Elvis Presley crooning about a blue Christmas.

When he arrived, he found Hannah swaying her hips, the scarf and dark abaya gone. Her short hair was smoothed to the side and clipped with pins decorated with ceramic roses. She wore a blue dress that turned her skin the color of cream. It was long-sleeved and belted closed, leaving a generous view of her chest above the crossed-over edges that formed the neckline. The fabric was a light knit that hugged her voluptuous figure adoringly.

Lust punched him in the groin. His wife was actually very, *tremendously*, hot.

She dropped her voice to croon a low "But *I'll*— Oh, hello." She jolted with surprise, then blushed and laughed at herself. "You caught me playing Santa."

There were a dozen gift boxes on the table. She was using ribbons to secure the lids and attaching name tags. Off to the side were cartons of unwrapped boxes of chocolates, books and colorful scarves.

"Are you sending things back to New York?"

"They're for my staff. And Qaswar's. He has thirty people dedicated to his care! I make thirty-one." She chuckled. "I'm counting the team who delivered him, of course. And I added my dentist to our list today. He said I could have my braces off early if I promise to be diligent with my retainer."

"We don't celebrate Christmas."

"I know. These are just tokens of appreciation that I'm choosing to distribute on the twenty-fifth of December. I've invited people to stop by for coffee and cookies if their time allows. Would you like to spend the day with us?"

"Us?"

"Qaswar and me." She leaned over the table, gathering bits of ribbon and scraps of paper.

The pendant he'd given her fell forward, drawing his gaze to those magnificent breasts. He indulged himself with an unadulterated eyeful, mouth going dry.

She glanced up and he realized she was waiting for an answer to a question he had forgotten.

She self-consciously straightened and adjusted the pendant. "I don't think I've thanked you in person for this. It's lovely and completely unnecessary, but thank you."

The color of the stone had reminded him of the oasis, the one place he was able to completely relax. He hadn't visited in nearly two years and usually went alone. For some reason, he had imagined sharing it with Hannah when he'd picked that out.

He didn't tell her that, only dismissing her words with "It was nothing."

The sweet light in her eyes dimmed and she dropped her touch from the pendant.

"Well, it's nice to be thought of," she murmured and gathered a stack of gifts with determination. She brought them to him. "Will you carry these for me, please?"

She picked up another stack and led him into the lounge. She set her lot on the coffee table and began fussing with them.

He left the ones he'd brought where she could reach them and moved to take in the framed black-and-white photos of New York that hung on the walls. There were a couple of photos of her as a child with an older woman—her grandmother, he presumed—and a terrible painting of a tropical waterfall. It had an HM signature, so he imagined it was something she'd painted herself. There was a colorful throw over the back of the sofa and an antique lamp with an elephant base and bronze fringe on the shade that was an absolute eyesore.

"This wasn't here when you moved in." It couldn't have been.

"It was Grammy's. When I look at it, I see her reading next to it."

A book with a bare-chested man sat beneath the lamp, a tasseled bookmark sticking out of it.

"Is this her book? I would have thought a librarian would read something more literary or academic."

"Everyone thinks that. *I* thought it. For years, I made myself read the most depressing tomes out of peer pressure. It was like eating overcooked brussels sprouts because I'd been told they would put hair on my chest."

"Do you want hair on your chest?"

"No. Which is exactly what I'm saying. It was a dumb thing to do, so I put 'Read what I want to read' on my happiness list and you know what? I'm happier. Go figure."

"You have a happiness list?" She was piling up bemusement in him the way she was stacking wrapped gifts on the table.

"It's a work in progress. 'Try a new hairstyle' didn't land where I'd hoped." She pointed at the little pins crisscrossed to keep wisps off her face. "But I'm happy I *tried*. In that way it's a win. I also decided to only wear clothes that are comfortable, then I got pregnant and nothing felt comfortable, but I'm coming back to making that happen. I wanted a baby and got one. That has also deviated from plan." She sent him a look over her glasses that could only be called a "librarian scold," but it was such a good-natured one he rather liked it on her.

She moved a miniature Christmas tree to the top of her column of gifts.

"That looks ridiculous."

"I know. Isn't it great? And look." She showed him an envelope while making an O of her mouth. "What does that say?"

"Did you write that?" He took it and looked at his name neatly executed in Arabic.

"How's my penmanship?" She wrinkled her nose.

"I'm impressed." And confounded yet again. "You're learning Arabic?"

"Nura is an excellent tutor. My maid," she said at

his blank look. "We're starting with the basics. Colors, clothing, food. Printing the alphabet."

He glanced at the name labels on the gifts, all written in her tidy hand. He knew the names of his key staff and approved raises and bonuses yearly, but he would never go to this sort of trouble.

He absently started to open the envelope, but she gasped in mock outrage and held out a hand to take it back.

"I don't think so. If you want to know what this is, you can come back in two days."

"I can't take an entire day off and spend it with you, Hannah." It was absolute fact, but he felt like a jerk when her cheeky smiled dimmed.

"It's not a holiday you observe. I understand," she said, covering up her disappointment. "But if you can spare a few minutes to drop by, I hope you will."

So naive. "I don't take any days off," he clarified. "Even on the holidays we observe."

"Why not? Tell me a little about what you do all day." She waved invitingly toward the windows that looked onto the courtyard where her maid was setting a table.

What didn't he do? He followed her outside, thinking it was odd to see the pool from this angle along with his own lounge through the screen of greenery. It didn't bother him that she could see into his apartment. He was rarely there to do anything but sleep.

He sat and they served themselves from the tray of flatbread and dip, dates and cherry tomatoes. Hannah poured two cordials and tipped sparkling water into them.

"Is the supervision of the military still under your purview?"

"Completely. I meet with my commanding officers and advisers first thing every morning." And read their reports well into the night. The country's security required his constant attention. "I meet with members of parliament daily, as well."

"I've been reading about Baaqi's history. Your brother's decision to move Baaqi to a democratic parliament sounds as though it happened very quickly."

"Dreams happen overnight," he said flatly. "One can't expect to wake up and find they have become reality, though. It's been two years, but our neighbors, even some of our citizens, find the idea too western. My brother was trying to appease those who conspire to abolish the monarchy, but history is loaded with horrific examples of what happens when there is a power vacuum. The worst of society's evil moves in to seize it. My armed forces are kept busy ensuring our transition remains as civil as possible."

She sobered. "Should I be concerned about our safety?"

"I stay vigilant so no one else has to be," he said dryly.

She remained somber. "That's a lot on you."

"I'm used to it." He lifted a shoulder, finding her acknowledgment unusual enough to be uncomfortable. "There's no one else to do it when our government is still so new. My intention is that we'll continue to transition peacefully to a broader share of power, one that Qaswar can rule without the threat of constant uprisings. It's a delicate balance. When you saw me this morning, I was on my way into a trade negotiation. Those take time and they're draining, but diversification is necessary so we won't be dependent on oil resources forever."

"And the King? Given his health challenges, I imagine some of his responsibilities fall to you?"

All of them. He bit back a sigh.

"My father finalizes newly passed laws, but he doesn't have the stamina for reading long briefs. I review and approve them before he signs them off. He and my mother have ceased all of their ceremonial appearances, so I cut ribbons and visit hospitals. There is no end to petitions for our attention to smaller, more personal matters that we have historically settled. Today I learned of a Baaqi student who has gone missing in Australia. It's likely a hiking accident, not foul play, but a telephone call and a release of some funds go a long way to resolving things like that. I do as much as I can."

She closed her lips in thought. "That makes me sad. I mean, of course you should serve your country— you're above reproach for all you do, but I had hoped you would have time for being a father to Qaswar. Was your father this busy? What sort of time did he spend with you and Eijaz?"

Akin silently scooped dip onto a triangle of bread and ate it, considering whether there was any value in telling her how it had been. He rarely let himself dwell on it, but it had shaped him into the abrupt, uncommunicative man he was today.

That shell he'd adopted was as much a repellent as a defense, though. Since Eijaz's death, he had wondered if he and his father might find some approximation of the camaraderie or regard Eijaz had shared with the old man, but Akin was so used to not allowing himself to want it that he refused to let down his guard and make it happen.

Nevertheless, "I do want to be a father to Qaswar,"

he stated, even as he wondered if he had the capacity, given the fathering he'd had. "Eijaz had nearly thirty years to prepare for a role he was ultimately unable to fulfill. Qaswar will begin assuming formal duties as a child. He will rule at eighteen, sooner if he shows himself capable and willing."

"I was barely ready to look after myself at twenty-five. You really expect him to rule a country when he ought to be at college? I have very strong opinions about education, Akin."

"I'm sure you do, but you have to stop thinking of him as one of your middle-class American children." They had arrived at his purpose in coming here. "Qaswar is a prince, Hannah. And you are not a housewife who can throw Christmas parties for your staff and walk out with *our future ruler* as if you're part of some 1950s' television sitcom. We have protocols. Rules. I expect you to abide by them."

One spoiled, unpredictable future king was enough for his lifetime. He wouldn't raise another.

She sat straighter. "See, I knew you were annoyed with me, but how was I to know how you would react? This is the first conversation we've had in weeks."

That annoyed him. He was stretched so thin he ought to be in half a dozen other places right now, but he was here taking flak from her because he hadn't been dancing attendance like a newlywed?

"What did your staff say?" he challenged.

She hesitated before conceding, "That the dentist could come to me. But I was feeling cooped up. It's not as if I took him out of the palace."

"There was no need to take him out of these rooms."

"Is this my cage? Am I one of these birds?" She

flicked a hand toward one of the cages. "Because I didn't see 'prisoner' in the fine print of our agreement."

"You're overreacting. I only want to be informed. We might have had guests."

"And you don't want anyone to see your hideous wife?"

"Don't be ridiculous."

"Oh, excuse me. Your *ridiculous* wife," she shot back. "I have spent my whole life trying to justify my right to exist. Do you even realize how many allowances and compromises I've already made to come here? How homesick I am?"

"For what? Syracuse?" he snapped. "Because you didn't make it sound as though you were that happy in America."

She sucked in an injured breath and sat straighter. "I was *trying* to be happy. I had a *plan*."

"You had a list."

"Don't disparage me for trying to achieve goals. I left everything that is familiar to me, and my *goal* is to make *this* feel like home," she spelled out. "So I went for a walk with my son. I could have left him behind, but I feel sick every time he's out of my sight. And you're taking me to task for that? You need to back off."

"I can't!" He slammed his hand onto the table, making her jump.

And now she'd goaded him into reacting and he was angry with himself. He rose abruptly, making his chair scrape, and strode several paces around the edge of the pool.

"I just told you what I'm up against, Hannah. This—" He circled his hand to encompass the paradisiacal courtyard that was his only refuge and only when he stole an hour late at night. "This is not real life. I give this to you and everyone else by keeping a firm grip on everything that happens in Baaqi. Don't fight me on that. For Qaswar's sake, you and I cannot be in conflict."

"I didn't ask to go to an all-inclusive resort for the rest of my life!" She stood, too, gesturing wildly.

"Neither did I," he bit out. "Yet here we are. And we can be enemies, or we can be allies. I make a particularly unpleasant enemy. Ask the ones I have."

"I can stand having enemies." She stalked toward him. "If you don't like me, that's your choice. What I won't do is allow an enemy to bully me and change my behavior. I won't buckle to your dictates and beg for your approval."

"Do you understand…" Warning rang from deep in his chest as he stepped close enough to bracket her toes with his own. "How much power I have over you?"

"Yes." She swallowed but met his gaze. Her lashes were quivering, her mousy brown eyes bright with fear behind her glasses, but she held his stare and crinkled her chin in determination. "You can threaten me and hurt me. Kill me, even. You can lie to my son and say I died or didn't want him. You hold all the cards, Akin." Her voice shook with intimidation that turned to resolve. "But I can never raise a son strong enough to face all he faces if I can't stand up to the man who will have the most influence over his life."

This woman. She had to know she was playing with fire. He wanted to crush her, he really did.

But there was something so glorious about the way she held his gaze and held her ground when her hands were in anxious fists and he could see her pulse racing in her throat. It wasn't just her son she was standing up for. It was for herself.

That conviction of hers struck a match in him that was the furthest thing from anger. It was hot and passionate and possessive. It was a fire so bright it could destroy him, yet he wanted to throw himself into it.

"This is who I am." Her voice shook. "I refuse to backslide into waiting around, hoping my life will drift in a certain direction. I'm going to go after what I want. Do whatever you have to in response to that, but this is who I am."

He did. He gave in to the compulsion to set his hands on either side of her head and tilted her mouth up to his as he swooped down, remembering at the last second not to rake her lips against her braces as he fit his mouth to hers.

She gasped and stiffened, hands flying up to take hold of his arms.

He braced himself for a scream, for an attempt to shove him into the pool. He would have released her, he wanted to believe he would have, but she only dug her nails into the tender skin on the inside of his wrists and stood very still, mouth trembling against his own.

He had never touched a woman in anger and that was not what this was, although there was anger in him as he took ravenous possession of her mouth. Sexual frustration had its talons in him along with a deep, indignant fury that he was being overthrown in a way he couldn't combat—because he didn't know how to fight her. He didn't want to fight. That was the issue. These lips said the most outrageous things and he wanted them to *do* outrageous things. He wanted them everywhere on him. Whispering against his ear and biting his neck and closing around his stiffening sex.

He wanted *her*.

He couldn't deny it any longer. He absorbed that undeniable fact as he roamed his mouth across hers, learning her edges and corners and softness and taste, coaxing her to kiss him back with a soft cling of her lips to his own. It became the tenderest act of punishment he had ever delivered. He was the one being punished. He understood that at a hidden level as a wildfire he couldn't douse swept through him, burning past any good sense that remained, urging him to beg for her to *meet his expectations*.

A baby's cry reached them, and Hannah gave a fresh gasp as she jerked her head back, staring at him in abject shock.

CHAPTER SIX

Akin let his hands fall to his sides while she turned and hurried inside. Shame hit him in another lash of punishment. They couldn't be enemies, if only for his nephew's sake, but he'd taken the first steps of aggression himself. How would she retaliate?

Akin watched her through the glass. Her voice carried in a muted, flustered sound. Her body language was tense, but her entire demeanor changed as she gathered the baby and crooned to him, nuzzling his cheek.

Firstborn, Akin thought enviously, punched in the gut so hard he had to look away. Another proverbial welt rose as he realized he could never give her another baby. He couldn't put his own child through the agony of being the unchosen one.

I feel sick each time he's out of my sight.

The Queen still felt that way about Eijaz but had never once behaved as if she wanted Akin anywhere near her.

He hadn't realized his gaze had fallen into the middle of the pool until a noise drew his attention back to the table where Hannah was retaking her seat. She'd draped a light blanket over her shoulder. Qaswar fussed with growing ire.

"I know, I know. I'm hurrying," she assured the baby. "Poor starving thing. You'd think you were abandoned on a doorstep. If this king thing doesn't work out, you definitely have a career on Broadway."

"What are you doing?" Akin hadn't expected her to come back out, let alone—

"He's hungry. So am I." She fiddled beneath the blanket and adjusted the baby.

The frantic wails ceased. She sighed and took a long drink from her glass. "Nursing makes me thirsty, too."

Akin looked toward the pool entrance into his own quarters. "Should I leave you alone?"

"Does it make you uncomfortable to be here while he eats?"

Was that what he was? This wasn't a circumstance he'd ever encountered. He wasn't used to being drawn into private moments of any kind. It felt like an overstep, the same way it had when he discovered she read romance novels and had a happiness list.

"Can I say something before you go?" Her voice was tentative and not quite steady. Her lashes stayed down, hiding her eyes while her cheeks wore scorched flags of heightened emotion.

He folded his arms, certain she would berate him for kissing her. He ought to regret it, but it wasn't that simple. Not when she had responded with a sweet heat that had been as unexpected as it was exciting. He was still hard and wanted more. He wanted to delve the very depths of her passion and she was going to call him a brute and tell him to go to hell.

"I'm trying to make the best of this, but it's been a difficult adjustment. Motherhood is. You can't imagine any of this has been easy for me, Akin. But every time

I hold my son, I'm reminded that I'm here because your brother helped me make him. Not intentionally, but the stars aligned, and now this is my life. You're right that I can't deny him his birthright. I want to prepare him as best I can, and I want him to be safe while he grows into it. I didn't mean to sound ungrateful for all that you do for his sake. I'm incredibly grateful for *him*."

She lifted earnest, damp eyes, saying nothing about their kiss.

He was arguably the most powerful man in this country and definitely on the top ten list in the world. He was revered and feared in military circles, known for his clever strategies and triumphs against grim odds.

Yet Hannah undermined him with a few words that weren't even flattery. They weren't about him directly, just sincere sentiments that took all the air out of him. He would be furious at this ability of hers if he wasn't so fascinated by how artlessly she wielded that particular weapon.

He sighed, pushed his hand through his hair.

"My brother was very unpredictable, Hannah. It's disloyal of me to criticize him, but his nature was very mercurial, and he was always given absolute freedom." Never held to account. Never forced to pick up pieces. That was Akin's job. "Thankfully, he was essentially good at heart. He wanted progress for Baaqi, but in a very idealistic way, not with a desire to do the hard work of it."

Akin pressed his lips flat, glancing toward the open doors and lowering his voice so only she would hear him.

"In many ways, he was motivated by the fact that ruling a country *is* work. With my father ailing, Eijaz was being called upon to do more. He thought he could delegate to a parliament and continue living however he liked. There was no sense of order when he declared we would hold a general election. No plan. He threw a rock into a nest of hornets and ran away to post photos of himself climbing glaciers in Antarctica. I had to deal with the fallout from all his whims. This has been a particularly challenging one." Akin sealed his lips against any further disparagement of a dead man.

"You're worried that I'm like him, doing things you can't predict."

"I know you're like that. You surprise me every time we interact." And much as he wanted to dislike her for it, he found it made her that much more appealing.

"I want to reflect well on my son, you know. And you." She said that with a deeply vulnerable look.

You don't want anyone to see your hideous wife.

Her self-esteem had been thoroughly trampled and he didn't know how to address that. He wouldn't have kissed her if he didn't find her desirable, but he was regretting that he'd lost control and broken his word. The one thing he'd always prided himself on was having more self-discipline and forethought than his brother. A sense of consequence to his actions.

"Will you eat with us so you and I can make our peace? I don't want us to be enemies."

Every time he thought he was being given more than he could handle with her, he just as quickly discovered there was an opposite side to the coin, one that put a completely different face on the situation. She was generous and forgiving, and he was drawn to that strange fire in her like a lost traveler in the desert on a cold night.

He retook his seat. He was hungry and the food was here. That was what he told himself. He was only being practical.

"Do you visit Qaswar when he's with your mother because you wouldn't have time to see her otherwise?"

He could have agreed and left it at that. Allowing people into the private spaces of his own life was as foreign as being granted admission to hers, but the situation with his mother was one of those excruciating realities where denial only made it worse.

"She needs a full-grown reminder that Qaswar is not Eijaz. In her mind, Eijaz has been reborn. Qaswar's presence brings her comfort, which I can't begrudge her, but she wants to believe he *is* Eijaz. She verges on taking credit for him." He feared if he wasn't strict about how much she saw the baby, she might try to claim him completely.

"Does she suffer dementia or some other condition?" Hannah asked with hushed anguish.

He nodded. "That's confidential. Not many know, and her grief has made it worse. The reality of Eijaz being gone is beyond what she can accept, not when a beautiful replica of him allows her a more comfortable delusion. It's not healthy for either of them, but I don't have the heart to force the truth on her. Her pain is real. Her mental state is irreparable. There are no solutions."

"That's tragic. You must be awfully worried for both of your parents. I'm so sorry." Her hand came out to clasp his wrist.

He looked at her narrow hand, so pale and delicate, smooth and warm. He was baffled by it. Perplexed by her words and tone. Comfort? *For him?*

She withdrew self-consciously. "My grandmother

had arthritis and some heart trouble, but her mind was always sharp. I can't imagine how difficult it must be for you."

A strange sensation ballooned in the base of his throat. He swallowed it away before it could take hold.

"We do what we have to." This was why platitudes existed—to be used to gloss over otherwise intolerable moments.

"Would it be helpful if I visited with your mother when Qaswar goes? I had the sense she dislikes me, but I understand now."

"I can manage," he assured her.

"But you don't have to," she said gently. "I wish I was reading above a preschool level in Arabic. I can't offer to help you with your law reviews, even though I have a reputation for being both a miracle worker and a complete pest when it comes to thorough research."

"I have no doubt." He smeared up the last lick of dip with a corner of flatbread.

"You've seen my work with ribbons. Feel free to put me to work on cutting some."

"None of this is necessary, Hannah."

Her good humor faded to a crestfallen hurt that she tried to disguise by looking toward his side of the courtyard.

"Are you trying to let me down gently? We promised each other honesty, Akin. If I'm not presentable enough to reflect well on the palace, please say so."

Your hideous wife.

It galled him that anyone had ever said a harsh word against her. *Stay here*, he wanted to command, so he would know unequivocally that no one could touch her.

"I'm not used to accepting help. It hasn't been an option. When we married, I thought it was purely for his sake." He averted his eyes as she started to withdraw the baby from beneath the blanket. "My mother gave up her duties sometime ago, so it didn't occur to me that you could, or would want to, take on any of them."

"I would be honored to do anything you need." She handed the baby across. When he stared blankly, she added, "Can you hold him please?"

Akin hadn't wanted to admit this morning that he hadn't actually held his nephew. He'd observed how the boy needed his neck supported and was handled like a sculpture made of spun sugar. Akin didn't want to be the one who broke pieces off him.

But here the infant was filling his hands, light yet sturdy, fighting fists clenched, naked brows scrunched as he blinking crossly beneath his cap of wispy black hair.

Akin couldn't help the twitch of empathy that quirked his mouth. "Nothing good ever lasts, does it?"

"Nothing bad does, either." Hannah finished her wardrobe adjustment. "I've always needed to believe that, anyway," she said as she snapped the blanket away and draped it over Akin's shoulder. She then guided him to bring the boy up to rest against it. "So he doesn't spit up on you. Rub his back until he burps."

A nanny was hovering on the other side of the glass, ready to step in. Akin had far more important claims on his time than coaxing gas, but he kept the little body cradled to the hollow of his shoulder, one thumb making passes across the boy's tiny back.

The scope of responsibility Akin carried on this boy's behalf often threatened to break him, but for one moment, Akin was drawn into the bubble of safety and contentment he created for everyone else. Relief sank through him.

Hannah sighed. "I wanted to see that." Her expression was so full of sweet enchantment that Akin nearly lost a tooth.

Holding the boy became an indulgence. A weakness. He shouldn't be gaining anything from the baby, only giving. Akin glanced and the nanny rushed out to whisk the boy away.

Hannah's expression turned doleful. "You don't want to be friends with me, do you?"

"I said 'allies,'" he reminded.

"That's all?" She searched his expression, her own gaze confused.

It was the moment to address the kiss. The moment to admit he would like a more conventional marriage that included the sharing of his bed, but sex meant children, and "friends" was far safer.

"You may have Christmas," he decided abruptly. He wasn't a monster. "And I will give thought to the formal duties you might take on for the palace. If observing tradition is your thing, perhaps you'd like to supervise the ceremony that will mark my father's formal retirement, where I will be appointed Regent in his place."

"Really?" Her smile burst like sunshine. "I would love that! I organize the dickens out of a cap-and-gown ceremony. You won't be disappointed. As for other duties, I would be happy with anything to do with literacy or education, particularly for girls. Women's health or childhood immunization or—"

He held up a hand. "There's a saying about idle hands that applies double to you, doesn't it? If I don't keep you busy, you'll plan a wet T-shirt contest before I can stop you."

"I'm holding one during the Christmas party. I'm pretty sure I'm going to win."

He closed his eyes, refusing to laugh. "Talk like that does not make your case as a suitable representative of the palace."

"But it's on my happiness list."

"Winning a wet T-shirt contest?" He was so tempted to pick her up and throw her in the pool.

"No, but I should add it, shouldn't I?" Wicked laughter was dancing behind the lenses of her glasses. "No, saying funny things is on my list. If I think it, I have to say it and not worry how people will react. Most people like funny people, though, so the odds are good it'll be a win-win."

"The day your bra size is announced in the headlines is the day I seal the doors on this apartment myself."

"See? I like you when *you* joke. It makes you seem almost human."

"I'm not joking." He rose.

"Where are you going?" The way she tilted her chin up made him want to cup it and kiss those lips again.

"I have been idle long enough."

"But that was only the appetizer."

Exactly. And like holding the baby, bantering with her was beginning to feel like an amuse-bouche before a grander meal. Like there was more to come. Courses to be savored that would be infinitely satisfying. "My people will be in touch to discuss the ceremony."

He walked around the pool to reach his own wing, mostly so he could spend those extra few seconds with the feel of her gaze on his back.

* * *

Hannah was lost in a cowboy catching a barrel-racer under some mistletoe when a tingling awareness had her absently glancing up.

Akin had appeared from seemingly thin air and stood watching her.

A jolt of electric surprise shot through her. She had been thinking nonstop about him and his unexpected kiss. How he'd cupped her cheeks as though sipping from a china bowl yet managed to shatter every thought in her head.

She'd been so shocked that she had hurriedly stammered right past it, using Qaswar as a shield, talking about anything *but* their kiss, but the memory hadn't left her. It rushed to the forefront of her mind now and caused an acute blush to sweep over her. She lowered her gaze.

The image of him stuck in her brain, though. He wore black trousers and a light gray tunic that closed with three snaps at his shoulder and half a dozen down the side. It was long-sleeved and plain, but it clung to the contours of his shoulders and upper chest, accentuating his physique.

"Where is your maid?" Akin moved to glance at Qaswar sleeping in his cradle.

"I gave everyone a few hours off."

His cheek ticked. "Because it's Christmas?" He eyeballed the pile beneath the tree that had been reduced to three small boxes. The trays on the sideboard held mostly crumbs.

"The guards are still at the door. They have even more adherence to duty than you do. Help yourself."

He did, demolishing a square of shortbread in one

bite, then used one hand to stack the remaining ginger-snaps and dealt them into his mouth, one by one.

She plucked the envelope from where it sat in the branches of the tiny tree and rose, suddenly deeply self-conscious about the gift she'd prepared. It had seemed like a nice gesture at the time, but that had been before their strange blowup and makeup the other day.

Was their kiss part of the former or the latter? She still didn't know.

She cleared her throat and said, "Merry Christmas" as she offered the envelope.

He turned over his free hand. She hadn't realized he was holding anything, but it was a small box with a silver wrapping.

"You don't celebrate Christmas."

"In the interest of diplomacy, I reciprocate gift-giving when it seems appropriate."

"Ah. This must be a lapel pin of your flag, then?" She shyly accepted it.

"Crib notes on your Constitution?" he guessed as he took the envelope.

He had to know how disarming he was when he showed her those glimpses of humor beneath the intimidating mask. He probably did it specifically to disarm. The way he watched her might have been designed to make her aware of herself as a woman. She became hyperconscious of every small thing about herself, from how she stood to the fit of her bra to the faint tremble of nerves in her fingers as she began to peel the gift open.

She watched surreptitiously as he broke the seal on the envelope with a practiced flick of his finger and withdrew the pages. It would take him a moment to realize what it was, so she quickly finished unwrapping hers. It was a beautiful pair of earrings that matched her pendant.

"How did you know that getting my ears pierced was on my list?"

"I didn't realize they weren't." His gaze flicked to her earlobe and swirling eddies of tension invaded her belly. From a *look*. At her *ears*. How would she react if he ever genuinely ogled her?

"Well," she babbled self-consciously. "This gives me the motivation to get past my squeamishness. Thank you. They're beautiful."

"You're welcome," he said absently, face hardening as he returned his attention to the outline before him. "You're giving me a biography?"

It had seemed like such a nice idea. Now she felt like a rock god's most enamored and possibly annoying superfan.

"I mentioned that I've been reading up on your history," she reminded him. "Your mother has one, your father has four and your brother has nine—but only two of them are authorized. The palace refused to bring in the ones that weren't." Heaven help them all if Qaswar developed his father's streak of self-indulgence. "Everything on you is piecemeal articles in a dozen languages all over the place, even though…"

She didn't want to criticize her son's father or grandfather, but from what she'd read, Baaqi's current state of tentative peace and growing prosperity was more Akin's accomplishment than the King's. Akin hadn't got a quarter of the credit he deserved.

"Well, it seemed as though it was a missing piece of a puzzle. The palace librarian said it was a matter of someone leading the charge and putting up funds. I have a ridiculously generous allowance, so I contacted the history department at your university. A professor agreed to select a group of students to make it happen. Are you pleased? Irked?"

He let his hand drop to his side. "I'm not looking for accolades, Hannah."

"That's not what it is! *I* want to know about your actions and accomplishments. Think of it as a record for Qaswar and his own children. You can't have a near twenty-year gap in Baaqi's history that just says, 'His uncle held the fort for a while.'"

His mouth twitched with dismay, but he conceded her point with a half nod. "I suppose if it's a factual account, you may continue. Do not paint me as any sort of hero. I've been doing my duty to my king and country. That's all."

"Of course." She opened her mouth to say more but closed it again.

His brows went up. "If you think it, you have to say it."

She bit her lips. "I only thought there was a joke there about your heroics in saving him from being the son of an academic librarian, but it didn't arrive fully formed."

"Don't disparage yourself." It wasn't a quip. He used the commanding tone that held such authority it seemed to land in the middle of her chest and expand, knocking apart all the old framework and leaving room for new views.

She folded her arms defensively as she realized she was still denigrating herself when she had promised herself she would stop. It was even more disturbing that he had noticed and refused to hear it.

"You see?" he said, voice pitched quieter but becoming more impactful. "I protect him against everyone, even from insults to his mother when she forgets that she deserves respect."

She could have cried. Really. She blinked hot eyes and admitted, "Sometimes it's easier to make a joke than feel all the feels." She fought to keep a smile pinned onto her mouth, but it slid sideways.

"Sometimes it's easier not to feel anything at all," he said with a gravity that kept sinking deeper and deeper into her.

His gaze hovered on her mouth and she thought he might be thinking about kissing her again, but his attention flicked away. His eyes lingered on the baby before moving to the door.

"I've asked the chef to roast a chicken for dinner if you'd like to stay and eat with me?" she offered.

"The helicopter is waiting."

Her heart pretty much dropped off a cliff. "I didn't realize you were leaving. Will you be gone long?"

"Two weeks."

An eternity.

"Will you go with Qaswar to visit my mother?" he asked.

That took her aback, but she nodded. "If you want me to, of course."

"Thank you." He started to turn away, looked at the paper in his hand and came back. His hand cupped her cheek.

She lifted a hand to his chest as his mouth came close. He paused. "There are more things we should talk about. I don't have time right now."

"Does it have to do with the fact we're people who kiss now?"

"It does." He waited another beat, as though giving her a chance to argue that development.

She only looked at his smooth lips and watched his head dip, willing her heart not to race so hard it ran itself into the ground. Her eyes fluttered closed as she savored the way he took her mouth captive. Her fingers unconsciously closed in the fabric of his tunic while her lips flowered in offering.

His arms went around her, and she melted into him. He was so tall and strong, holding her nearly off her toes as he gathered her into his chest and crushed her tight, his hunger making her feel infinitely desirable as he consumed her.

Far too soon, he set her back and steadied her. She was utterly befuddled, panting and blinking eyelids that felt too heavy to keep open.

He nodded as if that was the reaction he'd been looking for and left without another word.

CHAPTER SEVEN

KNOWING THE QUEEN suffered cognitively allowed Hannah to let the older woman's vague hostility roll off her back. If Queen Gaitha didn't want to speak English or acknowledge her at all, that was fine. There was nothing wrong with the older woman's maternal instincts. She might call Qaswar by his father's name, but she held him with incredible tenderness and murmured lovingly to him the entire time.

Nura's mother, Tadita, was Her Majesty's personal attendant. She hovered attentively, agreeing with the Queen if she happened to say something. Her tone was always soothing, as though she was actively working to keep the older woman's mood calm. The Queen grew despondent when it was time to give up Qaswar to the nannies but otherwise seemed in good spirits. She always brightened when they arrived again the next day.

All went well until about the fifth day. The Queen had just given up the baby to Tadita, who gently placed him in the buggy. Hannah always brought the baby into Queen Gaitha's private parlor herself, leaving the nanny and bodyguards outside the room.

The Queen frowned at her as she rose to take him out. "Why is the nanny dressed like that?" she asked Tadita.

"This is Prince Akin's wife, Your Majesty. Remember? Princess Hannah." Tadita's smile at Hannah begged for understanding. "She is Qaswar's mother."

"Who is Qaswar?" The Queen frowned in confusion, looking between Hannah and the buggy. "And she is married to Akin? No. I hate Akin. I love Eijaz. Why is she taking him?"

Tadita glanced helplessly at Hannah, mortified by her mistress's words.

"Qaswar is Eijaz's son, Your Majesty," Hannah said in the most gentle and reassuring tone she could muster. "Akin married me so I could bring Eijaz's son to be here with you. He will rule one day, as your husband does."

"But where is Eijaz… Oh." The Queen remembered and her eyes filled with sorrow. "Akin should have been the one to die. I never wanted him. I loved Eijaz so much."

Hannah was appalled, but she didn't let it show on her face. She might even have dismissed the Queen's sentiment as the ramblings of dementia, but the guilty horror on Tadita's face left a lump of icy understanding sitting heavily in her belly.

Tadita was making noises of comfort as if she'd witnessed this kind of resentment many times.

Hannah slipped away, but she could hardly breathe. Little things clicked in her mind—the way Akin always seemed to be recognized as being ancillary to the rest of his family. Eijaz was clearly the favorite who had been allowed to do anything he liked, while Akin was the one to do the real work of running the country. She remembered what he had once said about his mother. *Do not take her cold shoulder to heart. That way lies madness, trust me.*

"Are you feeling unwell, Princess? May I get you something that appeals more?"

Nura's voice snapped Hannah out of her reverie to an awareness of birdsong and the tinkle of the pool fountain. She was eating her midday meal in the courtyard as was her habit, but she hadn't touched her lamb and rice.

"I'm thinking about my visit with the Queen today," Hannah admitted. "She said something that left me wondering."

"My mother feels very fortunate to see the young Prince each day when you visit Her Majesty. I tease my mother and say, 'Yes, but I see him much more.'" Nura topped up the water in the glass that Hannah had barely touched. It was the sort of banter they often enjoyed, but Hannah had the strangest feeling Nura was trying to distract her.

"Nura, I know you and your mother are very loyal. You would never gossip about me or the Queen, not even with each other."

"Never, Your Highness!" Nura seemed to blanch beneath her light brown skin at the mere idea.

"But can you tell me, when you trained to become an attendant, did you work with your mother directly in Her Majesty's presence?"

"Oh, yes." Nura was shifting her weight, clearly wary of saying too much but wanting to impress on her how well qualified she was. "The Queen has retired from many of her duties, but when she was active, she required many hours of preparation and clothing changes. I assisted my mother as soon as I could fetch and mend. Later I arranged much of the incidental shopping. I cleaned shoes and jewelry and tended the Queen's birds in her courtyard. I was the lead maid of four who kept the royal chambers under my mother. Is there some particular task I've neglected that you need me to do? Please tell me."

Hannah started to say no, but turned it into, "I think there is some information you might be able to give me, something that will help me as I learn to make my home here. I need to know more about the Queen's regard for my husband."

If Hannah had ever seen someone confronted with the barrel of a gun, the expression on Nura's face was it. Hannah's niggling intuition turned into a heavier dread.

"I understand that Her Majesty has not been herself since losing Qaswar's father," Hannah said gently.

"No mother should have to face losing a child," Nura said with anxious sympathy. "And she lost a daughter many years ago. You may not know that."

"No, I didn't. That's tragic." It was. From the outside, Akin looked as though he had everything, but she was getting the sense he'd had very little of the things that counted. "It sounds as though she loved Prince Eijaz very much."

It sent her into agony, thinking of Akin risking his life for his country—for the very brother who had been favored over him. What if he had died in battle? Would his mother have mourned for him the way she did for Eijaz? She wanted to believe the Queen would have but had to wonder.

"Everyone thought very highly of the Crown Prince," Nura said, her voice barely above a whisper. She knew what was coming and so did Hannah.

"But how did the Queen feel about Prince Akin?" Hannah prompted, bracing herself.

"I—" Nura was wringing her hands, gaze casting

about as if she were hoping a dropping piano would save her from continuing. "My mother once said that every mother loves her children, but some mothers love one child a little more."

"And some love certain children less?"

"Not through any fault in the child," Nura said hastily. She looked miserable as she gazed toward the aviary. "But I think that can happen sometimes, yes."

Hannah's heart grew thin as it stretched toward the doors to Akin's empty chambers and further afield to wherever he was. She drew a pained breath and nodded understanding.

"Thank you, Nura. When I visit the Queen, I see how much your mother cares for her. It must be a great comfort to Her Majesty to have someone she knows so well at her side when she is not feeling as well as she could. I know I'm very fortunate to have *you*. Like you, I only want good things for Baaqi. Thank you for helping me understand the things that affect my son and my husband."

"Of course." Nura looked relieved to escape as Hannah let her take her plate. They didn't talk about it again.

Akin was exhausted. He took his scotch—a vice he'd picked up from a friend at Oxford—to his lounger beside the pool. His butler had taken to leaving a towel out here so Akin wouldn't affront Hannah's maid if she happened to glimpse him entering or leaving the pool, since he never wore a bathing suit. He stuffed the roll behind his neck and sighed at the stars.

He should have gone straight to bed, but he had come outside to feel closer to Hannah, as if coming home wasn't enough.

He had missed her while he was gone, much to his chagrin. And the baby, which was even more baffling. The most notice the boy had taken of him had been to curl a surprisingly firm grip around Akin's finger while half asleep. From what he'd observed, the infant did that with anyone who held him, so it was no great sign of affection, but Akin was looking forward to those tiny fingers holding him so trustingly again.

Pathetic.

He heard a soft noise and opened his eyes. There was flickering movement across the pool. Hannah's white wrap fluttered like an apparition as she slipped it on while weaving in and out of the moonlight and latticed shadows, making her way around the pool toward him.

He didn't move, wondering if he'd fallen asleep and was dreaming, because why would she come to him this way? She tied the light silk at her waist as she came around his end of the pool, but it did nothing to quell the free movement of her ample breasts or disguise their beautiful shape.

The banked fire in his blood flared and he dragged his gaze up to her faltering expression.

"Is the baby all right?" he asked.

"Sleeping. I just fed him and sent him back to his room, but I noticed you're back, so I came out to say hello." She crossed her arms as though regretting the impulse.

He cocked his head. "Am I wrong or does the dentist remain at the top of your Christmas list?"

Her white smile flashed briefly before she said, "The very tippy top."

"Let me see." He shifted his legs to the side a few

inches and patted the space on the lounger beside his thigh.

She nervously lowered to the edge, tongue sliding across her teeth behind her lips, silk wrap tinted blue by the lights beneath the water.

"I thought you would be smiling nonstop."

"Like a crocodile, all day." She bared her teeth, then chuckled and ducked her chin. "But I've been trying to hide my teeth most of my life. Strangely enough, the braces felt like armor. I wasn't as self-conscious when I wore them, but now they're gone I'm back to thinking I can't let anyone see me smile."

"That would be a shame." He touched her wrist, enjoying her soft skin with a light caress, a strange tenderness rising in him as he regarded her. "It should be on your list. If you feel an urge to smile, smile."

A small one struggled to stick on her lips while her gaze flickered to where he was touching her. She swallowed and he noted her nipples were jutting against the silk she wore.

Was making love on her list? He would add it to his own, he thought, as he brought her hand to his mouth. Lying with her would make him incredibly happy. He kissed the back of her knuckles then turned her hand so he could taste the thin skin inside her wrist, where her pulse was tripping so hard he felt it against his lips.

"I feel like I should tell you—" she blurted while her fingers flexed in reaction. "While you were gone, your mother said something that made think…"

Was there a more effective death knell for amorous thoughts than invoking a man's mother? He lowered her hand to the middle of his chest and waited.

She looked deeply uncomfortable. "It seemed very

personal and I thought you would want to know that I…have an inkling your childhood might have been difficult."

His inner guardedness had relaxed at the sight of her, but it now clanked to attention, standing tall and ready to go on the offensive. He released her hand. "I don't want to talk about my childhood, Hannah."

"I don't expect you to." She tucked her hands between her knees, but the straight-up compassion in her tone landed on him like a lead blanket. She knew without him saying a damned thing. He could see it in her face, all soft with gentle concern.

It was the most exposed sensation he'd ever experienced. Like his throat was bared for a sword and his chest bared to a cannon. He rarely even acknowledged that old pain anymore, but she stood staring at it. *Seeing* it.

He held his breath, waiting to learn what she would do with her knowledge. With that weakness of his. That *flaw.*

"I hate talking about my childhood, too," she murmured, shifting her gaze to the pool so the lights threw ghostly shadows onto her face. "My mother died of a drug overdose and I didn't know anything about my father. My grandmother had a house, but only a tiny pension. I wore secondhand clothes and ate plain sandwiches in my lunch. I made them myself and did my own hair because of her arthritis. I didn't want to be a burden on her, but I was. All of that made me withdrawn. Libraries became my second home. I like learning, but libraries are a safe space too, where people have to behave. Other kids couldn't tease me or play jokes on me there."

He was going to build her a library, he decided.

"Grammy would tell me to just ignore them but pretending something doesn't affect you isn't the same as not being affected. She would also say things like, 'Bloom where you're planted.' You've done a good job of that." She tilted a shy smile at him. "I know you don't need to hear that. You know who you are. I admire that about you. It's something I want to become better at."

"Come here." He gathered her into his lap, not knowing how else to express himself. He didn't open himself the way she did. He only had this—action.

Her gaze flashed to his with surprise. "Don't feel sorry for me."

"I don't. I admire you, too." It was such a strong, sincere sentiment coming straight from his gut that it shook his heart on its way by.

Then he kissed her. Because this was the only way he knew how to let tenderness out of himself. She was lovely and pure and shockingly earnest, and she terrified him because she could be hurt so easily. How could he possibly protect her from the inevitable scrapes of existence? How could he protect her against himself?

Hannah didn't know how to kiss him back, not in a way that could compete with the way his mouth slayed her so completely. She felt utterly weak when his lips claimed hers so commandingly. Somehow he made her feel taken while giving so much, and she trembled under the intense feelings he provoked. The entire world stopped to hold them in a timeless place yet whirled so fast beyond them that she was dizzy.

In the back of her mind, she knew much of her reaction was infatuation. She couldn't help falling for a man who ticked all the alpha male boxes like great looks, money and power, but also had inner strength and a deep sense of loyalty that wasn't impacted by the injustices done to him.

The more she learned of him, the more she was humbled to be in his sphere. And she was *married* to him. Touching him. *Kissing* him. She would never measure up to all that he was, but she wanted to. She wanted to give him this same sense of being wanted that he invoked in her.

He couldn't know how deeply the heat of his hands moving on her back and the hardness of him against her hip thrilled her, but they did. She'd only been mocked for wanting love. For thinking compliments and caresses had been offered as heartfelt sentiments instead of a manipulation into the bedroom. This didn't feel like mockery, though. She cautioned herself against reading more than proximity into his desire, but it felt like genuine desire, which was enough.

He shifted her, deepening their kiss so his tongue pierced into her mouth, shooting a jolt of pleasure straight to her loins. She blatantly sucked on his tongue and he groaned. His big hand gathered her breast and he opened his thighs so her hip sank more firmly against the hard shape of him.

"I want to touch you everywhere, but I don't want to hurt you," he said against her mouth, then kissed her again with more head-spinning greed. "What can I do? Tell me."

"I want to touch *you*," she said, overwhelmed as it was. Letting him have his way with her would be too much—and maybe not enough. The little sex she'd experienced hadn't been as earth-shattering as she'd been led to believe. She didn't want that sort of disappointment between them, not when they were in such perfect accord right now. "Can I?"

"Touch me anywhere you like. I'm yours."

He wasn't. She knew better than to believe that, but she wanted to. She wanted to claim him in ways she barely understood, but as he trailed his mouth into her neck, she pushed aside the edges of his robe and ran her hands across his pecs to find the sharp poke of his nipples.

She liked the way his chest swelled as he drew in a deep breath of reaction. It made her feel mighty and *equal*. She tilted so she could run her mouth to his nipples and lick around and across one then the other.

He hissed out a curse and his hand curled into her hair. "Let me do that to you."

She smiled against his skin and dabbed kisses down the trail of hair leading to his navel, opening his robe further as she went.

For all she'd lost in coming here, there were incredible things she'd gained and one of them was this. Him. He stunned her, this man who carried the weight of the world and was straining with arousal as she revealed him, but said, "You don't have to do that."

"I want to." She started to kneel and a rolled towel arrived to cushion her knees.

She barely noticed, too fascinated by the shape of him. With a tentative touch, she explored him. Kissed with parted lips, taking light tastes as she worked from the base of his shaft toward the tip.

His breath grew jagged. His stomach contracted. His foot fell off the far side of the lounger, opening his thighs so she had more room to caress him. She'd read about this more than she'd done it, but enthusiasm had to count for something? She closed her fist around the thickness of him and drew the velvety tip of him into her mouth.

"Hannah." His hand was on the back of her neck, not forcing her to take more. It was a reverent touch that moved into her hair, playing softly as she moved her mouth and tongue on him, discovering all the ways to make him twitch and stiffen and stop breathing altogether.

It was a magnificent experience. She loved how much *he* loved it. He was shaking, and when she lifted her lashes, she saw his eyes were on her, not closed and blocking her out as he drowned in what she was doing. His stare was alight with something fierce and hot as he watched her pleasure him. She could taste his growing excitement. Felt him swell to impossible hardness in her mouth.

"Stop," he said in a guttural voice.

No, she thought, but consent went both ways. She drew back, hurt, worried she'd done something wrong, but he closed his hand over hers and guided her fist to stroke. Once, twice—

Now his eyes closed and his head went back as he released a groan to the starry sky. He pulsed strongly against her palm as he crushed her hand on himself in a way that ought to be painful, but…

But his gratification was so tangible she couldn't help her secretive smile. She had given him that and it had been a lot better than the blunt orgasm he'd given himself. She could tell.

He swiped the edge of his robe across his stomach, then gathered her into his lap. "Let me touch you. Give you that," he murmured as he nuzzled her cheek and the corner of her mouth.

"Can it just be this for now?"

"If that's what you want." He sounded drugged and slid a tickling caress across her shoulder and up to her nape. He tilted her head so he could kiss her, long and thorough. "Thank you."

She tucked her nose into his neck where he smelled divine and his pulse was still strong but slowing. His arms around her grew heavy and she knew he was falling asleep.

She was wide awake and tingling with arousal, but it felt nice to be cuddled, so she stayed exactly as she was, listening to his breaths settle into the slow, deep soughs of sleep.

She didn't realize she had also fallen asleep until he brushed her cheek and said, "*Ya amar.* The other man in your life needs you."

"Oh." The stars were gone and the sky pearlescent with coming dawn. With it came the realization she was lying on his mostly naked body out in the courtyard.

When she'd run her tongue all over him last night, she hadn't considered that she would have to make eye contact with him at some point. *Too soon!*

From the door to her apartment, she heard Qaswar's muted cry, as though the nanny was trying to appease him with his Binky or a bottle, but he knew what he wanted.

"I'll go." She stood so fast her head swam, and she nearly wobbled into the pool.

Behind her, she heard Akin leap to his feet, but she quickly got herself under control and hurried away.

CHAPTER EIGHT

NURA APOLOGIZED PROFUSELY for waking Hannah, but Hannah hadn't even seen her. She was too befuddled and embarrassed to do more than brush the whole thing off, assuring Nura she'd done the right thing.

Hannah pumped for emergencies, but she had made very clear to all the staff that she preferred to breastfeed her son even if it meant waking her. She only wished she hadn't fallen asleep so soundly, forcing Nura to come out. The poor woman had only wanted to gently shake her awake, but whatever she'd seen in Akin's eyes when he snapped them open had spooked Nura into believing he wished her staked on an anthill.

Hannah tried to reassure the girl that Akin wouldn't have been upset in any way, but she suspected Nura was as relieved as she was when the only word they had from him that day was the message that he would like Hannah to continue visiting his mother in his stead.

Hannah was a tiny bit stung but reasoned that he had just returned after being away two weeks and would have a lot of work to catch up on. She wasn't ready to talk to him, anyway. Going out to greet him, she'd only been seeking a chat, not...*that*.

Then the pearls arrived. The necklace was like an infinity scarf that could be twisted and turned into drapes of three or four or five strings. Nura was thrilled and couldn't wait to try all the clasps and pendants so she could rehearse a full repertoire of styles, but Hannah was appalled. Was he sending her some sort of *reward* for what she'd done?

Akin hadn't included a note and, as two more days of silence passed, Hannah made a couple of discreet inquiries about the King. He hadn't taken a sudden downturn, so that left Akin's reason for ignoring her a mystery.

As her hurt and pique grew, Hannah decided she would rather not hear from him. There was no way she was reaching out to him, either. Not when he was ghosting her worse than a frat boy who'd passed his final and no longer needed a free tutor. Been there, done that, and made all the poor excuses for jerks who didn't deserve her benefit of the doubt in the first place.

On day five after their encounter by the pool, she arrived at his mother's parlor to find him there. He wore the green robe that usually meant he'd been with foreign dignitaries, and looked as though he'd had a fresh beard trim. He stopped whatever he was saying to swing his attention to her.

Damn him and his bedroom eyes. She hated that the sight of him made her feel as though a wave picked her up and tried to float her toward him.

"Oh, you're here. How nice," she forced herself to say, as she handed the baby to Tadita. She didn't show her teeth when she stretched her lips in a flat smile and sent it in Akin's general direction. "I'll leave you to your family time."

"Hannah," he said in *that* tone, the one that instructed missiles to launch or armies to halt.

It hit her in the middle of her spine, but she ignored it. She ignored him *hard* as she stalked away with her eyes on fire.

He didn't come after her, which was even more insulting than if he had caught up to her and chewed her out in public.

Maybe she was overreacting, she cautioned herself as her belly churned with misgiving. She lived in her own bubble here. Perhaps the zombie apocalypse was in full swing and Akin had been tied up with digging a moat around Baaqi. Perhaps zombies choked on pearls and that was why he'd sent them instead of a note that said something like, *I'll be tied up for a few days and will call as soon as I'm free.*

There could be any number of rational explanations for his ignoring her, but letting a man treat her like garbage was not on her happiness list.

Prince Akin could go to hell and he was *not* taking her with him.

Akin probably should have checked the palace library first. He probably should have read into the fact that she'd *gone* to the library, and not have entered the hallowed space the way a bull entered a china shop.

However, by the time he had sat with his mother, explained that the "white nanny" was actually his wife, been berated *again* for marrying the mother of Eijaz's son, he was already aggravated. And he'd walked all the way across the palace to discover Hannah hadn't returned to her rooms—suffering a stark moment of panic when he thought she'd gone missing, even as her bodyguard took his own sweet time to reveal her whereabouts. *Then* he'd paced all the way across the palace again to the library, his patience thinning to its very last thread.

"Out," he barked to the cavernous room, startling a handful of clerics and Hannah, who lifted her nose from a book she was browsing near a shelf on the upper gallery.

She gave him one very haughty look, then slid her book back onto the shelf and came down the stairs with her gaze on the door, as if she was calmly exiting during a fire drill.

"Not you," he said. "And you damned well know it."

She stopped on the bottom step, one hand on the top of the post. "You're supposed to talk quietly in a library," she reminded him stiffly as the door closed behind the last straggler.

"I don't have time for games, Hannah. Ever. If we have a problem, let's confront it and get through it."

Her fist closed on the post, the only sign that she wasn't comfortable with facing conflict head-on. "I find gifts for sex insulting."

Wow. She might not be comfortable with fighting, but she didn't pull her punches when she decided to throw some.

"That's not what it was. I knew I wouldn't see you for—"

"I don't care." She spoke over him. "I don't care what you thought you were saying by sending it. It came across as paying me for sex. That's gross. If you want to say something to me, do what you're forcing me to do and say it to my face. Don't encode it. I'm not going to guess. Obviously, mistakes can be made," she summed up tightly.

Anyone else would understand what a land mine

they stood on, talking to him like this. Not Hannah. She was as infuriatingly magnificent in her temper as ever.

It was moments like this that had imprinted her on his thoughts. He'd been reliving their intimate encounter almost continuously. She had leveled him, virtually leaving him in a coma. Which was one of the reasons he hadn't made a point of seeking her out right away. For those exquisite minutes, she had been his entire world. It was humbling to realize how helpless he'd been while she'd caressed him with her mouth. His climax had been incredible. He'd succumbed to such a deep sleep afterward, her maid had been on the point of touching Hannah's shoulder to wake her before his awareness of the young woman's approach had penetrated his consciousness.

He typically slept very lightly. *No one* surprised him.

Whatever had been in Akin's eyes when he snapped awake to see a shadow reaching for his wife had sent the maid running back in terror to Hannah's chambers.

Everything had added up to a level of vulnerability that disturbed him. Akin didn't allow himself weaknesses. Softness and distractions got a man killed. Caring was a one-way endeavor that ultimately left him empty.

"You know I have many demands on my time. I've made that clear," he reminded.

"And you understand that my desire to have a baby alone was for this reason right here. I don't want to expect anything from a man. I *don't* expect anything from you," she insisted, voice growing strident. "I won't, in future anyway. And you shouldn't expect anything from me. What happened the other night will never happen again."

A clammy hand folded around his entire being. "We're married," he said grittily, as if that had anything to do with anything.

"It's not a real marriage. You've made that more than clear, as well."

He stepped forward into the fray, as he would to rescue anything that was important to him.

She stepped back, stumbling slightly on the step above the one she stood on. She caught her balance with a hand on the wall behind her and pressed her back firmly against it.

As insults went, that retreat was one of the most cutting she could deliver.

"I'm never going to hurt you, Hannah."

"But you did!" She leaned into that accusation, pointing at him. "I thought you were starting to like me. That you kissed me because you wanted us to be more than allies. We agreed not to lie to one another and what you let happen was a *lie*."

He was not the romantic young fool he'd once been. That was what he'd been telling himself these last few days as he fought the craving that had begun to eat at him from the moment Hannah disappeared into her chambers.

"I'm not like you, Akin. My self-esteem is an eggshell. Every man I was ever involved with stepped all over me. They acted like they wanted to be with me, but they only wanted to copy my homework or tell their friends they got the frigid librarian to give it up. They were mean and they *didn't care*. You should have warned me that you were *just like them*."

As fights went, he was taking the beating of his life. His ears rang, amplifying the injured tone in her words.

And he wanted to kill those other men. Actually erase them from this earth.

"Where is the man who keeps telling me it's his duty to protect Qaswar's mother from harm?" she charged.

"I was trying to protect you," he ground out. Both of them, really, but he'd gone about it backward. He saw that with blinding clarity now.

"By running hot and cold? Thanks," she scoffed derisively, tears standing on her lashes.

Akin scowled into the middle distance, heart pounding. He ran a hand down his face.

"I'm not like those men. I do like you." He hated to revisit the past, but he could see it was necessary so she would understand why his ignoring her had made twisted sense to him. "But I was in love once."

Her breath hissed in as though he was the one who'd landed a blow. It only made him feel worse as she stood there so white-lipped and injured.

"Perhaps it was infatuation. That's what I was told it was." He spilled the words dispassionately so he wouldn't dwell on the layers that went beyond a bruised heart to profound scorn from the people who were supposed to love him. "We were young, but I wanted to marry her. I knew I was expected to wait until Eijaz married, then accept the bride my mother chose for me. I planned an elopement anyway. My father sent me into the desert on a mission that kept me there for months. When I emerged, she was married and living in Australia. They have two daughters. I've heard she's very happy, so I suppose we weren't in love. Still, I'm careful about revealing where my affections might lie."

"You thought someone would put me on a ship to the colonies if you treated me with an ounce of respect?"

"I don't know, do I?" he snapped. He had his own back to a wall, and he *hated* it. "I still have a king who has the power to make brutal decisions without regard to how they affect me. I have been soundly schooled on that, Hannah. My feelings have never mattered. If I let *you* matter beyond the duty I have toward you and your son…"

He didn't want to finish that sentence. He didn't want to contemplate any scenario where this very nascent thing between them was snatched away and given to someone else.

"That's how you made me feel." Hannah's subdued voice seemed to fill the empty room. "Like I don't matter. It doesn't help that you're saying you fell in love once and wouldn't dare take that risk again."

"You do matter," he growled. "I should have made that more than clear to everyone, including you. I see that now. My mother thinks you're the damned nanny and I've allowed that to go on because…" He waved a hand.

Some of the starch left Hannah's shoulders. "I don't care about that," she mumbled.

"*I* care, Hannah. I just don't have the ability to change her mind." He'd never had, and these days her mind was next to impossible to reach, let alone fix. "I can't be seen as trying to snatch power from my dead brother and weak father, either." He sighed, exhausted by a sense of futility. "I've been holding off on taking any bold steps until…"

"The ceremony." She had hold of her own elbows.

"Yes." The official handoff from King to Regent wouldn't happen for another two months. "You had enough on your plate with the move and having a new baby. The press was all over you. I thought keeping you tucked out of the way was in your best interest. I see now that it's not."

"What does *that* mean?" She seemed to try to blend into the striped wallpaper.

"It means it is time for you to take your public position as the mother of Baaqi's future king. As my wife. You'll stand at my side as I go about my duties and my people will see by my regard and respect for you that I'm caretaking our country, not taking it. They'll recognize your value and protect you as I do."

"No, they won't! They hate me!"

"Who does?"

"Trolls," she said with an abstract lift of her arm. "All those people who were saying things online. The press."

"*Were.* They aren't anymore. I've forbidden it."

"Pfft! I should have thought of doing that myself! They stopped because I've been hiding, Akin. Leave me tucked away. I'm sorry I said anything."

"No. This is the right thing to do. You'll see."

"You are *so wrong.*"

"Hannah."

"Don't use that tone on me. I don't like it."

"Hannah," he said as gently as he could, while closing in on her.

She shook her head and the scarf over her head was dislodged because she was still trying to disappear through the solid wall at her back.

He set his hands on the wall on either side of her shoulders, liking that she was up on a step, because it brought her high enough her eyes were even with his mouth. He wasn't bullying or intimidating her. They *were* equals.

"You will not ask to be ignored, because you just told me that it hurt you when I did that to you," he pointed out.

"That was because…" Her bottom lip wasn't quite steady. The heel of her hand pressed the hollow of his shoulder.

"You thought I didn't respect you. I do. We are more than allies."

Her gaze flashed up to his.

"We're partners," he said.

Her lashes swept down again to hide whatever came into her eyes at that.

"You will not run from me or anyone who sees you as less than you are, because you are not a coward. Look who you are standing up to right now."

"Is that what I'm doing?" Her hand was more resting than resisting, but he wasn't pushing into her space, either.

He wanted to, though. He wanted to flatten her to the wall and feel every soft curve cushion him. He wanted to run his hands over her, his mouth…

He wanted to take because, "I'm not used to being given things," he confessed. "I've trained myself not to want anything, but suddenly the world is in my lap."

Literally. Her in his lap the other night had brought on the most profound rest he'd experienced in years.

"I'm taking my brother's place as father and ruler. His *son* is mine. Pleasure of any kind has always been a fleeting thing to me. Incidental. Yet you gave it to me with such selflessness." He grazed her cheekbone with the pad of his thumb. "I didn't know how to accept it gracefully. I still don't. But I want this marriage to be a real one. I want *you*, Hannah. It's not comfortable for me to admit that."

Her brow gave a little flex of agony and he set his mouth there, trying to ease whatever hurt he was causing, because it was the last thing he wanted to do.

Hannah didn't know if she was being the biggest fool alive, falling for a line, or reaching for salvation when she let her hand slowly slide up from Akin's shoulder until her arm was twined around his neck.

Akin seemed to shudder as she stretched against him and let him take her weight as she came off the wall, but she thought she might be trembling, so it was hard to tell which one of them shook. Either way, he wrapped both his arms around her, drawing her into his embrace, and the shaken feeling between them became mutual.

At the same time, he felt warm and solid and secure. Safe. Maybe it was because she was at such a close height to him. She felt like she might be able to handle him right then. Almost. Because as she drew her head back to look at him, he swooped to capture her mouth.

If she had doubted his claim that he wanted her, she had her proof here in the greed of his kiss. Not selfish—oh, no—but hungry and thorough. The control that was so much a part of him was gone as he cradled the back of her head and devoured her lips and swept his tongue into her mouth.

It was overwhelming and might have left her hanging weakly off him another time, but a hot, brilliant need flashed alive inside her, one that wanted him just as fiercely. A dim voice warned caution way in the back of her head, but she ignored it in favor of catching her fist in the back of his collar and clashing her tongue against his.

He groaned and backed her into the wall again. Her foot caught again, and she would have stumbled, but he was right there, so steady, anchoring her to this world even as she spun off to a new one. Their mouths parted and crashed together again and again in a mindless gluttony that was pure hedonism.

She forgot where they were, who they were. All that mattered was his mouth and the silken scrape of his beard against her chin, the scent of him drugging her senses and the feel of his hair between her fingers as she got under his kaffiyeh, dislodging the cord that held the headdress in place, so the square of cotton slid away.

Her scarf was long gone, brushed away by busy hands that roamed from her hair to her shoulder, down to her ribs and her backside and up to her waist and splayed over her breasts so she danced and twisted into his touch every which way, thinking, *more. More.*

When his mouth trailed into her neck and his clever fingers drew down the zip of her abaya, she only sighed in relief at the rush of cool air that wafted into her cleavage.

"What the hell are you wearing?" He pushed it open to reveal her sport bra and yoga shorts topped by a loose tank.

"I've been going to the gym after visiting your mother." There was an all-women Zumba class she liked. She had thought to bide her time in the library today, rather than go all the way back to her chambers. Sometimes abayas were superconvenient since no one knew what she wore underneath, but what she was wearing right now, that Akin was seeing, made her feel really self-conscious of the fact she was showing a lot of skin. "I still have baby weight." On curves that had been pretty curvy in the first place.

"In all the right places." He gave her thigh a gentle squeeze, then sent his palm on a slow circle over her butt cheek before grabbing a handful and making a noise of satisfaction. "You're incredibly sexy, Hannah."

She wasn't. He was being kind, but she would take it. Although she said, "We probably shouldn't do this here."

"Do what?" His mouth was nipping and nibbling along her jaw while his fingertips traced along the edge of her tight shorts, teasing the exposed skin of her upper thighs. "This is your happy place, isn't it? Let me make you happy."

She choked on a laugh since his hand was traveling up the inside of her thigh to cup her mound.

"I—I couldn't," she gasped as his lips found a spot on her neck that weakened her knees.

"No? Let's try."

"That wasn't what I meant." She unconsciously tried to squeeze her thighs together, mostly in reaction because she had never been very comfortable with being touched so intimately. This was different, though. This was Akin and, if anything, she was trying to slow him down so she could think, but he was taking his time anyway.

"Hannah." Sometimes the way he said her name made it sound pure and divine. "Accept this gracefully." He drew a light touch with his fingertips, up and down. The tightness of her shorts accentuated the sensation so hot tingles rushed into the flesh he caressed.

She quivered and a sob sounded in her throat.

"Where are my earrings, *ya amar*?" He sucked on her earlobe and cupped her again, this time firm as he began to rock his hand.

"W-what?"

"You're so hot here. Move with me. Show me how you like it." His mouth came back to hers and he kissed her passionately, encouraging her to rock against his firm hand.

It wouldn't work, but it felt good and she wanted to keep doing it. She'd only had about a million fantasies that involved being seduced in a library, so she kept moving, but it wouldn't work because she was too repressed to give herself over to anyone.

Still, when Akin abruptly stopped, she could have screamed in panicked frustration. He slid his hand upward, though, under the edge of her tank to caress the skin of her midriff, then he slid his fingers under the tight waistband of her shorts. He struggled to work his hand back down within the confines of the spandex.

She caught her breath, thinking she should tell him not to bother, but she held very still, paralyzed by the glitter of heat in his dark eyes. When his fingertips found her slippery folds, she jolted.

"*So* hot," he breathed against her lips as his fingertips did wicked, magical things, moving incrementally against the constrictive fabric, but with untold power. "I keep thinking of the way you looked when you had your mouth on me. I want to do that to you. Make you orgasm so hard you pass out."

"I—I—" She had no words. *Don't watch me*, she wanted to plead, because despite how flagrant this was, she was thinking now about how he had hardened in her mouth—

Two firm fingers right *there*. Like he was pushing a button. She had her hand over his, trapping his hand in her shorts as she lifted her hips into his touch and closed her eyes, moving against his fingertips as she succumbed to a sharp orgasm that rocked her loins. It was so strong it made her breasts hurt and her womb contract while luscious waves of pleasure engulfed her.

She knew she was making noises of abandonment that echoed to the high ceiling and she didn't care because it felt *so good*.

His voice rumbled words she couldn't understand, and his lips were teasing her ear and neck and stealing kisses while she shuddered and gasped and very slowly came down from standing on her toes.

They kissed passionately, but even though she gave him her tongue, he began to withdraw. His hand left her shorts and he made a noise of reluctance as he steered her touch from the firm shape she found through the layers of his clothes.

"I would say we are even now, but you still owe me one," he teased to soften his rebuff. "We'll revisit this later. I'll dine with you."

And that was it, she realized. All the cards were falling.

She *was* a fool. A bigger fool than she'd ever been with any other man. Those past crushes of hers had been experiments and attempts to find a like-minded companion and accept sex in place of the sincere regard she longed for.

This was completely different. This man now had a hold on her in a thousand subtle ways. She didn't just want him to like her and be friends with her. She wanted to *deserve* him. She wanted to make *him* happy. She wanted to gift herself over to him and yearned for him to do the same for her.

She was falling in love with him and he had just told her he was afraid to let her matter. He had trained himself not to want anything.

He might not be like those men who had hurt her in the past, but he could definitely hurt her in the future, and she had no defenses left against him.

CHAPTER NINE

WHEN AKIN DECIDED to take bold steps, he took them in bounding strides that left Hannah breathless, trying to keep up.

He dined with her that day and held his nephew, kissed the hell out of her and apologized when phone calls forced him to disappear for the rest of the evening.

She had half expected to be ignored again, but first thing next morning, while she was still eating her grapefruit and slice of toast, she received a message that she should meet him at his offices across the palace.

Nura, bless her, put Hannah in a flowing pantsuit that was trendy and smart, yet demure enough that she was perfectly attired for her meet and greets with armies of staff.

Akin was by her side through all of it, keeping things short and on task, reminding everyone she had a new baby so would only work a few hours a day, but he made it clear Hannah would gradually take on all of the Queen's previous duties.

"I don't actually know how to be a queen—you know that, right?" Hannah said when she finally had him alone in *her* office.

It was a stunning space with an adorable neoclassical French decor, built-in shelves she could pack with books, and abundant natural light from the doors to the balcony that overlooked the palace gardens.

"Did you know how to be a mother before you became one?"

"Oh. Same level of life-and-death stakes if I screw up, I presume?"

"See, you're a natural."

"Please don't make light. I'm terrified." She opened a door and interrupted a half dozen worker bees setting up workstations for her new battalion of assistants. They froze and looked expectantly at her. "Sorry," she muttered and closed it again. At least she would only be taking meetings in the palace at first and mostly in organizational capacities. "When do I have to, like, be in public with you?"

"How do you define 'public'? We're hosting a dinner tonight."

"Tonight! No, we're not. For whom?"

"Neighboring royalty. Kings who are allies and have a lot of influence, as do their wives. You'll like them."

Wives. Oh, dear God. How could he be so smart, yet so dumb?

"Your maid will show you to the harem once they've arrived—"

"You have a *harem*?"

"What do you think a harem is, Hannah? Sex slaves in a genie bottle? It's a set of rooms for female visitors so they have as much privacy as they desire. Their husbands have accommodation in the same wing if they'd rather sleep with them, but there is space for servants and children if they bring them. It's convenience and culture, not dictate. Greeting them there will allow you to visit in a casual setting before dinner. I'll do the same with the husbands in my private lounge."

She shoved her fists under her elbows. "Can I take Qaswar?"

"As a human shield?"

"People like babies."

"Hannah."

"Don't tell me I'm not a coward." She jerked her chin away from the light hand that tried to force her to look at him. "You be the girl in middle school with acne and the wrong label on her jeans, then tell me how brave *you* would be, walking into a room full of *queens*. This was never part of our deal, Akin."

He took hold of her fists and unbent her arms, trying to lever her closer.

"No. You don't get a kiss." She turned her face away. "I'm mad at you. You sprang this on me without any warning."

"This is your warning. I didn't invite them until yesterday, after our talk in the library." His mouth twitched on the word "talk." She gave her fists a shake, trying to get him to release her, but he only slid his hands up her arms, keeping her before him. "They confirmed this morning and now I'm telling you we have an engagement. Take Qaswar if you want to, but you won't need him."

He drew her close, but she stayed stiff as a board, determined to convey her displeasure, but he ran his magic hands over her, and she began to melt.

"You can sleep with your husband, you know. Come to my room. We don't have to meet like teenagers sneaking out at night."

"You're never there. Are you?"

"I haven't had a reason to make getting to bed a priority. Have I?" he countered.

She would have her post-childbirth checkup in a couple of days and be ready for what he seemed to have in mind, but she ducked her head, not prepared to contemplate how thoroughly he could destroy her with an all-night seduction.

"This is a lot of performance anxiety to put on me all at once."

"Yesterday was a 'performance'? Let's have an encore." He started to back her toward a desk where his mother had sat for decades, signing checks for charities and answering letters.

Thankfully, there was a ping from her new tablet.

"The other man in my life needs me." She patted his chest and made her escape.

Hannah very miserably put on a floral dress that would be awful to nurse in and a pair of heeled shoes that rubbed her ankle. Nura did her makeup and draped a light scarf over hair that had grown out to midway between pixie and bob.

At least her son was pretty. He took after his father, with his dark eyes and black hair and thick, curling lashes that belonged on a supermodel. Which made him resemble his uncle, not that Hannah had spent much time mooning over *that*.

Nura accompanied her along with a nanny to a section of the palace Hannah had never been. A handful of bodyguards stood outside an unassuming door but let her pass after briefly checking their screens to ensure she was who she claimed to be.

Hannah walked into what looked like a boutique

hotel. There was a desk where one of the palace assistants sat to greet them. Beyond it, there was a hallway with a half dozen doors and stairs and an elevator. On the other side was a small dining lounge with doors that opened onto a private courtyard smaller than her own, but similar.

Through the glass, Hannah saw three women sitting at a table. Nura had coached her that the one with typical Arab coloring was Galila, Queen of Zyria. The ivory-skinned redhead was Fern, an Englishwoman who had become Queen of Q'Amara, and the brunette was Angelique, Queen of Zhamair.

They were talking over each other and laughing, clearly familiar and comfortable with one another. They all wore casual western day dresses like Hannah's but somehow looked incredibly beautiful and relaxed while Hannah felt like a prickly frump.

She wanted to cry, she really did, but the wretched greeter hurried to announced her.

"May I present to you the Crown Prince of Baaqi and his mother, Princess Hannah?"

All the women stopped talking and stood up with an air of expectation as she came outside. Hannah forced a smile.

"Welcome to Baaqi. I hope you've settled in? Please call me Hannah."

They introduced themselves. Galila was pregnant and made it look effortless. All of them cooed over the baby and begged to hold him.

No, he's mine, Hannah wanted to growl but had to say a gracious "Of course."

Fern had two older sons who were elsewhere, but her four-month-old daughter came out moments later, having freshly woken. She had black hair and two small teeth and came to Hannah with a big smile.

Babies, Hannah discovered, made for very good ice-breakers. And great equalizers. They all had questions for one another and stories of their misadventures as new moms.

When Angelique talked about all the twins in her family, Hannah realized she hadn't recognized her famous guest—the first of what she assumed would be her many faux pas for the evening.

"Forgive me. I didn't make the connection. You're one of the Sauveterre twins! You and your sister had the design house. You must think me an idiot for not putting it together."

"We still own it. We just don't get to do as much of the actual work as we used to. It turns out mother-hood is a full-time job. Who knew?" she said with facetious humor.

Somehow an hour passed, and Hannah discovered she was as comfortable as if she had joined a handful of librarians to talk shop in the break room. She had forgotten she wasn't one of them, but as Galila excused herself to lie down before dinner, Hannah realized she still had an entire evening—the rest of her life, in fact—to get through.

"May I ask you both something?" Hannah ventured after Galila left. "I know you've spent a lot of your life in the public eye, and I wondered if you've struggled with all the publicity?"

"You mean when my husband got his nieces' governess pregnant out of wedlock? It was a cake walk," Fern said in her dry British accent. "Karim's mother was terrified for my life, so *that* helped."

"Oh. I'm so sorry. I'm not facing that, I don't think. I'm just worried about online haters. They've already had a go at me, but it died down while I was out of the spotlight. Now Akin wants me to start making appearances and…" She hated admitting she was a target. It felt too much like admitting she deserved it, but she had to voice her need. "I wondered if you had any advice on coping. I dread what they might say."

"You know what they say about haters," Angelique remarked. *"Nothing."*

Fern's laughter bubbled up and Hannah snickered, as well.

"I can't take credit for that," Angelique confided. "It's my sister's, but she was treated horribly for *years.*" Angelique's gaze dimmed with introspection and her jaw set. Her phone buzzed and she smiled. "There she is, wondering what's wrong." She tapped a heart and set the phone aside. "It's awful that people think they can behave that way. All you can do is remind yourself that the things they say aren't true."

"But what if they are?" Hannah asked faintly.

"What do you mean?" Angelique had the most compassionate eyes Hannah had ever seen. She was so beautiful it was intimidating, yet there was an incredible softness to her that made it possible for Hannah to reveal her darkest hurt.

"I'm…" She stopped short of saying *ugly.* "Not pretty."

"Hannah." Angelique turned in her chair and picked up her hands. "I'm going to say to you what I've said to my own sister. If you feel down on yourself, if you feel bloated or you have a spot or some other thing that makes you feel less than beautiful, that's okay. Your feelings are yours and I'm not going to tell you not to feel them. And if a stranger says something that hurts you, your hurt is valid. But they're *trying* to hurt you. That's not honesty. It's cruelty. Believing what they say is like believing you would deserve it if they hit you. They're not the type of people you would admire or respect if you met them, so please don't give more weight to their remarks than the things said by people who care about you."

"I—" Hannah had to take back one of her hands to press her trembling lips. She'd been struggling to believe she had anyone who cared about her here. What she really feared, deep down, was that Akin would believe those remarks and realize what a mistake he'd made. "I know I shouldn't let their opinions matter so much, but it feels so much like the truth. I've never felt pretty," she confessed with wet eyes.

"Angelique made me cry the first time we met, too," Fern said, rubbing her shoulder.

"I know in my head it shouldn't matter how I look," Hannah continued. "I'm never going to be tall and skinny, but when I look in the mirror, I don't see 'pretty' and that makes it feel as though what people say is true."

"When I look in a mirror, I see my sister, so I always love what I see," Angelique said wryly. "But the things that make me feel pretty are things I can literally feel. Soft fabric and my hair loose on my shoulders. Laughing. Showing my husband my new lingerie." She cast her gaze to the sky, making them chuckle. "But I did make a career in helping women feel confident and beautiful. You have incredible skin, Hannah. And nursing mothers have a built-in advantage. Look at Fern making the most of what's she's got."

"Use them 'til you lose them." Fern sat taller, straining the buttons on her bodice.

"What are you wearing tonight?" Angelique asked. "Can I come help you get ready?"

"Do a makeover?" Hannah shook her head. "It would look like I'm trying too hard."

"You don't need to be anything but who you are," Angelique said firmly. "You're perfect. But I miss playing dress-up with my sister. It's great bonding time and I *do* know a few tricks that might help you feel you're getting the most from your wardrobe. Please?"

The word "bonding" got her. She needed friends, so she nodded, hoping Nura would be able to tone things down if Angelique went too far.

Fern elected to stay back and call her sons, so Hannah promised to see her at dinner and nervously brought Angelique back to her apartment.

Akin believed in diplomacy over combat, which wasn't to say he wouldn't resort to combat if it came to that. Tonight was meant to be ambassadorial, but there was every chance his actions would be seen as aggressive. They were definitely tactical.

He had invited three of the most powerful kings in his region for an unofficial meeting he had billed as a social opportunity to introduce his wife to theirs. None of them were stupid. They knew more was afoot or they would have had more notice.

To call them friends would be an overstatement. They were traditional allies and all well acquainted from years of attending weddings and funerals, coronations and the occasional crossing of paths near a desert border.

They were also circumspect men who would make up their own minds. Whatever opinions they shared outside the palace after this visit would carry a great deal of weight around the globe.

After tonight, Baaqi would either be seen as vulnerable, with a weakened king and no confirmed ruler, or in steady hands with Akin at the helm.

Akin brought each man into his father's chamber to briefly pay his respects, king to king. His father's ill health and lack of interest in continuing to reign was painfully obvious.

Afterward, they all convened with drinks in a private lounge reserved for mingling with exalted guests such as they were.

"Take heed, men," Zafir said as they clinked glasses. "Our fathers stood like this at one time and thought they would be our age forever."

"We should be so lucky as to enjoy a long life," Karim said. Both he and Zafir had lost their fathers when they were young.

"It's sobering to confront mortality at any time," Kasim agreed with introspection. "I'm reminded of my own father in his later years. The delicate tightrope that has to be walked."

It was an acknowledgment of the difficult position Akin was in, finding the balance between his father's right to rule, his regal pride, and the fact he simply no longer had the capacity to do it.

"It's an equally difficult balance to be the uncle who raises a king," Karim said with a nod of acknowledgment to Akin that was also a subtle warning. "Mine was much like you. A firm, steady influence who modeled the devotion to duty I've carried with me to this day."

We know what you're doing, Karim was saying. *We're watching and can make things uncomfortable internationally if we don't like what we see.*

"At least you were old enough to have learned basic manners," Akin said dryly. "I held Qaswar the other day when he visited my mother and walked around the rest of the day wondering, what is that smell?"

"Ah. The bewitching aroma of new father. I'm likely wearing it myself," Zafir said with a grimacing glance at his own shoulder.

They chuckled and moved on to discussing other matters, but Akin knew he was still on trial. If Qaswar had not existed, Akin would have been recognized as the rightful heir and allowed to take control without question.

He was not, though. There was a baby who held that title and these men wanted reassurances this was not a power-grab that could destablize the entire region. They would bring their own armies to stand behind the infant against Akin if it came to it. Without their support, Akin had nothing.

Which was why he needed to push Hannah into the spotlight, despite her voiced reluctance to be anywhere near it. Until Qaswar was old enough, she was the placeholder to whom Akin would demonstrate his dedication. It was a play to reassure the public, but it was sincere. Ironically, his life would be so much more straightforward if Qaswar hadn't existed, but Akin couldn't find any regret in him that the boy did.

A subtle knock announced the women were joining them.

Akin suffered a moment of concern. If Hannah walked in looking hurt and ill used, he would have to take a completely different tack, starting with banishing any catty queens who had dared to claw at his little mouse. She might not be the most glamorous wom—

As the hostess, Hannah led the parade of graceful beauties and Akin's mouth went dry as she moved with assurance among them. *As one of them.*

His heart swelled with such pride he could barely see over his chest.

They all wore long dinner gowns. Hannah's was bronze and poured down her voluptuous figure like caramel syrup over ice cream. It offered a generous view of her upper chest and coated her hips, puddling in a small train behind her. Her hair had been trimmed and reshaped into a smooth cap and was topped by a small tiara that leant her an air of quiet sophistication.

Her glasses were gone, her lashes decidedly false, but her smile was genuine and so filled with confidence that he was utterly dazzled. She wore heels and came across to him with a roll of her hips that was every man's wet dream.

"My wife. Princess Hannah," he introduced as she arrived at his side. He wanted to throw her over his shoulder and take her somewhere private to ravage her. For *days*.

She greeted each man in turn with a personal comment. "Your daughter is so precious. I'm hoping Fern can coach me on how to raise such a happy baby... Galila was telling me about your country's literacy endeavors. I'm looking forward to stealing all her inspired ideas... Thank you for loaning me Angelique this afternoon. She's been so generous and has been enduring my practice of very rusty Spanish."

Every single one of the men managed to keep his

eyes on her smile, but Akin knew that despite the fact that each was completely enamored with his own very beautiful wife, they all noted Hannah's loveliness. Any male with a pulse would.

He experienced a surprisingly deep stab of possessiveness as he perceived it and closed his hand over hers in a blatant claim that was a betrayal of his inner barbarian. Not like him at all to feel it or reveal it, but he couldn't stop himself.

They all chatted a little longer before moving into the small dining room, where a square table put each couple on a side so as not to put a prince above a king, even though Akin was the host.

"No glasses?" Akin murmured as he seated Hannah.

"Contacts. That's why I'm blinking like a first-class flirt."

She was and it was adorable. Probably the sexiest thing she did, however, was reveal how incredibly intelligent she was. As conversation meandered from mild gossip about a scandal at the boarding school Zafir's son attended to complex political issues, Hannah listened attentively, asking incisive questions and offering smart, fresh perspective.

It was the most relaxed and genuinely social evening Akin had experienced in recent memory. When the women rose to retire for the night, they kissed each other's cheeks and promised reciprocal invitations soon. Akin would have dismissed it as a meaningless courtesy, but their husbands backed them up.

"We're in England next month, but will you accompany Akin when he attends our trade forum in June?" Zafir asked with a glance at Akin, who nodded. "I'll arrange rooms for you at the palace."

Akin had rooms booked at the hotel where all the meetings would be held, which would be more convenient for him, but this was the seal of approval he'd sought with tonight's dinner, so he said, "Thank you. We'd be honored."

Hannah wouldn't say that she magically felt beautiful and confident and fit to be a queen after eating dinner with royalty, but she did feel less of an imposter after spending the day with those women.

Galila had been raised a princess, but even though she looked amazing, and wore the title of Queen without any seeming effort, she'd confessed that pregnancy had taken a toll. Hannah had very much identified with that.

And how could she not relate to Fern, a single mother's daughter with education her only real asset, who had accidentally become pregnant by a man with royal blood?

Then Angelique had been so warm and encouraging and an absolute genius about the colors and styles that best suited Hanna's figure. The whole evening had gone so well that Hannah was unable to focus on anything but the positives.

It had added up to the boost she needed to step into the role Akin demanded of her. Well, the public role, anyway. She had since held a tea for a handful of chairwomen running charities the Queen sponsored, and had accompanied Akin to a ground-breaking for what would eventually be Baaqi's parliament buildings.

Her private role as his wife was making her wring her hands with nerves, though.

She hadn't actually seen her husband since the night with the royals. A land use dispute at an oil field had taken him away for two nights and he'd been up early this morning, texting that he was needed in his office and couldn't breakfast with her, but...

Come by my office on your way to yours.

She did, but even though things had been going really well between them, butterflies invaded her stomach when she heard his voice as she was shown through the catacomb of offices occupied by his assistants and advisers and approached the one that was his.

It was an imposing room that reflected his military service in its ruthlessly practical decor. A handful of dignitaries were leaving so there were introductions all around before she was left with only him and two of his assistants, both anxious to pour water, slant the blinds so the light wasn't in her eyes, hold her chair and fetch cake and coffee if she so desired?

"I'm perfectly comfortable, thank you," Hannah assured them.

"Close the door on your way out," Akin ordered dryly.

Hannah waited until they'd done so before brushing her scarf off her hair. "Far be it from me to complain, but you may have made *too* big a deal about their giving me every consideration."

"No one offers *me* sweetcakes with my coffee," he grumbled.

"Because they know you eat the hearts of your enemies with your morning coffee."

"I'll eat certain sweetcakes." His hungry look was not an appetite for food. "If they have a sprinkle of spice."

"Flirt," she accused, blushing as she looked to the closed blinds.

"You started it, coming in here with that chic haircut that makes me want to muss it up. How much longer do we have to wait, *ya amar*? Did you see the doctor while I was away?"

"Yes." She had an urge to open the neck of her blouse and let some of the heat against her throat escape. "He gave me an IUD and said it's effective immedia—"

Akin hit a button on his desk. A distant buzzer sounded and the door promptly opened. A young man poked his head in. *"Sayidi?"*

"Clear both our schedules for the rest of the day."

"What?" Hannah blurted.

"Nem, sayidi." The door closed.

"I didn't think—I wasn't—" She cut herself off, unable to form words as Akin stood and held out his hand to her. The heat in his eyes made her throat go dry. "Right *now*?"

"I don't intend to seduce you here," he drawled. "Not this time, anyway. Not our first time. But I've been thinking about this long enough that if I have to spend the day in a state of anticipation, I'm liable to last about five minutes when we get to the good part. Come."

CHAPTER TEN

SHE NERVOUSLY PUT her hand in his and he drew her to her feet. Then he kissed her, just once, and her heart raced as he smiled conspiratorially, as though they shared a secret.

They did, as it happened. He used his thumbprint to unlock a door and showed her into a private passage, which took them past an unmarked door that she vaguely suspected was the throne room. She got turned around after that. They passed an emergency exit and went up and down a few flights of stairs. He had to use his thumb on three more doors, or they would have been trapped in dead ends. She didn't see one camera.

"You're not lost, are you?"

He sent her such a pithy look she chuckled away her nerves.

"I had to ask. We're going to need a tent and campfire soon."

"This is why I don't commute this way. I had these security doors put in place myself so I have no one else to blame, but these passages had ceased to provide the privacy they were designed for. When I was a child, Eijaz and I played hide-and-seek for hours here, but servants began using them as a shortcut. Doors were being left unlocked and propped open. Today, however, they allow me to steal my wife to my own chamber, with no one the wiser."

He touched a final sensor and a wooden panel swung inward, revealing that this particular entrance was disguised by a bookshelf inside his den.

"Almost no one," he corrected as a bearded man in a white tunic and plain cotton pants appeared in the doorway, a surprised look on his face. "My butler, Ulama. The Princess and I do not wish to be disturbed."

"Unless the baby needs me," Hannah added as the man dipped his skullcap-covered head in a bow and evaporated.

"He will need me, you know." Not for a while and it might be time to see if he would take a bottle, but she would make that decision when her phone buzzed.

For the moment she was fascinated to be in her husband's private space. Like his office, this place didn't have a lot of froufrou touches, but the soothing colors made it a place of retreat. He had windows looking out into the real world, not just the courtyard, which briefly distracted her.

"You don't have a dining room," she noted. Only a table in a nook that offered a view of the desert. She and he shared a chef, though. She knew that much.

"I don't entertain. You have the dining room and the bigger lounge for hosting family gatherings. Everything else is hosted in the formal rooms of the palace."

She would have dismissed this as a bachelor's apartment, but when they arrived in his bedroom, she saw that it was even bigger and more sumptuous than her own. He had a massive bed and a full sitting room with a window overlooking the pool area. There was also a screen of greenery, but she still had a moment of shyness when he stood behind her, clasped her shoulders and kissed her neck.

"What's wrong?" he asked, lifting his mouth as he sensed her tension.

"What if Nura can see us?"

He moved away to touch a button on the wall. Bone-colored drapes whispered from the corners to cover the glass while the room remained softly lit.

"Don't you have blackout blinds so you can sleep if you have to?"

"Yes. But I want to see you."

She shook her head in automatic rejection, linking her hands nervously as he came back to her. "I don't want that."

"No? Then how will I see this dimple of yours?" He tilted up her face and set his thumb in the middle of her chin. "It appears when you're digging in your heels. It frustrates the hell out of me, but it's so damned cute I always want to kiss it."

He was barely moving his thumb, but it felt like the most erotic caress. The heat in his eyes scrambled her brain.

"I want to make love, Akin, I do." She heard the plaintive note in her voice and hated herself for being so insecure. "But I have a lot of hang-ups about sex. I never felt attractive or like anyone really wanted m-me." Her lips trembled despite how hard she fought to speak evenly. "I know that no one is perfect, and you don't expect *me* to be perfect, but I'm still really scared that I'll disappoint you, either in the way I look or my lack of experience…" She shrugged to encompass all the many ways she could fail to measure up.

He didn't laugh or dismiss her. His dark brows quirked with concern. "I've been nothing but satisfied and delighted every time I've held you. I hope you know that. I hope you've felt the same?"

"Of course, but that was only fooling around. I got to keep my clothes on."

His mouth pursed in thought, then his hand moved to her neck. "Let's try this."

He unwound the silk scarf she had draped over her hair this morning. It tickled her nape as he gently slithered it free. He made a band of it in front of her eyes and started to tie it over them.

"Wait! No. *You* should wear the blindfold," she protested, catching at his strong wrist.

"I'm the one who wants to see, *ya amar*. You're the one who doesn't want to see my reaction. You'll feel it, though. I promise you won't have any doubt how desirable I find you."

He waited a beat, then stepped closer so he could see behind her head. He smoothed her hair out of the way before he tied the scarf in place. When he dropped his hands, they lightly traced her spine, drawing her into him so she could feel he was already aroused.

"Feel how irresistible you are to me? Do you hear it?" His voice was husked in a way that seemed to abrade her all over, sensitizing her skin. His hot breath grazed her cheek before his lips nuzzled across her skin, seeking her ear. "These are not my earrings."

"No." She started to bring her hand up to the sleeper hoops she'd let Nura poke in when she pierced her lobes. They had stung for about five minutes, leaving her to wonder why she'd been so scared for so long.

Her hand bumped into his arm. She let her touch rest

against his ribs, disconcerted by the fact she couldn't see. It was silly. She mostly closed her eyes when they kissed anyway, but this was different. She *couldn't* open them. It was like making love in the absolute dark and it emboldened her to let her hands explore where her eyes couldn't, trying to get her bearings that way.

He made a noise of satisfaction and his mouth trailed to capture hers. Here, when he kissed her with this depth of passion, everything was right in her world. They kissed like that for long minutes, exactly as they had on other occasions, hands whispering over linen and charmeuse, slipping free a button or delving beneath an edge to find warm skin.

Except, rather than fondling under her blouse, he opened it completely and brushed it off her shoulders. Rather than lifting her skirt, he unzipped it and dropped it to the floor. And rather than hug her close, he stepped back so there was nothing but cool air around her.

"Akin," she protested, automatically shielding herself with her arms.

"Oh, no, *ya amar*." He took her hands and held them out to her sides like wings. "You are far too modest if you think that what I am seeing is anything less than perfection."

"That's not true." She wore low-heeled sandals that were pretty enough. All her clothes came from top-end designers now, but despite lace panels and jewel tones, her underwear was still the least sexy style. Thongs and cheekies were way too uncomfortable, so she wore high-waisted, maximum-coverage panties. And she was wearing a nursing bra, for heaven's sake.

"How does this come off?" he asked, touching once

between her breasts before stepping to follow the bra to its clasp below her shoulder blades.

"Akin." She tried to be brave, she really did. He was her husband, she wanted to make love with him, and he would see her naked eventually, but she felt so *vulnerable*. When he dropped the bra away and stepped back again, she curled her arms to hide her breasts.

"Hannah." His voice was that commanding tone, but there was a catch in it. Just enough that she didn't take umbrage. In fact, her nipples hardened against the press of her own arms. When he took her wrists and set kisses in each of her palms, tingles spread from her nape into her shoulders and down her whole body, weakening her knees and making them shake.

"If these hands continue to get in my way, I'll have to tie them behind you." He crossed her wrists behind her. "Keep them there. Pretend you have no choice but to let me see as much of you as I wish."

"That's kinky," she accused.

"Only if it excites you. Does it?" His hot hands gathered her breasts, gently plumping them. She could tell by the heat of his closeness and the angle of his breath that he was staring at the pale globes laced with fine blue lines. He was watching his own thumbs make circles around her distended nipples.

She shifted restlessly, thought about breaking her invisible bonds, but it was a little bit exciting to pretend she couldn't. A little bit freeing to imagine he had tied her up so she would be at his mercy.

"I think it does excite you." He sounded pleased. "Your panting is making your breasts shake in my hands. It's the most beautiful sight I've ever seen."

"It's fear," she lied. "I'm being held hostage, if you recall."

"Oh, I am well aware. You are completely mine to touch and admire. If I wish to slide these down just a little…" His thumbs caught in the band of her panties and took them down so they cut low across her hips, exposing the fine hairs at the top of her mound. "Then I may do so. I can do anything I want to you and you are utterly helpless."

As she stood there trembling in a strange, erotic excitement, deeply aware of how exposed she was, his fingertips traced the line of elastic from hip to hip, pausing in the middle to pet and discover, ever so briefly, the place where her folds began to part.

Heat flooded up to her hairline and down to her loins. She was aware of a rush of damp arousal into silk and grew more and more sensitized, and more and more frustrated, as he continued to caress her with such teasing lightness.

"You are so lovely." His voice was guttural and rough while his touch stayed light.

"You're enjoying this," she accused, scandalized by how much he seemed to be embracing their fantasy.

"Believe it. It's all I can do not to bend you over the foot of my bed." He drew her into a hot kiss, pressing her naked body into the hot linen that still covered him.

She almost forgot she was "bound," but he loosely grappled her wrists in one of his hands while the other slid beneath her lowered panties to cup her backside.

He seemed to love her bottom. He never missed an opportunity to touch her like this when they kissed, stroking in a way that made her squirm against him, then firming to press her mound into his shape.

Today he traced the line between her cheeks, slowly, slowly easing her panties down until they were fully off her butt and cutting across the backs of her thighs. Then he drew back again and his hand gave her wrists a reminding squeeze before he said, "Are we coming up to Valentine's Day? Because I have a gift to finish unwrapping."

She heard his knee click as he crouched before her to take the lace and silk all the way to her ankles. Her elbows twitched as she fought her invisible cuffs. She clenched her eyes behind her blindfold, unsteady on her feet as he lifted them one by one to remove her sandals.

He rose with another click of his knee and she heard all the clothes being flung away from around her feet. He touched her hip to shuffle her a few steps, perhaps moving her closer to the bed. She heard him remove his clothes and licked her lips, waiting, but there was only silence now.

"What are you doing?"

"Looking at you." His voice was behind her. "You're in front of a mirror so I can see everything, Hannah. Your round ass and lush breasts and pale thighs and soft stomach. Your obedience." He touched her crossed wrists.

She had started to draw them apart, but firmed their cross, releasing a small whimper of helpless frustration as she did.

"I'm looking at that mouth going all flat with annoyance and thinking about how much pleasure you give me with it. So much, I can hardly speak. I'm looking at your hair." He touched where it stopped at her nape. "So soft I want to sleep with my cheek on it."

He stepped up behind her, so his hot frame brushed

her back and pinned her crossed wrists between his hard abdomen and her lower back. His thick sex rested against her buttocks, hot and heavy, while his hand came around her. His fingertip offered a barely-there caress along the seam of her folds.

"I'm looking at the dampness here that tells me you're aroused," he said huskily against her ear. "I feel so impatient to have you, I'm shaking with it. Do not ever let me hear again that you're anything but beautiful, Hannah. That is an order."

She might have had an intelligent response if he hadn't chosen that second to sink his touch into her damp folds and gently part her. She stumbled back into him and he caught her close, pinning her arms even more firmly so she was trapped as he sought her swollen bud and encircled, gliding his touch over and around and across.

Intense pleasure was jolting through her. White light flashed behind her eyes. Her knees nearly gave out on her.

"Akin," she gasped, hanging in his arms.

"Poor little captive, so helpless. Let's tie you to the bed." He removed his intimate touch and steadied her. She could have wept; her sense of loss was so profound.

Moments later, cool sheets were at her back and he was guiding her hands above her head.

She scrabbled ineffectual nails against the quilted leather of his headboard while his cropped beard tickled her chin and throat and between her breasts. Her stomach muscles contracted as he arrived there, and she realized where he was going. She pressed her thighs together. "You don't have to do that."

"You are correct. I am in absolute control of everything that happens here. I may do whatever I want, *ya amar*. Do I have to tie your legs open?" He used effortless strength to part her thighs, but she was shaking more than resisting.

"You're a barbarian at heart, aren't you?" But she pretended her legs were bound, as well. She could do nothing but let him have his way with her. It was titillating to believe but liberating in how it allowed her to accept his caresses without guilt that she was being selfish. Without fear that she didn't deserve to be pleasured and worshipped this way.

"I will be satisfied with nothing less than your complete surrender." He was looking at her; she knew he was. Delicately parting her and letting his hot breath waft across her sensitive flesh as he spoke.

The anticipation was so palpable she was ready to scream with frustration.

"You are magnificent, Hannah. Feel it. Believe it."

He claimed her, stealing across intimate territory with his lips and tongue. He undermined her resistance and staked a claim, easing two fingers inside her.

She writhed with pleasure. She could have broken her pretend bonds and reached for him. She could have torn off her blindfold and made this a more mutual act, but as much as she wanted to give him pleasure, she wanted to give him *her*. He wanted her unequivocally. Why else would he pleasure her like this?

With that realization, she understood that whatever had held her back in the past might have been real, but there were no shackles today except the ones she allowed herself to believe in.

She let go of her old hurts once and for all. She didn't worry how she looked to him, only that he knew how magnificent he made her feel. She abandoned herself to the agonizing joy he was bestowing on her, holding her body open to him while holding back none of her moans and sobs of pleasure. She cried out his name again and again. When her climax hit, she held herself taut, hips lifted in offering, absent of inhibition as she exalted in his unrelenting ministrations.

As she panted in reaction and her flesh sang and her abdomen shook with reaction, his hands roamed from her thighs to her breasts. His mouth followed, taking restrained bites from her stomach and the inner swells of her heavy breasts and he sucked a decided mark against her neck.

Then he shifted so he was aligned with her entrance and brushed the blindfold off her eyes. Here was the barbarian, eyes glittering, cheekbones sharp as knives, the weight and strength of him caging her.

"You're mine," he said in a rasping voice laden with passion as he slowly, inexorably pressed into her.

She wouldn't dream of arguing and couldn't speak anyway. The sensation as he filled her was too intense. She abandoned her invisible restraints and closed her arms and legs around him. Claimed him as hers. She wouldn't entertain any other belief as they kissed and he sank fully into her, so hard, so hot. So deeply a part of her that it was unescapable and profound.

He gave an abbreviated thrust, watching as he did, testing her readiness.

She didn't shrink from his all-seeing gaze. She probably still wore the flush of her recent climax. Her eyelids were heavy, and her lips tingled. Everything about this moment was deeply intimate, but they were in it together. She drew his head down to kiss while pressing his shoulder with her other hand.

In an effortless twist, he hugged her tight and rolled so she was on top. She smiled and caught his arms, finding his hands and pressing them to the mattress beside his head.

One dark eyebrow went up, then his gaze narrowed as she sat tall upon him, running her hands over her body as she began to undulate upon him.

"Vixen," he bit out.

"You unleashed the savage in me. You have no one to blame but yourself."

"Use me, then." He lifted his hips, encouraging her to ride him. "Show me how much you want me."

She splayed her hands on his chest, bracing herself as they began to move together. It was raw and wild. Blatant and intense. Her breasts jiggled and their bodies slapped. When her thighs tired, he clamped his hands on her hips and guided her rhythm. She curled her fingers on his chest and thought she must be pulling his chest hair, but the tension was coiling in her and she was nearly there, as was he.

She bit her lip and watched him bare his teeth. She wanted to close her eyes as the wave began to engulf her, but she held his slitted gaze as dark color washed into his chest and face and the tendons in his neck stood up.

At the same time orgasm struck deep inside her, dragging a cry of repletion from her, he shouted and arched and let out his own shouts of release.

An unfamiliar intermittent hum woke Akin.

He dragged his eyes open to find his wife in one

of his robes, leaning into pillows pressed against the headboard. She was nursing Qaswar, who was gulping loudly between humming in the way of anyone who was enjoying a hearty meal after a long fast.

"Is he always like that?"

"I don't know why I thought I could do this without waking you. He's like a starving wolf on a lamb, aren't you, my little glutton?" She tenderly stroked her son's hair. "Growling and gobbling."

"I don't mind." Akin absently reached for the boy's foot, which poked from his knee-length pajamas. It wasn't even as long as his thumb, and his small toes curled as Akin ran his finger into the boy's arch. He had the most ridiculous urge to press his cheek to the soft sole and let the baby feel the texture of his beard.

He released him and fell onto his back, curling his arm under his head, disturbed by how hard he'd slept, but damn, he felt good. Relaxed. He could get used to this, he thought, but immediately a cool draft entered his chest. A harsh recognition that nothing in life was permanent, so he shouldn't let himself get used to it. Even people who seemed to care could cause pain and disappear.

He realized Hannah was looking at him with a small frown. "Problem?" he asked.

"I just wondered…" She touched the baby's foot. "You said you and Eijaz used to play in the passageways. That makes me think you were friends, but… I know you said you didn't want to talk about your childhood. It's fine if you don't, but I always wished I had a sibling. I wondered if you think we'll ever give Qaswar brothers or sisters."

"Ambush me in my own bed when I'm too weak to

walk away, why don't you?" he muttered, frowning to the ceiling.

He loathed dragging open heavy doors inside him, scraping across the grit of the past, but her expression was very naked and vulnerable. Their physical intimacy had formed a connection between them that was delicate and so tenuous it terrified him how easily it could be broken. He couldn't shut her down.

"We were friends. Very different because we were raised very differently. He was the future king and mentored for that role. Spoiled. So spoiled," he sighed. "But charming and likable, and I was his confidante, the only person who really understood the pressures he faced. The expectations he feared he couldn't meet. In that way, I sometimes think my parents did me a favor, making me work like hell for each tiny shred of approval. Like how the straight A students fall apart when they reach university, but the ones who are used to getting Cs already know how to dig in."

"I thought it was just your mother who was...less than forthcoming with her affection. But I don't understand how any parent can favor one child over another," she protested.

"My mother had a stillbirth after me, a daughter. Seeing how Eijaz's death devastated her gives me some indication how thoroughly the loss of my sister must have broken her. She had two sons, you see. If she had to give up one of her babies, her daughter should have been the one to survive."

Her arms tightened around Qaswar. "That's so wrong, Akin. I'm sorry she's lost two children, but no. That was deeply unfair of her. And you're here. That ought to count for something."

He didn't bother pointing out his mother's reduced mental capacities these days.

"I'm really sorry you lost your brother, though. He must have been your confidante, too? Did he never stand up for you against them?"

"In his way," he said on an exhale. "He told our father I was planning to elope."

"He *did* that?"

"He thought he was helping."

"You believe that?"

"I do." He'd been furious at the time, but it had been typical of Eijaz to do what he thought was best without thinking through to the consequences.

Akin watched her shift the baby to her shoulder and pat his back. The day he'd met her, he'd thought Eijaz must be laughing at the predicament he'd thrust Akin into, but now he wondered if any divine intervention might have had a more benevolent motive. The things he felt for Hannah were infinitely deeper and more complex than that youthful crush he'd once entertained. Had his brother tried to repair that long-ago injury from beyond his grave?

"Do you want more children?" he asked her.

"Not today," she said with a wryly slanted glance. "But I will." Her nod held calm certainty. "I thought when I got pregnant that one would be enough, but now I want someone for Qaswar to play hide-and-seek with. I want a family." She knitted her brow anxiously. "I want *this.*"

She shifted to set the baby on the mattress between them and slid down to face him across the wriggling little boy.

"I want to make love and tell each other things no one

else knows, and I want us to play with our children." She held a hand against Qaswar's foot so he could work his tiny leg muscles against it.

"Children don't stay children," Akin warned. "Happy moments are only moments. Everything changes eventually. You know that, don't you?" It was a harsh reality that had been drilled so deeply into him he couldn't see outside it.

"Sometimes things change for the better. A baby can grow up strong and capable of handling the challenges he faces. A life alone can turn into one with...a partner." The emotion in her eyes grew even more undisguised.

He withdrew slightly. She didn't understand the risk she was taking in opening her heart that much. Hurt became inevitable and he would do anything to keep her from being hurt.

Not that he wanted to yank that trusting innocence away from her when they were tucked so safely into a rare pocket of contentment. Hell, there was a part of him that longed for partnership and family and belief in the future, too.

But he wasn't a fool. He didn't *ask* for disappointment and loss and pain.

He dropped his gaze to Qaswar.

The baby cycled his legs and his abstract gaze moved aimlessly then snagged on Akin's. His tiny mouth stretched in a smile so much like his brother's it kicked Akin straight in the heart.

It was such a powerful moment it shook Akin to the core. Hannah and Qaswar were already rattling the gates of his heart, threatening to make him even more vulnerable than he was.

"I've only ever protected what everyone else has,

Hannah. I don't know how to imagine more for my-self, let alone make it a reality. Maybe..." He stopped himself, embarrassed.

"What?" she prompted.

"I don't know. I can't help thinking it will be differ-ent after the ceremony. Once my father recognizes me as— Not his heir, obviously, but his temporary succes-sor at least. Something more than..." He peeked down into the basement of his soul. "More than a second son. That's been a stain. I would never condemn my own child to that position."

"No, you wouldn't." She set her hand on his cheek. "*I* wouldn't."

He wanted to believe that, but there was a part of him that refused to see and want and accept that he de-served the life she described. If he let himself yearn for it, any ultimate denial would destroy him.

"My life does not get reshaped by a happiness list," he said gently, cushioning his words by holding on to the hand she tried to draw back. He moved it from his bearded cheek so he could kiss her palm. "I admire you so much for going after what you want out of life. I want to give you everything you could ever desire, but can we talk about more children another time?"

She bit her lip in hurt but nodded. "Of course."

CHAPTER ELEVEN

I WANT YOUR HEART. That was what Hannah had wanted to say.

Ironically, the one thing she had purposely left off her happiness list was anything to do with winning the love of a man, yet here she was with pretty much the whole list achieved and she wasn't happy.

She couldn't resent Akin for holding back, though. She understood how his parents had taught him not to trust that he was as entitled as anyone else to a fulfilling life. She also understood how hard it was to decide what personal happiness looked like and go after it.

The worst part was, she couldn't change his mind for him. All she could do was believe that time would heal all wounds and try to give him that time. At least she had the reassurance of his physical attentions. They made love every chance they got, which was pure magic, but she didn't realize how completely he wanted to share a bed until he showed up in her room in the middle of the night, sounding quite annoyed.

"Why didn't you come back?"

"Qaswar took forever to settle. I didn't want to wake you," she murmured drowsily as he joined her in her own bed and dragged her into the spoon of his body.

"I was lying awake worried something was wrong. We're changing wings after the coronation, so this won't happen again."

He made it sound like a dire warning, but it made her smile with gladness in the dark before she drifted back to sleep.

The coronation was only a few weeks away and final plans were falling into place. Akin had approved all her arrangements and offered special praise for her attention to detail—as if she'd never had to organize a faculty lunch that satisfied vegan, kosher and nut allergy requests in the same meal plan before.

Hannah was in the middle of a meeting that would put the final touches on the celebration when her assistant touched her elbow and whispered she had an urgent call from her husband.

"My father passed," Akin said abruptly. "I've just informed my mother. I have to make more calls. Can you bring the baby and sit with her? She's asking for him."

"Of course. I'm so sorry, Akin."

He said something noncommittal and hung up.

A cold premonition entered her heart. She didn't make any announcements to the staff, unsure if it was her place, only hurriedly called the nanny to meet her in the Queen's chambers. But the whole while, she was thinking about what he'd said that day about how the coronation would change things. That if his father recognized him, he would start to feel accepted as something more than a stain.

The next days were difficult, as all such losses were. She barely saw her husband except when she stood beside him to greet visitors who came to pay their respects. It was an endless procession of long faces and hushed voices. Between that were spells of placating his mother and reminding her that her husband was gone. The Queen had taken a very hard turn with the loss.

Hannah also had to call off the coronation. Instead, the day after the King's funeral, they were visited by the representatives from parliament. If Akin had been sleeping, it hadn't been with her. He looked like hell.

"By unanimous vote, we have cemented your authority as Regent of Baaqi until our Crown Prince is ready to assume his duties," one of the men said—or so it was translated quietly into Hannah's ear.

The formality lasted ten minutes. They took their leave and Hannah finally had a moment alone with her husband. He looked so drawn, with his hollow cheeks and bruised eyes, that she reached for him.

"Is that really all that was required? I thought the coronation was meant to prove...something." She shrugged ineffectually.

"It was." Akin's voice was empty of emotion. His arm was cold and unresponsive. "It would have proved my father wanted me to have the appointment. That he trusted me and recognized me as his surviving son and a competent leader. It was pure vanity on my part," he added in a bitter scoff at himself.

"Don't say that." His despair broke her heart. "It's okay that you wanted his recognition. That's not vanity. That's being human."

"Wanting love as a child is natural. Wanting it as an adult is immature and self-indulgent."

"No, it's not! *I* want love. Everyone does." Anxiety clawed at her along with inner warnings that he was in too much pain to hear through it, but she kept speaking. "I'm sorry your parents withheld their love for you.

You deserve it and I know it's no substitute, but… I love you." It hurt to say it the way it might hurt to pull her own heart out of her chest and show it to him, but she offered it to him all the same.

He sucked in a pained breath, not moving, but visibly withdrawing from her.

Don't, she silently protested.

"Hannah, I can't… I told you I would give you everything I could, but that life you want? It's not in my power to give you that." His eyes and voice were bleak. "I'm not the man who can make that happen for you."

How do you know if you haven't tried? That was what she wanted to say.

"I'm not going to stop wanting it, Akin. Who will give it to me if not you? Am I supposed to find it with someone else? Or just accept a life that falls short of…" She couldn't disparage the life she had. The son she'd been given. The life he had already given her.

But she was greedy. She wanted more. And she couldn't imagine being with anyone else, not when she loved Akin with everything in her.

"Yes," he said distantly. "Find someone else." He walked away.

CHAPTER TWELVE

HANNAH WAS DEVASTATED, but she let him go because he was obviously in too much pain to be rational.

He didn't just walk away, though. He *left*.

It took her two days to realize it, but she finally ran the gamut of his assistants to reach his top aide. "He went into the desert. I didn't realize you didn't know, or I would have informed you myself," the man apologized.

"What does that mean? Like…where in the desert? For how long? Why?" How could she possible reach him there? Was she supposed to not even *try*? Her desolation was so profound it was a type of grief.

"That is very hard to answer," the aide said with remorse. "I can make enquiries. It may take some time."

"Thank you." Hannah walked out, crushed, but more than that, she was *mad*. Maybe Akin had never promised to love her, but he had promised to treat her with respect. Maybe he hadn't promised to make her happy, but he wasn't allowed to hurt her. Not on purpose.

While an old, fragile part of her wanted to crawl away and hide from the pain of his abandonment, she let her anger at him fuel her. Maybe she was kidding herself, pretending it was pique, not a broken heart that had her make her own inquiries, but it was safer than believing she was foolishly chasing a man who didn't really want her.

She deserved better than this, she told herself and made herself believe it as she texted Galila for advice.

Do I let him grieve in his own way? Will he be angry if I go after him?

Galila was not only intimately connected to the nomad families who traversed the deserts, she understood best the sort of man she was dealing with. Her response helped Hannah decide on her next course of action.

Probably. Men like ours are too proud to lean on a woman if they can avoid it. But if he's hurting and you love him, be there for him anyway.

Galila arranged a helicopter herself.

Which was how Hannah got to the oasis ahead of him.

The sizable pool was a jewel of blue in an ocean of sand that charmed her immediately. A small tribe was in residence. Hannah and her entourage of bodyguards and nannies, cooks and maids were greeted warily until they realized Qaswar was with her. Then the entire mood became celebratory, and they were all welcomed warmly.

Hannah wondered if Akin would welcome the sight of her. He would likely be furious, while her own anger had dissipated into uncertainty. Had she really come all this way to be rejected? Again?

She had to wait two full days to find out. It was nerve-racking but pleasant to be out of the palace. The nomads were happy to educate her on native plants and their culture, and help her practice her rudimentary Arabic.

She was in the middle of learning a traditional lullaby when a thundering commotion and a huge dust cloud appeared at the edge of the bowl that surrounded the oasis. A half dozen camels bawled as they were galloped down the slope into the encampment.

It would have been terrifying if Hannah hadn't recognized the tall bearing of her husband within seconds. Elemental and dynamic, he took her breath with his imposing presence. She handed Qaswar to a nanny and met him as he dismounted.

"What happened? Is the baby okay?" He was covered in dust and sand.

"He's perfectly fine. Smothered nearly to death by all the adoring arms who want to hold him." She glanced toward the tent where Qaswar was being put down for a nap in the shade, a dozen minders hovering nearby.

"Then what brought you here? My heart stopped when the hawkers told me you had been here two days, waiting for me."

"Where am I supposed to be?" she asked with a flash of the anger that was the only thing she'd been letting herself feel. "If not with my husband. What are *you* doing here?"

"You did not come all the way out here to ask me that." The thunderous look he gave her nearly made her back up a step, even though there was a flash of something behind his outrage that she couldn't interpret.

"I did." She held her ground, but it felt as though she stood on insubstantial dunes that shifted beneath her feet. "Was I supposed to wait back at the palace for you until you returned to inform me what sort of future I could expect? Live whatever pale, useless life you told me to live?"

His expression didn't change.

The sand was slipping away beneath her, and now she felt like she was sliding through an hourglass.

"I love you, Akin. I told you that. And even though you were in a lot of pain when I said it the first time, your reaction left a lot to be desired. Think long and hard about how you react today."

The lift of her chin was pure bravado, because inside, she shook worse than she ever had during one of their confrontations. Those other times, she hadn't had nearly so much of herself invested. Before she'd felt his touch and his lips and shared secrets across a pillow, she would have been able to bear his anger and rejection. But now she loved him and that was her heart right there on the sand. If he kicked it away this time, he would do irrevocable damage to the fragile bond between them.

He said nothing. He stood there coated in dust, nostrils flared, eyes going black as his pupils expanded.

Inexplicably, her heart began to pound in panic. She swallowed and started to lean onto her back foot, sensing real danger.

Before she could whirl and run, he swooped and caught her and swung her over his shoulder. It happened so fast her nose was in the back of his dusty robe before she realized what he intended.

He barked something in Arabic and she heard someone answer him, but she couldn't tell who or what they said, or even where he was taking her.

"What are you doing?" she cried, wriggling enough to test his grip, but also hanging on because he was starting to walk.

"This is who I am, Hannah. You say you love me, but you've only ever seen my civilized side, when I've been trying to run a country and earn my parents' respect and keep from scaring the sexually repressed librarian."

"I'm not sexually repressed."

The cadence of his steps slowed as he began wading into the water.

"What are you *doing*?" She kicked her feet, pretty sure he'd lost his mind.

"I'm filthy." He swept her around so she dropped into the cradle of his arms and her startled eyes were even with his. "And I'm furious. I would have settled for my father telling me I was doing right by my nephew. I would have settled for my mother calling you my wife, not the nanny. I was furious that I let you see how much those things meant to me and how little I meant to them. I was hurt and angry and worst of all—"

His mouth flattened.

"I was furious that I couldn't see myself giving you the thing you want most. I don't know how to make someone else happy, Hannah. I've never *been* happy."

Not even with her? A little? Her heart clutched in agony.

"So when you asked if you should find the life you want with someone else, I thought, yes. She deserves it even if I can't give it to her. And I did what I've always done. I went into the desert, where life is pared down to the basics of survival. Where the things I want, the things I *need*, are purely physical. Those are needs I can meet myself. But you have *ruined* that for me, Hannah. The whole time I've been out here, all I could think was how stupid I was to have left you. So I'm furious with you, too."

He threw her.

She screamed and flailed and remembered to catch

her breath at the last second, right before she hit the water in a giant splash and plunge into its blessed, silent chill.

When she came up and toed to find the bottom, she was up to her breasts in the water, her abaya tangled around her.

He stood with the water at his waist, dragging at his clothes and throwing them toward the shore.

Beyond him, she saw that he'd managed to clear the area. Flaps had been pulled down on tents and voices were drifting in retreat as the camels were drawn away to the corral set on the far side of a dune. Not a single pair of eyes so much as peeked from behind a dangling bit of washing on a line.

"I'm not going to leave my son to go looking for some other man. Did you think about him at all? Because this is your chance to be a better father than—"

"I'm already a better father than the one I had," he snapped. "And I do want more children, for your information. Not because I want one that's 'mine,' either. Qaswar *is* mine in the ways that count. But I want that far-fetched dream of yours where we make love and play with our children and get through the bad times on the belief that they don't last. That good times will come again."

"Is that belief really so far-fetched?" she cried, hurt that he sounded so disparaging.

He sobered. "Being out here was bad, Hannah. It was nothing but loss and a feeling that sat like a sick pile of rocks in my gut, that I'd thrown away my soul by leaving you. That what we had was gone forever and it was my own fault that I was suffering."

"So why didn't you come back to fight for me? *Us?*" That hurt. It cut so deeply she could hardly breathe.

"I didn't get the chance, did I?" he said gently. "Because here you are. Proving that the good shows up, whether I know how to accept it or not. Finding you here is good, Hannah. Seeing you when I was feeling like hell is *good*. I shouldn't have left without speaking to you. I shouldn't have shut you out when letting you in is like…turning on a light inside myself. Like setting down the heaviest weight. Like sinking into cool, clear water when I'm hot and sweaty and filthy." He waded in toward her. "I don't understand why you would be this good to me, but you are. I won't throw you away again."

They were ignoring the part where he'd thrown her into this pool, she presumed, but she was beginning to tentatively hope.

"You're on my list," she said with a lift of her shoulder. "Even when you're sweaty and grouchy and uncivilized, you make me happy, so I had to come after you."

Tender agony clenched across his grimy face for one moment, the way emotion overpowered him sometimes when he didn't seem to know what to make of her.

"Even though I'm liable to be that way often?" He splashed the dust from his face. "I've thought about making my own list, you know. But you're the whole thing. What else could I need?"

"Akin." She dipped her chin, blinking more than water from her lashes.

"Why aren't you keeping up, *ya amar*?" He nodded at the clothes she still wore. "Too angry? I've hurt you too much?"

Her hurt and anger were dissolving beneath the emotions he was making no effort to disguise. In fact, the gleam in his gaze was so intense she wound up shyly looking down to unzip the garment, trying to escape how monumental it felt to be the subject of that much admiration and value and regard. Something inside her was growing too big for her skin to contain it. Her throat ached in a good way.

"My top is white," she said huskily as she let the abaya float away. She was using levity to keep herself from dissolving into emotive tears. "We could hold that wet T-shirt contest we talked about last Christmas."

A brief pulse of surprise, then he said, "Let me see," and drew her to him.

She was so buoyant it took no effort for him to draw her up so she could wrap her legs around his waist and reveal her soaked torso.

"It's not ideal," she murmured. Her nursing bra was clearly visible.

"It's a preliminary round," he allowed. "But you're definitely on the way to the finals."

"We could hold another qualifying contest later," she suggested, linking her hands behind his neck. *In the future*, she intimated. The one they would have. Together.

His gaze stayed on her chest. "A tournament circuit. I like that idea."

"Despite the lack of competition, I believe I have a shot at the title. One of the judges seems very biased in my favor."

"The *only* judge," he said in stern warning, "is extremely biased. He also has an uncanny ability to spot excellence. Eleven out of ten. Without the bra, your score will triple."

"Hey." She cupped the sides of his face. "My eyes are up here."

"You started it." He made no effort to disguise the lust simmering behind his love.

"I think I fell in love with you the first time you made a joke. Do you know that?"

"I have never made a joke in my life. I am always completely serious," he assured her.

She gathered all her courage, even though this gamble wasn't nearly as frightening as she had always feared. Happiness was right here. All she had to do was grab it.

"Do you love me, Akin?"

"I love you so much I cannot breathe, Hannah. I am terrified that something will happen to you, because I do not know how to face life without you anymore. But I am so glad to have you by my side. In my arms. In my head and in my heart."

Her mouth trembled and her throat could only manage a thready whisper. "That is a much better reaction than the first time. For the record."

"For the record, there is no contest. You are the most beautiful, perfect woman ever created. But as beautiful as you are, especially in the throes of passion, I am going to make love to you in your tent. Your body is very much my vision to enjoy and no one else's."

"So possessive," she teased, secretly delighted.

"Believe it."

A few minutes later, when their damp, naked bodies were coming together on the cushion-strewn bed in her tent, he paused to take in her pale curves. His reverent hand stroked the back of her shoulder, down her back and waist and hips to her bottom and her thigh.

"You really are the most beautiful, perfect woman," he murmured worshipfully.

And she believed him.

EPILOGUE

"EXPLAIN THAT AGAIN." Qaswar might only be seven years old, but his dark brows were perfectly capable of a thunderous frown of astonishment.

Akin loved him so much his chest could barely contain it sometimes. His son-slash-nephew had so many of Eijaz's physical traits it was unquestionable whose son he was. He also had Eijaz's outgoing personality and idealistic vision of how the world should run. All of that was tempered with glimpses of Hannah that showed up in an expression of curiosity or an incisive way of seeing things or a quiet moment of compassion.

Not that Qaswar was in any mood to hear about his inherited traits today.

Akin glanced at his wife. She was biting her lips together as she closed the children's book that seemed to be prompting more questions than it answered.

"Which part is confusing you?" Akin asked. "Because you've always known that I'm actually your uncle." They had made that clear from a very early age in ways that had been appropriate at the time, pointing to other blended families as examples. "And we talked a little about where babies come from when your sister was born." That had been last year and Qaswar hadn't been that interested.

"Yes, but—" A dimple appeared in Qaswar's chin and he looked between them with disbelief. "You *do* that?"

Akin took Hannah's hand. "Yes." They special-hugged the hell out of each other as much as their busy schedules allowed.

"But I didn't do that with your biological father," Hannah clarified. "That's why I wanted you to read the book, so we could explain that part."

Qaswar had *not* been eager for a reading assignment when it wasn't a school day, particularly one on reproductive science that included illustrations of smiling sperm and ovum with eyelashes.

"This is information we wanted you to learn straight from us," Akin said. "We thought you were old enough to understand it, but we don't have to talk a lot about it right now if you don't want to. You can bring it up anytime in future, though. And when your brother and sister are old enough, we'll explain it to them, too."

Akin hadn't known it was possible to love this wide and hard, but he would have ten more children if Hannah was up for it, he loved his existing three so much.

"Okay but tell me again how the doctors just *mixed it up*," Qaswar said. "Because it's not like when the maid accidentally puts your socks away in your brother's drawer, is it? It seems like something that's pretty important. Shouldn't they have been more organized?"

"Yes," Akin assured him. "And I am not one to excuse incompetence, but in this case, I can't regret their lack of attention to detail. In fact, I think it was the best thing that could have happened for all of us."

Qaswar shook his head in bemusement. "I guess."
In the next second, he had shrugged off one of the most
profound, defining moments of his parents' lives. "*Now*
will you play hide-and-seek with us?"

"Sure," Akin said dryly. "Go get Kamal." Akin had
promised to take them into the passageways where they
slipped out of sight around corners then leaped out to
scare one another from their skins. He had to warn security when they were going in, because their shouts
alarmed the staff who heard it through the walls, but
his boys loved it, and Akin did, too.

Hannah sagged into him before he could rise. Her
shoulders were shaking. He realized she was gasping
for breath, she was laughing so hard.

"What—?"

"Am I the drawer?" she sputtered.

A crack of laughter left him. He hadn't heard it like
that, but now he absorbed Qaswar's remark about the
socks put away in the drawer and laughed so hard his
eyes grew wet.

The boys came back and Kamal cocked his head, his
grin the most endearing replica of Hannah's cheekiest
smile. "What's so funny?"

Akin was too weak to speak. He squeezed Hannah.
She was wiping her eyes.

"We're just happy," she said around her lingering
chuckles. "Very, very happy."

They were.

* * * * *

MILLS & BOON

Coming next month

AN HEIR CLAIMED BY CHRISTMAS
Clare Connelly

'I will never understand how you could choose to keep me out of his life.'

Annie's eyes swept shut. 'It wasn't an easy decision.'

'Yet you made it, every day. Even when you were struggling, and I could have made your life so much easier.'

That drew her attention. 'You think this is going to make my life easier?' A furrow developed between her brows. 'Moving to another country, *marrying* you?'

His eyes roamed her face, as though he could read things in her expression that she didn't know were there. As though her words had a secret meaning.

'Yes.'

For some reason, the confidence of his reply gave her courage. One of them, at least, seemed certain they were doing the right thing.

'What if we can't make this work, Dimitrios?'

His eyes narrowed a little. 'We will.'

It was so blithely self-assured, coming from a man who had always achieved anything he set out to, that Annie's lips curled upwards in a small smile. 'Marriage is difficult and Max is young—only six. Presuming you intend for our marriage to last until he's eighteen, that's twelve years of living together, pretending we're something we're not. I don't know about you, but the strain of that feels unbearable.'

'You're wrong on several counts, Annabelle.' He leaned forward, the noise of his movement drawing her attention, the proximity of his body making her pulse spark to life with renewed fervour. 'I intend for our marriage to be real in every way—meaning for as long as we both shall live. As for pretending we're something we're not, we don't need to do that.'

Her heart had started to beat faster. Her breath was thin. 'What exactly does a 'real' marriage mean?'

'That we become a family. We live together. we share a bedroom, a bed, we raise our son as parents. It means you have my full support in every way.'

It was too much. Too much kindness and too much expectation. She'd thought he would be angry with her when he learned the truth, and that she could have handled. If he'd wanted to fight, she could have fought, but this was impossible to combat. The idea of sharing his bed…

'Sharing a home is one thing, but as for the rest—'

'You object to being a family?'

He was being deliberately obtuse.

She forced herself to be brave and say what was on her mind. 'You think I'm going to fall back into bed with you after this many years, just because we have a son together?'

His smile was mocking, his eyes teasing. 'No, Annabelle. I think you're going to fall back into bed with me because you still want me as much as you did then. You don't need to pretend sleeping with me will be a hardship.'

Her jaw dropped and she sucked in a harsh gulp of air. 'You are so arrogant.'

His laugh was soft, his shoulders lifting in a broad shrug. 'Yes.' His eyes narrowed. 'But am I wrong?'

Continue reading
AN HEIR CLAIMED BY CHRISTMAS
Clare Connelly

Available next month
www.millsandboon.co.uk

COMING
SOON!

We really hope you enjoyed reading this book.
If you're looking for more romance, be sure to
head to the shops when new books are
available on

Thursday 12th
November

To see which titles are coming soon, please visit
millsandboon.co.uk/nextmonth

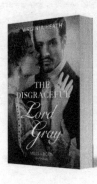  

MILLS & BOON
DARE

Sexy. Passionate. Bold.

Sensual love stories featuring smart, sassy heroines you'd want as a best friend, and compelling intense heroes who are worthy of them.

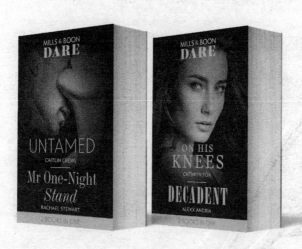